D0953046

The Road to Esmeralda

ALSO BY
JOY NICHOLSON

The Tribes of Palos Verdes

The Road to Esmeralda

JOY NICHOLSON

ST. MARTIN'S PRESS NEW YORK

FOR JEFF

NGH^3

www.stmartins.com

Book design by Irene Vallye

Illustrations by Maximilian Bode (www.maxbode.com)

Library of Congress Cataloging-in-Publication Data

Nicholson, Joy.
The road to Esmeralda / Joy Nicholson.—1st ed.
p. cm.
ISBN 0-312-26863-7
EAN 978-0312-26863-3
1. Americans—Mexico—Fiction. 2. City and town life—Fiction. 3. Prejudices—Fiction. 4. Travelers—Fiction. 5. Mexico—Fiction. I. Title.

PS3564.I2774R63 2005
813'.54—dc22

2004065832

First Edition: June 2005

10 9 8 7 6 5 4 3 2 1

Acknowledgments

I'd like to thank the writer Robert Stone, whom I don't know, but whose writing is a constant inspiration.

Thanks to Betsy Amster for everything.

Thank you, Elizabeth Bewley, for your patience and care in editing. Thank you, Frances Sayers, for your sensitive, smart, and thoughtful copyediting.

Green

He awoke at dawn to the sound of cicadas in the mangrove swamp. A hot *suroeste* wind blew from the south, screaming through the mosquito net, pressing it to his face, then ballooning it outward like a sail. As he unstuck his perspiring thigh from a tangle of hammock strings, an image flashed across his consciousness: His girlfriend slamming the door, leaving him alone to sleep on the rickety second-story porch. There he still was, suspended in air, spine throbbing.

"Sar?" Nick called out toward the shuttered bedroom.

To escape the clouds of insects during the night, he'd crafted a tent of mosquito netting, adhering the material to the porch with gaffer's tape and twine. Still, countless insects had gotten past the defense, buzzing his ears, then landing on the exposed skin of his neck. When he'd finally gotten comfortable, a gull had crashed into a windowpane behind him, shocking him enough to rip the net in half. He'd then fashioned the useless thing into a grim reaper–style robe. It was this robe he was wearing now.

"Sar? Are you already awake?"

As he struggled upward, swatting sand off his mouth, he felt something lying next to his thigh. A smooth, oval dinner plate. No, it wasn't a plate. It was a bone. What was a bone doing in the hammock?

"Jesus Christ." The bone started running; silken filaments skittered across his fingers.

He sighed. Nick had just spent the night with a crustacean.

He was still a little drunk. For a while, he frowned at the Yucatán sky. He frowned at every Mayan god in it. The mouth on the mask over his desk began to open and close in the breeze. There was no mystical connection between the mask's actions and his own thoughts—the mask always waggled. Still, the motion disturbed him.

He had gotten no writing done at all last night—millions of moths, throwing themselves against the screen, had made sure of that. Every moth was potentially the embodiment of Chac Tut. Every goddamn living thing in the Yucatán jungle was potentially the embodiment of Chac Tut. So if the inspiration god had happened to be a moth, and had happened to bash into the screen at the same moment Nick was chipping away at his ridiculous little story, something good might have happened.

But it had not.

What had happened was that the moth noises, the sea noises, the bird noises, the noises of mating monkeys, had kept him from being able to think, much less write. Only by pretending he was an extra in a castaway film had Nick been able to endure the elaborate setup Sarah had created to inspire him: the relocation of his desk and writing items to the porch, the altar of candles, flowers, Mayan tchotchkes she'd carefully arranged on the desk's rickety rim. Of course, the altar had toppled forward when Nick mistakenly jiggled it. All at once, in slow motion, molten incense sizzled in Nick's lap, a stone jaguar head careened onto his left toe, a votive candle disaster was pretty much nigh.

Even then, with a sizable char-hole in his research notes, Nick had tried to keep going. Even then he'd tried to believe tequila and wind and candles and legal pads were not a hugely unfortunate idea. But soon enough, the chore of listening to the moths, of rubbing the sticky residue of salt from his arms and legs, of trying to feel wise and knowing and at peace in nature, while simultaneously knowing he was not feeling those things, and would never feel those things, and would never write a book, made him certain he would never care to visit the great outdoors again.

Look, he'd told himself, he was just feeling eco-hysteria, just serving a Mexi-punishment, a nature vacation gone wrong.

Look. Things could be worse. He wasn't a soldier on his way to Iraq. A writer, he simply had to pick up his weapon, try again.

Still, as he'd stared fixedly at the jaguar head of the war god, he'd gripped the pencil tighter and tighter. The sensation of ambush had been uncanny.

He'd closed his eyes, waiting.

Soon enough the air assault had come.

When Karl Von Tollman, their host at the guesthouse, had begun to play his nightly accordion concert last night while Nick had been trying to write about soldiers dying in Vietnam, Nick's pencil snapped in two. Louder and louder, the music continued to waft over the vines that separated the main house from the guesthouse. Each note left a cold spot on Nick's skin, and on each cold spot a goose bump rose. With every goose bump came a singular lack of ideas.

As the night progressed, as the noise continued, Nick had begun to imagine the music overriding him, obliterating his concentration, pushing him downward into the deepest Mayan circle of hell. Perhaps the Mayan war gods were in league with Karl's accordion, the two forces united in a mission to destroy Nick's book. Perhaps Karl had conjured the gods; the altar had surely been his idea. In any case, Karl had given the jaguar head to Sarah. And if there was a Yucatec god of inspiration, this icon could certainly represent a brother deity, the Yucatec god of dull, laughable prose. If there was a Yucatec god of petty vengeance who ruled over the human realm of bee stings, dog bites, and scorpion stings, the god of medium-sized vengeance could, almost certainly, commandeer a hand organ at will.

For a while, Nick had continued to stare into the dense foliage, imagining strangling Karl Von Tollman with the accordion's neck strap. The jaguar head, it could be said, was badly carved, vaguely leering. Bad art. Bad ideas. Bad, bad, bad.

His toe hurt like hell.

"Come on, Nick," is what Sarah had said earlier when Nick had tried to discourage the desk altar, when he'd pointed out that Karl always *waited* to play—waited until nighttime when Nick might write his best material. At the same time Nick had pointed out that "Liebensraum" was, in and of itself, simply wrong for a Mexican vacation.

"And since when do Mayan skulls dovetail with iconic German drinking songs?"

"And since when did typical Yucatec lore include a polka?"

"Come on," she'd said, laughing. Karl's music was, "lovely, and part of an old culture."

Though Nick hadn't grabbed and shaken his girlfriend, or even come close, the very idea that he'd thought of doing so made him sick, and he'd walked to the edge of the room and had beaten his chest like an ape. *An ape!*

"So, give a little shout if you need anything. I'll probably hear you," Sarah had said.

He had shouted with vigor and volume. She had not heard a word.

And so, last night, stuffing wadded toilet paper in his ears, taping the mosquito netting like a vacuum bag around his head, he had given up on his girlfriend, tried for just one breakout sentence. Christ almighty, just one good *page.*

From the main house, he'd heard material swirling, toes tapping, Sarah laughing, Karl laughing: *oom pah pah oom pah pah oom.* The sea crashed, the sand blew, the violet moon seemed to ring in his ears.

"Nazi," he'd found himself writing incessantly. *"Nazi, Nazi, Nazi, Nazi."*

Nick had spent half of his evening resharpening the tip of his broken pencil; the lead breaking off every ten minutes from the violence of his dotted "i"s. He'd spent the other half drinking tequila and liqueur from an empty Advil canister, trying to put things into needed perspective. It *wasn't* a great tragedy that Nick Sperry was a failed writer being assaulted with an unwanted accordion concerto; not when the poor—and that was literal—jarhead kids were about to invade Iraq any day.

It *wasn't* so bad that Karl Von Tollman was trying to seduce Nick's girlfriend with the nerve-destroying, ear-melting instrument—the pump being pressed fervidly between sweaty palms with a lascivious grin—kids were about to *die* out there.

Being on an ecologically sound vacation, learning about new cultures and religions, just wasn't so bad. It wasn't being a soldier on the way to Baghdad. It wasn't being blown up in a berm.

He drank and drank and drank.

"Shut up, shut up, shut up, shut up, shut up, shut up, shut up . . ."

A man could be in a million worse situations than being in a Swiss chalet in the Mexican jungle, trying to write a serious novel about a war. If Nick's father had gotten his way, Nick would now be a soldier, shipping out to Afghanistan, Turkey, Iraq. In Mayan times, children were the favorites of the war gods. That meant they were dressed up in little costumes with little hats, knifed, drowned. In those times, a man would have been *lucky* to live to thirty years. Nick was now thirty-two.

Nick still had a *head.*

Still, it was pretty bad to be a bad writer when one dreamed of being a good writer. Nick had come to Mexico with the expectation of writing two hundred good pages in twenty-one days. Last night, he had written the word "Nazi" 130 times.

It was now a humid, yellow morning and he was bleeding from the nose. He was empty of ideas, being watched critically by a crab.

Looking at the sky, he heard his father's spidery laugh—*Eeeeeeee.* "You'll never write a book, boy."

He fancied he heard the sun rising. It made a burning, charred sound like meat.

Or maybe the meat sound was coming from Karl Von Tollman's prized Yucatán smokehaus. Maybe Karl had killed a few bats, was now roasting their tongues and cheeks in heavy cream for a secret German breakfast. Maybe Karl was making napkin rings from their hides, maybe he was making a stylish bat-hide bikini for Sarah.

"Can't you see Karl's lived through a lot? Can't you just look beyond the World War Two clichés?" Sarah had asked him last night. At first, her voice was soft, not accusing.

Unusually soft-spoken, Sarah was the possessor of a fantastically calming voice. Under the dark blond bangs were the eyes of a child once fat. Wounded. Smart. Smarting. She was the smartest person Nick had ever known.

Still, what Sarah didn't seem to grasp was that clichés were a necessity when rage was the point. And if rage wasn't the point of this vacation, Nick no longer knew what the point was.

Sar? It was the Midori. I shouldn't have mixed liqueur with tequila."

Of course, there was the problem that melon-flavored alcohol should exist at all. But Nick had unfortunately unearthed the old bottle, left by a previous guest. The vaguely female bottle shape had intrigued him, as had the color: plutonium-green.

"The stuff should be outlawed. It probably is."

He waited for a sign of his girlfriend's presence, but all he heard was the distant waves, the crow of a rooster, the hissing and crackling of the nearby smokehaus.

He gagged.

It was clearly too early to be roasting meat. The sun was barely up, Nick's eyes were barely open, but flaying, chopping, gutting were already cheerfully in the works at the Gasthaus Esmeralda. Which went to prove that Karl was absolutely an escaped Nazi, no matter what Sarah believed. With his piercing blue eyes, his propensity for poking and prying, his summary pronouncements over where to deposit the toilet paper; not in the bowl, *never* in the bowl, *"Ve vill have a backup if you put it in the bowl";* Karl could have once manned a work camp in the Grünewald.

Nick's mother had been Jewish and he knew a fair bit about Nazi evasions and Nazi hiders in tropical countries. The type was certainly not unknown in Mexico. Karl had breath like a Nazi. He was a prick like one.

Of course, it had been said some Nazi soldiers weren't real Nazis. It had been posited they were just caught up in the times, trying to grow their Nazi turnips, raise their Nazi families like anyone else.

But what would a Nazi say except he was *not* a Nazi? he'd told Sarah last night. Who else would operate a private smokehaus, with a long stack belching black streams of stench into the sky?

"I'm going to call the Mossad when we get back to LA," was what he'd said, exactly. "He must be on some kind of list."

"How silly. Karl wasn't even born when the war was on." She'd laughed uneasily. "Take a moment and do the math."

"He could be lying about his age," Nick had insisted. Besides, why else was Karl hiding in a jungle without a phone?

Her smile had grown less easy still. "Did you drink that weird, old bottle of green stuff? Is that what this is about?"

"The Simon Wiesenthal Center," Nick had said. "Right when we get back."

"Nick, you're scaring me," she'd replied.

As gently as he could, Nick now snorted, tasting the dregs of Dos Hermanos, Midori at the back of his throat. He did the Nazi math. He snorted again.

So who cared if Karl wasn't a Nazi. He was anyway. Clearly all the guy needed was some Wagner, the German flag in the background—the old one that pictured a dormouse being squeezed to death in the talons of a falcon.

In addition to roasting flesh at dawn, the man made his own soap. Rendered from thick, sick "veg-e-tah-ble" glycerin—"Not from porks." As if a man who spoke five languages fluently couldn't use the correct term, "pigs." As if Karl was opposed to the use of blood and gristle in personal hygiene products.

Nick looked at the rising sun with alarm.

If this was what the world had come to: Nazi-almost-rans owning Yucatán eco-lodges, Nick could be excused for ramming his fist into Karl's smooth teak balustrade. He could be pardoned for gritting his teeth until they made an unattractive sound. God, he needed Sarah's large, cool hands on his forehead. When she massaged his temples, she knew not to laugh, exactly where not to press too hard. If she would only appear, he could get up, face his hangover. If she would then only admit to Karl's treachery, Nick could do anything.

He felt a prickling on the back of his neck. All night he hadn't heard a single sound from inside the room. He'd thought he'd heard muffled footsteps going down the garden path to Karl's house. Then again, he may have been dreaming. In Nick's dreams, Sarah was often darting into secret passageways, making muffled, disturbing noises. Lately, Karl figured, too, in the murky nightmares.

"And you, my friend?" The crab sidled farther away from Nick.

Something it its movements suggested revulsion. "Did Karl eat your wife last night for dinner?"

Karl, who had graduated from Nazi-infant to shoemaker to shoe factory–owner to innkeeper in the Yucatán jungle, was certainly capable of anything. When the man wasn't busy bowing elegantly for Sarah, pulling polite chairs for her, he was busy showing off by making his own tools, drying his own boar jerky. Always up at dawn, after showering and shaving in cold seawater, he delighted Sarah by naming every insect, bird, mammal, and invertebrate by a careful scrutiny of its dung.

Poking around in crap did not embarrass men like Karl. They simply called it "droppings," or the ever-elegant "spoor."

That is, "ssspoor," with a Germinglish accent.

"I'm just saying he talks to you in rather suggestive ways," Nick had said to Sarah's back, last night. "I'm just saying just because he's old doesn't mean he's not a maniac."

"You could come to their house, too. He's invited you many times."

"Ah, but I'm afraid I'd mistakenly flip a switch. A secret wall would give way—Wait! Sarah! Where are you going?"

Even though Nick tried to smile at her, Sarah had made a *sss* sound, slammed the door, gone inside.

For a while he'd lain quietly, doubled up in disbelief.

Nick had never heard Sarah make a mean noise at him. Not in all their years together. The noise hurt him, physically.

Germanically.

A slit of sunlight now made its way through the vines, into his headache. A blinding flash like television. The smashed jaguar head grinned up at him.

Yessssss.

Hissed at, as if one were a paranoid, as if one were a piece of effluvium under a German boot. A man had to fight back, he did.

And so, yes, after Sarah had left him, after he'd whistled the "Horst Wessel Song" a few times to no response, it had been Nick's duty and privilege to smash Karl's jaguar statue. It had been his obligation to smash it and keep smashing until his hand gave out.

God, for a moment he'd felt like a god.

Even now, even though his hand hurt, even though Sarah had not thought the idea funny when he'd told it to her through the open window, Nick knew that if Karl Von Tollman lived in Los Angeles instead of the Yucatán jungle, he'd have his own cable show. *The Gemütlich Nazi's Militia Hour.* On his show Karl would discuss how he had foreseen events like 9-11, the ensuing downfall of Western imperialism, the breakup of the United States, and, having predicted it all, had cleverly found himself a piece of land that would be untouched in the coming global nuclear meltdown.

"Ju moost go south of the equator!" Nick had mocked Karl's incredible accent. "The fallout vill be lighter south of the equator. Ju moost have a large store of underground water, and guard it with your life."

When Sarah had closed the window, Nick had jimmied it open again. It had only opened a half-inch. Karl's lock had seen to that.

"Maybe Karl could become a cartoon character, picked up by the WB!" He'd stuck his lips through the half-inch crack again. Sarah had been reading and frowning.

"Nick. Go to *sleep.* I can't even understand you, you're slurring your words so badly. And if this is for Karl's benefit, he can't hear you, either. The wind's blowing the wrong way."

Instead of sleeping, Nick had imagined how, were Karl's show animated, it would gain underground status among the leisured and ironic and anarchical. On it, the cartoon-Karl would point at maps, wear his fatigues, his Alpine hat, and hawk his own line of survival products on the screen.

"While some Americans fight wars on one channel, others can get radical by switching to your buddy's show! Help me think of a slogan, babe."

She still hadn't looked at him.

"Use a MasterCard! Be the master race!

"Some moost die, some moost buy!"

She'd turned off the light.

And so, he'd smashed the jaguar head. And so, she'd finally gotten up to look.

And now the guilt and anger had escalated. Nick hadn't yet moved from the hammock, and already he was under siege. True, he was guilty of breaking statues to get his girlfriend's attention.

True, he'd shouted nasty things, and his goose-stepping wasn't as funny as it seemed at the time. True, liquor could make a person a real shit.

And yet, what did it matter *which* word he'd shouted at the top of his lungs while Sarah appeared for a moment, held the broken jaguar head in her hands, bit her lip, and gone back inside? "Terrible"—that's all the word "Nazi" meant these days. It made Nick sick how the word had been co-opted by people who had no right to it. Right-wing Republicans, left-wing Democrats, fashion mavens who mandated no white shoes after Labor Day. Whoever had a strident, unalterable point of view that differed from one's own: that's what a war criminal was now. People in Nick's office even called his boss a Nazi. What they meant was that Larry was a hard-ass, cruel about deadlines and vacation time. Which he certainly was. But if being a Nazi now just meant a person was unduly irritating and harsh, that made everyone in Nick's *life* a Nazi. Certainly everyone he'd met on this vacation.

"Americans are the real terrorists," the rich Russian bond trader had told Nick and Sarah in Ensenada with a flick of his haughty wrist. "The Americans and the Jews."

"Yanqui fock. No war Iraq!" a Spaniard had said in Acapulco, flicking an olive most cruelly.

"Americans are the new Nazis," the French girl had said, drunk, flicking her stringy hair.

All in all, flicking gestures were like Mexican vacations, like the word "Nazi."

Oddly painful. Shoddily insulting. Certainly overused.

The theory that an American citizen could escape his nationality, the target on his back, simply by purchasing car insurance and crossing a border, had proven a particularly popular one. Since the World Trade Center had come down, since war was all but declared on Iraq, every beach Nick and Sarah had attempted to escape to—from Ensenada to Acapulco—had been packed full. Every other license plate read CALIFORNIA, ARIZONA, NEW YORK. (The sixty-foot, satellite-equipped RVs always read TEXAS.) The good hotels were full of nervous escapees, the so-so hotels, too. The bad hotels were airless, brown, damp. Beds in them were the lazy shape of tacos.

The anxious Californians trying to escape suitcase nukes that might and might not go off in LA harbor any moment would not have been so bad if they had not shown up in Nick's secret spot, each carrying an identical bright yellow copy of *Let's Go: Mexico* (why did the thing have to be so goddamn *yellow?*), each copy promising each person the same "secret spot, without tourists." The prowar Arizonians always brought Jet Skis and radios. Male Texans had careful, shellacked hairstyles, like holiday wreaths.

It was wartime and every American with $19.99 was at war.

And so, tooth against nail, wallet against wallet, *Let's Go* against *Fodor's,* Americans engaged each other in grisly acts of road rage, furtive *mordida* battles for cheap beachfront rooms. It was the tourist gold-medal challenge; casualties mounted.

"Maybe we should keep going south," Sarah had said. Then, "Maybe just a little more."

Nick wouldn't have minded driving a *little* farther south. He wouldn't have minded flinging *Let's Go* out the window, even if the act made him a litterer. Still, given the fact they'd propelled him, downward, southward, toward Karl's guesthouse, Nick had two words for his countrymen in Mexico: "Default Nazis."

A notch below satanic. That is, evil by mistake.

He mused for a moment. Yes. It was a good idea. The first good idea of the morning, maybe even of the whole trip.

"Satanic" had no gender bias, no racial overtones. One could use the term quite guiltlessly.

"*Hola.* I come from the Great Satan."

"*Allô.* I see you're flicking at me, French person! I guess that's because, *mais oui,* I'm Satan."

"Good day! Two cold *cervezas* for two traveling Satans!"

Mostly it was a perfectly politically correct word that one could use when describing Karl to Sarah.

"I didn't say anything racist! Just that Karl was a friend of Beelzebub."

"Not Nazi. *Satanic,* Sar. Not germane to a country of origin, or political parties therein."

Yes. Satanic. It had a ring to it.

But where in the *hell* was Nick's girlfriend?

He addressed the window, the chain lock, again.

Nazi. Christ. The word didn't *mean* anything anymore. Now no one cared how it was thrown around, which made it doubly stupid that Sarah wasn't speaking to Nick because he'd called Karl a Nazi last night. She wasn't speaking to him, and she probably wouldn't screw him, either.

Nick needed sex with Sarah. No, what he needed was her warmth, her laughter, her affirmation that she'd chosen him from among all men. It was her habit when unsure to smile distantly, withdraw behind her long curtain of bangs. Similarly, it was her way to instinctively step back instead of forward when meeting a stranger. That this tended to bring the person farther forward sometimes made for great comedy. She'd step backward again and again, drawing the invading person ever closer.

Nick now cleared his throat, glancing nervously toward the glass door. When Sarah first met Karl under the shade of Karl's pepper tree, she hadn't shied away. A writer noticed these things. *Especially* a nonwriting writer with a tall, blond girlfriend.

He cleared his throat again. Perhaps during the night a diseased moth had flown into it. Perhaps he would get sick, and Sarah would take pity on him.

She was like that.

And he was like this.

Dressed like a death's-head. Plotting.

Having studied fiction in college, having fully imagined he would have a serious, well-reviewed novel by the time he was thirty, it was still impossible to believe that he was now older than thirty, mostly writing puff pieces about movie actors. He'd imagined that he'd get married along the way. But Sarah was the woman he wanted to marry and she did not know if she "believed in marriage per se."

He didn't understand what she meant by "per se."

His stack of dew-soaked papers fluttered in the breeze. The salty air brought the ocean's smell. If he didn't move his head, it was mostly all right.

A beetle landed on his open eye. A page blew away. He let it.

There would be another opportunity to write in, say, ten million years. Nick, of course, worked long hours at home, had no savings. His savings account had been low in the first place, and now had gone to pay for this writing vacation: a holiday on which Sarah had not wanted to come. Now, on this vacation, Nick had spent his last thousand, had done no writing, and Sarah's life had, apparently, been transformed.

"I didn't say 'transformed.' " Sarah had laughed. "Don't make me sound like a twit."

"What in the world did you say, then? I thought you said, 'transformed.' "

"I said being out here makes me think of things *differently.* I'd just forgotten there was a world outside of LA."

The world Sarah spoke of so highly was the Gasthaus Esmeralda; the curious patch of Mexican jungle that had been crafted into a Little Bavaria, circa 11 B.C. Karlworld included sprightly canoe rides, horse husbandry, orchid-gazing, the crafting of herbal remedies for toe itch, eczema, nightmare. Jesus Christ, in a country where one could get any number of useful, controlled narcotics at the local pharmacy for less than a dollar, Sarah was bothering to relieve headaches with goddamn stewed pods. She was using a paintbrush Karl had made for her from a horse's mane clippings, a sheaf of paper made from dried, stretched coconut husk. She was making bread, making art, making life into art. Without a malicious bone in her body, Nick's girlfriend was making Nick feel he knew nothing and could do nothing for her at all.

Then there was the fact that the more time Sarah spent with Karl Von Tollman, the more she was absorbing the man's nasty, phlegm-filled geopolitics. Dried-up aquifers, plague, stick-children, kwashiorkor, teeming millions—all were sad subjects a woman with Sarah's sympathetic nature would gravitate toward quite naturally. Yet, until meeting Karl, she had done so with a great deal of charm.

Now, while she kneaded chunks of incredibly healthy brown dough, Sarah was talking about rats and cages, birthrate exponents out to there. She was waking at night worrying about world water tables, food sources. They'd only been at the Gasthaus Esmeralda for five days, and Nick was watching his girlfriend become a communist.

"What I love," Sarah had said when he'd tried to talk to her about it, "is having the time to work with my hands—with clay, or wax, or paint, even wires and plumbing. I love the weird little sense of happiness you can get from fitting the right groove into the right nubbin. And I love being outdoors all day. I should have been a carpenter with the size of my hands, anyway."

Of the classic, statuesque Scandinavian type, Sarah Gustafsson was much taller than Nick in heels (thankfully, Sarah never wore heels). It was easy to imagine her named Dagmar, Gretl, Ursula. It wouldn't be easy to believe she was shy, and yet she was. She had been thick-backed, broad waisted, large-footed, as a girl, and though now her features were elegant, suggestive of horses and riding crops, she didn't quite trust she'd outgrown the tedious nickname Sasquatch.

"I think this vacation is the best thing we could have done," she'd told Nick. "I'd forgotten what it's like not to run on deadlines, M&M's, and adrenaline."

Yes, it was true, Sarah had always been quietly stringent when it came to a cause. But at home, when Sarah agonized for old mutts, old trees, old buildings set for the wrecking ball, Nick counted her belief in civic responsibility as a plus. Here, from five-thirty A.M. to nine she was with old Karl on the deserted beach, working with homemade rakes and hoes. After ten-thirty she was with him again, shoulder muscles shining, sweaty, tireless.

"When the green line goes to two," she'd told Nick, having gained instant mastery of Karl's incredible solar lighting apparatus, "it means the power's on low, so we have to light candles until the battery recharges." She had little blobs of wax residue in her hair almost all the time now. She was learning, from Karl, how to make dripless candles from beeswax combs. Combs, of course, that came from Karl's hive.

Beekeeping was weirdly sexy, Sarah had related to Nick. "That hum, I guess. Though I don't have any idea why a hum would be sexy."

Of course Sarah was weirdly sexy. Long-necked, long-limbed, long-waisted, as any ballet dancer, her broad shoulders gave her the impression of health, strength, not a ballet dancer's fragility. Though her face was a perfect oval, the bones in her cheeks were high, strong, almost Indian. Her arched blond brows, wide mouth, subtly slanted eyes, were saved from doll prettiness by the intense gaze, the slightly too-high forehead, the ever-present squint that left premature wrinkles around her eyes.

Men, especially, were terribly smiley in her presence.

"I just don't see the relaxing aspect of insect-viewing!

"I just don't want you in dark, unsupervised corners with *that guy!*"

Her answer—that Karl was just showing her "what a queen looked like"—was *exactly,* precisely what Nick could not bear.

And because he could not bear how she had wrongly separated men into two camps—those who were wise and those who were carnal—Nick had no recourse but to pace and lecture some more.

"I'm just saying attachment to the power grid does not denote evil.

"I'm just saying the bees might want their wax themselves.

"I'm just saying the man is after you. He'll use any trick in his book."

Sarah had gone quiet, and had not mentioned dripless candles in Nick's presence again. Still, he couldn't forget how she'd said Karl was "amazing, eccentric, like Crusoe."

Like a literary giant.

That was to say, exactly *unlike* Nick.

"But you're just *not toxic* to begin with," Nick had exclaimed when Sarah later admitted that she had not only stopped eating refined sugar, but that her weight loss was due to "detoxing" with slippery elm, slithery snakeweed, Karl's slimy teas. Little by little, she'd given up alcohol, coffee, pot, meat over the last year.

With each eschewal, she glowed a little more.

"Why not eat some sugar? Sugar is beautiful. You're already doing yoga, running. You're not fat anymore, Sarah. Aren't you letting this health stuff get out of hand?"

No, she was not. Her detox had nothing to do with fat. It was other things, "hard to explain" things, she wanted to be rid of now.

"I'm just saying I don't want you to turn anorexic."

"I know, I know. And you're sweet."

And so now, to keep mosquitoes away, she was rubbing her body with citronella leaves, lime ash, rinds. Off! she believed, got into the mucous membranes during coitus, burned.

"Besides, who wants to fuck to the smell of Off!?" she'd asked.

"People who don't want to contract malaria and die."

"Oh, Nick." She'd laughed, catching his impatience, patiently correcting it. "No one's going to *die.*"

And yet, Nick was slowly, quietly dying inside. He was dying of malignant innkeepers, incurable, suave know-it-alls, his own fatal map-reading that had led them to this place. This was their vacation, *theirs,* and the great love of Nick's life was spending it all with Karl I'm-Not-a-Nazi Von Tollman in his I'm-Not-a-Nazi A-frame chalet. What could *be* trickier than Karl's predawn wind farm walks, his lectures on solar power, vegetable gardening, animal rehabilitation, habitat loss? How cunningly Karl had commanded Sarah's attention with his fatherly smirk and Teutonic accent, bending so close while giving her lessons on homemade electricity, handmade benches, sun-brewed honey-ginger ale.

Just before the trip, Nick had written a piece about a minor movie star who, when not busy with appearances, shoots, and modeling assignments, cooked exotic foodstuffs, designed her own chairs. The article was meant to call attention to the actress's intelligence, her probing forays into the neo-modern aesthetic. The actress had large breasts, full lips, a Chinese Hairless dog.

For nearly a week Nick had struggled with how to best incorporate chairs, nude dogs, morels, Mensa into an intelligent interview. His dissertation had been on Sartre. He tried to read *Granta* magazine. Still, meeting that starlet, he'd felt acutely that he was, and apparently always would be, from California's depressed Yucca Valley with its military bases, lack of museums and libraries, its ROTC, its single celebrated attraction—"Home of the World's Largest Papier-Mâché Missile." As a youth, Nick had never had an *idea* there was such a thing as the superior, neo-modern aesthetic. Dogs *with* fur just didn't seem bad to him.

When he'd asked the actress's opinion of war, she said: "War is not the answer."

Apparently chairs, charbroiled mushrooms were.

"It's not that I'm suddenly 'enthralled with chairs,' no," Sarah had said gently of Karl's driftwood benches, his beaten-tin boxes, his conch-shell showerheads. Her gentleness with Nick seemed more and more forced. "But it feels good to make something with your your own hands. What's wrong with Karl wanting to do that?"

"I like to think my chairs express an inner philosophy," the actress had chuffed.

"And who in the world doesn't know how to make a simple chair!" Karl's argument against Nick had been.

Nick wasn't opposed to nice chairs. He wasn't opposed to frilly mushrooms, or writing puff pieces to make his rent. He wasn't even opposed to sizable papier-mâché missiles, if that made people happy.

What he was opposed to was the hijacking of his every goddamn waking moment.

"Sperry, you're on the edge here," his boss had said to Nick when he'd turned in the article about the actress's chairs.

Apparently, although Nick had decided against, "A Chair Is Apparently the Answer," his second-choice title, "A Surprisingly Intelligent Person," had made the actress mad.

He was getting mad. This was madness. His current furniture was made of string. He could not move his head. Sarah was sneaking out on him. A war was starting any week now. Movie stars worried about clean lines, while the war against terrorism might not have any end. Karl spoke five languages, played nine instruments. Sarah claimed to be leaving Nick alone so he could "write his little heart out." His girlfriend was leaving Nick alone all day *on their vacation* so he could struggle with the novel she "knew was in him."

For a long time, in his youth, Nick had assumed a great novel "was in him."

Then again, as a youth, Nick had believed the world outside a military town would be less stupid and peculiar and painful. At least, he'd believed, he would keep a full head of hair. As it was, his girlfriend was flirting with an *Obersturmführer* and Nick was balding—not even in the attractive high-crowned way. On this vacation, like a Neanderthal, Nick had cracked peanuts against his chest. He had balanced beer cans on his belly. He had grown comfortable using himself as a dining table.

It was after dawn in the remotest, thickest stand of jungle on the Esmeralda Coast, and Nick Sperry had majestically risen to an upright position. Every muscle in his back seemed to have fossilized, his neck swiveled slowly, slowly ten degrees. With every millimeter he felt the taut pulley that was attached to a rusty chain in his spine.

My God, he thought. I am a trilobite.

Wrenching himself forward, trying to touch his hands to the floor, he felt the sensation of helplessness, of his father laughing.

"What a good soldier does, son, is eighty knee bends a day."

There was just enough light to show the shadowy vines and ceiba trees in the jungle below. The browns and greens reminded him of his childhood bedroom, the sensation of smoke, the smell of rot, too. On the floorboard of the guesthouse a tiny spider was attempting to catch a huge red ant by running in circles, depositing sticky silk around the ant's sturdy legs. Hopping and jumping, the spider headed off each of the ant's forward movements with a thick outlay of goo. Refusing to back up, perhaps unable to, the ant plunged onward, leaving one of its legs behind.

For a while the spider continued its careful, demented orbit. Then it began wrapping the leg.

If an insect could be a Nazi, the spider certainly was one.

Nick stretched farther forward, frightened himself.

Had the spider–ant war been lost or won? Was the ensuing carnage satisfying to either side? How much nutrition was in an ant leg anyway?

Every childhood morning Nick had risen to the battle lessons of Sun Tzu, George Patton, Mountbatten. Every day, he'd saluted his father, held up his fingernails for inspection, taken his place in front of pasty, reheated eggs with currant jam.

Because Nick might and might not have been kept awake the night before, because his father might have fed him whiskey during an interrogation session, Nick might and might not have the answers to the posed military questions.

And because Nick's father had fully expected his son to join the

Corps, all Nick's life he'd been aware of what he was not man enough to withstand: not Verdun, not Vietnam, not Nicaragua or even Grenada. Nick would not have been man enough for the Afghanistan War, and was apparently not even man enough for the new one.

The war against Karl.

Nick knew very well that while he sat immobilized and impotent, Karl was setting an ambush, a selective jamming, a simultaneous land and sea raid. If Nick's father were alive he'd be pointing his vigorous finger in Nick's face, ordering Nick up, off this porch, *Get your useless ass in gear;* to do something about the "lessons" Sarah was receiving while half-naked and beautiful.

But what could Nick do without a neck?

Counterattack? Ha! Nick could not even *see* his own toes.

It was his third-to-last day of relaxation, and already he felt hot and fat. He gave up on the toes. He didn't need toes, didn't like toes. Toes were slug-shaped, slug-colored. Karl didn't cut the nails on his toes often enough, and if Sarah could not understand curly, thick, yellowed toenails were a sign of deep psychological disturbance, Nick could just not help her. A lizard zipped past. It was the bright green, nauseating color of Midori. The hangover clanged between his temples like an accordion song.

And what would he tell Phil Sperry?

"Sir, I just do not trust his toes, sir?

"Sir, I would like permission to shoot, sir?

"Sir, the enemy is very wily, sir. I find myself quite at a loss, sir."

For the most unreal thing about Karl, the very most hateful, wasn't his seductive accent, or his toenails, or even the fact that he made his own toothpicks out of slivered shards of beech wood. No, the worst thing was that with his heavy-lidded stare and the spiny hair sticking out of his chin, Karl Von Tollman should resemble an old carp. And yet, though he was old, though he had the pointy beard, though he wore absurd fatigues, the Alpine-style hat, though *he was at least sixty* and short, and had terrible dental habits—Karl

Von Tollman could not rightly be called unattractive. The man's light blue eyes were lit from within, set widely in a tanned, finely boned face. His Fu Manchu was guerilla-chic, his agelessly thick gray hair climbed halfway down his back, blunt-cut and severe as any Indian chief's. Muscles and sinew had taken the place of what should be, in a fair world, an old man's flabby skin. He built and manned canoes, swam a mile a day in the sea, disdained a telephone as "irrelevant."

Just yesterday the man had taken a lump of burnt wood from his fireplace, and crafted it into a cunning little charcoal pencil for Sarah to sketch with. He'd come close behind her, showing her how to sharpen the tip with a knife.

"Funny. I've wanted to start drawing again." Sarah had smiled up at Karl. "But I forgot. I didn't bring any supplies."

"You just need a hand, young lady," Karl had said, bowing.

Or maybe he'd said, "You just need a man."

Maybe Nick had said "crap" to Karl under his breath. Maybe when Karl asked him to repeat the unheard word, Nick had said, "Nothing! Nice pencil. Good flaying there, man." Maybe it was okay if a man lacked the inherent instinct to whip out a knife, stab at a handy pig or goat or stick or human. It was okay if a man didn't want to spear and gut, if he did not fancy shooting another through the head, or lobbing a cluster bomb at him through the scope of a faraway aircraft carrier. It was okay if Nick was not a fighter. This is what he'd tried to tell his father: It was all, in the end, okay.

"It's not *fucking okay,* Nicholas, to be a coward and a disgrace to your country. If you can't or won't show some gratitude for your freedom, how in Christ's good name can I stand to look at you?"

Yes, it was all okay, Nick used to tell himself, that he couldn't quite see himself snapping a man's neckbone with his bare hands.

Bayonets scared the shit out of him. He didn't care for medals. His honor would come in recording things other people were too busy to notice, in making people feel less alone.

Now, Nick had to laugh. Phil would have laughed. Karl was certainly laughing.

"What? You think writing is *brave?*" Phil, Nick's father, had said. "What are you going to do? Protect women and children with a *pen?*"

"What are you going to do?" Karl had asked. "*Write* your life away?"

"Don't you dare forget the veterans who made it possible for you to be free, Nicholas," Phil Sperry used to say to Nick quite often.

"How in the world did you capture such a pretty girl?" Karl had winked.

"Oh." Nick had grimaced. "You know. Chloroform."

Of course, the men going off to Vietnam hadn't died so that Nick Sperry could write about movie stars and vacations in Mexico. Of course, the young soldiers probably never believed they would die.

Of course, Sarah didn't know she was killing him now.

"The only *healthy* work is the *physical* labor," Karl had told Nick, waving his shiny rake.

"There is only one job fit for a son of mine," Phil had said through clenched teeth. "And that job is the Corps."

As it was, physical labor didn't require a "the."

As it was, "the" Corps did.

And as it was, Nick might not have been conceived had Phil Sperry gone to Vietnam the way he'd meant to in his mind. There, Phil might have died in the name of God, fighting gooks.

Furthermore, Phil might have lived to fight camel jockeys, sand niggers, sheet-wearers.

Evildoers.

Eenie, meenie, miney, mo.

And so the book Nick was not writing was a book about the treachery of war. He'd been not writing the book for exactly ten years now. He'd told himself he was in a "research phase."

"You were not even in Vietnam. You joined up, but they didn't take you. You were an insurance agent."

That was as far as he'd gotten in the war novel that was not about Phil Sperry. It amazed and dismayed Nick how his father kept worming his way into that first line. Nick had done years of reading on truly courageous men—the battles in which they had lost arms and heads and families and minds.

"It's none of my business, but why not just write your own story?" Sarah had asked two years ago, when he'd tried to explain that he didn't have writer's block, his slowness was simply due to the complexity of the book he was outlining—the book where he'd follow six young men into the rice paddies of Vietnam.

"Don't they say to write what you know?"

"They say anything."

Besides, Phil Sperry, whose punctured eardrum had kept him in the insurance game, Phil, who had not even gone through basic training, who nevertheless liked to employ military slang, who, for twenty-five years, sported faux dog tags, who wore a close brush cut oiled with Brylcreem, who kept every war movie ever filmed on a specially built shelf in the living room, who got teary-eyed at the sight of a celluloid GI in a back lot trench, but could not spare a tear for his own ruined life, Phil did not deserve to be the focus of Nick's breakout novel. Still, the first sentence continued to plague Nick. No matter how many times he erased it, he always wrote it again.

Nick heard Larry Scakorfsky's laughter in his mind.

"You want to write your book, don'tcha? That's why you're asking for this *unprecedented* favor."

"It's been eight years since I've gone anywhere, Larry," Nick had pointed out to his boss at the magazine.

"Get out of here, Sperry. Eight years!"

Nick had agreed the time frame was disturbing.

"But Mexico!" Larry had whistled through his thick grouper's lips. "I hear they wait for you to come along the highway, then throw a donkey in front of your tires, and when the poor bastard dies, they make you pay them *mucho.*"

Nick hadn't bothered with the logistics of the argument. How reasonable was it to believe a man could lift and toss a donkey? Instead he'd held firm.

To his surprise Larry had given in.

"I'm giving you the time because you're cracking up, Sperry. You've been giving us a little scare here."

What Larry had been talking about was Nick's drinking. Or Nick's sarcasm. Or Nick's propensity for referring to actresses as "the great nattering goatherd of tits." Or maybe it was his gray skin.

"Your face is actually the color of computer casings, Sperry," Larry had said.

"Here. Bring your face next to my iMac!" he'd laughed. "See? Exactly the same shade."

Nick hadn't pointed out Larry's beard and Botox shots gave Larry the expression of a surprised wildebeest. But he'd thought it. He'd later screamed it, very loud, in his car.

And so it had been decided Nick would take some time off.

"While you're down there, I hope you take a load off, Sperry," Larry Skakorfsky had said. "I've been covering for you since your old man died. But, man, I run a pop culture magazine, not a sniping range. After 9-11 people want a little less *hostility* with their celebrity profiles."

Because Sarah did not want to fly while the terrorist warnings remained high, the idea of Mexico had been raised.

It had been raised to a singularly underwhelming response.

"I thought you hated Mexico," Sarah had said. "I thought you said big hats and ruffled pink shirts irritated you."

"Did I say such a stupid thing?"

In fact, Nick had been to Mexico only once. With his father, he'd visited a Mexican military show for the 121st anniversary of the Battle of Puebla. His father had been jovial, vigorous, slapping people on the backs. The Mexicans didn't like to be slapped so hard, or spoken to in English, but Phil had been drinking. Through his grin, Phil sneered at the *militaria* tanks, calling them subpar. Unsure of what to say, Nick had agreed.

"Since you know so much, tell me what's wrong with the tanks, son," his father had said. He'd repeated the question twice, each time more dangerously.

Nick's answer, that the tanks were too small, had been wrong, of course.

Phil had spent the remainder of the trip quizzing Nick on the regurgitative slow-point output of Mexican tanks, and on topics like how, on May 14, 1926, Captain Emilio Carranza had flown nonstop from San Diego to Mexico City in twenty-one hours, four minutes in a Ryan Brougham Special named *Mexico-Excelsior.* And how on June 3, Major Roberto Fierro Vilalobos had flown the Tijuana-built *Baja, California* No. 2 parasol monoplane nonstop from Mexicali to Mexico City in fifteen hours, and nine weeks later, on August 11, he flew the same aircraft from Mexico City to Havana, Cuba.

And so, Nick, at age ten, had decided never to come to Mexico again.

At age thirty-two, Nick had regrettably overturned the ruling.

The trip had been meant as a solitary writer's kind of trip; the kind that might get him in touch with exactly what was eating him alive. But American tourists were too numerous in Baja for that kind of trip. Every beach was full of Cadillac Escalades sporting tiny American flags. While the flag-owners frolicked on the shores, wiping their hands assiduously with Handi Wipes after touching doorknobs and cutlery, the beggars stole the flags for resale.

"Aren't they inspirational?" the vacationing secretaries and lawyers said of the cardboard homes. "They have so little and yet they're so happy."

The limbless beggars spoke English, trailed doggedly on skateboards and dollies. They often called Nick "my friend."

"Of course, Mexico is going to get behind us in the end," the flag-bearers said of the Iraq War, the UN Security Council.

"Of course, Mexico is a friendly democracy."

"Of course, Mexico depends on us for aid."

Thus, the Americans dispersed coins and cold Coca-Colas into the democracy, using the word "amigo" while the beggars smiled and used the word "friend."

Six-year-olds curtsied, did native dances. Native trinket-sellers sniffed glue from imported sandwich bags.

Nick took photos, took aspirins, took a look at his map of Mexico.

"What do you think?" Sarah had said in front of the gated condo community of blond ex-Texans and blond ex-San Diegans.

"Maybe we keep going?"

They'd walked around, tried to walk off their depression, watched their countrymen shop for antidepressants at half price.

They had lasted exactly three days in Ensenada.

They had lasted fewer in Acapulco, Mazatlán.

One thing Nick wasn't prepared for was six-year-olds working a crowd. Another was the ancient, wheezing donkeys painted to look like zebras.

"And so we'll make it an adventure," Sarah said. "We'll drive. Who knows where we'll end up?"

"And those poor old donkeys. Painted with latex housepaint. How in the world are the things supposed to *sweat?*"

They'd thought they'd escaped, but farther south, they'd met backpacking Europeans. That had been scary, all right. Why was the US government trying to overthrow the UN? Why did they want to invade helpless countries? *Mon dieu! Mein Gott! Ay Dios! Ach du lieber!* For six days Nick had been held personally responsible for bombing Afghani children, undoing the Kyoto Accords, starving the people of Africa, raping the land of Palestine.

While lying on a beach south of Los Reyes it had been Nick's privilege to hear: "If the terrorists want to get the worst Americans, they can forget New York, hit Los Angeles instead."

A German had relayed that piece of knowledge.

"It's so much better not to be the most hated country in the world anymore," the German had said conversationally.

A German drinking Coke, wearing Ray·Bans. Who made films.

The call to battle had become more insistent with every new beach. Nick learned long before Cancún never to accept a drink from a continental with a distended vein on his neck.

"I guess we'll just stay to ourselves," Nick told Sarah. "They're the ones who should be embarrassed. I mean, Christ, we agree with them about the war."

The lazy, tropical beaches swarmed with skinny, angry, voluble Italians in Speedos, erstwhile UN envoys wearing jute crisscross sandals, native ponchos, string jewelry.

"Why are British people dressing like Guatemalans when we're in Mexico?" Sarah asked.

Later she had asked, "Why are they dressing like Guatemalans at all?"

"No, I don't *think* we should pretend to be Canadians," Nick said. In fact, he had been debating whether to cover their license plate with masking tape. "I'm not going to let some rude, hairy Belgian in a Che Guevara T-shirt ruin our first trip together. What does a Belgian know about revolution anyway?"

"The difference is they all hate us *personally* now," Sarah had sighed. "When I've traveled before it was never this personal."

Nick didn't like to be reminded Sarah had traveled before. Traveling "before" meant before Nick, when she had other boyfriends with more money, more free time, possibly larger and more engaging penises.

What in the world would Sarah's "before" boyfriends have done if they'd been asked, over and over, why Americans thought they were entitled to steal the world's oil supply?

Why in the world had Nick not suggested Maui, Miami Beach? Surely a war book could more easily be written in *peace.*

"What we're going to do is ignore all café revolutionaries," Nick had said to his girlfriend.

Later he'd said, "What we're going to do is pretend we're Canadian."

Spit was a hard one. Angry spittle was difficult enough when it came from braying Flemish dudes, but when the moisture came from bikinied French beauties, lovely Swedish girls, beautiful Mexican señoritas it was worse. It had always puzzled Nick that love-spit, the kind that came with kissing and fellatio, was delicious, but anger-spit, no matter how beautiful the spitter, was gross and bitter and untenable.

"With the unfortunate 's's placed at strategic spots, 'USA imperialist' *is* a particularly spit-laden phrase." Sarah sighed.

"Scud missile," Nick had agreed, was not good on the saliva front either.

"Honestly, we need to do something about our license plate," Sarah had said.

"Honestly, these peace-lovin' backpacker types are getting pretty scary."

He wasn't culpable for an Iraq invasion, Nick wanted to tell the magnificent Euro-women who wanted to spit at his country. He had nothing whatsoever against the UN. He hadn't even *voted* in the last election—like most Americans he'd been too busy working to pay off his credit card bills.

Sarah had tried to disappear behind her bangs. She'd tried to wear dark glasses. But it was no use trying to fit in, she told Nick, no use trying to hide. The two of them were absolutely imperialists. Their imperial blue passports said so.

"So what should we do?" she asked Nick, in a low, depressed tone. "One of them is going to start a fight. It's not like I don't stand out, even here."

"Just keep going south, I guess."

"How far south should we go?"

"Until we find a beach with no one on it."

"That could take a while."

"Larry gave me a lot of time, for some reason."

In the out-of-the-way motels, even in the car on a dead-end road, sex between them had been unaccountably hot at first.

"I guess it's because everyone wants to kill us," Sarah said.

And yet, she'd started to get less effusive around about Los Amelinos.

"Is there something wrong?"

"No. I came twice. It was good."

Nick knew what was wrong: no woman wanted to watch a man lose a geopolitical debate to a kid in dreadlocks. No woman could be expected to come after *that*.

"No. I came. I did. I promise." She'd smiled a soft, sad smile.

"Do you think they're spitting in our food?" she asked nervously in the roadside café with the English-language menu. As her uneasiness steadily increased, her detachment from Nick had seemed to grow.

"Nah. They're probably just laughing into it."

Having grown up believing every person in Mexico envied and emulated the free, rich citizens of the United States, Nick hadn't been prepared for snobbery *a la Mexicana*. Who would have guessed the low-rent perception of American citizens by Mexico's middle class? Any Mexican who owned a sport jacket or even a blender exclusively admired Europeans. "Americans have no culture," they said, clicking their tongues. "All they do is watch robot movies, eat *los* Big Macs all day."

Even the working classes in Mexico tended to use the term "yanqui" (yahn-key) in place of *"Americano." Americano* or the hideous "gringo" were at least somewhat friendly. Canadians could be gringos, for instance, as could Swedes, Dutch, even light-skinned Chileans. Yanqui, however, was reserved for aggressive, bullying, north-of-the-border menaces. The term, Nick had learned, was synonymous with "stupid prick."

And so for many weeks before the trip, Nick had worried the Mexicans might think his BMW coupe arrogant. Now it was clear there was no point in not washing his car for two months before leaving LA. Plenty of middle-class Mexicans had plenty of shiny BMWs. Plenty had art-school educations.

"Yanqui Go Home" was a popular techno dance tune.

"And there we have it," Nick said to the air.

Blue

And here he sat, watching dragonflies alight in the pools of sweat in the folds of his stomach. The charming *Swiss Family Robinson*–esque waterwheel could be seen in the distance churning water from the underground lake. Jute wash lines hung in orderly rows among the slender coconut palms, stone washtubs were camouflaged with thatched overhangs. Poured concrete outbuildings were decorated with painted coconut shells, driftwood sculptures, conch shells, coral shards. Here and there the Von Tollmans had even attempted a bit of whimsy: a gold-leafed motor oil can, a shimmery flip-flop encrusted with barnacles. They'd installed brightly painted birdbaths, Toltec-inspired hummingbird feeders, copious Germanic-Mayan statuary (blocky yet toothy), for the further delight of their guests.

It was all so goddamn *wrong*. Like a medieval beer stein come to life.

Which reminded Nick of the wrongheaded reason they'd driven all the way to the remote Yucatán Caribbean: the beer-throwing incident. The Yucatán was approximately three thousand miles past their initial plan.

"I couldn't hit her," Nick had told Sarah, sorrowfully. "She was a girl."

Were he a Neanderthal, or a jerk, or a better nihilist, Nick could have hit the Austrian girl, and then her Mexican hippie boyfriend. He might have guessed there would be trouble when the Austrian asked if they were Canadians.

"Everyone knows the Americans engineered the 9-11 to help Israel," the Austrian said. "Everyone knows your country is ruled by Jews for Jews."

"*Ándale!* Israelis planned the attacks and their lapdogs, *claro que sí,* invade Iraq," the Mexican boyfriend had continued.

"Nick, let's just go," Sarah had said.

The outline of the Austrian girl's nipples, the hatred in the Mexican's eyes, had flummoxed Nick so that all he could do was defend himself with a stammered, "Hey, now, let's not get anti-Semitic! That's hardly reasonable!"

The Austrian girl had soon been joined by her French friend. The French friend seemed lovely and fresh-faced and youthful and gorgeous, even in her *solidaridad con los Zapatistas* garb.

"Reasonable! So your treatment of the Arabs is reasonable?" (Pronounced "rhy-sonable.") "You even treat your neighbors the Mexicans like dogs. Look at NAFTA. You will chain all the poorest Mexicans into sweatshops so you can have your cheap telephones and Nikes and stuffed animals." The French girl accentuated her words with a skewer of charcoal-grilled beef.

"Me? So *I'm* the one buying all those low-priced teddy bears? It's been *me* all along?" Nick, who knew almost nothing about NAFTA, and in fact, thought it something Mexicans were happy about, nevertheless decided to take on the French girl's wild inaccuracies. If nothing else, he'd thought, standing up to them would make Sarah want to fuck him again.

"Americans are *just like* the Nazis," the girl had said, as the night went on.

"More worse," the Austrian chimed in.

"Absolutamente," the Mexican said.

"Americans are the worst criminals"—the night had degenerated—"look what they did to the Indians! The blacks!"

"And now the Jews behave *just like* Nazis to the Palestinians. And they get paid by the USA."

"Solidaridad con los pobres Palestinos!"

The trio had clasped hands.

"Hey! Jews and Israelis are not synonymous," Nick had cried out, upsetting the table. "Just for starters."

"Don't talk to my girlfriend like that, *cabrón,*" the Mexican had said.

"Nick, let's *go.*" Sarah had tried to take his hand.

Nick had not gone and had, in fact, asked the French girl if she'd ever learned the charming history of her own country. He supposed he'd shouted a little, rolled his eyes around like a maniac.

Blinking, he recalled the shock of the beer being emptied in his lap.

"American pig," the French girl had said. "Sixty-three percent of Europe *knows* the Mossad and your CIA was behind the attacks."

And nearly the exact percentage of Americans "knew" Saddam Hussein was behind the bombing of the World Trade Center. Nick had fumed and burped.

"And now you're going to kill Arab children!"

And now the soldier-kid was on his way to Iraq.

"And now you've insulted my girlfriend, yanqui!"

When the Mexican boyfriend had waved to his chums sitting in the back, Nick had raised his hand and grabbed a large, blunt saltshaker. The Mexican had raised his fist, grabbed the empty bottle of beer. There the implements had stayed, wavering, in the air.

"Stop this! Stop it!"

All at once, Sarah had gotten quietly to her feet. She was Nick's height, exactly. He had never felt so small, so diminished.

"This isn't solving anything. This is so incredibly *dumb.* You, please put your beer down. Nick. Put down the salt."

"They were just rich kids high on amphetamines," Sarah had later said.

She'd been distant while he kissed her. "Let's forget them. Let's keep going south."

And now Nick and Sarah were very far away from beer incidents, possible gang rapes, Mexican snobs, USA hat-wearers, European model/revolutionariettes. They were here at the Guesthaus Esmeralda—eighty acres of Caribbean beach, so far away from everything it was as if they'd arrived at the end of the world. Nick was finally alone with his girlfriend, but Sarah was charmed by Karl's eco-beard and shrubbery lectures, his predawn bird walks, his five A.M. berry-gathering sessions, his "fascinating"—probably faked—extemporizations on sexy, savage Mayan ritual.

She was charmed by his "life philosophy."

There was no sense in shouting at Sarah that the use of a bow and arrow didn't constitute a philosophy, or threatening to call the Simon Wiesenthal Center on Karl when they got back to LA. Sarah was right: Karl, at sixty-three, was too young to be a Nazi.

He closed his eyes, letting the velvety dew collect on them.

"It's just that you're so consumed with making me sound like a dimwit," she'd said last night, closing her harlequin's eyes. "It's like you're taking pleasure in mocking things I enjoy."

Not mocking, he thought, rubbing a leaf until it was dust under his fingers. Not mocking.

A bird cried out: *haw, haw, haw.*

"I'm not the enemy, Nick."

That was a problem with Sarah—she was always right. She would always do the right thing. Upright and earnest and strong and even and measured.

A good soldier.

"The girl's too good for you, son."

Nick had now wasted a beautiful sunrise thinking about Nazis, talking to insects, grimacing at waterwheels. As he fished around for his keys, he began to make a plan.

The plan for the day was to forget about war, think about happy things, bright things. He was against war. He was against Nazis. If one needed war to get rid of Nazis, well that was just too much wigginess to fit into one hungover mind.

Goddamnit. He was doing it again.

Nick's mornings had not been particularly peaceful or cheerful this year. Most had started with a nightmare involving Phil, a hangover. From there they had segued into checking the latest Osama news.

"Something could go off in a supermarket," CNN commentators had said. "A Wal-Mart. Anywhere."

"Something big is in the planning stages, according to Al Qaeda."

"Americans will never know what it is to feel safe again."

Nick had pasted an antiwar sticker on his bumper, pasted Phil's picture on his lightweight punching bag. Still, he had preceded every elevator ride to his office with a secret sniff to test for the scent of marzipan—sweet almond—the smells of a gas attack. Still, Sarah stocked up on canned beans, water, matches.

Still, the Terrorist Threat-o-Meter continued to swing from moderate to high.

Goddamnit. Why couldn't he stop worrying and losing his hair?

Nick, it could be absolutely said, was against the Iraq War. The war had caused Nick to drive three thousand miles out of his way. It had caused Sarah to meet Karl. Meeting Karl was a terrible mistake. The Iraq War was a terrible mistake. Boys were going to die so pricks could drive Cadillac Escalades. Boys were going to die and it was going to hurt.

In Ensenada, Nick and Sarah had met a young soldier taking his last holiday before being sent to Kuwait. The kid was a shy, muscled vegetarian. His tattoo read JESUS LIVES.

Nick had made it a point to buy the young soldier a beer. He thought the kid might give him an interesting insight into a mania for war, but all the young soldier had said was, "I just don't like meat."

Nick's father had tried to join the service in 1966, and had been rejected. Phil Sperry was a Catholic. Nick was a hopeful atheist.

"God hates evil," Phil had said.

"I guess God will watch out for me," the soldier had said.

"Allah will praise those who obliterate the infidel," said the boys on the other side.

It was said the Pope would come out against the war on Iraq. To kill, the Pope had apparently said, was against God.

But then again the Pope wasn't an American.

Allah, apparently, wasn't either.

Nick listened to the sound of the waves. Waves were supposed to soothe, to replicate the sounds of the womb. Why then, did every wave, every new liquid crash against the shore, bring with it so much *agony?*

Phil had believed in the infallibility of the Pope.

"The body's a temple, dude," the soldier had said.

Beer didn't belong in a temple. Apparently 7UP had been okay.

"If I die, I'm going to go to heaven."

"Seventy virgins in heaven," was the promise from the other region.

Nick didn't understand the appeal of virgins, particularly. Nick didn't understand Phil's logic about guns and God. Nick would die and hope there was a heaven with Sarah in it, no guns, lots of screwing. A hopeful atheist, he would persevere.

More and more it all seemed so fucking *unlikely.*

The psychiatrist on TV claimed Nick's present nervous mania was part of posttraumatic stress. Nick, who had been three thousand miles away from the Twin Towers when they'd fallen, couldn't *possi-*

bly suffer from what the Vietnam vets all had. If he did, the whole country had post-traumatic stress disorder, ergo everyone's trouble was comparable to a Vietnam veteran's.

"Maybe just a little Prozac to get you through the rough months," Sarah had said.

"The guy's a fraud. It just makes me sick."

In point of fact, Nick would like to sic his father on all handsome TV doctors, their peddling of nerve pills, their easy co-option of the aftermath of 9-11. For once in his life Nick would have looked forward to his father's rant. The doctors would hear about Danang '67, Penang '67, Tet, Quang Tri '68, Que Son '68, Hue '68 until they begged Phil to stop. But Phil wouldn't have stopped. He would have pinned the doctors down with a huge, meaty forearm, worked himself into such a lather that he would begin using the pronoun "we," as in, "We saw combat in Hue." "We fought for our country." "We know post-traumatic stress."

Of course, the doctors would never think to ask whether Phil had served.

The guesthouse keys were in his pocket. No, they were on a chain around his neck. No, they had slipped during his rant last night, and were somewhere on the deck.

But, no.

He was crazy to think things might be so easy.

"Crazy happy," that's how Sarah had put it. It made her crazy happy to wake up, get in a canoe, slice through the water, feel the roughened paddle in her hands.

It made her crazy happy, "like heaven, really."

The Yucatán sun was crazy bright in the morning. Between the beachfront and the northern limits of Karl's property were a chain of low hills that looked onto a lagoon and a series of underground cenotes. Fairies, apes, Sasquatchs could easily live here. Nick had to get out of bed. Start the day. A little sun and canoeing. A cheerful day doing healthy things. Crazy things.

Yep. That's how it would be.

Yep. Yep. Yep. All he had to do was find his keys.

A slight wind had come up, whipping the vines against one another. Massive dark clouds remained fixed against the Yucatán sky, neither moving nor shedding needed rain. Palm fronds scratched against the railing, splattering mud, insect eggs, and webby, mysterious fibers.

Even now, as Nick stood alone on the deck, he couldn't help but be unnerved by the purplish light over the thin Yucatán palm trees. The ruins of a small pyramid crumbled in the distance, parrots and monkeys could be seen darting in and out of its shadows. Other ruins and parrots lay beyond it—for fifty miles in either direction, the guesthouse was completely isolated. The gulls swaying in the slight wind, the ocher tint of the morning hibiscus, the nearby crash of waves—it was all, in some way, telling Nick to look lively, soldier on, pretend.

Not a particularly adventurous soul, not a tent-user, a backroader, or a chic hippie-type, Nick had nonetheless endeavored to become such a soul. On *this* vacation, on *this* occasion of his thirty-second year, on *this* first year without his father's living presence looming over him, he'd sworn to become a happy-go-lucky guy. To this end he'd forced himself to dry shave, to eat goat, to smile while showering with plastic bags on his feet. He'd climbed to the top of a pyramid, trekked through a mosquito-filled jungle, ridden a horse fast on a nasty beach. He'd made use of a Swiss Army knife (albeit as a corkscrew), and had drunk from the bottle itself. He'd stayed calm during the snake episode, the hurricane warning, the odd rash on his inner thigh. Before they'd come upon the Gasthaus Esmeralda, before she met Karl Von Tollman, Sarah had smiled at him a lot.

Her smiles had spurred him on to pretend a little more.

Sarah seemed so happy after he'd lied to her, telling her his book was writing itself.

"I told you I could write the thing. All I needed was a little time off."

The lie had made her want him, and want him badly. With Karl's half-assed ceiling fan clicking morbidly overhead, Sarah had dragged him to bed, sat atop his erect penis, came not once, but three times. Moreover, he'd been sure, absolutely sure, she had come because of *him,* Nick Sperry, not because she was imagining fucking Karl Von Fucking Tollman. No, because of the lie, she'd come hard and bad, and flushed red across her chest. Because of the lie she did not regret being with him, did not feel revulsion, did not feel gypped—even *if* he was a pacifist who did not even make his own pencils and chairs and canoes.

He decided that today he'd learn to make a pencil.

He'd stop drinking.

He'd look her deeply in the eyes, grab her. "Here's a pencil for you," he'd say.

As he continued to look for his keys, picking up pieces of his novel that had been largely filled with the penciled word "Nazi," his smile dropped away. It was he who'd insisted on leaving Playa del Carmen for the wilds of the Esmeralda Coast. Though Playa had seemed like a perfect writer's destination—a town written up as "still pretty remote, while retaining much of its lazy charm"—Playa had turned out to be mostly ravers and ecstasy dealers.

In retrospect the raver kids had been all right, mostly too stoned to get into political discussions. The sea was pretty enough from a distance. Up close, however, the charming beaches had been full of diapers, Coke cans, raver kids smoking joints. Twice he'd tried to walk a mile or two, scout out his own patch of pristine sand, but beyond the line of hotels and bars, the plastic bags whirling in the offshore breeze, the plastic bags impaled on fence posts and cactus, the plastic bags floating in the azure water, had made him sure a writer could do better.

Though Sarah had patiently pointed out that beaches all over the world had trash on them, and that Playa was peaceful enough for her, Nick had decided to head straight toward a great blob of green on the map.

"If it's all green there, it means 'undiscovered,' because the tourist areas are colored pink," he'd reasoned. Cities were mostly shaded brown.

After two more days driving, he'd landed them in a swollen, billowing gob of green—green vines; green ivy, emerald kudzu, thick jade-tinted sapsago, cascading, verdant, impossibly overgrown ceiba—a place so green and abundant and humid and remote and thick, the very air seemed to drip moisture.

"No, I'm not nervous at all," he'd told Sarah.

Once, as a kid, when Nick had been scared by a neighborhood dog, Phil had seen fit to show him *Apocalypse Now* as a punishment. Key scenes Phil rewound and repeated.

"Do you see *these* boys crying under *these* circumstances?" Phil Sperry had said, disgusted.

No, I'm not nervous at all," Nick had repeated to Sarah throughout the journey to Esmeralda Beach.

Several times they'd come upon unsmiling, possibly hostile, bands of men who'd looked at the BMW with stony silence.

"Why should we be nervous? They're just guys."

Humping over mountain passes, lagoon byways, campesino roads, palm tree after palm tree, he'd kept up the adrenaline pace. Consulting maps, consulting his *Let's Go: Mexico* guide, taking wild turns, scanning motel parking lots for rental car stickers (which meant hassle and Europeans), he'd driven the BMW coupe as if possessed.

Around the time a group of pickax-toting Mexicans had asked Nick how much his car cost, Nick had started to hear Phil Sperry laughing in his mind. Phil had enjoyed adventure to the exact degree Nick did not.

"In the 'Nam bugs were ten times this size," he was wont to say on camping trips.

"I guess we could always use the tent we brought for emergencies," Sarah had said in her melodious way. "We could probably just set up on the beach. Make camp."

But there was the fact of the unsmiling locals on their turkey shoots; *their* Che berets were not affectation. There was the fact that Phil had once knocked the wind from Nick for being slow at setting up a tent. As a father, Phil favored the quick left hook.

"It would be fun to pretend we're the only ones left in the world." Sarah had laughed and stretched. "It might even be kind of ridiculous."

Yes, it might have been fun to play survival games, except that on camping trips with his father, Nick had been forced to play "Vietnam." Toy guns and knives were divvied up, hoods and army-navy surplus gear were taken out of suitcases. Whiskey was drunk, eyes were narrowed, temples throbbed. Usually Nick was the gook. Phil was the general.

As it was, camping seemed unfun, sick-making, murky.

As it was, camping called to mind "capture," "prisoner," "interrogation tent."

"No problem. So we'll just camp," Nick had told Sarah. "Good plan—buying the tent."

At least the emergency tent was an Eazy Erect model. Nick hated when "z"s were used instead of "s"s. Already the marketing people presumed you were dumb and skittish.

Which Nick certainly was.

"It'll just be for one night. And I'll be right there." She'd laughed and kissed him. "And nothing bad will happen. I promise."

And then they'd seen the sign.

GASTHAUS FOR RENT. HALFWAY DOWN THE ROAD TO ESMERALDA. NO CHILDREN. DOLLARS ONLY. UNDER THE STONE ARCH.

The weather-beaten sign had been lashed to a palm tree. It had come at them almost from nowhere. When they'd seen the advertisement for the Gasthaus Esmeralda, Sarah had laughed, kissed him deeply, said, "Ah, too bad. I was starting to get ideas."

"We could—"

"Yes we could." Sarah had stretched, luxuriously. "But then again . . . hot water. Towels. Mmmm."

"Still, I'll leave it up to you."

She had crossed and recrossed her long legs, leaned back in the seat, studying Nick with a teasing expression. "Hmmm. We could destroy all of your bad memories of Phil in one fell swoop, or we could take a shower with actual soap."

Then, she'd laughed. "Oh, I'm just teasing. It's going to be fantastic waking up at a gasthaus. Whatever *that* is."

At that moment, she'd been so golden and glowing, so patient and handsome, so weird and weirdly delighted, Nick had loved Sarah more than any person ever before.

A thought had occurred to him: Phil's.

"That girl's too good for you, son."

Since meeting Sarah, Nick had been marking Phil's words, marking them with a precise, insistent inner dialogue: *Salman Rushdie is hideous enough and no one questions his lovely gal. V. S. Naipaul is a toad but look what he's got.*

"Of course, she's too good for you," Phil had said. "Girls like Sarah want a rocket scientist, a Corpsman, a member of a biker gang. They don't want something regular."

"I like how you do exactly what you want," Nick had overheard Sarah saying to Karl not too long ago. She'd been trying to explain to him the life of a freelance graphic designer.

"Computers! *Ach!* What a waste of time, *Liebchen!* Why don't you young people want fresh air? Why save up all your money for a two-week jaunt into fresh air when it's all right here! Pretty soon, you're all going to be born with pointed fingers, all the better to push toggle switches, buttons, knobs, and keypads."

Sarah had laughed dangerously, helplessly, a way she never laughed with Nick. She'd stretched out her arms to the sun. Given Karl a friendly squeeze.

"We're not all so lucky, Mr. Von Tollman," she'd teased, "to have our own little seventy-acre nation to escape to."

"*Ach,* luck has nothing to do with anything, girl." Karl had winked at her. "If you want something you do it. There's always a way."

And now the keys were gone, and so was Sarah. It was a betrayal, Nick thought. A sensation of ambush. Of course, he'd been drunk and obnoxious. Then again, he might have been set up. Karl might have left the Midori in the bottom cabinet for Nick to find. Karl might have told Sarah to take the keys, meet him on the beach last night.

"I've never really felt right in my job," she'd told Karl in a dejected voice. "But you can't always make a living doing things you feel right about."

Freelance, Sarah worked at home, often in her tailored pajamas, head bent over a project, nodding coolly while arranging pixels and fonts into intricate formats. Photoshopping double chins, slenderizing thighs, rosy-ing cheeks, there was an endless supply of work for her. Her hours were long, her office door often closed.

Sometimes, he'd hear her sobbing in there.

"Not crying, no. But please don't come in."

Because Nick was fully apprised that PMS could make a woman cry for no reason, and because PMS could not be reasoned with, and because Sarah didn't even have to talk to anyone while earning the same pay as Nick did, he'd mostly let her cry without too much grilling.

Maybe it wasn't perfect, but she didn't exactly have the world's worst job.

"What if we just gave it all up and joined the Peace Corps?"

Every once in a while Sarah emerged from her office, talking about going to Somaliland, Palestine, Burundi. And every once in a while she smoked a cigarette, or tried a new haircut.

"I know. I know. I'm just having white-person guilt. It's all this bad news, and Anglo-Saxons are always in the center of it."

"That's because you're not watching African CNN."

Like a gallstone, like Nick's eczema, Sarah's guilt broke out from time to time. Then it went subterranean, and she'd coolly and competently pass out pamphlets to save a park. He'd always envied her practical remedies.

"I guess what I feel," she'd said to Karl, "is sadness. Almost all the time."

"Nonsense, girl." Karl had laughed. "What you feel is rage."

Here she was endlessly happy, sweating, peeling, moist—dirty fingernails, hot earth etched deep below her anklebones. As he took her from behind, he watched her grit-stained backbone move up and down. But no matter how he pulled her to him, pushed himself inside of her, he wasn't reaching anything. The diaphragm between them felt vast and dry.

"Of course I came." She'd laughed. But her chest had remained a telltale white. The noises she'd made weren't right.

A rushing, twittery feeling came over him. The noises just *weren't* the *right* ones.

They were guilty noises: Nick recognized them. He'd heard them many times before.

"Like Crusoe, don't you think?"

"Karl's doing exactly what he wants to do."

Even now Nick could imagine Phil Sperry lifting a decaying, bony finger out of the grave, pointing in a ghostly-yet-insistent manner toward Karl Von Tollman's house. The finger was shaking with undisguised mirth, as the corpse lifted itself, higher and higher, and Phil Sperry's ghoulish face appeared.

"Mark my words, son. She's interested in the man."

Nick had been imagining the very finger, the very corpse, yesterday afternoon, when he'd come up behind Sarah, kissed her shoulder, sucked on her neck. The skin had tasted faintly of bitter lemon, herbs. When he'd lowered her straps, cupped her breasts, her nipples felt like jumping beans under his touch.

"I was just about to meet the Von Tollmans for tea. Do you mind if we have sex later?"

He'd tried again. The breasts were unresponsive: cold lard.

"I thought you were just with him."

"I *was,* but we'd talked about having tea. The truth is, I've already promised them. They're having some kind of problem with the locals, and I want to hear about it. I thought you'd be working."

Sarah had not been shaving her armpits, Nick had noticed. The hair was getting to the point where it had to be deliberate. Her breasts had become smaller, more triangular in shape as she shed water weight.

"If you ask me, their problems aren't with the locals," Nick had said, unhappily. Just the day before Cordula had hidden Sarah's underwear on the wash line, stringing towels around it in an attempt to hide it from Karl's view. "I've never known a woman to have so many peculiar pains. And if I have to hear about those aching teeth again, I'll scream. Why doesn't Karl carve her a wooden set? She already calls to mind George Washington."

"I feel sorry for her. She's been begging Karl to move back to Mexico City," Sarah had conceded. "I guess she's lonely out here. Though she says that's not it."

"Look, forget them and their weird, steaming bowls of twigs. Stay here with me."

In the end, Sarah had sex with him anyway, and it had been bad.

It had been bad because he'd been aware she'd made the cardinal sin of calling sex sex. When you had to call it sex, sex was already over.

Ffft. Fffft. Ffft.

From far off, among the trees, Cordula Von Tollman, Karl's wife, could be seen chopping logs into firewood, her brows drawn together in a single, harassed line. Cordula's gray mountain of hair swung in time to the staccato motions. A few of the shepherds nosed at the stone wall behind her, terrorizing lizards. From far off a dog was yapping, roosters scratched and pecked.

The smell of the sea was strong in Nick's bruised nostrils. When he looked up, his eyes rested on a necklace of birds circling a stand of thorn trees. Their swoopings, glidings, seemed a physical representation of his hangover.

"Excuse me?" Nick swung around. Cordula was talking to the dogs. The conversation seemed intense and private. Spooky.

He tried the door of their guesthouse again and again. It was impossible to believe. The room *he was paying for* was locked. Cordula was not with Karl. Sarah had deliberately taken his keys, kept him off-balance, away.

He knocked on the window hopelessly, peered in.

Done up in high-Heidi style with a pitched roof, brightly colored window boxes, jaunty curlicues carved into the molding, the structure might have been set down, intact, from Zermatt. The enormous bed was covered in a lace mantle, a cutie-pie quilt; both contrasted sharply with the frayed mosquito netting. An antique oil painting of a snowbound scene in the Alps hung over a purely decorative fireplace, little elfin tables were strewn with doilies. Overhead, heavy support posts painted to resemble pine bowed inward from years of relentless tropical moisture, lacy curtains moldered along a bamboo pole, a WILLKOMMEN welcome mat sat on the doorstep. The flooring was speckled with blue Dresden tile. The chairs were sized for gnome-people. Cordula, it could be ascertained, enjoyed miniatures.

"Crap."

There was no doubt anymore that Sarah was not asleep inside. But maybe she had only risen early, gone for an eco-lesson with Karl. That the "lesson" consisted of tugging a homemade sled through the sand, loading it up with articles washed in on the night tide, was disturbing enough. But if a choice find was discovered—say a cache of old driftwood, or a tossed outboard motor—Sarah could be away for hours while she helped the old cheapskate bundle and sort the wreckage.

Sarah. Sarah. Doer of good works. Valkyrie with a pickax and a smile.

Bending over the railing, Nick tried to calm himself by breathing rhythmically, fixing his gaze on the ocean just visible through the trees, but the liquid movement of the waves only stirred his bladder. When he closed his eyes, a glowing bladder appeared on the inside of his eyelids.

"Oh, it's less noble than it sounds." Sarah had laughed. "This place used to be a Mayan site so I keep thinking I'm going to find some wildly valuable artifact, but usually we find stuff people threw out of the passing cruise ships. Deodorant from Lichtenstein. Coke cans from Brazil—it all comes in on the Gulf Stream. Scary, really."

"Most people try to avoid scary things."

"Most people don't know what they're missing then," she'd said lightly. "Karl looks for old wood because it has a beautiful grain. And he fills the cans and bottles with sand and uses them for insulation. See? Not so weird or crazy. He's like one of those guys you'd want to be stuck in a life raft with."

"Karl Von Tollman would kill and eat you in a life raft. And no doubt his industrious wife would make a nice slaw from your innards."

"Frightening," she then agreed. "How you never know what a person would do."

But tell me what you'd do in this scenario," the old man had started up yesterday in the canoe. For a while they'd been paddling along the lagoon quite peacefully. Nick had been quite prepared to have a good time. "They wait a few years until you're all calm and lulled, then they poison the water supplies of ten major cities at once, at the same time bombing a few major oil fields in the Mideast. While the world comes to a halt, they drive a few planes into nuclear plants, and they—"

"In *that* scenario I'd walk out and demand a refund for the bad movie I'd somehow stumbled into," Nick had said, paddling furiously.

"But no, really," Sarah had interjected. "Karl has a point."

"Which is?"

She'd looked up, swiveling her neck, a rubber band being pulled too tight.

"Well, that he's right. It could happen. Something's going to happen, anyway."

Because Karl had displayed the irritating teeth, and because Nick had noticed Karl's hairline was perfectly intact, Nick had been moved to comment that Karl was, in fact, quite wrong, that nothing spectacular would happen to end humanity. There would be no mobs of well-planned suitcase-bomb attacks, no tit-for-tat rain of missiles, no World War Three, no dramatic, flash-fried moment whereby populations came to a sudden, fiery end. Humans would follow very much the same slow breakdown his father had when he'd died of cancer, the long, excruciating payback for each bad habit and vice—first the stomach lining goes, then the liver, the lungs, the brain.

"So your father was a drinking man, then?" Karl had said.

"That wasn't what I was trying to say. I was attempting to point out you might be overly dramatic. They thought the end was near in the year 1000. They were sure of it—the Bonfire of the Vanities. All the cults."

He emphasized the word "cults."

"They say if a man has a problem with drinks, the son will have the problem, too." Karl emphasized the word "drinks."

Karl did not, of course, "trink the likkids," or smoke or take drugs. Karl shot his own "sustainable" meat, ate vegetables pulled from his own garden. Karl thought he was the president of his own tiny nation.

Later in the same canoe ride:

"If you grimace and groan and hide from the sun all day, what in the hell do you want to write for, boy? There can't be any money in it."

"Well, wait a minute, Karl!" Sarah had argued. As they'd passed under vines, she appeared to dissolve, reassemble, dissolve again. She moved the paddle with disarming grace. "The money doesn't matter, and you know it. If you're doing something you love, that's all you can ask for. You said that, yourself."

Karl had tossed a piece of salami to a submerged crocodile with a placid flick of his wrist. Nick had been annoyed by the warmth with which Sarah called Karl by his first name. Also, her argument with the old man struck him as too intimate by half.

"Ach." Karl watched the crocodile surface. "But do you *love* writing, boy? Do you love it so much? That's what I want to know."

"In what way do you mean 'love'?" Nick sat up straight. Then, thinking better of it, he slouched.

"How many ways are there to mean it?"

"Probably ten or twelve distinct ways in English alone."

"A book about your father, isn't it?" Karl had paddled a little more slowly.

Nick had kept his eyes trained on the crocodile swimming close to the boat. Its skin looked like an old, moist purse. It seemed to emanate a sulfur smell.

"You hate him."

Sarah opened her mouth.

"No. My book is fiction, *actually.*" Nick had closed his eyes tightly after giving Sarah a warning look. "It's not really about any one person in particular. It's set in the Vietnam War era, when I was a kid. It incorporates a lot of research I've done in the prewar structure of—"

"*Ach,* wars! There's no structure to wars, boy," Karl had interrupted. "Wars are all about land grabs. Grabs for water. Grabs for gold. Nothing more and nothing less. Nothing romantic in war."

Nick had gritted his teeth.

Still, Karl's chopping gesture managed to indicate there was no purpose to Nick's existence. Or maybe it was a mosquito on his hand.

"People make the same mistakes over and over and over whether things are written down or not. People are animals, boy, just stupid animals, no matter the crown of intelligence they've so placed on their own puffed-up heads. Like the bark beetles that eat a patch of forest until there aren't any more trees and they die out, people chew down the world and will keep chewing until they eat themselves out of house and home." He waved his hand again. "Get some unspoilt land. Build a fence around it. Try to keep the bark beetles and other parasites from getting in. And tell your father to go to hell and be done with it."

And still later, when the interminable canoe ride had ended, he had accompanied Sarah to the main house for an interminable dinner:

"What we've got ourselves is a *buk* writer and a *guerilla* girl, wife." Karl touched Sarah's shoulder in a friendly way. Tropical, heated smells blew in off the Caribbean, ripening the platter of cold meats, cream, cheeses, pickles that spun slowly on a jerry-rigged lazy Susan. A bowl of sardines in oil had been placed just near Nick's nose. "I don't know about the young man's books, but the girl's a fearless type. A fighter. She even likes crocodiles."

"Is that so?" Cordula Von Tollman was wrapped in a black rebozo reminiscent, to Nick's mind, of bat wings. All through the dinner she'd looked at Sarah and chewed.

"I'm afraid your husband exaggerates," Sarah said uneasily.

"No, no! For a vegetarian, she's remarkably intelligent. She tracked our way back with no help from me at all. There's a brain underneath that fancy hairdo with its streaks and chops and whatnot."

"Is that so?" Cordula had repeated. She was hunched in the too-small chair, in the inelegant, bearing-down posture of a farmhand. Her chewing became measured and ferocious.

Sarah's hand had moved, self-consciously, to her collarbone. Then and there Nick decided to smash one of Karl's Delft figurines by "accident."

"What we've got here is an adventuress, Corde," Karl continued. "They don't come along very often, so we'll have to take full advantage; put the girl to work. She learns faster even than our Al. Though I can't say I'm in favor of decorating one's toenails with pink lacquer. Not in the jungle where the color attracts wasps."

"Karlchen," Cordula reprimanded softly, "not everyone enjoys seeing the butter encrusted with crumbs from your toast. And maybe the young couple would like to be left alone on their holiday."

"Hear! Hear!" Nick had managed to say, before being interrupted.

"Pink toes. I suppose that's how they're attracting mates these days. Rings through the noses. Bones through the ear." Karl was talking to Sarah alone. "In my day we simply took what we wanted—after asking permission from the father, of course."

"But then, Karl wanted my pretty sister," Cordula offered into the silence. She smiled prettily. "There were five of us back then."

"Don't start in with the sister nonsense, Corde." Karl pointed with his fork. "Actually I wanted all five sisters. So I suppose even in my day it wasn't fair." He was about to go on, his mouth stuffed with toast, when Cordula said:

"My sister resembled you, Sarah. Wouldn't you say so, Karl?"

"I'm an old man, Corde. How can I remember what your sister looked like? Anyway, I got the best of the sisters, and that's the end of it."

The two couples sat at a picnic table under the stars, Nick stabbing a wedge of salami off the chipped bone china, while fighting the beetles that landed on his plate. Candles, flickering inside hurricane lamps, cast a wild glow over the blowing foliage.

"And so how is it, child, that my husband has convinced you to muck out the stables on your holiday?" Cordula finally said to Sarah. "Are you interested in one day becoming an innkeeper yourself?"

Sarah took a long, careful sip from the glass, avoiding Cordula's scrutiny of her. Only with a careful sideways glance could Nick see her bottom lip tremble. "I'm trying to stay out of Nick's way. That's why I've been tagging along with your husband. I hope I'm not making a nuisance of myself."

"Not at all, not at all," Karl had boomed. "The boy's got to write his weighty tome that might save the world from its foolishness. You can't be crowding him in there if the future of the human race is at stake!"

Nick clasped his hands ever more tightly.

"How many pages of this book have you finished?" Cordula turned to Nick with a show of interest.

"Uh," Nick had replied. "A hundred or so."

"I thought you had two hundred pages," Sarah said, jumping in gratefully.

Nick wiped sweat from the underside of his nose. "A hundred good pages. The rest need a lot of work."

"You mean to tell me you haven't read any of this book!" Karl bellowed suddenly. He looked relieved to turn his attention to Nick. "You're his woman, child! You owe it to him to give an opinion. My wife has an opinion about everything I do."

"And what is your opinion of Karl's . . . many fine hobbies?" Nick asked the woman, smiling. "Since we're on the subject?"

"A wife must finally agree with her husband if one hopes for harmony," Cordula said, seriously. She had mused Nick's question at length, as if her answer might solve a great philosophical conundrum. "But then, of course, you're not married, are you?"

She looked at Sarah.

"My prettiest sister never married," she'd continued. "She lived like you do, very free. She was quite adventurous. Spoiled, said some. But I always thought her marvelous. And all the men loved her, of course."

"I'd love to read Nick's book, and I will." Sarah leaned away, trying to draw herself out of the conversation, and at the same time keeping her physical distance from Nick, who was insistently squeezing her shoulder. To Cordula's profile she said, "I'm dying of curiosity, but Nick won't let anyone read the manuscript until it's finished. It's a superstitious fear a lot of writers have. But he promises I'll be the first."

"Nonsense," Karl said with great joviality. "Why don't you bring your book here, boy? Read it to us tonight? It's the kind of thing we like here—a nice evening by the hearth. Fictional accounts of this and that human folly. Besides, I'd like to hear your musings on war. I hear it's quite a terrible experience."

"Oh, yes," Cordula said to Nick. "We could invite Al, our hired man. He gets lonely in his lodgings, though he never complains."

"Except," Nick demurred, "I just don't do that."

Karl was running his tongue slowly against his teeth.

"See?" Sarah smiled. "What did I tell you? He's intractable."

"Or he's not writing a thing." Karl laughed.

And still later:

"In the autopsies of drinkers, the brain looks exactly like a hammock. Stretched out and full of holes."

The comment had been spoken by Karl to Cordula, aimed at Nick. Nick, who had been drinking from a bottle of tequila he'd brought, stopped himself from filling his glass again. He'd been the only one drinking at the table, though he'd noticed Cordula staring at the bottle a few times.

"Now, now," Cordula had said. "The children know your stand on the matter of drink, Karl. We all do."

Her use of the word "children" had been aimed at Karl, meaning Sarah.

" 'Drink' is a funny word," Sarah said, trying desperately to dispel the tension. "In German."

"Not so funny when they do your autopsy," Karl replied.

"I'll drink to that," Nick said.

Sarah bit her lip.

There had been a long, tense silence, broken by Cordula's passing a dish. For dessert was a jar of wild honey, a plate of arrowroot biscuits. The honey contained fine grains of sand. To Nick it called to mind miserable days masturbating—grains of sand in the Vaseline. The sea wind blew and blew.

"I think I'll have a small glass," Cordula finally said. "To commemorate our nice dinner party. It's been nice, hasn't it?" To Nick she then said, "We hardly ever have guests to dinner, you see."

Nick poured her a small one and she smiled.

Karl pushed his elbow under Nick's pouring hand, levered it to raise Nick's forearm.

"*Ach,* my lovely wife deserves a drink! A bigger one, fill it up to the brim, boy!" He had winked at his wife. "I know I've been nasty tonight and that I've spoiled yet another dinner with my poison tongue. But if I forget how to be nasty all is lost for me. You'll be begging for a computer and an easy chair, wife. You'll think your life is a tragic one, and that I've made a mistake spending every penny we had to move us out here away from the social whirl of Mexico City."

"That is quite enough tequila, thank you," Cordula said primly.

"No! More! More! Drink and be merry, wife!" Karl cried out.

A subterranean tension crept into the conversation.

"More cookies?" Cordula said.

"You see, it's not easy being an innkeeper who doesn't care for tourists," Karl then said, not losing his cheerful tone. "I find I've lost all my good manners, and worse, I've begun to envy the luxury of good manners in anyone else. But I'm sorry, wife, that I've embarrassed you. You deserve better."

Sarah laughed, uncomfortable.

Cordula chewed more and more precisely.

"More cookies, absolutely," Nick said.

"My wife is a gem among women, and I don't tell her so often enough. We didn't plan to take in paying guests," Karl had said. "But then those fools got into power and the bottom dropped out of the peso, and poof! We lost half of our savings overnight. And now Corde is destined to wash tanning lotion from sheets while I sanitize the jungle to our guests' liking—the dog poop picked up, the mosquitoes killed, the vines trimmed and pruned, the snakes put away in their holes for the night. It wasn't the life I'd promised her. No wonder she wants to *trink.*"

"Any life has its troubles, Karlchen," Cordula said, pushing the glass of tequila away.

"*Ach,* troubles! There's no trouble we can't handle." Karl reached out, gave Sarah another biscuit. He pushed Cordula's glass back in front of her, indicated she should drink, enjoy. "Not from scoundrels, idiots, idiot neighbors, or governments."

Cordula gave the drink a wary look.

"Let me tell you why the neighbors want my land, and they all do," Karl said to Nick. "Here at my rancho, people get dangerously happy—at first, anyway. They say it's a Mayan curse—that the first years are such heaven, anything that follows seems worth slogging through. One might get back just a *measure* of that initial happiness, you see. One becomes enchanted. Then obsessed. Then broke."

"Al's happy here," Cordula said quickly. "And he's been here quite a while."

"Well, they say being a Canadian is the secret to happiness," Nick replied.

"Telling people to go to hell," Karl said pointedly to Nick. "Protecting a good woman and a good piece of land. *That's* the secret to happiness, my young friend."

Excuse me, but where exactly is Al from?" Sarah had asked, mildly, when Cordula had continued to speak of him in glowing terms. "He seemed vague on the question when I asked."

". . . once they *know* you're happy," Karl had continued to speak of the neighbors trying to take his land, "they'll come after you. And they'll keep coming—wave after wave like Dresden when I was a boy."

"But that's terrible!" Sarah had exclaimed. "I didn't know you were in Dresden."

"Al's from Saskatoon," Cordula murmured. To Karl she held up a pleading hand. "He's hardly vague. I don't know why you would say he was."

"Just like in Dresden, the obliterators obliterate for no reason," Karl had continued. "Just to hear the loud sounds they can make. Just to try out their new bombs and zillion-dollar noise-making devices!"

"Karl lost his mother to the bombings in Dresden," Cordula

sighed gravely. She crossed herself. "His childhood was spent in a most terrible way."

"Oh, go on, wife. You talk about Al. It's a much happier subject." To Sarah, he grinned. "Al's my wife's pet project. Her golden bird with a broken wing."

"Alchen is hardly broken!" Cordula exclaimed. "And Canadians are, anyway, quite neutral and sensible. They're against this new war. Al tells me America is quite in favor of it."

"Of course, it's easy to be neutral knowing the American army is just next door," Nick pointed out.

"Then again, it could be seen as rather frightening," Karl said.

"And see what we've all become!" Sarah exclaimed. "A bunch of cynics—trusting nobody's good intentions, talking about war at dinnertime. It was a delicious dinner, Cordula. I enjoyed it. And Karl, I'm so sorry to hear about your mother. I'm especially sorry it was us."

"O Canada," Nick said, toasting.

"And Dresden." Karl clinked Nick's glass with a fork.

"And peace," Sarah joined in. "At least a *little* peace, I hope."

When Sarah had tried to single-handedly take responsibility for World War Two, Nick had tried to discourage her from playing Karl's game.

"It's not *us,* first-person plural, who killed Karl's mother."

"Of course I know that. But if we don't apologize who will? He still hurts so much. And besides, the war was almost over before Dresden. They didn't need to level it, not honestly."

He'd tried to explain that people like Karl didn't feel pain. Crazy in, crazy out.

"If the guy was from Chicago, he'd have a different excuse to hate the world. Most people from Dresden didn't go nuts. I mean, look at this place! Need I say more?"

Now, as Nick tried to jimmy the lock of the guesthouse door, he recalled the fact that the high stone wall that encircled the entire property, cutting off the sea view, had been made triple-thick by Karl "to withstand even a motorized attack." The nonexistent neighbors were also the reason Karl sported a rifle on the beach, why there were gates and locks every three hundred yards, why there were nine shepherd dogs, why Karl and Al Greenley walked the perimeter of the land every morning and evening, looking for signs of "tampering."

Because Karl didn't trust that the tools he bought in Esmeralda Town weren't booby-trapped to blow up in his face, a bank of solar panels attached to car batteries powered his jerry-rigged handsaw. His electric planer, resting on a melted-down car door, ran on wind power alone. Though the rancho was ten miles from Esmeralda Town, down a potholed road, across a narrow spit of land surrounded by water on either side, Karl felt "certain" the rancho was being spied on by the locals. To this end, he'd topped the gargantuan wall with jagged pieces of broken glass against rappelling. Peepholes featured upended nails.

Tourists were encouraged to soak their fruits and vegetables in a mild bleach solution, and then scrub them "absolutely vigorously" and "absolutely thoroughly" with a brush. The dogs were not to be given any of the tourists' scraps. Tourist tortillas should be purchased sealed from the factory—as should any and all foodstuffs entering the gasthaus property.

Of course the Von Tollmans didn't eat "factory rubbish." Safe food from their garden was available for a fee.

Cordula's vegetable garden and fruit orchard were fed from a complex irrigation system originating at the freshwater lagoon—no potentially poisoned water for them. Sprinkled throughout the vast property were thick-walled, adobe-style storerooms, each holding canned goods, firewood, candles, home-jarred pickles, fish, oils, meats. Bell-shaped cisterns collected rainwater. In short, paranoia absolutely reigned.

"Somehow I just can't believe that hordes of angry natives are willing to storm the rancho walls just to come into possession of a Bavarian chalet and a collection of Delft figurines," Nick had told Sarah, exasperated. "Call me simple, but there are *hundreds of miles* of empty beach just outside the wall. They can build their own chalets, any time they choose."

"I don't know," Sarah had said. "I just don't know."

"I mean, what's not to *know?* The guy's got hidden pans and pots hanging on tripwires in the vines in case anyone breaches the security wall and somehow escapes the extremely acute hearing of nine shepherd dogs. Who's he going to stop with a hanging omelet pan anyway? And who even knows this place *exists?* Who even *cares?*"

"It's just that he asked me not to say anything," Sarah had replied, guiltily. "I'm sorry, Nick. I promised. But he might not be as crazy as he seems."

"What?"

"He has good reasons for the security measures. You'll just have to try to believe me. If you can't, we just can't talk about it anymore."

In thinking about it, Nick didn't really care if Karl wanted to believe the world was after his sad little hotel. Everyone knew schizophrenics could not help themselves. Especially schizophrenics born in wartime Dresden. In thinking about it further, Nick decided the galling part was the secret. Everyone knew secrets were a tactic to get a woman into bed.

Though he'd pretended not to notice, the flirtation between Karl and Sarah had started almost immediately. Just as quickly Nick had begun to hate the man's guts.

"You've got a problem with that vehicle," were Karl's first words to Nick after finally opening the gate. "What you'd be wanting in Esmeralda is a Jeep. Something sensible in the sand."

"I'll keep that in mind."

"I vud."

Nick and Karl had looked each other over, Nick in his BMW wearing a Mets hat, Karl on his bicycle, wearing camouflage. It had taken many, many sweaty moments pulling the bell (an actual bell attached to a pulley), before the old man had deigned to even open the peephole.

"Go away, now," Karl had said to Nick. "We have no beds to spare."

"Mr. Von Tollman, we're exhausted," Sarah had said, smiling through the peephole. "We'll take anything you've got. Really. Even if we could pitch a tent on your land. We'll pay to use a shower, or share bunk accommodations with some of your other guests."

"Actually we're closed this season." Karl had an exceptionally hearty laugh.

Cordula's eyes had appeared through the slot. "We have no guests at all."

"That's even *worse* news, then." Sarah had sighed. "Because this is exactly the kind of place we've been looking for. I'd like to stay practically forever."

There had been a long silence.

"And what kind of place, child, have you been looking for?"

"A place that's exactly the opposite of where we came from." She'd added, laughing, "With no computers. And no television. And no *people.* Especially, none of those."

A blue eye had locked onto Sarah's brown one. The trapdoor had closed. Raised voices had been heard. Then the gate swung slowly open, as Karl turned a series of locks and keys.

"For the tired young lady we might be willing to make an exception. That is, if you don't mind waiting for the room to be made up."

Cordula had been seen stalking off toward a stand of lush trees.

"Frankly, I don't care if you give us a hammock." Sarah laughed, looking around at the vine-thick grounds, the statues, the fountains, the bright birds. "To sleep right here would be fine. Oh! And you have horses! What are their names?"

"A true horsewoman always asks the names first." Karl's smile widened. "*Ja, ja.* Later today my wife will go bathe them in the sea, and you can assist her if you like."

With each of Sarah's cries of delight, Nick could feel the price of the room going up.

Karl smiled.

"So I'm betting there's no air-conditioning in the room." Nick didn't believe for a moment the Von Tollmans weren't ecstatic they'd trapped a few paying customers, and Karl was playing out a game in order to tack on a few extra dollars. It was imperative Karl understand Nick knew the charade.

"None of that here," Karl had agreed.

"Not even a ceiling fan, then?"

"A little fan, maybe," Karl yawned. "But you'd have to open the windows." He'd winked at Sarah. "Mayan air-conditioning. It was fine for a thousand years, it should work now."

"It's perfect, just perfect," Sarah was saying, her eyes fixed on the horses.

"It's going to be hot at midday, babe. We might just swelter with no air-con."

"For twenty dollars a night"—Karl had winked at Sarah—"I can assure you that you'll be cool enough. And if you like animals, you'll also enjoy our wild monkeys. They come and go as they please, but they'll probably come after your sunglasses at least once."

"A bit of thievery, then, I think we can handle that." Sarah had laughed. "But I don't care what the room looks like, you should be asking more." She smiled into the craggy old eyes.

"You're a shrewd businesswoman, I see. And so, for you, I'll make the price nineteen dollars," Karl had then said. "And I'll knock off the tax."

"And does the room include, um, refrigeration? A private bathroom?" Nick had interjected. "Do the monkeys come *into* the rooms?"

"From the city are you, young man?" Karl adjusted his shotgun, and then put it on the dirt. He gestured for Sarah to climb the stone ladder, survey the rest of the place.

Nick had indicated the license plate of the BMW with his thumb. "That's what it says."

"*Ach*. Hasn't that place been swallowed up by the earth yet?"

"Nick! You've got to see this. It goes on forever." Sarah had waved him over. "We're the luckiest people alive!"

"Nope. Still standing."

"Los Angeles," Karl repeated, looking at the BMW. He whistled. "That's a long drive in a car with no real shock system."

"There must be a hundred parrots sitting in a single tree." Sarah again.

"We managed, apparently," Nick said.

"Los Angeles, California," Karl repeated. "Do they have private toilets there? *Mein Gott!* It sounds like heaven!"

Nick had smiled tightly, walking toward Sarah. He was being made fun of by the old man, or he was not. Either choice was disturbing in its own way.

He now closed his eyes, pictured himself standing in front of an open refrigerator door. The blast of imagined cool air, the icy, frosty relief, made him able to bear the sudden heat. The refrigerator trick was one he'd learned from Phil on a camping trip to Joshua Tree. Phil had gleaned it from a "Letters Home from Vietnam" issue of *Reader's Digest.*

Sarah had laughed just yesterday, while operating the hand-cranked water spigot. "It's hard to believe I would ever have looked forward to a cold shower. It's much easier to understand hippies now. You just kind of scream for the first minute and then it passes."

Nick had been moved to explain that people—great, bearded hordes of them—had already tried going back to nature. It hadn't worked in the sixties and it never would.

"Still, it was probably exciting." Her jerking of the spigot became rougher. "Being a hippie, I mean. But that's not what Karl is, anyway. He's more of a—what?—a man who just dropped out. I don't think you could classify him."

"If you notice, most people who drop out, drop back in sooner or later. Wearing tunics while hunched over a solar oven and a loom doesn't seem to have staying power as a solution for happiness. And neither, I posit, does this Tarzan life."

"Okay. I was just saying—forget it . . ." She'd disappeared behind her bangs. "It doesn't matter what I was saying, does it?"

Nick, whose left eyelid had begun to sting and twitch at Sarah's giddy delight in the old-fashioned appliances, had felt as if he would break out into leprosy any moment from her refusal to concede his point. The truth was that one out of every one person was going to die. It was a bad statistic, but there you were. If Nick was going to be hit by a global nuclear meltdown or a terrorist's bomb, he planned to go with a goddamn flush toilet to pee in and a Starbuck's Grande in hand, with air-conditioning and a couch. He was going to go in a society with roads and street lamps, and clear separation of man and parrot.

Her frown did not go unnoted.

"You're still having nightmares, I might point out. So the simple life isn't *quite* perfect."

"Or maybe I'm scared of going back." She smiled up at him. "I honestly haven't thought of Osama bin what's-his-name once since we've been here. That's reason enough to endure cold showers."

Nick felt the flesh of his tongue melting to a shriek.

"Right," he said.

"My God, I was stockpiling rolls of tape! What was I going to do? Adhere the terrorists to the curtains? Hope the sarin and anthrax spores get stuck to the cellophane?"

She laughed. "Don't you get sick of laughing bravely, pretending?"

She'd stopped laughing. "God, I'm sick of laughing bravely," she'd said.

"Mr. Sperry? Are you talking to me?"

A nasty, hot sensation rose in Nick's stomach as he glimpsed Cordula advancing through the palm trees. As usual, the missus wore a rattling armor of garden trowels, clothespins, rags, and dog leashes in a curious tangle of bags and belts around her waist. Today she was accessorized with a chain saw.

The wet canine odor that always preceded Cordula's presence seemed unbearably strong this morning. The dogs now came into view—all German breeds. Besides the numerous Alsatians, giant schnauzers predominated.

"Lovely morning, isn't it? If one were a bird?" he babbled. Christ, what kind of headgear was the woman wearing today? The sombrero was as huge as an upturned card table. "It was a beautiful sunrise, I was thinking of taking a picture, but then I got sidetracked by the . . . uh . . . the birds."

"But the sun rises and sets every day in every locality," Cordula said in her singsong voice. "There's no need for a photo of it."

There was no point in picking over the fine points of logic with a woman as slow and methodical as Cordula. Not when he had to pee.

"You're right, of course. You are absolutely right."

Her mouth smiled a little more. "But what I don't understand is why you're taking aim at our window with a rock."

When she ascertained Nick was locked out, the change in Mrs. Von Tollman's face was immediate and chilling.

"You've *lost* our keys?" The Butoh mask cried out.

"No. Not *lost*." Because the Von Tollmans had a morbid fear of their keys' whereabouts—it had been explained to Nick and Sarah, upon checking in, that the keys must always remain in their possession, even when swimming—Nick had to work for an extra reassuring tone. "Not at *all*. They're hanging right there on the rack. I can see them. My, uh, girlfriend hung them there."

But he didn't want to get Sarah in trouble. Trouble was already brewing between the women. Trouble like a cloud getting blacker, thickening, without purpose.

"I mean—I asked Sarah to hang them there, and then I fell asleep. I was writing. It was—"

"*Jünger Mann,* I must ask you to keep your keys with you at all times."

"I should be able to do that for the next three days," Nick conceded.

He climbed through a window, Cordula looking on. The unflattering image of his ass squeezing through the tiny window annoyed him.

Still, she continued to watch, and called out for him to show her the keys.

"Only three more days? Odd, I had thought you might be staying on an extra week." Cordula cocked her head.

"Well." Nick laughed. "No."

Cordula's face remained perplexed. Then it brightened. "Anyway, now I won't change the linens if you don't mind. We'd like to conserve the water. And the soap."

"No problem. Sorry to disturb you about the keys."

Cordula stood a long while, shaking her head. "It is all very disturbing these days," she finally said.

To escape the detailed rundown on Cordula's aching teeth, her back problems and stomach complaints, Nick waved while firmly shutting the sliding door. No wonder the woman was hysterical. The Von Tollmans just weren't doing good business. "Closed this season for maintenance," Nick's eye.

Though Karl claimed a locust-swarm of guests would descend if he allowed it, the second rental chalet remained boarded shut, its windows overgrown with vines. A rusty key-and-chain setup guarded the cobblestone path, overhung with thick, rubbery vines, flowering jacaranda trees.

The beach was consistently empty. Except for a few fishermen and a military tank now and then, no tourists or wanderers ever appeared on it. Farther down, next to a waterfall, was a native settlement. Hardly customers, the natives barely had shoes, and almost certainly had no jobs with which to earn money for an eco-holiday.

In another situation, Nick might feel pity for the WILLKOMMEN TRAVELERS! sign, the obvious care and money that had once gone into the place's design. Like many personal monuments run amok, Karl's place was quite astonishing in its way. Behind the wall, among the cascading vines and greenery, the temperature seemed to dip fifteen degrees. The scent of flowers and coolness lingered under stone archways, cobbled paths, mossy benches, a natural waterfall pouring from bare limestone. Giant land crabs skittered across sand walkways, neon-colored birds flitted in the many stone baths carved into the wall. The breaking waves were cinematically perfect.

The signs of economic distress: missing tiles, chipping paint, termite damage on the steps, seemed to call out for pity, and yet Nick could summon none. It was as if, he had decided, the place had been wrongly situated in the first place. It was quiet, yes, but could be too easily absorbed back into the jungle. The vines would quietly encroach, strangle you in your sleep. You'd scream, but instead of a sound, tendrils would poke out. You'd scream, he thought now, and no one, not even one person would hear.

Or maybe it was just too eerie to be alone in a property meant for a minimum of eight or ten guests. Even the bitterest European anti-American Mexicrasher would be better than the present lack of company. As it was, the only reasonable occupant to converse with was the tall, blond handyman who lived in the smallest chalet at the far end of the line of structures. Always kept busy scraping, painting, repairing fences, building new pathways for the guests that never came, Al Greenley worked with curious and tireless enthusiasm.

Nick had made it a point to talk to the guy every day, trying to discern the source of his happiness. Other than his haircut, his homemade flip-flops, Al Greenley seemed a perfectly rational young man.

"It's all good, buddy," was the guy's cheerful answer to everything. "Esmeralda's got its pastimes."

Considering the lack of women, the preponderance of farm animals, Nick had elected not to explore the matter further.

"And Karl's always interesting to talk to. There's no one like the old man for giving advice."

Nick had elected not to explore that topic, either.

Topics, therefore, sometimes ran short between Nick and Al. Nick had never before met a man who smiled contentedly while picking up dog droppings.

Sometimes he'd come upon Al smiling at the air. He was impossible not to like.

Sarah, for some reason, hated him.

"He watches *you,* Nick," she'd said incredibly. "All the time."

"So maybe he's gay." The thought had occurred to Nick. He didn't care.

"No. It's not that."

"Of course it couldn't be because I'm interesting."

"I didn't mean it like that."

But she did. Exactly.

Down a few rickety stairs, the guesthouse WC was humid and sticky as a cave. With its ovoid rainwater tank shower, chunks-of-stone sink, and toy-sized commode, the bathroom might have been lifted from the pages of *The Hobbit.* As Nick flipped up the toilet seat, dislodging a centipede, he marveled at the seat's decorative aspects—shells, old keys, bits of tumble glass were embedded under the epoxy—and it occurred to him that Karl had crafted the thing himself. What kind of person planned and executed an artistic pit-toilet seat?

He planned to bring the matter up with Sarah. No doubt she'd blame it on Al Greenley.

In any case, he may as well engage in a round of pointless hygiene. If nothing else, wash the tequila droplets from his chin. Nick's curved, white toothbrush was dry and clean, though its Clinique stamp was covered in sea salt. He began to dry-drag it across his incisors and molars. Then again, insect excrescence *disguised* as salt might be what was going on here.

"Agh." Ten-hour-old tequila rocketed up his throat.

Outside a bird was saying, "Sick, sick, sick."

The waves were gurgling and churning.

His girlfriend was nowhere to be seen.

Fear of vomiting was worse than the act itself. All morning he'd been afraid he might upchuck but now he was clean and empty, and had plenty of time in which to consider Sarah's words last night. Cojoined, the words "sad" and "silly" were insinuating, suggestive of a dupe. No woman wanted intercourse with a man whom she found "sad" and "silly."

Nick was just not silly.

He found himself feeling around on the feather bed for indentations or warmth; there was no way of knowing whether she'd slept in the bed at all. While he'd been passed out behind a locked door, she easily could have met Karl on the beach—in the darkness the teeth would have been invisible. The age, too. In the dark Karl might just be sexy, calling to mind an aging French commando. Which had been Sarah's description of him that first day.

Faster and faster Nick's eyes roved the stack of reading material provided for amusement—German periodicals many, many years out of date. An ancient map, which still showed Vietnam as belonging to France, hung over the mantel, its weather-beaten edges carefully taped against damage. The sky was momentarily a brilliant blue, though in another hour it would cloud up completely and the rain would begin to fall. There would be thunder. Sheet lightning. He looked at the gulls circling, knowing the more gulls there were, the more rain there would be. The scorpions always came out just before the first drops. The leaves shivered lightly.

The thought of Sarah, shivering with the old man, caught in a rainstorm, brought a feeling of revulsion so strong Nick held his stomach with his hand. Then again, Sarah would just not screw another woman's husband; it wasn't her style.

Christ, I don't know what her *style* is, he thought nervously.

Her style was to be so free, so independent, she didn't need any style.

Which was, of course, the best style of all.

He found one of Sarah's long, soft hairs on the pillow, held it up to the light. Yep. The end was split, as usual. She always combed ferociously.

No one dressed themselves more carelessly than Sarah did—though, of course, it was only her natural elegance that allowed such a stance. Impossibly tall and graceful in anything, she'd throw on a simple white T-shirt, laughing, appalled, at the cost of Nick's designer suits. Her hair hung down in a bobbed sheet that might or might not have a peculiar chop mark denoting lack of care. Her Birkenstock shoes were always ratty and rat-colored. When he'd met her, she'd actually been wearing socks with them.

And yet, she was vain, Nick had come to find out in the four years he'd known her. Vain about her disinterest in trivialities, vain about her conscious lack of vanity. Sarah was vain about things most vain people couldn't pinpoint and judge. To be judged as trivial might just kill a girl like her.

And on the opposite side of the fence was a man like Greenley. Simply living his simple, little life. Not caring, not knowing, not even conscious he was an object of envy at all.

Nick smiled in wonder at the revelation. To Sarah, Handyman Greenley was perfectly unforgivable. In a war of authenticity, Al Greenley had Sarah Gustafsson beat by a mile.

And now, finding the chink in her armor, he was of the mind to be critical of his girlfriend. He felt the sulfur taste rise. The heavy, torpid clouds hung down.

"Ah, you're *pissed*." That was how she'd put it the first morning when he'd woken to find her gone with Karl. She'd put it with nonchalance.

Continuing the act, she'd rubbed up against him, gently sliding her hand into his trunks. "I know you don't want to hear this right now, but at the lagoon, the water is so clear you can see the bottom twenty feet down. We've got to get out there and swim before breakfast."

He'd tried to resist the hand that was stroking his balls. What he wanted, *before* sex when he would forget to want anything, was an apology.

Instead, she'd continued to talk of the sorry state of things when a person couldn't swim every morning. A person didn't even have time to make love, read a book. A person almost went crazy. As she spoke she continued rubbing him.

Then her hand had stopped moving for a split second. In that second, he'd known he wouldn't get the apology. "You and Karl hit it off badly. But—"

"I don't need to hit it off with my hoteliers."

And yet, fucking her had been especially mystical that first wet morning at the rancho.

But the next day she'd snuck out with Karl at dawn.

Writing was the thing. Writing in the morning. While Sarah was out bird-watching and sketching and trash-picking and giggling into the beard of a madman, he, Nick, would studiously knock out a few pages, show her how busy he was.

"They have special chairs for computers?" Cordula had said doubtfully, when Nick had exclaimed over the pains in his back. The cries of pain had been real. No one in the world could be expected to write on a plank balanced atop a milk crate. "Why in the world would they need a special chair?"

Nick had started to explain, but Karl started faster.

"*Ach!* First they sell the computers, then the chairs, then the chair-cleaner, and the computer-wiper, and the fluids and replacement gears—"

"Actually a computer chair tilts so that"—Nick cut in furiously—"so that your head and forearms can rest comfortably in a position that doesn't strain the—"

"As I said," Karl interrupted. "Straining! Pain! And then pay to relieve it! Don't even get me started on the doctors and the pills."

"Let's not get started on that," Nick agreed.

"He gets particularly tense when writing," Sarah had rubbed his shoulders sympathetically. The rubbing had gone a long way toward Nick's not bashing Karl's head in with a stone.

"Not when you're there, Sar. And now I think I'd like to be alone with—"

"And how much are they charging for these torture chairs?" Karl had interjected.

Nick opened his hands to signify pure frustration.

Karl had not stopped talking. "The doctors probably have a stake in the companies that sell these chairs. No, listen! It's not funny, boy.

The people broil and bubble plastic food in a microwave oven and then ladle the stuff in front of a television. Later they insert some kind of medicine from a bottle onto their molars to dull the pain as they continue to change the channels and shovel it in. At a young age their teeth are ruined and their gums hang loose like sacks, and they go to doctors who give them more medicine—"

Nick squeezed his knuckles. "And now we're back to doctors again."

"Doctors!" Karl had crowed. "If you want to talk about doctors, my wife could tell you stories. Pull up a chair, Corde, tell these young people about the 'doctor' who was charging five hundred pesos to run an electric current through your spine! You see the man built himself a miracle box from extra radio parts and bilked unsuspecting women—women who should know better—of their hard-earned money . . ."

At that moment one of the shepherds had urinated in a clump of bushes nearby. Finishing, it spun around, kicking urine, grass, vine waste in Nick's direction.

Nick, unable to stop himself, kicked the stuff back.

The miracle-box story had continued, unabated, unabridged.

The dog had growled at Nick. The cuckoo clock had struck twelve, one, two, three.

He's just lonely. Why not let him talk?" Sarah had said. "Besides, he makes me laugh. I *like* his stories, especially when they're ridiculous."

The guy had night-vision binoculars. He didn't have electricity, or a normal fork, or even a clock but he had the latest mail-order night-vision binoculars! It was cheating—you couldn't be Amish or a survivalist or a neo-cavemen or whatever Karl thought he was and have designer spy equipment.

"They're regular binoculars," Sarah said, with a mystified expression. "Probably fifty years old."

So that was okay with her? To be peeped at by *vintage* binoculars?

Yesterday, while they swam in the warm, clear, aquamarine sea, he'd waited for Sarah to ask how his own story was going. But when he'd brought up the book, she'd only glided slowly through the water, her arms motionless, body propelled by a bright orange flipper.

"I'm glad to hear it," she'd called out. Her movements in the water were clandestine, slidey. She wouldn't meet his eye. "And swimming is probably good for your back. The salt water relaxes the spine."

Trailed by a large barracuda whose only desires seemed to be to remain in Nick's line of sight, grin with a rictuslike overbite, and scare the crap out of him, Nick had paddled and boiled.

"You're spending a lot of time with a guy who has a crush on you. That's all I'm saying. And you're acting a little guilty. A little bit like you have something to hide."

Of course he'd only said this in his mind.

In fact, he said, "Good idea. Salt cure. I'll file that one."

When she bubbled up from underneath, the snorkel mask pinched her nose, bloating her cheekbones, distorting her voice. "Come look at this grouper. It looks like a little man wearing a bow tie. I swear that fish could be a professor."

"Uh-huh." He wondered why she was so falsely bright, so twittery, nervous. Sarah was just not the twittery type.

"And the brain coral has even got both hemispheres going on." When he swam up next to her and kissed her chin, her eyes bounced away from his.

"Okay, so we won't kiss or talk about anything. We'll just goggle chastely at sea life."

Nick had suddenly stroked quickly toward the horizon, the warm water filling his trunks with disagreeable weight. Even once they'd swum all the way to the reef, were treading water among the waving sea fans, hulking masses of brain coral, brilliant colored fish, the barracuda could be felt nearby.

Sarah swam in the direction of his pointed finger. She ripped off the mask. Around her mouth was an angry, red, indented ring. "Nada. Zip. There's no barracuda in sight."

He dove under, pretended to scan the bottom of the sea. A large eye blinked slowly from behind a rock. The hairy sea grass moved to and fro in an unchanging rhythm. Moving through the aqueous blue, hearing the clicks and whirring sounds from the bottom of the seafloor, he felt suddenly afraid the scene was mechanized, staged. He knew it couldn't be true, and yet the thought had persisted.

Now salt and sweat ran down his cheekbone. Over the ocean a storm was gathering, wet, black clouds stacking up on one another. Nick sat scrunched against the far wall at the slab Karl had provided for him to work on. The tabletop, Sarah had informed him, had washed in on the tide, as had much of the wood used to build the guesthouse. Sitting at the low, warped, hideously uncomfortable thing, Nick held a pencil in his fingers, clacking it against the wood. Cordula could be heard nearby, hoeing the rows of avocado trees, whacking at the ever-encroaching vines. Every so often he heard her mutter German or Spanish endearments to the dogs.

Either language made him sick.

He checked his watch again. Though the watch was useless after he'd forgotten to take it off while swimming, the checking of it was habitual. It was habit, Phil Sperry had said, that would keep a POW sane.

It was half past moist. A quarter to ruined. Foggy and silty on the dot.

Phil. What would he know about POWs, sanity?

Whatever time it *was,* Sarah was not back and the old man was with her.

"Ladies love uniforms," Phil was wont to say.

"Ladies just need a man in control."

Nick's hands shook as he walked to the small sink and took three aspirin with a swallow of bottled water. The liquid tasted like warm plastic, and a furred brown object that appeared to be a large bee's stinger floated in the ridged bottom of the bottle. A beetle whirred around his ears, and he clapped his hands to rid himself of it.

I will never take another drink, ever, he thought to himself.

"I will not drink until September first," he wrote down.

"A soldier drinks just enough so he never falls down."

Nick's ears rang. A sound escaped from his lips, unbidden.

Two scorpions were fornicating on the wall.

According to his watch, no time had passed. He'd been lying down for a long time, considering what his foot might look like wearing a toe tag. The sun was full and white. The pillow was bleached gray, smelled of salt.

He imagined mounting Sarah from behind, the way her backbone rose like a string of beads under her skin. She liked it that way these days. Or maybe she didn't like to look at him.

Yep. That had to be it.

From the window, Nick watched Al Greenley sort twigs into a basket, humming a song Nick recognized from one of the popular hair bands of the eighties.

The song was about how many times a lady someone was. Nick didn't get it.

Boy, he was getting mad.

"Hey, happy Al," he finally called out the window. His voice was more aggressive than he meant it to be.

"What's going on, writer?" Al looked surprised and pleased. But then he always looked that way. "Hope I didn't disturb you. I'm getting Cordula's herbs." He pronounced the "h."

"Nah. No problem. Have you seen my girlfriend anywhere?"

"She's out with Karl. I think they're fishing this morning. Or anyway, *he* is. I think she's drawing him."

Nick bit back his sickness. He thought of inviting Al Greenley for a coffee. Then there was the fact of the rattail.

"Sorry, man. For bothering you."

"No bother. You think you might want to get a beer in town later? I've got to do some errands for Karl, and you look like you might want to get out of here for a while."

"Actually, yes. I think I would like that. Thank you for asking."

Nick imagined grabbing the guy, taking a scissors to the unnecessary thin braid lurking underneath an otherwise reasonable haircut. The absurd haircut was almost a deal-breaker. Al had explained it as having come from a "friend at Unisexy"—Esmeralda's only beauty salon.

"You just have to laugh and go with it," Al had said. "It's the only style they teach 'em here in beauty school. Besides the short-on-top, long-in-back thing. I wore that one for a while. People kept asking if I played guitar."

"I'm about to die of boredom." Nick sighed. He was going to cut off the rattail if it was the last thing he did. Yes, the silliness and sadness was going to go.

"Not a bad way to go, actually. Did you know fifty-one people were killed by pirate attacks last year?" Al laughed. "Mostly in the Caribbean, actually."

"I did not know that." Nick laughed.

"But sea monster attacks are way down since Mayan times. The natives used to record about eight a year. And twenty attacks by the *chúpacabra*—the flying goat-devil. That thing was the Ted Bundy of its time."

"You're right. I prefer death-by-boredom," Nick said. "And thanks again, for asking me to go to town. I like that bar, in spite of the disco ball."

Al laughed. "Good, good. We'll meet up with a friend of mine. He's a trip."

"I always like a trip."

"You won't be disappointed," Al said.

Previously, Nick had met two of the handyman's trippy friends. In the interest of widening his world to include trippy people, and in the interest of drinking in a place where Karl could not find out how much he'd drunk by reviewing the empties at the trash pile, Nick had sat through the two meetings with some trepidation. The first had taken place at the Coco Palms Bar in Esmeralda Town, and the first trippy person had been Chaz. The initial impression Nick had gotten was of a Baltic warlord, a green-eyed, sun-frazzled monster of a man who smashed heads and used torture devices in dank rooms. The first impression had been a wrong one, and Nick had been surprised to find that Chaz was giggly, friendly, and fluent not only in English and Spanish, but also in Quiche Maya, the local language.

Chaz, it had come out, was a former American citizen. He had been in the army, then had studied botany, then worked for Fish and Game (FAG he called it, "because that's what they all are"). While at FAG he'd had "troubles" in his office, most notably with his superior over the disputed classification of a certain fungus ("The guy couldn't classify his own ass") and had come, on a Musgrave grant, to Mexico to study a certain fungus that might and might not be promising in the cure of headaches. The grant had run out, and now Chaz was simply, "Hanging around. Having some fun. Great town for fun, Esmeralda."

Nick's other outing with Al had resulted in a somewhat inebriated discussion with two handsome Mexicans about the word "kingpin."

It had derived from a bowling term, Nick had put forth. The guy with the better English and schnauzer mustache had said no, it had come from the movie *Scarface*.

"I'm talking about *before* that," Nick had said. "They were already using the term before *Scarface.*"

The friend had affected not to understand Nick's English.

At that point the conversation had moved safely on to soccer scores. But at another point the guy had brought up *Scarface* again.

"He took it like a hero. In *el fin.* That's what the movie ees about."

"Scarface was a cretin." Nick had been drunk. "*That's* what the movie is about."

"You don't know *nathin',* yanqui. Peoples down here *loves* Scarface. He not only gets the yanqui girl—he *focking* slaps the yanqui girl."

Nick had rolled his eyes slowly, "He lost the girl. If I'm remembering correctly."

"*Ay ay ay.*" The guy had laughed angrily. "Who cares a shit? He rich man. He have many yanqui girls. He don need *nathin'.*"

Later, when Nick had recounted his evening to Sarah, she'd bitten her lip with delicate concern.

"What? I'm not being racist. The guy really talked that way."

Her bare legs had snaked around his for a moment. The warmth had been unexpected. Very nice.

"It's just that the guy's probably a dealer. Karl told me they drop kilos of coke over the reef with floaters and it washes up to the beach around here. Most of the local guys are in on it."

"Nope. Karl's wrong again. The guy runs the phone booth. The other one is his semiretarded cousin."

"Just be careful at that bar. *Please.*" She'd stood up, smelling of salt and cinnamon. "Those tanks we see sometimes on the beach. Those ultralights coming from the direction of Belize—it's a weird place for a drug-drop but that's I guess what it is. And they probably all drink at the Coco Palms."

Nick had done a lot of thinking about it. He'd considered the taller guy's way of opening a beer bottle with his teeth.

He had come to the conclusion that drug dealers would not quote *Scarface.* Things were just not so postmodern down here. The guys were a clerk in a phone booth and his cousin—machismo on overdrive to help them forget the fact. For that, Nick supposed the men deserved his sympathy.

But then again, in another age they would have been sacrificed to Chac Tut. All things considered, they had it pretty good.

The shower had a seawater spigot. Because it was still a picture-perfect morning, sunny with just enough wind to keep the clouds moving in neat little stacks, he felt he should wash his armpits, take a walk in the open air before the storm began.

Shampoo and salt water were an unfortunate combination. Salt water and razors were an even more ridiculous pairing. He'd taken to shaving with upended bottles of Evian and stuffing toilet paper into the cuts before anything scurrilous could land, drink his blood.

When he heard the sound of the lock he jumped out of the shower.

"Hey. I'm so sorry. I forgot to unlock the door when I left!" She was clutching a white object to her chest. And there it was again, the faint smell of cinnamon. Karl's tea.

"Willkommen." He looked at the watch. "Or should I say, *'Willkommen Fräulein'* ?"

"Let's start this again. Hi," Sarah said, wiping the sand from her bare feet, putting the white thing down. She didn't look sorry, he noticed, only tan. At the sight of the shell necklace she was wearing, he sucked in his breath.

"Don't you look sexy and wet in your towel?" she continued. "A little hungover, but not bad."

"And don't you look . . . *Lord of the Flies* . . . in that necklace thing. Did Karl make that? Doesn't Al have one of those, too?"

"*Al.*" He watched her shiver distastefully. "I'll tell you about that . . . phony later. But first tell me—how did you get in?"

"Pure rage."

"Good for you."

He looked at the shells again. The smile. The blondness. The sweetness.

No response occurred.

They talked for a while, Sarah resting her bare feet on the table's bench, carefully avoiding mentioning Karl's name or the fight last night. They ate toast. They spooned jelly. She seemed to be enjoying him, and yet who could tell? Maybe it was just the cheerful, tanned color of her skin. Still, the easy conversation, her smile, the languid way she stepped out of her dress, the ease and familiarity of her nakedness, stirred him against his will, and he decided to let the matter of the locked door, the stolen keys, drop. Her long neck, so white it shone against the dim interior, looked impossibly angular, balletic. Shadows arced across her collarbone and torso, giving her the dramatic look of a Horst photograph. He was about to comment on the likeness, when she unfolded the white object, stepped into a smock. He gaped. She was pulling on a balloon-like, white, *bee-keeping smock!!!* Her head stuck out the top of it like a grape impaled on a tent.

"Ugh," he said. "No. That's just too weird for words."

"It's just loose. It keeps the sun off. All my comfortable clothes are dirty. I hung them up to dry last night, but for some reason they were covered with mud this morning."

"So Karl is dressing you in loose, white clothing now? Are you getting my general, cultlike drift?"

Because she decided to act like he was joking, even though it was obvious he wasn't, he decided to remind her what had happened to Patty Hearst.

"Funny you should mention her." Sarah pointed out that Patty Hearst had received a presidential pardon, was now in Connecticut, wearing hair bands, shuffling her children to elite private schools and equestrian events. That is, when she wasn't penning books, appearing in movies and on talk shows.

"You know what I mean."

"I don't know what you mean," she'd said, "actually."

"What I mean is I don't want you wearing his old clothes."

She didn't lose the patient smile.

"Good then. It's Cordula's, and it's the only comfortable thing to wear with a sunburn. Now we can move on."

Moving on meant moving on to the subject of Al Greenley: an apparently pressing bit of urgency in Sarah's mind.

"What was he doing up here?" Finally the good cheer wavered. "I don't really want him in this room. Even less so after today."

"He was being rather entertaining, actually."

"Now I *know* there's something weird about the guy. First of all, I think he put the mud on my clothes last night. And then, when I was with Karl on the beach," she said, still wearing the smock, tapping her finger on the table, "he threw a ring on the sand, and pretended to let Karl find it there. I mean, I saw him bend down and flip the thing out of his pocket. Of course Karl got taken in by the whole thing."

Nick noticed the angry flush creep against her collarbone. She flicked her hair contemptuously. "Then he winked at me. *Winked,* like I was in on it. And because I didn't say anything, I guess I am."

So what was the point? Who in the world *cared?*

"The point is, that was a creepy thing to do."

"Or maybe Karl wouldn't take a gift because taking things from people as opposed to trash piles is against his code—whatever *that* is—and Greenley wanted to make his day."

"It wasn't like that. He was just trying to let me know he could."

The shells tinkled in frustration. The long legs folded and refolded. "Anyway, it gave me a sick feeling all morning. I should have said something to Karl, but how could I? And then, just after Al left, we saw a manta ray trying to beach itself. It was horrible to watch." Her look was of barely constrained irritation. "The ray kept ramming and ramming the sand, like it couldn't wait to be dead." A burst of wind slapped a piece of hair against her cheek.

"What? Greenley drove a fish to suicide? He's flinging dirt on your laundry? Sarah, listen to yourself."

Instead of getting mad, Sarah walked behind Nick, put her hands on his shoulders. She then walked to the stove, stood pouring red liquid from a red can. Soup. "Karl said he'd never seen a ray do that before. Not in all the years he's been here."

"That doesn't explain what Greenley had to do with it. And I don't want tomato soup. Not for breakfast. But knock yourself out."

"Okay," Sarah said. "Okay."

"No, it's not okay." He tried to make her look at him, hating the high tone of his voice even as it came from his mouth. "The geezer has a crush on you. He's trying to impress you. *You're* jealous of his handyman. You're competing with Karl's goddamn hired help for his attention. And Karl is loving it all. Don't think he doesn't know exactly what's going on." He couldn't keep the disbelief from his voice. "I'm sure the ray was just sick or lost. And it's the wind that screwed up your clothes! The crap drops out of the trees here and slops on everything! And now the soup is on your smock-thing. Just FYI."

Every muscle, sinew, and cord on her thin body stood out, her bobbed hair, with its bobbed bangs, whipped wildly as she swung to face him.

"There's a Mayan legend that says rays beach themselves to foretell disaster."

"Fine. But since when did you start believing in crap like that?"

Her voice was absolutely calm; the tomato soup spatters looked like the aftermath of a murder scene. "You want me to know about my beliefs?" Her eyes looked challengingly into his. "Are you sure about that?"

Nick looked at his nails. They were veal-gray.

"I'm just saying Karl might seem like a father figure to you. You're scared about terrorists. *A lot of people are scared.* Strangers who want to kill you *are* scary. But Karl Von Tollman's belief that hiding from the world, instead of facing it, is not an answer. He has no answers for you. He's just as screwed up as anyone else and probably a little more so."

Her smile dropped away.

What then? Come on." He smiled and yet felt his pulse jump. When she'd said, "I guess it's time to talk to you," her lips were slightly bared, the eyes flat and expressionless. Looking at her face, a phrase came to mind, "the zone of frightening."

"It's not fair to get mad at you, because you don't know."

She was pacing the floor, looking out at the sea and shivering. Her silent pacing had continued for some time.

"What don't I know?" he said slowly.

She started to speak, then waved her hands uncomfortably. "You've always seen me as even-keeled and practical. It's been convenient to see me that way," she said.

Nick stopped and stared at the anger in her tone.

"One of us has to be sensible, right? One of us has to keep it together, while the world fucks up."

"Okay," he said in a neutral voice. He wanted her to stop pacing. What in the hell was she shivering for?

She took a deep breath. "Except I'm not what you think. Not at all.

"Remember how I told you I felt a little depressed, and that maybe I should take something," she then asked, into the silence.

"A few years ago, yeah."

"It didn't just stop . . ." She broke off for a moment. "Forget it. I'll just say it straight. I went to a shrink. A couple of them, actually. Not that it did any good."

"But why didn't you—"

"I knew you were against pills and they all wanted to give me pills. Besides, your father was dying. You hated your job, and weren't writing anything of your own. You were drinking a lot. Then planes were bombs. Anthrax was zooming through the mail. That's why I rented so many movies—so we didn't have to talk." She grimaced. "Didn't it seem strange to you? All the comedies all the time? I mean, we never *talked.*"

Nick blinked, unnerved, thinking of all the times they'd sat in front of the VCR, laughing at the antics on the screen. She hadn't been *acting.* Sarah was just not an actor.

"Also"—she fluttered her hands—"I wasn't going to PETA meetings on Thursday nights this past year. PETA doesn't even have meetings."

Nick tried and failed to conjure up what PETA was. One of her groups. An image of pumping fists, frowning, flannel-wearing brunettes, came to mind. At the same time he was getting chilled.

"But that's so *weird.*" His first reaction was to laugh. The chill spread up his spine. "You're the last person who—"

She sighed, interrupting him. "For the last year on Thursday nights, I was going to a test group at UCLA. A new drug for anxiety. A so-called therapy group."

"I could have told you—"

"Wait. For a while I tried to imagine killing myself. But the thought of skulking around some alley someplace, looking for an overdose of heroin, was too absurd. The thought of hanging from a rope, with my tongue hanging out, was too weird. I realized I couldn't ever be serious about suicide. That made it even worse."

"You can't be serious." His disbelief was total. He was expecting her to smile and tell him it was all a bad joke, and at the same time knew it would not happen.

"I *wasn't* serious, as I just said. But I was getting worse, so I decided to give their drugs a go." Her hands continued to move in an effort at silencing him. "It was the pills that gave me the headaches and ruined my sleep. Karl's detoxing me from them. Apparently they affected my liver."

"But wait a minute! You can't trust *that* guy with your *liver.*" Nick felt his heart revolve slowly in his chest. "*He* doesn't know what he's doing. If there's something wrong with you he'll make it worse!"

"Please." She took a deep breath. "There's nothing wrong with *me*—that's what I've figured out. *I've* been fine all along. The scary part is that they say there's nothing to be afraid of. That it's all in your mind."

Sit or stand, Nick wondered. Rage or understanding? Fight or flight?

"So far we have pills, suicidal thoughts, secret test groups, and Karl's pod remedies. I can't just connect the dots here. Not to wellness."

She looked forlorn and frightened.

"Let me put it this way." She laughed suddenly. "It gets worse."

Nick steadied himself.

She was shaking her head.

"At the group they told me I was having mild panic attacks. *Mild,* when all of a sudden your body is ten feet away from you and your heart is beating so fast you think you'll die. The worst is when it happens in public and you have to keep smiling and talking like it's *not* happening. A hole is opening, you're falling through, but you just keep jabbering away."

"You should have told me."

She shivered lightly. "I told you I was scared, I just didn't tell you how scared. And besides, you didn't really want to know."

The beginning of a confession, yes. But underneath it something terrible waited.

"And so, I'd go into my office to cry. And read the news."

He waited a little more.

"Anyway, the episodes got worse, so I decided to sign up for the group, try to talk it out. Imagine trying to talk to a psychiatrist with a Mercedes-Benz and four-hundred-dollar sunglasses. To him, the problem was my brain chemistry." She was talking so fast Nick couldn't keep up. "Shit was going bad out there, people were going cruel, planes were bombs and anthrax was zooming through the mail, kids were shooting up schools, but my *brain* was faulty. Just slow on the synapse uptake."

She laughed again.

"And the other patients didn't care. They just wanted to relieve their own pain. And how could I fault them?"

"But you did."

"I did, yes." She gave him a desolate look. "It's true. I got sick of hearing them talk about themselves. I felt sorry for them, but I was sick of them, too."

Nick stopped hearing her while he held an image of her purse in his mind. Her grayish, oversized tote always neatly brimming with what he assumed were papers, books, and pens. He had never once thought about going through that purse to examine its contents. Suddenly it seemed he should have been rifling her drawers, perusing the contents of her glove box, checking the folds of her underwear.

"And then two months ago, I stopped working."

He turned away physically from the words.

"I couldn't do anything about the anthrax, or the bombs, or the kids, so I was going to the dog shelter, petting the dogs. I spent afternoons there, just scratching their ears through the bars."

She grew more distant, still.

"The dog I'd fallen in love with the day before would have been killed already, but there would be new ones. Every day new ones. And so I had to keep going."

"Sarah," he said.

But she continued. "And then I'd go into the parking lot and watch the people dropping off their dogs. The poodles and shepherd mixes would be on their leashes, just looking up with the purest happiness. They'd think they were going somewhere to play. But then, all of a sudden, they'd *know.*" Sarah stopped a minute to shush Nick's protests. Her eyes widened. "It happened to all of them—they'd have to be dragged through the door. And the worst thing was people would *do* it. They'd just drag them, practically breaking their necks. And then the people would come out smiling, telling themselves the dogs would get a new, better home."

"Sar? *Where* were you getting money if you weren't working?" He was thinking, My God, my God.

"The dogs would wait around a few weeks in their cells, and then they would die," she finished. "But the people were still feeling good about themselves. Because their lives were fine. Their lies worked to ease their pain. Like a pill."

After a beat she said, "I sold things."

Nick grimaced as a slow flush spread up his neck.

"My grandmother's jewelry. That gold antique set. The bonds I had."

"And now?"

"And now I'm out of things to sell."

They sat in silence.

"Good God. This must be shocking to hear. Thanks for not screaming." She smiled at him, gratefully. The smile kept him from exploding. And yet it also kept him in his place, he noticed.

She'd just told him she couldn't see herself working as a graphic designer for advertisements anymore. But she had "ideas" for new clients.

"I want to do something better with my time, Nick. I loved being with those dogs. For once I felt like I was doing something useful. And then good things started to happen."

The realization that he loved this woman, that there would never be a woman to whom he was more attracted, kept coursing through his mind. It wasn't just her long legs, her decisiveness; Sarah's credulity was also part of that attraction. He allowed himself to entertain the idea her naïveté could be overcome, but the goodness would remain. He had to keep thinking along these lines because the alternative wasn't possible.

And yet, the *tap, tap* of her fingernails was driving him to an obvious fact: she had hidden things. She had done it very easily.

"Don't worry." She drew her arms around herself as if guarding her next words carefully. She couldn't seem to find them. "We'll have money. I know you can't carry us both.

"Don't *worry,*" she then repeated. "I'll *work.* I know exactly what's going through your mind."

"What I'm worried about is you."

"But I've never been better."

Her calm was reassuring. Why, he couldn't decide. Convenience, maybe. Her insistent smile was definitely not reassuring.

He had now heard about many dogs, all long dead from phenobarbital. All through the stories, Sarah had been giving him a look that seemed to express surprise at how little Nick knew about it.

"It's what we're paying for with our tax money. And not only against animals. Against people—in that secret US military jail in Cuba, for instance. There are Web sites you can find, if you have the time. Which, when I quit working, I did." She shuddered deeply. "It's worse than anything you can imagine—electrodes, acid baths, rape. And those are the good guys. Those are *us.*"

The air was bathwater warm, looked dark. Outside, small waves rolled up against the shore, spewing foam and salt. He tried to stop looking at her with faint disbelief.

"No, I'm not crazy. They put hoods on people, chain them to chairs—worse. A thousand people like your father, Nick. Except they're real soldiers. And some of the people they have in there are kids."

She took in a sharp breath.

"Sarah. I have no idea what you're talking about. But you have to—"

"No. I *don't.* I don't have to calm down, or pretend it's not happening. Because I tried that already. It doesn't work for me. I'm not going to be part of it. I'm not going to work to support that kind of world."

Nick bowed his head, kept his fists clenched, tightly. He hoped they were too far apart, physically, for his skepticism and anger to reach her. Still, the chasm between them widened with every word she spoke.

"It's better now." She went around the table and put a hand on his shoulder, suddenly changed the subject. "Because Karl told me he used to feel the same way I'm feeling." She squeezed Nick's muscle too hard. "He knows what happens when a country turns to the right. He knows the signs. He sees it happening in the USA, and I think he's right."

She continued to talk about cabals, conspiracies, Karl's "intuition," while Nick got more confused and furious and ashamed.

"So you were spending a lot of time reading . . . unsubstantiated . . . Web sites. Don't you think if there was real evidence of torture it would come out?"

"Oh, it's all going to come out," she said, irritated. "And people won't believe it even then. Because they'll be working so many hours for such shitty pay, they won't have time to care. They've got it all sewn up, Nick. I thought I was the only person in the world who could see it."

The wariness, the wan lines between her brows, was new. Or was it? Even as he watched, she pushed her bangs in front of her eyes, receded. Her eyes flickered for a moment, then were still.

"Put it this way," she then said. "The leader of the free world believes an angel impregnated a virgin and that God whispers in his ear. That's some scary shit, hon. If you think I sound scary, look at that."

Her smile was beautiful and calm and scary.

Nick looked away.

Brainwash, brainwash, was not a thought as much as a rhythmic cry, said in time to a strumming in Nick's head. Faintly, her argument that US soldiers, specially trained in Israeli torture techniques, were reason enough to quit paying taxes, shimmered around him. It was a crazy argument, a hysterical argument, Karl's argument.

"Anyway, they're not telling us a lot of things," she said. "The point is—what I'm going to do, now that I know."

Nick kept his face very, very impassive. He was imagining the pay scale of a kennel worker, a nurse, a Red Cross canvasser. At the same time he was ashamed of himself.

"Is this what Karl talks about during your cheerful walks on the beach?"

"Sometimes," Sarah said quietly. "But actually, we talk a lot about birds. He wanted to be a vet, you know."

"So he says to *you,*" Nick said, savagely.

Sarah looked absolutely radiant.

"Oh he's good with animals. They all like him."

The punch-in-the-stomach-feeling spread. His face stung.

"Of course, Karl would tell you anything to get you on the beach alone with him." A mystical connection with her. A shoulder to lean on. Nick's skin began to itch ferociously. "The man's been stranded with Mount Cordula for twenty years. Don't underestimate that fact."

The comment didn't seem to reach her.

"Not everyone has your good motives," Nick said, "is what I'm saying. Photos can be doctored—you should know that more than anyone. And lonely men say anything. I should know. I was one of them."

"He's a good man, even if you won't let yourself see it." The wary, concealed look was back. Quickly she said, "Anyway, Karl and I also talk about what's going on in Esmeralda. It's so typical, you could almost laugh. Except you can't."

"Americans just don't torture prisoners—there are too many rules, Sarah. And Karl's not like you," Nick insisted.

"Listen to this. The American hotel chains want to take Esmeralda Beach and make it wall-to-wall high-rises. Septic tanks. Jungle rides. They've been pressuring Karl to sell. They plan to kill everything, all the animals, just mow them all over." She tipped her head, gathering momentum. "Someone's been actually threatening him." She paused, with a sad smile. "What? You don't believe me? You think I'm making it up?"

Nick filled his cheeks with air. Let it out slowly. "What I think is that he'll sell." And he would get rich. And be even more insufferable. "And he'll blame it on the Americans like everyone else does. So he can still look good."

She was staring at him like she was trying to make sense of a foreign object.

"Don't tell me the guy doesn't see dollar signs, and isn't just holding out for a few more of them. Don't tell me you think he's noble. Don't go down that road, Sarah. You're very vulnerable now and that's when people like Karl make their moves—"

"What am I going to do with you?" she interrupted. He was astonished to see a tear snake down her cheekbone. She picked up a T-shirt, wiped her eyes. Then she folded it into a neat, tight square.

He continued to watch her, speechless, as she folded many other T-shirts into similar squares. She had once worked at the Gap. Her folding was masterful, fluid.

"He doesn't want their money. He'll never sell." She yanked at her hair, suddenly in motion again. "And I can't tell you why it feels so good to be with someone like him because *you're* worried if I'm fucking him."

She wasn't denying she was fucking him, Nick noticed.

She lowered her head into her arms.

"Look. Karl came out here to keep animals," she finally said, into her armpit. "That's Karl's secret, evil Nazi life. He keeps nearly eighteen endangered Mexican species including jaguars and peccaries on the land behind the lagoon. He's trying to keep them alive—just a single, healthy gene pool. That's where his Nazi money goes."

Nick, who continued to look at his fingers, took in the uneasy information. He could see the heroic figure of Karl grow and grow.

"So you see, he's got bad table manners. He's mad and he doesn't hide it. He's loud and rude. But he's actually doing something good, my friend."

The words "my friend" were almost unbearably painful. The sun was full and gigantic, the smell of the sea bitter against the sweet jasmine. Sarah placed a stack of dirty folded T-shirts on the floor, then stood there, listening to the waves crash against the beach.

"Anyway, what are we going to do now?" She threw up her hands, took off the red-splattered smock and folded it. "Right now. This uncomfortable minute? Because you think I'm crazy. You can't think, even for a minute, it might be you who doesn't see."

She regarded Nick with extreme caution. She was naked now. The sunburn on her shoulders now became apparent to him for the first time.

"That's what I worry about all the time. How much can I tell Nick?" she continued. "How much is he willing to face? Because I'm frighteningly good at not telling, I'm not *good,* you see."

"Here." Nick finally sighed. "Come over here."

For a long time she wavered, then she came to him.

"Nick?" She opened her mouth, closed it.

He was careful with her sunburn, put pillows under her back, but again the sex wasn't right. It was banging against a door that had opened, but was empty inside. At the exact moment of release he thought of an empty red room.

"Oh, yeah, I definitely came. You must have felt it."

"Well . . . no."

He could feel her skin jump, hot, restless. Underneath it was a part of her Nick did not know and Karl did. He needed her to lie still. To show her he wasn't as much excited as disturbed.

"Hey, fella, we can't do an instant rewind, so you'll just have to take my word for it."

The cheerful, glittery smile was back.

"Why are you getting up? I should at least put some cream on your shoulders."

"We'll have time later. And there's just birds that I wanted to see. To draw."

"Birds?"

"Yeah."

"Birds."

"Come on. Don't grab me. I want to go think. Besides, that stuff drives the mosquitoes crazy." She indicated the bottle of Lubriderm he'd picked up off the table. "It's time for you to work anyway. Right? That's what this vacation is about."

She reached out to touch him, but her hand knocked a glass over.

"Hey!" she cried. "Your handyman friend is looking in the window, hoping for a good display."

Her jerky movement further unnerved him.

"Greenley's just raking leaves. He's not even looking over here."

Al was at least three hundred feet away. His back was turned. But pointing this out would do no good. Nothing Nick could think of would do any good. He began to sweep up the glass with a newspaper in long, fluid motions. The red of her shoulders continued to bother him. So she hadn't been lying about that.

"You have to stop this stuff about Greenley. The guy's got nothing but blue skies between his temples. And frankly when you talk about him, you seem a little . . . unhinged."

"Of course I do." She laughed. "Of course."

To soften the edge, he said, "At least let me put some olive oil on your skin, Sar. I can hear it broiling from here."

"Okay." The smile wavered. "I'll stop talking about him. *If* you stop about Karl."

"Deal," he said, through gritted teeth. But of course there was no oil in the guesthouse. He watched her put on the smock.

"And no more secrets. I'm not completely against pills, you know. Not if there's a reason for them."

"There's no reason for them now."

She said nothing else while he finished the sweeping, but he felt hot breath on his neck. He thought she was about to whisper something into his ear, but she only waited for him to move aside, then knelt to find her flip-flops under the bed. In a small voice she said, "How is the book going, anyway? I've been meaning to get an update."

"The best thing I've ever done."

"Liar." She laughed, ruffled his hair.

He swallowed.

"Escaping Phil. That's the best thing. And now I'm going to go, let you work."

You were never even in Vietnam. That's where this story begins."

The chill against his neck came from a wet towel he'd iced and placed there. But beneath it was a worse feeling. Like something small and tight filling up, little by little. Sarah had promised to come back within an hour. She'd been too quiet, too casual.

"I'd like to read a little of the book," she'd said casually.

"When we get home," he'd said.

"You were never even in Vietnam." He erased the second sentence, panicking. All week he'd been erasing the second sentence.

"Family," he then wrote, *"is overrated."*

He erased that. "*Family is a cancer.*"

Then: *"War is a cancer . . . Family is a war . . . Cancer is a family . . ."*

He erased again, obliterating the idea for the paragraph he meant to show to Sarah when she got back. He couldn't show her crap, but all of his thoughts were crap-thoughts. Whether this reflected a surfeit of crap inside him, or an overriding anxiousness was another matter he could not discuss with her.

What mattered was that this was not a book about Phil, about Phil's cancer. This was the great war book he'd promised. If he wrote about Phil, it would all start going wrong. The masks would come off. He would be spineless, floating, one-hundred-percent void.

"Can. Cer. Can. Sir," he wrote.

He steadied his pencil again.

"You were not in Vietnam, and you are dead anyway."

"You, you, you, you, you, you, you, you, you, you."

This was not a book about how Phil hadn't sweated the first lesion. The first cancer of Phil's was a laughable enemy: only skin. That first month, Phil was going to "Beat this thing, beat it good." He was going to annihilate the lesion, neutralize it, smoke it out of its hole. It was war, and Phil had been waiting for war all his life. So, when the doctors found the second and third cancers, Phil had been only slightly irritated. Irritated, he had gone into the hospital, he had not come back out. The first week of the second cancer the nurse had been accused of sabotage, of watering down Phil's Haldol, so she could use it herself.

The nurse was a gook nurse. Phil knew about them.

The nurse was a Filipina nurse. But that didn't matter. Phil "knew very well" where her sympathies lay.

Nick had been called in more and more often to mediate and apologize and pace the halls, sheepishly.

"No one's watering down anything," the pretty nurse assured Nick.

Phil, attached to a glucose drip, violently denied she was the same nurse.

"They switch, you see, tricky little people. They like to play games with you."

Phil had then ordered Nick to return at 0800 hours to check on the morphine drip in case the thief-nurse returned, tried to water *that* down. For two months Nick had risen at five thirty A.M. to check a bag of liquid he would have no way of knowing anything about. He'd always pronounced it, "All there." Phil always nodded his head.

"You keep watching my back, son.

"You just keep those sneaky nurses in line.

"Tricky little people, don't you apologize to *them*."

As the other cancers made themselves apparent, Phil couldn't eat, couldn't chew. The nurses would patiently feed him. He screamed in pain, went yellow and skeletal, often shat himself. Even then he didn't soften, get humble, didn't do what he was supposed to.

"If you have anything to talk to him about," the nurse had said to Nick, softly, "you'd better do it now. It's just a matter of time."

Due to his frequent visits, Nick had come to look forward to the tiny nurse's soft, padding sounds. In time, she'd started smiling at him a lot, and he'd become confused in his feelings toward her. Once they'd grabbed a taco together across the street. "My husband used to be afraid I would leave him, so he set out to get me fat," she'd told Nick through her charming under bite. "He was incredibly weird. He tempted me with Ding-Dongs before my monthly."

At about the time Phil had been diagnosed with the first tumors, the nurse had left her husband, and had now met a new guy. "It was the best thing to do," she'd told Nick. "I had to let go. That's when it all got good."

The new guy was a singer in a hotel jazz band. His singing wasn't very good.

"No one's ever as good as you hope they are," the nurse had said after Phil died one evening while watching the Afghanistan War on TV. "The thing to do is move on, remember the good parts. Come on, let's hear some of the good parts."

"Nah."

"Yes, yes. And then there's something I'd like to share with you."

At first Nick could only wonder if the nurse was going to tell him she'd fallen in love with him, and how strangely erotic her under bite was. To make her happy, he'd recounted how Phil had once been in tears when he'd mistakenly rolled Nick's head in the electric window of his Chrysler Brougham. It hadn't hurt, and, in fact, the ensuing bear hug had been more painful.

As the nurse encouraged him, other memories had come, too. Sometimes, when Nick was a kid, he and Phil played soccer in the desert sand. They'd wrestled. Kicked up dust.

There were the times Phil had taken him to visit the world's largest papier-mâché missile.

They'd shot targets, human outlines, sometimes plain circles.

They'd eaten ice cream cones with half-frozen gumballs embedded in them.

"You *see,* there's good in everyone," the nurse had said joyfully to Nick. Then she'd handed him a pamphlet. It pictured a smiling, multiethnic rainbow of people. Smiling dogs. Grinning psychedelic parakeets. It was titled: "Have You Heard the Good News?"

Nick hadn't attended worship services with the nurse and her jazz singer. He'd declined comment when she'd said, "The Lord loves your father just as He loves you."

And yet, sins had weighed heavily those last months with Phil. Sins had been the point of Nick's visits to the hospital.

The sins of the father. To be exact.

Yes, it had been uncharitable, bringing up Phil's failings, while Phil lay captive in the hospital bed. Yes, it had been psycho. A little wrong.

Phil's game, for instance, of Vietnam. Phil's favorite drinking game that often lasted until Phil's bottle was finished, or until Nick had run to the neighbor's house, or if Nick couldn't get away fast enough, or was on a camping trip. In the end the game lasted until Nick didn't flinch anymore.

The game of Vietnam, as far as Nick could tell, had no clear, definable objective, no time limits, no absolute goal. Stalking and ambush seemed to be the only constant: sometimes hostage-taking, sometimes just pure quiet, waiting for the worst.

There had been good times yes, and gumballs, and missile-viewings, but the games always took place during the bad, drunk times, when Nick was rousted out of sleep, given a green oil pencil to camouflage his face and ten minutes to hide in the backyard. If Nick had not done the dishes correctly, or if his room was not in the order Phil expected, or if Phil was especially drunk, or if things had not gone well at Phil's insurance office, the game also began with a hand around Nick's neck. A hot whiff of drunken things to come.

"One. Two. Three . . . Ten . . . Eighteen . . . Twenty."

"Just a game, boy. Now we'll see how smart you are."

Nick would be waiting, not breathing, not moving a muscle, while slowly, slowly, through the yellow light of the bug lamp, Phil would make his way across the yard, toy rifle and toy knife at the ready. Weaving through the desert sand, Phil would "hunt" the Cong, drinking from the flask.

Sometimes the questions were logical. Had Nick really thought he could get away with not making his bed? Had Nick left egg on the dish just to defy his father?

And sometimes the questions were not logical. Sometimes they were not questions at all.

"I can hear you, fucker. I can hear your fuckin' heart."

"You think, you little gook, you can do my buddy McCollim like that?"

If Nick picked the right spot, sometimes Phil would be weakened and exhausted when he caught up to Nick—there were only so many cactus and scrub bushes to hide behind—but sometimes Phil's rage and shame had not yet been spent.

At those times, when the answer to Phil's questions were not in the logical world, but somewhere in the quantity of whiskey Phil had drunk, Nick's heart would race madly. He would try to disappear, try to scale the neighbor's fence. He had to run.

Because at those times, Nick was not even Nick anymore.

When Nick was the traitor who'd gone AWOL and left McCollim to die alone were the worst times, even worse than when he was the Cong. At those times, he would often piss himself, get cold and blubbery, make things worse for the interrogation.

Had he thought he would get away with his cowardly shit?

Had he?

Did he know what happened to fucks who went AWOL and shamed their buddies?

And yet sometimes, just sometimes, Nick *was* the buddy.

"Found you, buddy." Phil would clasp Nick to his chest, move his hand tenderly across Nick's hair, talk of medals and bravery and courage while Nick still didn't dare move.

"You're gonna be fine—just a little shrapnel in the leg, see, McCollim. Let's get you out of here."

The times Nick was McCollim he was carried gently, heroically, safely to bed, Phil grimacing, breathing gin, even crying while saying, "You're gonna make it, McCollim. We got ya. We got ya. Hang in there. Don't die."

In the mornings, the game would not be mentioned. If Nick's eye was blackened, his mouth swollen, he would be kept out of school, told not to answer the door, or call anyone. Phil would give him a little whiskey for the pain, tell him not to be so clumsy while playing in the yard. He'd leave Nick with the bottle, and a canister of Tylenol.

"You're too fuckin' clumsy, boy—you get that from your mother's side. Always falling down. Always breaking your goddamn teeth. It costs me a fortune."

The bruises would heal and things would be okay for a time. Phil would get Nick a new bike, or share a cigarette with him, and Nick would start to love him again. No one else's father let them smoke. No one else's father in a military town was around all the time like Phil was.

And so, Nick had been prepared for the amnesia while grilling Phil in his hospital bed about the game of Vietnam. He had been prepared for more of Phil's denials, the "Bullshit. You get that lying tendency from your mother's side." He was ready for the excuse of "a little game being blown out of proportion so you can make a sob story out of it, like you people always do."

What Nick hadn't figured on was the movie channel: the impossibility of competing with the racket of machine guns at top volume.

"Who in the fuck was McCollim, Dad? Who was I *supposed* to be? Just tell me *that*. Were you supposed to go to Vietnam with him?"

Rat-a-ta-tat-brubba-brubba-boom.

We got 'em cornered, Major.

Agghhhh!

As Nick had listed the childhood choke holds, the coldcocks, the drunken kicks, the split chins, the maddening mystery of McCollim, he had not been allowed to turn off the movie. The guns drowned out the nights Phil had menaced the Cong with an open plastic bag, the nights Phil had shoved a traitor up against a wall and kept shoving him and mashing him until Nick heard a little *ftttt* or a little *ssssst* or once a *pop,* the nights Phil had simply sat Nick at the kitchen table, shined a light in his eyes and dared him to deny he was a coward.

"*Who* was he? Forget the rest. Who was McCollim?"

"Don't touch the remote, son. I'm watching this movie."

"It happened. You know it did. All I want to know is *why?* You don't even have to apologize. I just want to know *why.*"

"Goddamn, this is a good movie."

Phil would turn up the volume, and Nick would continue to speak.

With less and less control, Nick had talked through the sounds of napalm striking foliage, the sounds of machine guns, the unearthly screams an actor made while dying into a microphone. Once he'd even read Phil a story. Phil's own story. Phil hadn't once looked away from *Platoon*.

"You were never in Vietnam," Nick had read, in a loud voice.

"That's what your people teach you in writing school? To make up lies about the father who did everything for you?"

Then, "I didn't have to keep you after your mother died. I didn't want a kid with her. Your mother knew that."

Then, "I paid for your writing school when you should have joined the Corps, and this is what I get? I wanna laugh. In fact I'm going to watch my movie and laugh and forget you even exist."

In the end, Phil did not talk to Nick about the drinking or McCollim or the hot, sick fear Nick felt every day when coming home to the house that might and might not hold Phil, a bottle, a pickup game of Vietnam or McCollim. Phil did not talk to Nick because Phil's throat grew a cancer in it, then his ear and his tongue. As he died, he believed he was being burned alive.

"A man tries to teach his son values, but if the bloodlines are wrong . . ." And so began the first paragraph in Phil's final letter to Nick. The letter had ended with the frosty phrase "Good luck."

"Poor man," the nurse had said after Phil's death. "So many of them die guilty if they had friends over there.

"Poor man," the nurse said, when in fact Phil had been rich.

Phil left all of his money to a Vietnam veterans' fund, "In memory of Tom McCollim. Fallen. Brave."

"For the proud, brave veterans of Vietnam," Phil's will had said, "I leave my effects. My worldly goods. And my gratitude.

"For my son," Phil's will had said, "I leave the rest."

"You were never even in Vietnam," Nick wrote now, *"You stole your sadness from your high-school friend who went."*

Nick erased the second sentence. The rest of Phil had been cremated, and the ashes had come to Nick in a plastic bag.

Even wet, in the garbage disposal, Phil's ashes had looked like rat powder. Like Comet. Like a bag of cyanide.

Nick had flushed and flushed.

Even skeletal, even powdery, Phil didn't get an explanation that might absolve him. Phil didn't get Sarah's explanation of "an ignorant man trapped in adolescence." Or the all-purpose apologia from the nurse that he was "a man whose friend had apparently died over there."

Mostly, Phil didn't get his prediction of Nick writing a ridiculous, unpublishable book.

Nick knew very well every first-timer wrote a coming-of-age story, and that if the tale involved drunken fathers, scenes of child abuse, the tendency would be to discount the tale as clichéd. Nick had read many, many reviews of such books, had sweated many nights. He could take anything, but not sneering. Not humiliation. Not when he'd lived through Phil's.

And so as not to be ambushed by agents, fathers, hostile humiliators, a first-time writer's safety was in writing a *great* book, a sweeping book, a book that could not be confused with the kind called small. Therefore Nick had decided that in the Great Vietnam Story, Phil would be but an opening paragraph, a little man selling homeowner's insurance to the men going off to their deaths in the Tet. Each soldier would pass through Phil's insurance office, each soldier's story would be ever larger in scope. Each soldier would drive Nick's point home with beauty, subtlety, rings within rings within rings.

The rings were his escape if only he could jump high enough.

Nick could hear them clashing, clanging, tripping him up now.

"You were never even in Vietnam," Nick wrote, over and over be-

tween the rings and the blank spots on the legal pad. Real writers wrote on legal pads. *Real writers write on legal pads.* He found himself looking at the absurd, new sentence, sobbing and striking the tabletop. He then lay his head on the plank, thinking of the interview he'd once done with a minor actor from *Platoon.*

"He Made It Through the Nam," Nick had titled the piece.

He'd slaughtered the poor actor with his smile. His disarming kindness. Then his pen.

"*In the Nam they wrote home on legal pads. But you were not in the Nam.*" The pen broke and mashed under his fingers. Pen number eighteen.

Putting the mess in the trash, covering it with good paper towel camouflage, Nick's eye caught the mound of moist flour resting in the ceramic bowl. Next to it was a block of goose fat, a greased pan ready to be popped into the oven. He stared at the mound, poking it in despair. Sarah must have been planning to make another batch of rolls—heavy, wheaten, blocklike things that called to mind Cordula's midsection. A line of rolls stretched out like dog runs in front of him.

"Hey-o."

Al knocked on the window, turning his face discreetly from the glass.

"He's doing this," Nick said bitterly.

"Who, buddy?" Al pushed opened the door slightly, looking at Nick with a pleasant, calm expression.

"Karl. The simple life." He glared at the dough.

The familiar rage descended on him. So Sarah had been pretending things were okay. There was not going to be any pretending now.

"How am I supposed to afford *serenity?* Only the very richest can afford that shit in LA."

"I wouldn't know," Al said, eating the last of a banana. He held up a tube and a can. "I was just coming to spray."

"The dough! It can't just come from a store. It's got to be ground in a mill that runs on a waterfall, that comes from the earth. The earth has vibes, you see, and those vibes fill the mill with vibey goodness. Those vibes cost you triple if you don't happen to own a mill."

Nick was looking at Al, not seeing him. Even through his anger he remembered Sarah didn't want Al in the room, and that she had no good reason for it. And yet now he had to take every one of her worries, worry it. Make things all right for her. Spend. Write faster. Write at *all.*

"Jesus, armpit hair, and serenity. And huge bills from Nature Mart. Do the three always have to go together?"

Al shrugged. "Maybe," he said amiably, "it's just bread."

Sometimes Al wore good shirts with his buglike surfer sunglasses and pukka shells. Today he was wearing a shirt featuring a native drawing. A Mayan glyph with an ugly little hopping man. Big machete. Just enough detail to express extreme violence.

"Where'd you get that shirt?" Nick said, trying to calm down. Of course, Karl already had the things Sarah craved. Dogs, mills, sympathy. If Nick didn't calm down he would start drinking.

"My pal Chaz had it made."

"Chaz, the guy I met? The fungus guy?"

"That's the one. Among other things he's an *artiste.*" When Al said the word he fluttered his hand. He seemed to possess a humor that surpassed his haircut.

Nick rested his mind of Chaz, but not for too long. "That is one creepy dude on your shirt, man."

"What that *is,* is a symbol for the Great Toltec Renaissance," Al said, lifting the can of bug spray.

"Oh, man." Nick was looking at the dough. He didn't want to look at the shirt.

"That's when the Mexicans rise up and take back California and

Arizona. Chaz is talking about handhelds and rockets and meetings with the sheiks. Making treaties with certain interested parties. He's studying up on Arabic, I hear."

Al laughed. Soon enough the room smelled acrid, tinny, and sweet. Raid. Insect napalm. Or some natural mustardy facsimile Karl had brewed up.

"Am I wrong or is Chaz an American? Doesn't he know the sheiks want to kill him?"

"Chaz is a cokehead who doesn't want to see his beach get invaded by the hotel chains, so he figures a little preemption is in order. He'd like a Mexican jihad against Radisson and Hilton. And if the sheiks want to help, well, he'd be down with them. Meanwhile, he'll just make up some shirts."

"Piquant bit of logic." Nick considered the shirt again, shivered.

"Ah, he's harmless. Until he's had a line, anyway. Then he's just bugged out."

"So they really *are* going to build it up down here? Sarah was saying so." Nick shook his head at the specter of Chaz bugged out. The smell of the bug spray was nauseating. There was definitely mustard in it. Garlic and cayenne pepper, too.

"Sooner or later the entire coastline of the world'll be a resort or a drug dealer's house. I guess it's our turn, soon."

"You don't seem particularly upset about it."

"I'm not, particularly, but Karl is. He's with Chaz on that one." Al laughed, seeming to find the pairing of Chaz and Karl very funny. "It's heating up around here, all right. Factions are forming."

"Karl and his dog army are going to fight Radisson? Your friend Chaz is going to fight all of history, and believe he'll win?"

"Chaz'll just make T-shirts. It's Karl who'll do the fighting. Everyday he's out there with his blunderbuss and binocs, looking for the enemy. I gotta hand it to him."

"Well." Nick shrugged. "An enigma. Wrapped in an Alpine hat."

"And now if you'd give me a hand," Al said.

When Al turned around to spray under the cabinets, Nick held the hose, trailing slightly behind. As he bent forward he saw a book sticking out of Al's back pocket: *The Pocket Guide to Philosophy.*

Two points off for Al.

"Don't tell me you're reading that book."

"Nah. Cordula gave it to me." Al spritzed while Nick aimed. "It's an improvement course, among other improvement courses. Part of life at the Gasthaus Esmeralda."

"Bam. Splat. Eddication flies."

"Ha." Al was finished. "That's how it is."

"Jesus," Nick said, wrapping the hose neatly in a coil. He noticed the stamp—HOOVER. Karl had made the contraption from a vacuum. He sighed. "The simple life. Nothing simple about it, apparently."

"Did you ever notice . . ." Al looked up.

Nick backed out the door. The mist was settling on top of the dough.

". . . that Aristotle was a psycho?"

Nick waited for the punch line.

"No human endeavor is of any importance," Al said. "Nothing you do means anything so do whatever you want. Doesn't get more psycho than that."

"Something tells me," Nick said, "something was lost in the translation."

"That's what the guy said, exactly." Al was leaving. "So I was thinking we'd go to town at about three? I told my buddy you're a writer. He's looking forward to meeting you."

"Your trippy friend?'

"Yep." Al grinned again, as if in surprise. "He's a Mexican cop in Esmeralda Beach. Doesn't get trippier than that."

Something ran across Nick's side vision. Crabs again. They were living under the WILLKOMMEN mat. Every time he wiped the sand from his feet, a crab scuttled out, maneuvering itself slowly, claw poised in an angry challenge.

Now, as he wiped out the bread bowl, he wondered why Karl's homemade mustard gas didn't kill the things. Flies were already buzzing around the dough in the trashcan, then dropping into it, surprised and leaden, like pebbles. He considered leaving a bit of dough on the floor for the crabs to eat. Maybe smearing it violently against their mandibles.

"You see," he imagined telling Sarah, "it's not necessary to live this way. We're in the post-post-classic-*millennium* and we have exterminators now. We have cars and airplanes to escape from these primitive places, and nice, comfortable cities in which vermin-free environments are entirely possible."

He aimed his blunt Top-Sider shoe at the crabs. Boating shoes weren't stylish anymore, no, but they were useful all the same.

Then again, he didn't even have any reason to kill crabs just because they made hideous noises and sat, humping and clicking, on the floor. His respect for life, if that's what it was, was too built-in.

"Man." He was shaking, laughing, conjuring the *click-clack* of Sarah's keyboard. In his mind, her hands had taken on the form of a crab's pincers. In his mind things were starting to warp.

"I just can't *use* a computer with these weird new hands," Sarah was saying. "But it's okay. I'll get a new client."

God, God, God. She'd promised there would be money, but how in the world was he going to pay the bills *as soon as they got back?* She knew very well he'd been counting on her paychecks for half.

"Weirdly, I'm not worried," she'd said just before she left. "Except, a little bit for you."

"Hey, writer," Al called up again, "mind if we take your car? My van is shot." He added, "Or we can probably take Karl's Jeep. It's up to you."

Nick smiled. Karl's Jeep didn't have doors, windows, or even a windshield. The seats, all except for the driver's, had been taken out and replaced with milk crates. Globules of dried cement littered the floor. Chips of wood whirled in the gusts of air.

"What's up with the Jeep anyway? Some kind of macho survivalist thing?"

"It's a mold thing," Al said. "A rain thing."

"It's a shitty thing," Nick said, "to drive in."

It was decided they'd take the BMW. Al, Nick knew, probably just wanted to ride in it. He probably thought it made him look good.

I've got a new idea." The words continued to plague him. He wrote them down.

As he became absolutely sure Sarah was planning on working for a nonprofit, taking a downsized salary—or worse, going back to school—he became absolutely convinced he needed a beer. But the drinking, at least in the morning, really, *really* had to stop. For one thing, he was going to need a raise and Larry Scakorfsky had joined AA a year ago.

After Larry's defection to workaholism, the people in the office, one by one, had joined the ranks of the smug and dry. Some had acquired motivating silver bumper stickers, placards for their desks. Some had started drinking coffee in huge quantities. All had taken to regarding Nick with sorrowful, concerned smiles.

"In a little late, are we?" Scot Brinkman had gotten a promotion to grade-A actors after getting sober and humorless.

"A little headache, have we?" Len Curser had done the same.

Nick sat back down at the table, determined to look both busy and sober when Sarah arrived. After taking a quick swig from the Dos Hermanos he crossed his brows, made a lipless iron bar of his mouth. It was the same forbidding expression he adopted around Larry. Over the years, it had served him only mildly well.

He began to write the very first things that came to mind:

"My grandmother's jewelry."

"Like Crusoe."

"I'm not worried."

"It works if you work it."

"Never happened."

Then:

"Every time a mighty tree is felled, so a star falls from the sky. When the last star falls from the sky, what is will be no more."

In seizing on the esoteric Mayan claptrap Karl rolled out for Sarah—"and the Mayan calendar ends in the year *2012, Liebchen!*"—Nick felt a momentary jolt of relief. For a while, he concentrated on the moneymaking breakthrough, trying to think of a story involving the end of the world and the Mayan calendar. One of those hopping guys with machetes. A sheik. A beautiful-yet-strong heroine.

"Christ. I can't write a screenplay."

He couldn't even breathe.

As he headed toward the seawall where Sarah might be sketching, a peculiar sensation hit him. The sensation was one of something just out of his line of sight creeping up, doubling back, almost on top of him, then sliding away again.

He saw the head poke out from the vines. Karl was standing over an open pit, pouring kerosene into it. As he set fire to the plastic bottles, paper packages, the bottles crackled, spit up flames.

"Hello, boy! *Wunderbar* to see you!" Karl said cheerily. "You're out of the cage quite early."

"Good morning to you, too," Nick said crisply. Up close, Karl's pointed beard, arched brows, and mustache seemed calculated to bring Eastern wisdom, guru-dom, to mind. As usual he had the old rifle, the passel of German dogs. One of the smaller Alsatians approached Nick and said, "Arf."

Karl stirred the burning trash, wrinkling his nose. "I've been wondering what kind of man leaves his pretty girl to walk along the beach alone in the morning with a stranger! Anything could happen." Karl regarded Nick with merry blue eyes. As usual, he wore the desert fatigue trousers, the same campesino shirt patched and repatched with grave care.

"You've got matters under control."

"Control, *ach!* If you're going to be in the jungle, you can't leave the control to others, boy. They might just use it."

"Well, I'm off to find Sarah." Nick continued to walk. As he covered ground, he imagined a time in the future when he might be able to tease Sarah. *"Remember when you had a crush on that German geezer with the gray teeth?"*

Karl threw a pebble in Nick's direction. It struck the back of Nick's thigh, perfectly.

"Wait, let's us talk, boy. Let's us get to know one another. I think it would be helpful."

Nick sighed.

Karl smiled.

Two roosters crowed in unison.

So I said to myself." Karl shook his head. " 'What could these two beautiful young people be fighting about?' I asked myself, 'Vat in *Gott's* green earth!' "

"Is that what you said?" Nick grimaced.

"Now, now, boy!" Karl bit down on a stick of jerky he pulled from a leather waist bag. "Please, indulge me. The only fun is hearing about the fights. It's the joy of being an innkeeper."

"Look, Karl—"

"No, you look, boy! The butterflies are fornicating, the grass is growing, and you can do nothing but stomp around and glower at the world. You haven't stuck your head out of your hidey-hole for longer than a few hours since you've been here, and I know it's not for love of the decor." He paused. "You seem bound and determined to have a terrible time, and if that's what you're after, *mein Gott,* you'll get it. You can't make your father a good man if he was a bastard. You're best off just to forget about him. Write about nicer people. Or learn carpentry."

A million responses went through Nick's mind—each beginning and ending with an expletive. He said, "That's a thought."

"And what's all this about calling me a Nazi? I'd say you have an unhealthy fixation on Germany, young man. My guess is that you should have that checked out by a psychiatrist. German-envy. It's a problem."

"I have no idea what you're talking about." Nick flushed purple. The patches of troubling weather were now visible offshore. "As usual."

"What I'm talking about is the charming page just filled with the word 'Nazi' I'm in the process of burning right now." He winked at Nick. "No need to upset the wife—an avid reader—I said to myself. I said to myself, what this boy needs is to understand is that Germans are a terrible lot. Liars, smiling liars, that's what they are. Sausage-eaters. Money-lovers. Nothing to get worked up about. I'll just have a little talk with him, I said to myself."

Nick started to move, feet trampling stones, brush.

"World War Two is long over, boy," Karl called out, "The smart money's on World War Three."

"If you could just tell me if Sarah is north, south, east, or west?"

"Oh." Karl regarded him lazily. "She's gone to town with the wife for a haircut. Al's friend wielding the scissors. Didn't I tell you the bad news?"

The Esmeralda shoreline was cinematically perfect—an endless white line of powdery sand giving way to brilliant, clear turquoise water. For a long time, perhaps an hour, Nick jog-walked along the shore. If Sarah came back with one of Al's friend's haircuts, how exactly was Nick supposed to greet the sight?

He scratched at a patch of eczema on his forehead. The eczema continued under Nick's hairline, and was the reason he wore his hair longish, styled, and didn't mind paying sixty dollars for the privilege. Of course another reason was that he'd worn a cheap brush cut, a military two buzz, for much of his youth. Sarah had pronounced the youthful photos of Nick sad. She'd saluted him once, coyly, while taking his cock in her mouth. "And now for some R and R," she'd said.

God, why did she have to cut her beautiful hair *short?*

When he could no longer see the beach wall, or the smoke from the German's trash fire, he stopped, went still for a moment. Trying to lift his knee to his forehead with closed eyes—an old steadying trick of Phil's—he toppled forward into the bank of sand. There he lay, for a long time, looking at the sky. After a while he felt a familiar dread, and the silence closing in. "You are all alone," the voice said. He opened his eyes, overcome by sadness and terror. Presently, he got up and ran.

As soon as his blood began to pump faster, thicken, redden, enliven in his veins, Nick began to feel weightless. He might be a rocket, he might be an atom. He might just be okay, in the end.

Coconut palms crowded the edge of the shoreline, every so often shedding a nut that fell to the ground with a soft, wet thump. Quite a few people died every year in the Yucatán from falling coconuts, but Nick knew he would not be one of those people.

No, Nick would die of rage, when he heard Karl compliment Sarah on her newly androgynous hairstyle. Nick would die, Karl would smile charmingly.

He felt his chest contract.

He stopped running, heard the buzz of mosquitoes—little buzz cuts to the quick of his neck. For so many years he'd tried to convince Phil not to cut his hair when drunk.

"Keep still, boy, or I'll take it all off." Phil had stood over Nick, the buzzer in hand, a beer in the other.

Sometimes, Phil mistakenly took it all off. Nick could use the slosh of the beer to gauge how bad it would be.

But then, it didn't matter how hard Nick pushed for the extra inches that might save the girls from Yucca Valley from looking at his crusty, peeling forehead. The prettiest Yucca Valley girls didn't look at "military trash." A perfect buzz cut was never longer than a quarter is high.

Sometimes it was quite a bit lower.

"How come you don't have a girlfriend yet, Nicky?" Phil always endeavored to shave Nick's hair to match his own. He always used a quarter. "You got your looks from my side. So how come you're so shy with the ladies?"

The prettiest girls didn't look at Nick, especially.

"Oye!"

Nick watched the Humvee snake around the beach. When he waved to the occupants—two men in military dress, he saw their gold teeth flash in the sun.

"*Qué estás haciendo,* yanqui?" one of the men said.

"La playa está cerrada hoy," the other man said.

Nick said, "Hi."

When the men continued to talk to him in their unintelligible sounds, Nick smiled, shrugged.

"I look like a fool in this haircut," he imagined one of them saying.

"I am a hedgehog," said the other.

The military men brought to mind Phil Sperry again. It was true with his too-close eyes, soft chin, Nick did resemble Phil. The older he got, the more he drank, the more he resembled him. Nick started to run, very fast and hard, the sand making crackling noises between his toes. At the very end, when Phil had been forced to whisper through a microphone embedded in his throat, Nick had been sure an apologia, a mea culpa had been close at hand. Phil's last wheezing words had been, "Change the keys as soon as I go, Nicholas, the maid's got a set, and I wouldn't trust her not to steal if she has the opportunity."

The fact that the maid could steal whatever she wanted, steal while Phil was helpless in the hospital, had eluded the old man. No. Phil had been secure in the knowledge the maid feared him, even from a distance, and he had been right. The maid had cleared the place out on the day of Phil's funeral—Nick had come in to find the TV, stereo, guns, car all gone.

The offshore wind let up for a moment, and a swirl of butterflies appeared from the dense jungle along the shore. Nick tried to beat them off, but they clung tightly to his forehead, rubbing their mandibles over his eyebrows, drinking the moisture from his skin. Butterflies hung from his nose, dripped down the front of his neck. He swatted at them violently.

He was so far from Karl's land now he couldn't even see the smoke from the trash fire. He had it in mind to walk to the native settlement, turn around.

"Today I walked to the native settlement," he would tell Sarah. Walking was something, anyway.

"I am a walking cliché," he said out loud. He kept walking, swatting butterflies.

As he walked away from the shore, taking the jungle path, he began to hear the sound of fast-moving water. He opened his mouth, feeling the waterfall's spray before it hit, ever so slightly, his tongue. Fifty yards away, bubbling up from a deep underground river, was a forty-foot-long lake—a rush of cold blue water that snaked upward, reaching for sunshine, before disappearing under the earth again. According to Karl, the Von Tollmans owned the water, as it sprang from the fountainhead on *their* property.

"And won't it put a bee in their bonnet when we put a wall around it!"

According to the gleeful Karl, in Mayan the place was called the Coil of the West Serpent of Divinity. In Spanish it was called, appropriately enough, El Hoyo—the hole. According to Cordula the Mexican name was more appropriate since, every day, the locals arrived in trucks and vans to wash their clothing and their dishes and throw their garbage. "Their own water source!"

In truth, Nick could agree the diapers, Clorox bottles, and Tide canisters that littered the craggy limestone bank were not a reasonable thing.

And yet he could not agree that taking El Hoyo by force, building a wall around it, was the solution to a happy neighborhood, either.

The only point of agreement between Nick and the Von Tollmans then was the few times a year the gringos arrived in a four-wheel-drive vehicle on expensive package tours from Chetumal. The European tourists were charged criminal fees to bathe in the "ancient Mayan bathing and ceremonial site," this, after precautions, such as cleaning the garbage from the banks, spraying for mosquitoes, sprinkling antifungals along the rocks, had been taken.

"Those French are swimming in a trash dump!" Karl was known to slap his knee. "Because they think God's in there, you see."

Nick was known to smile a little. Just a little. He did so now, in fact.

The path narrowed as it wound through a thicket of thorn trees and creepers, then widened again at a field of tall grass. Beyond the grass was a wide, green, lute-shaped lagoon. In the lagoon were several tiny islands where eagles, boobies, hawks nested. On the other side of the water, another mile in, was the path to the native settlement: a collection of huts like upturned baskets, goats, Coca-Cola signs. The word "settlement" rather than "town" was appropriate for the place. Unsure of what he meant to do by visiting the settlement—he would probably just bob and nod and project dutiful guilt—Nick stepped gingerly into the water to cool his feet. The lagoon bottom was silty, given to suction, and though repulsed by the slimy sensation against his toes, he stood in it for a moment, thinking to wade out to one of the islands. The thought only lasted a moment; the islands were all covered in bat guano, bird droppings. He'd get shit on. His feeling of general uselessness would jack up a level.

While he considered what to do next, certain long-ago conversations with Sarah continued to plague him. Watching a corn spider cross the wet stones, he suddenly remembered how she'd once dreamed she was suspended in a giant spiderweb, stuck for years and years. There was no spider, she'd claimed when he'd woken her, her blood did nothing except nourish the web itself.

"You were there, too, but you couldn't help me.

"I screamed, but you were screaming, too."

Upon exiting the lagoon again, Nick nearly tripped over one of the Von Tollman's shepherd puppies lying in the shade of a banana tree, gnawing on what looked to be a stick. One of Sarah's scarves was tied around its neck.

The scarf had been expensive. More to the point, it had been Nick's gift.

"Jesus, little guy! What the hell are you doing all the way out here? And you're wearing Hermès if I'm not mistaken."

He looked around, but no one was in sight. Only green and more green, spiderwebs, the faint sound of rushing water.

The dogs were not allowed out without Karl.

"Well, I guess you're trying to escape Herr Karl, too. But sorry. Too many dangerous coconuts around." He picked up a piece of vine, trying to fashion a leash. "Come!" he commanded, but the puppy jumped up, wiggled out of his grasp.

"Aus! Aus!" He wasn't sure what the words meant, and they had no effect.

Joyfully, the dog then showed off a caught lizard, entrails hanging out, and dropped a large piece of it on Nick's sandaled toe. Nick did not want to look at the gory reptile, but the thing kept waggling back and forth in his line of vision. Before he could stop it, the tail disappeared into the dog's mouth, switching back and forth like a metronome.

Nick watched the puppy eat the rest.

"That's better," he said.

The tail wagged happily.

"All the better to eat you with," he was saying to himself. Random phrases and snippets went through his mind. "Hi-ho the dairy-o."

Anything to keep him from grabbing at the dog, losing his tenuous hold on its attention.

The puppy's presence had given him a sense of purpose, and he'd backtracked to the waterfall, the dog following him at a careful distance. The whole time he'd been careful to keep a sheltering hand above his head against any heat-seeking leeches that might drop.

"Nick? I've been running around like crazy trying to find the dog! What are you doing here? How strange."

From the high promontory near the waterfall's edge, Sarah came up behind him, holding a sketch pad and charcoals. The smock was dirty now, black with mud from the shoulder blade to the middle of the back. Like she'd been lying in the cool dirt by the waterfall, which, in fact, she had.

"Hi! I thought you went to town with Cordula." Through his surprise, he noticed her hair remained beautiful and was glad of it. The dog slid easily into her arms, then wiggled free again. She watched as it dug a deep hole, rested its belly against the coolness.

"I was going to get a haircut with her, but she got weird so I decided to come here instead. I grabbed the dog, thought I'd go sketch where it was cool."

"She *got* weird?" Miniature silver-red bats fluttered from the trees, making rapid circles while chasing mosquitoes. He waited for Sarah to explain herself, but she only lowered her eyes slightly, looked out into the distance. "Isn't she weird already?"

"I mean she got mad. At me." Her faced paled noticeably. "It's a long story."

Nick took in the information with a suitably baffled expression. The fact that she felt comfortable taking Karl's dog also nagged at him. The mangroves swayed like wet black mesh against the papery sand.

"Cordula thinks I'm getting in Karl's way. I could tell she was going to lecture me in that dour way of hers—it always makes me feel like a ten-year-old—so I begged off and came out here. But the drawings were getting wet, so it was a bad idea."

"Why are you picking at your eyebrows?" Nick asked.

"Am I? I don't think I am."

"Look at your hand. It's digging to China."

"I'll stop then." She wrung her hands for him to see.

"I was wondering what you meant. About your new client. That's actually why I walked out here. It was bothering me."

"Oh," she said. "Yes."

"That wasn't a yes or no question, was it?"

She was absolutely shaking.

"Maybe it shouldn't be bothering me."

"No," she said. "I mean yes. I can see why it would."

Suddenly the bright sun took on a foreboding quality. A fat coconut smashed down, startling them both.

"And so—"

Letting his eyes rest on the open page of the sketch pad, Nick spied a blurred set of lips, a pair of teeth. Even through the wavy lines, his mind registered in an instant Karl's mouth.

"Wait a minute, Sar. *That's* pretty fucking strange."

She stared, wide-eyed, at him. Her hands flew back to her eyebrows, picking.

"Teeth and lips are the hardest to draw for me. I thought I'd practice. It's from memory, so it's not all that good."

"*Karl's* teeth!" Nick laughed a little too loud, gently stilling her hands. "I mean isn't that a little . . . macabre? A set of rotten teeth? Aren't you supposed to be doing jungle landscapes? Birds?"

She avoided his gaze, then put a finger over his lips and said, "*Shhhh.* You'll scare the puppy."

Now, Nick sat on the dirt, pointed at her with the tip of his shoe. The puppy grabbed his Mets hat and ran away, wanting to be followed.

In an instant he registered that he'd already left his other, second-favorite Mets hat in the *licoreria.* He'd meant to ask for the it the next time he visited the store, but by the time he'd gone back to town, the hat was resting squarely on the clerk's head, the hatband soaked with sweat and grime.

Sarah dropped the pad. With a mechanical, grim motion she retrieved it.

She took a deep breath. "But before we talk, let's walk a little."

"What do you mean *before* we talk? I thought we *did* talk."

"Well, we better talk some more."

"Does it have to do with Karl?"

"Wait. Let me breathe."

They walked and walked, until they reached a small pyramid that marked the beginning of a set of windswept ruins. His legs felt rubbery, he could go no farther. Now as he sat under the Temple of the Dwarf, a great chill overtook him.

"I wasn't planning for this to happen, you know," she said, squatting beside him. "And I told you I've been—"

"Unhappy. Yes. *Yes.*" He wasn't breathing, just staring at the ever-repeating geometric patterns on the ruined archway, watching an ant try to climb it. A few Herculean steps and a long slide backward. Another slide.

"It was a mineral deficiency."

"What?"

"There was a mineral deficiency in the soil when Karl was growing up after the war. That's why his teeth lost the enamel. It's not because they're dirty."

As she stalled him, Nick followed the interlocking "X"s and cubes into infinity. He could no more stop Sarah's confession of betrayal with Karl than he could interrupt the carved pattern. But if he could only find a break in the pattern, a flaw, it would be a sign that she did not mean to leave him for the old man. His eyes raked the long arch. The "X"s were in perfect shallow relief, the cubes in two dimensions.

"My news is: I'm a thief," she said.

The dog accompanied them with its proud, little gait. In its mouth was Nick's hat. Nick's stomach was weightless, he could not force a single word to his tongue. At the exact moment they passed the marker for Karl's land, Sarah stopped. For a while she shifted her weight from side to side. Finally she put her lips to his ear.

"I took some money. I mean, we don't have to go back."

Nick swatted unseeingly at the dog.

"What money?" He was confused and shaky, still waiting for the confession about Karl. "I don't understand what you're talking about."

He looked at his girlfriend. Her long face gave him no clues.

"I took my credit cards and went to a bunch of banks in Playa del Carmen." She swayed, started to walk away, kicking up little puffs of sand behind her. "I actually started in Ensenada, little by little. But in Chetumal I took the most, from the cash advances. I took everything I could."

She laughed, a nervous laugh. "I know it's wrong." He was still staring at her, unsure. "And yet I wonder."

"Help me out here," Nick said. "I don't understand a word."

It was because I couldn't think of any other way to stay and help out."

When Nick was able to speak, he moved slightly away from her, the better to look in her eyes. They were like pools, or blank mirrors. He could not see himself in them.

"At first, I just started taking the money as a hedge fund. Not for any particular purpose. I've done it before for us when things have gotten tight, but I've always put it back. I just thought we might need it." She hesitated. "And I suppose I knew they'd get suspicious if I took it all out at once."

"Ensenada was three *weeks* ago! You didn't even know Karl then. Or are you lying about that, too?"

"I've actually been lying for about two months." She illustrated the number of months on her fingers. Her voice was a monotone; she looked relieved to be stating facts. "That's when I first talked to Larry about things."

"Oh, my God. You talked to my boss? About what *things?*"

"It started when I ran into Larry at Trader Joe's, and he told me he was letting you go because you were drinking too much. He wanted me to have fair warning, since I'd have to foot the bills for a while. He knew I worked freelance and it was going to be hard. I almost passed out in the parking lot. Because I hadn't *been* working. I'd just quit."

"Oh, my God, Sarah. My God."

"Nicky? I didn't know Karl before. I didn't know I would meet the animals. I didn't know any of it." It was the first time she'd used the diminutive of his name in a long time. Yet, it wasn't comforting as much as minimizing. "Just hear me out. Please." She reached out for his arm, but didn't quite meet it. "I thought this trip was only going to be for you. We'd hide for a month in a cheap place while we figured things out. You kept talking about Mexico, so I gave in." She smiled a little smile. "I didn't know what else to do. I could barely handle my own reality at the time, as I told you." The smile wavered. "I knew we couldn't afford the apartment anymore, so I was going to have the movers come, put our things in storage while we were in Ensenada. Then Larry told me he could get a subletter. Jay Garner from your office broke up with his boyfriend and he needed a place—with furniture—"

Nick was blinking rapidly. "Larry can't *fire* me. He was the biggest wino in town before he got—"

"Larry *does* think you have talent as a writer," she interrupted. She seemed to take great solace in the phrase about Nick's talent. "Just not as a magazine writer."

"Bullshit. I'll just write somewhere else."

"There's something else Larry told me." Sarah looked at the sand. She opened her eyes wide, then closed them again. "Apparently it's not just him who's worried about you—word's gotten around that you went to that Scientologist actress's house drunk. She thought you were making fun of the furniture she makes. She thought you were making weird comments about her feelings on the war. In other words, you're blackballed unless you stop drinking."

"Don't." He felt himself lift upward, revolve slowly in the air. "That's not how it happened."

But it was, exactly.

She was rubbing her hands against her neck, struggling to maintain an expression of calm. Still, her eyes were bright. Too damn bright, he thought. "Larry didn't want to fire you. I swear he's been lovely, Nick. He's not at all what you think he is. And if you decide to go back—you can get the apartment again."

He did not want to look at her.

"If I go back alone, you mean?" He punched at the sand.

"Listen." Her brow furrowed into a thousand tiny lines.

I looked at your *pages* after that night with Karl. I started thinking he was right—you were being too secretive about it."

He paled, the hairs beginning to raise on his neck. A wave crashed in the distance. Sweat welled from his body.

"There are *no* pages, Nick. Nothing. Just scribbles and random, weird lists." Her look was of the worst kind. There was no defense against pure sympathy. "I had no idea what to think. Every time I looked at you I just felt so . . . odd. Obviously, I know how terrible it is to pretend like that."

Nick sat down on the sand.

"And yet, the truth is—"

"The *truth?*" He blinked up at her. "We're going to try that old thing?"

They both laughed uneasily. And yet, Sarah looked less uneasy.

"Why are you writing about Vietnam?" So gently he almost didn't hear her, she said, "You weren't there. Not any more than Phil was."

The blows fell silently, gracefully.

"A few of the sentences you jotted down about Phil are wonderful. You really *can* write, Nick. I'm sure of it. If you want my help . . ."

"No, no," Nick was saying. In his stupor the beach had gone surreal and blinding white. Sarah was still standing over him with her hand on his head, a curiously dominating pose. As if realizing so, she quickly ran her fingers through his hair, crouched down to meet him.

Five soundless minutes passed while Sarah kept talking, relating plans, budgets, possibilities, for the next year. He recognized her staccato cadence; it was the one she used to cover disbelief or embarrassment. In another age, the tone would have signified "good soldiering." Focusing on the problem at hand.

"I really want you to stay, try to work out a new book. Or if you don't want to write, you can help me with the animals."

Nick laughed, false hearty laughter.

"Wait a minute. Let's look at the facts here." If Nick wanted to make a go of it, the two of them could probably live almost as cheaply as she could, alone. She reached out, touched his arm in a nervous way. "I'm thinking a year."

He straightened his back, looked at her in fear.

"Maybe longer if the money lasts."

Karl, she continued resolutely, had agreed to a month-to-month lease, and would lower the daily price in exchange for help with the garden, the animals. As she talked Nick could not look at her—to do so would bring on a rage and shame so frightening in its intensity he didn't know what he might do. As the humming sound of the cicadas rose in his ears, he found himself violently shaking his head.

"Did you give money to Karl for the animals? Wait, don't answer that. I'm going to be sick."

"I tried, but he wouldn't take it."

"Yeah. Ha. Yeah." Nick turned his chin to the sky, heaved great quantities of bitter air.

"Karl didn't ask me to stay. *I* want to be here." Her voice cracked. "The animals *need* me, Nick. Can you understand that? Karl can't do it all alone, and he doesn't trust Al with them. Cordula's always sick." She smiled again, touching him. "*Can* you understand?"

"Yes. I can understand." Slowly the breath left him again. When he brought his eyes to hers, Nick felt himself begin to understand how she'd set it up so that they all needed her now: Karl, Nick. The animals. He was thinking of the heady sensation one might feel; the piousness, the highest kind of high. Yet, there was no tactic against righteous good intentions. His mouth lost its moisture.

Thump. A gull landed not far away.

"But I can't let you do it."

"Oh." She smiled with the utmost tenderness. And yet she did not back down. Not in her eyes.

When she said the number twenty, Nick latched on to the number as a welcome fact. What he needed were facts. Less nausea, more facts.

"Maybe it was nineteen thousand—the most you could get on cash advances."

"Nineteen, then? Did you happen to note the interest?"

His eye latched onto the sign warning intruders they were coming upon PROPIEDAD PRIVADA. EL GASTHAUS ESMERALDA. The sign was riddled, he noticed for the first time, with bullet holes.

Sarah shrugged, made a halfhearted lunge for the dog and caught it. The dog squealed indignantly, then began to lick her face. She laughed. "No. But I'll bet it's hideous. I'll bet it frightens the hell out of people."

The general wrongness of the laughter confused Nick's circuitry. He must be dreaming, or be on some kind of bad drug. Maybe the bug spray had short-circuited his synapses. Maybe he was still drunk.

"I didn't even count the final amount. They converted it into pesos, and anyway I don't want to start that—counting it up, counting down." She offered him her profile. Only then did he see she was sweating profusely from under her arms. "It was scary, though, at the bank. They put all the money into this plastic grocery bag. Then I had to walk to another teller, and give her the bag." She swayed, calmly removing a blond hair from her eye. "It felt so stupid and peculiar. Just little slips of *paper.* It was so goddamn strange. Everyone in the bank looked like they wanted to murder me, bash in my head and run with the plastic bag." She sighed a little more.

"Sarah, look at me."

She did not turn her head. "They would have stuck a knife in me, easily. Any of them. I've never felt anything like it before."

"Look at me."

"But I don't want to look at you," she said with a new, cold tone. "I don't want to be talked out of this. Every possible scenario has gone through my mind, believe me." She was walking faster now. As for when the money ran out, she'd worry about what to do at that time. It was like walking across a river, she continued, with every step a new stone would appear.

A jolt went through her. "Oh, I'm being ridiculous. There won't be any stones." She made a dismissive motion. "When I face them, maybe I'll wish I wouldn't have done it. Maybe I'll feel sorry then. But I'm not there yet, am I?"

In his imagination, he flung her to the sand, bound and gagged her, dragged her to the BMW. If he kept her bound, dumb, they could be in Los Angeles in five days. Less than five hours on a plane. He would take her directly to a hospital. They could do something electric to her with paddles. Something corrective to her brain.

As it was she remained free, standing, smiling.

"But you should see the animals, Nick. They're incredible. I've wanted to bring you to them so many times. You should see how they look at you. It's better than anything in the world."

As she continued to talk in the animated tone, he watched the woman he loved more than anything walk beside him, dragging the dog along with the piece of vine. The wide eyes, the smock gave her the aspect of being in a straitjacket.

Or a nun.

"They need help for everything. For food. For water. Just for everything. It's heartbreaking."

She smiled.

Yellow

It was hot.

"Hot like bitch," as Pablo liked to say.

As he smoked a cigarette behind Karl's old shed, Al Greenley smiled at a passing gull. Thirty-eight in four days, he was no longer sure that his own glide was coming to an end. Both a happy thought and an unhappy one, he was simply tired of waiting for the crazy traps to reveal themselves. And there was no particular reason to believe a snare was being set for him. Mostly, in Esmeralda, he was having a fine, easy time.

During the two years he'd been at the Gasthaus Esmeralda, Al had enjoyed smoking under the long stringy clouds, the lazy sky, the constant stream of moving birds. A fishing vessel had just passed the property, its deep hum reverberated against the broiling dunes. For the next hour the heat would continue to rise, and then the storm would break. It was a cycle he could set his watch to.

On the whole, Al thought watches a particularly comic item. Glittery slave bracelets. Though Al enjoyed the vibrant colors on his Swatch—an item he'd lifted from a guest last season, although he wasn't of the habit of lifting from the guests, but the watch had caught his eye—he'd used it not so much to tell time, as to remind himself he wasn't yet free.

Besides he liked the way it looked. Cheerful. Young. A little frivolous. Perfect.

It was his handyman's habit to wear the stolen Swatch a notch too tight so the plastic band wouldn't catch on a piece of fence as he worked. By noon, the knuckles on his watch hand were purple, the fingers slightly swollen, the carpal veins overpressurized like a thug's, a bodybuilder's. The sight was an unfortunate one; the mottled, crepey skin pricked at his vanity, still it was a temporary inconvenience he'd resigned himself to. A reminder he was squeezing out time. Selling his life, minute by precious minute. Or not so precious. Just a life. Just one of billions.

The word "precious" always made him laugh a little.

If Al Greenley was a little vain about his hands, he believed the narcissism was, on some level, inescapable. A little better looking than average—6.85 percent better according to his own calculations—Al probably wasn't great looking, not anymore. Nice-looking hands brought a man's average up, perhaps one's fingers in particular were often noted. Because of the elongated shape of Al's fingers, their hairlessness and taper, people had long assumed he was a good lover, played the guitar, the piano. Once an old guy had even cornered Al in a bar, claimed he could "discern" that Al played the flute. The guy had bent Al's ear with flute talk, gossip from the flute world, for the entire duration of three beers and two shots of mezcal. He'd been a loud laugher, a bad tipper, a tweed-wearer, and Al had only humored him for the hell of it. The guy's supposition—that being musical indicated a superior soul—was just another funny belief in a world of them. Al, of course, knew plenty of psychos who played music beautifully.

Speed freaks liked reed instruments in particular.

And yet, higher art had its good points. At times Al had been grateful for its largesse, indeed. For instance, because he'd humored the old guy, a surprise cache of symphony music had arrived in the mail—a fancily wrapped box with a long love note offering the usual love talk—and Al had been able to unload the thing for sixty bucks. Of course, he might have gotten even more cash if he hadn't unwrapped and listened to the CDs first, but animal curiosity had him there.

He probably should have saved himself the trouble. Classical music had been much as he'd guessed, very effortful and tortured. Pretty, yes. Also pretty bogus.

Which went along with Al's only rule: With too much effort there was no glide.

Without glide there was nothing to live for at all.

Again, he looked up at the birds, then at his watch. When the birds flapped their wings in time with the Swatch's ticking small hand, it gave him a great feeling of pleasure, indeed. It was true that life at Karl's gasthaus lacked certain modern entertainments that might otherwise help pass the time. Al had been known to enjoy an Atari game, a Floyd jam, a Phil Collins concert in his day. Still, he had to admit that bird motions were better than Atari, bird sounds were more agreeable to the ear than any sound created by man. Even now, when Karl played his accordion, he had to close his eyes, imagine how the instrument must sound to the nearby birds: graceless, thumping, earthbound. And yet, the instrument produced its share of amusement. Al had found particular delight in the variety of dance moves the guests concocted to accompany Karl's "Feuerwerks Polka." The writer's girl, for instance, seemed to morph into a claw hammer whenever the old man played. As if to kill, she steadied her hips, thrust out her chin, drove the nail home again and again and again.

Yes, Al enjoyed the curious guests, had taken pleasure in every last one of them, not expecting his days at the Gasthaus Esmeralda to last as long as they had, nor to be as lucky as they'd turned out to be. Certain his glide was over after he quit the cruise ships, when he'd discovered a carefree bartender at almost forty brought out a certain unease a carefree bartender at thirty did not, Al hadn't even expected to be in Mexico now. As a young bartender on the Funships between Mexican ports, he'd had quite a time, yes he had. But as the years passed, the old guys wanted younger guys, and the old women wanted boys. The young women had no money, and the young men made him work too hard.

Still, he'd played out the years so easily until the first, hard wrinkles had come, and even after the first Botox injections, it had all been fine for a while. In the end, though, he'd gone on a little too long, hadn't quite gotten out clean, and the fact nagged at him. In the last months, he'd allowed himself to settle for the bugs, the lowest and most desperate type of mark, and when a particularly odd night with a homosexual in Cancún went haywire, he'd had to snuff the guy with a pillow, watching the guy's bare ass flail against the bedspread. The image of that wrinkled, absurd ass had bothered Al for a long while. It had been his first act of violence, and his impulse had been to equalize the damage by cutting back on his own pleasure. For a while, he'd sworn off alcohol, which had been a painful punishment, indeed. It had gone against Al's easy nature to face the bugs without a single shot of tequila in his system, to face their swollen eyes, raptor smiles, their looks of such pure avarice he'd wanted to laugh and smother them all. Of course, he'd come to his senses during his peaceful stay at the Gasthaus Esmeralda. Even now he was thinking about the beer he would enjoy later on.

Maybe he'd have a beer and a bump. *Una cerveza y el* chaser.

It amused him to no end that the bartender at the Coco Palms Bar resented the Spanglish word, always pretended not to understand it. Al, of course, always pretended not to understand why the guy's nose was bent out of joint. "Ah! I'm sorry—*Perdón! Perdón, amigo!*" He liked to have a laugh. He'd make it so the other bar clients—all friends of Al's—would exclaim at the guy's sourpuss. "It's just a common word!" they would say in Al's defense. "English is creeping into our language, it's not Greenley's fault!" Of course the bartender always fetched Al's chaser in the end. He liked Al's tips, which were always good. Always tip a barman well, Al knew from experience. Fuck with them, fine, but tip big, and have a laugh, and all would be forgiven.

As he now imagined the barman's scowl, the bar's selection, which chaser he would choose—probably tequila but maybe bourbon or whiskey—Al remembered Pablo, and that the drink wouldn't be as enjoyable as it could be. Pablo and his knife tricks. Pablo and his favors.

Pablo and his pecking and cawing.

Al frowned.

The day had started out strangely, perhaps full of omen. Of course to believe in omens, a person had to believe in a great guiding principle. Al was of no particular mind on the subject, but thought it piquant to speculate.

"Piquant" was a word he'd just learned from the writer. The writer would never just say "hard" or even "harsh." No, he would say "piquant." Al liked him for it. The writer had also taught him the word "rancor," which wasn't as good as "piquant" but nearly. When Al had tried "rancor" on Pablo, Pablo had snorted. It had gotten under Pablo's skin that he wasn't one-hundred-percent fluent in English and his brother, Castillo, was.

"Fucking ridiculous language," Pablo had told Al.

In any case Al had awoken that morning when his arm burst into flames. The scorpion had been hiding in Al's sea-damp sheets. Apparently he'd rolled over on the thing, opening his eyes to see the segmented tail whipping down not just once but three times. As the poison began to move through his system, his gums had gone numb, he'd lost all sensation in his eyeballs for an hour. Even now the pain in his shoulder was such that someone might have been holding a cigarette lighter to it; Tylenol couldn't touch it. Heroin took away one's sharper instincts. In the end, Al had taken nothing and had considered hunting down the little creature and smashing it. He'd decided the effort wasn't worth the end result, and that the thing was well within its rights to sting. What he would do is place the bedposts in bowls of water; something a long-ago mark had shown him.

At the time he'd thought the idea bugged-out.

In truth, Al should thank the scorpion, because the sting had woken him from an uncomfortable dream, the kind he'd been having since things had begun to heat up between the Rodriguez brothers. There was Pablo with his grimy dictator's shirts. And then there was the quiet one—Castillo, with his fat belly, crisp European collars, handmade moccasin shoes. The dreams incorporating the brothers had begun to unnerve, to annoy, to destroy Al's peaceful glide, even while he was awake. For one thing, even conventional powertools didn't jibe with grogginess. Certainly not Karl's homemade ones. For another thing, the brothers' endless fighting shouldn't, probably *didn't,* concern Al.

No, a day's glide in his present situation could best be continued by sleeping well, waking rested, studying what gave the Von Tollmans pleasure, and giving it to them. Or not. One could not give a boss everything, spoil them too much. Still, Al had given a lot of good times in his years. He thought, a little angrily, of the flailing ass again—the sleep he had lost over that—but the fact was that if a bug was crazy enough it had to be smashed. If the bugged-out freak in Cancún would've paid the agreed on price, he would be alive now instead of lying under six feet of sand with that stupid look of surprise on his face. Al's prices had been reasonable, after all—a few hundred for the whole night, a few hundred more if the mark looked like he could pay. In Al's prime the lonely cruise ship patrons had paid a lot, and it had been a beautiful, effortless glide.

As he recalled his present circumstance, pain pulsed all the way through his arm, to his lower jaw. It was said by the locals that a scorpion's poison could be counteracted with twelve bee stings.

On the other hand, it was said that a scorpion's sting might be a punishment, inflicted by a hired priest representing the Mayan small gods of petty vengeance. To curse one's enemy in Esmeralda wasn't particularly costly; in fact, smaller curses were available for the price of a few shot glasses of tequila. Even the smaller punishments, however—nightmares, painful rashes, dog bites, hangnails—would come in irritating threes, and would keep coming in threes until the gods got bored, or the priests were too drunk to care. Therefore, because Al relished neither the idea of such gods existing, nor the idea of sticking his arm into Karl's hive to placate them if they *did* exist, he decided not to think about the locals and their beliefs.

He fished around for another subject. Anything pleasant would do.

"Another cigarette?

"Okay," he answered himself, laughing. Yeah, he shouldn't. Bad for the circulation. Bad for the skin. But fifty more sit-ups later. Balance in all things.

He'd had a laugh the other day when he'd read the president of the United States had sworn to go off sweets if he sent the army boys to die in the war in Iraq. It was curious to Al that a Christian president seemed to believe in a form of karma. Still, there was nothing more important than understanding a man's inconsistencies.

Al could absolutely sympathize with hedging a bet, he could.

When he'd come to the inevitable conclusion that his gliding years were over, he'd figured it was the logical thing to do himself in. Instead, he'd bought the gun, checked into a motel, stared at the gun awhile, and then had headed for Belize. Belize, the last lawless place, the last outpost for aging gigolos and bartenders, had appealed more than a bullet through the temple, though it was clearly the less practical of the solutions. In Belize City, Al would either find a good, long mark, or he'd be shot for ten dollars. But then the van had stalled in Esmeralda, and he'd met Cordula Von Tollman at the *ferretería,* and the winds began blowing his way once more.

"Alchen," Cordula had told him recently. She pressed a wad of moist peso notes into his hand. "You've become like a son to me. Please take this extra money. I know Karl isn't generous."

Al had spent the money on a silver filigree charm for Cordula—a peacock with emeralds for eyes—knowing it would not be long for her now, and that Karl would never spend money on charms for his wife. She had been pleased, and had squirreled the token away in her charm box where Karl was unlikely to look.

"Oh, Alchen! What would we do without you? Please be careful with your money! And be careful on the roads. You know it's not safe, now, for any of us in Esmeralda."

Dying with the flailing ass on his conscience had unnerved Al Greenley. But living without a glide had unnerved him even more. So to find Cordula just when he needed to find someone like her, to walk into the *ferretería* with the intention of buying rope to either have his van towed or to summon the courage to hang himself on Esmeralda Beach should the van cost too much to repair, had seemed the perfect solution. In any case, Cordula had arrived, smiled tightly, then commented on Al's good Spanish accent. Al had decided, on a whim, to make a favorable reference to the old woman's hat. The hat talk had led to other good-natured banter, and then a cold mamey juice—Al's treat. Esmeralda was changing, getting odd, Al been told by Cordula, as he sipped the sweetish, musky mamey. Not only that, but the Von Tollmans were having "perplexing troubles with the locals" and needed help constructing a new wall.

"But we can't hire any help from Esmeralda Town!" she'd continued in a slightly more hysterical tone. The flapping hat had emphasized the hysteria, and Al had seen fit to offer her a quick sip from the flask. She'd accepted, most gratefully. "We can't let any of them on the land, you see. They'll try to claim it as their own! Burial grounds or some nonsense! They actually believe they have a right to our land!"

As it turned out, the van needed a new muffler and Cordula enjoyed birds as much as Al did. Which was almost to the exact degree she didn't enjoy being called "ma'am." There were birds everywhere at the rancho, Corde promised. Of course, the wages would be low. "On the subject of money, my husband is, *ach,* very difficult."

"If he doesn't like my work, I'll leave, no hard feelings," Al had said. "I'm like a train; people can jump on or jump off whenever they choose."

"Like a train, boy, you're like a *train!*" Karl had laughed uproariously, upon meeting him.

And suddenly, without warning, Al's glide had begun anew.

Back behind the shed, he looked at the cigarette between his second and third finger with distaste, then affection, and puffed again. If he were on a desert island, having to choose—this desert island, this choosing, was often present in his thoughts—he knew he'd have to pick a carton of cigarettes over more practical items. The inherent trap—he'd eventually run out and suffer anyway—nagged at him.

Traps in traps in traps.

In any case, he was free for the moment. Cordula had come, the bug was long dead, there was no proof of karma and the president might as well pour pure sugar down his throat if he started the war. The way it had been explained to Al, acts of kindness built up good karma, while acts of unkindness didn't erase themselves. No matter how much good karma in the bank, an evil deed must be paid for separately.

Thou shall not kill, buddy, he thought. That's right there in your own book.

Still, he couldn't help but laugh sympathetically at the president's predicament. A few years ago, Al had been guilty of the same careful, human chit system. The bugged-out tradings and sleepless machinations. There was nothing easy about that kind of life. The president's mouth reminded him of a box turtle's—zipped up, without lips. Lipless people always spooked him a little; his own lips were full, red, even at thirty-something. Even as a smoker.

He closed his eyes, comparing his lips to the president's.

His were the better lips, no doubt.

Besides, if God existed and God forgave all, then God would just have to forgive Al. The problem of the flailing ass was all right there—built-in. If God didn't exist, the ass didn't matter. Nothing mattered. Curses didn't matter. Curses didn't exist.

As usual, he felt better. He exhaled.

Yes, a cool beer later would be perfect, if only he didn't have to share it in Pablo's company. Raul would be tomorrow's beer, tomorrow's problem. Raul at least always made Al laugh with his Lysol smell and furtive knee-knocking.

Pablo's brother Castillo, it was said, didn't drink at the Coco Palms Bar. Castillo apparently preferred sugared hibiscus tea in the room behind the meat shop, though Al couldn't confirm this, never having been invited to drink or speak with him. Castillo had only spoken to Al once, in all of Al's time at Esmeralda. "Watch your health," Castillo had said, with his blubbery, thick-lipped smile. His voice had been very soft, but his lips were like a turkey liver, cut in half, sutured precisely on. "Tequila is for young men, and for stupid ones. You don't strike me as a stupid man."

"Don't *ever* fuckin' talk to my brother," Pablo had warned.

In truth, Al did not know why Castillo had spoken to him all of a sudden. With the way things were going for Castillo, the guy shouldn't be talking. He shouldn't be mentioning Al's health. And yet, he'd done it so naturally.

Al had chosen not to relate the conversation to Pablo, and thought the matter had been dropped. And yet, in his mind he could not drop it.

He could not forget the liverish lips, the thin, dry sheen to Castillo's skin, the chapped, oblong skull, the sunken eyes. The man's physical appearance and mannerisms suggested not a bird but a prehistoric flying creature. Something that had survived too long, seen too many years.

He shivered and laughed.

Types of birds. It was always good to break them into types if one was unsure of one's position. Where Raul was quiet and sparrow-thin, Castillo was obese and quiet. Pablo was loud and tall. Pablo's elongated, yellowish face called to mind both an eagle and a doublet-wearer during the Spanish Inquisition. His voice called to mind nest-raiding, rodents squealing, teakettles boiling, children screeching, fingernails being dragged across a blackboard. Both Pablo and Raul enjoyed talking about revolution, accentuating their words with long, bony fingers. The way Pablo saw it, the spirit of his ancestors lived in the knife he carried in his belt, and at the appropriate moment they would emerge and whisper into Pablo's ear. War would begin. *La raza* would rise again.

It irritated Al that so much feather-ruffling, so much fevered talking would have to be done, ruining Al's cold beer, when Al already *knew* what Pablo wanted tonight, what Raul would expect tomorrow night. The last time Al had found the two a gringo to do a muling job, a "wet job," trucking the shit up from the lagoon to the Chetumal airport, things had gone strange and the Dutch guy had gotten shot.

Of course the Dutch guy had been a last-minute find of Al's: a macho soccer-playing type down on holiday, drinking too much. He, too, had been loud, reminiscent of a pouter pigeon. His chest had been broad, his lips thick, sloppy, Dutch. He hadn't believed in knife spirits.

"That's why they're going to get you first, Dutchman." Pablo had smiled in his particularly unpleasant way.

Al had truly believed the guy would work out fine when he'd found him playing volleyball in Chetumal. But when Pablo's boys had gone to do the count-up, they'd found him with an ounce in his pocket, and later someone had found him floating in a lagoon.

"Unbelievable." Al still couldn't believe the stupidity of the guy. A tiny ounce—grabbed with a fist. They'd caught the guy doing a line off his own index finger.

The guy had been a scavenger, a bad call, and it had been told to Al that he'd pled for his life all the way to the lagoon. His parents would pay, he had a rich uncle in Hoovenstratten or Sinkweiler or Dockdamm or some such place. It had been a fact that the Dutch language made Pablo's boys laugh. They thought it sounded like a plumbing backup.

Pablo's brother, Castillo, of course, hadn't found the body amusing. When Castillo got unhappy, things got particularly touchy between the brothers. "He was your find, handyman, and you gotta pay for upsetting my family." For several weeks Pablo had left threatening little messages—pages of Mayan glyphs—on Al's van in town, and Al had waited for the knife to fall.

By the third week, he'd lost ten pounds.

Then Pablo had reappeared, strolling Esmeralda's streets in his unbelievable new paramilitary getup. "My brother says I'm a pig." Pablo had laughed and imitated the immense Castillo's cheeks puffing out. Pablo was a gifted dramatist, in his way. He could really make himself look like a pig.

And yet, Pablo hadn't dropped the matter of the Dutchman. "If it wasn't for my brother, I'd probably've chopped off your fucking huevos. But he doesn't want any more dead gringos. My brother's got a fuckin' soft spot for gringos. So let's just say you owe me big."

Al continued smoking, considering the unhappy problem in front of him. To keep Pablo happy he needed a mule. The mules tended to disappear if they weren't clever. The business didn't tend to draw the clever. A particularly absurd cycle, Al felt, but there it was.

Al, himself, had done a few wet jobs for Pablo and Raul, and the craziness, the trip-wire wigginess weren't suited to a nice, easy glide.

First of all, Pablo's people were nervous. During a wet move the driver—the *cabrón,* the male goat—was blindfolded as soon as he parked, and the loader was poked and prodded with guns. Was there anything less productive than prodding a nervous man with a gun, while admonishing him to "be careful, *chingado* hombre, don't look at us"?

The driver was there in the unfortunate case a hostage needed to be pulled. The loader was the other guy. He just had to be big. Al wasn't big, and wasn't fond of being a hostage, or of being blindfolded. Therein, lay Al's problem.

Another problem with being the loader was that the stuff was packed into waterproof Baggies, the Baggies stuffed into more plastic. On false step and the plastic would burst open, the powder would ride off on a current in the wind. The nervous watchers insisted on dogging your every step, poking a gun in your face, snarling nervous commands. Even as you loaded the Baggies into a waiting Starjet, sweat dripping off your forehead, they stuck their guns into the back of your knees, so that you almost went down a million times.

And more and more, it was said, someone would go down soon.

Something crazy was going down between the brothers.

In any case, it wasn't going to be Al going down.

Al had no problem with cocaine; it was just another absurdity in an absurd human world that alcohol, an intoxicant, was legal while another intoxicant was illegal. It was also okay with him if people wanted to act illogically and dumb. They seemed happiest that way.

Still, Al didn't want to involve himself with Pablo's guys this time around—not even for two grand, not even to keep on Pablo's good side. After the Dutch guy had been shot, Speedy Chaz had been doing the runs with some hophead he'd met in Playa del Carmen, but Al knew the guy had overdosed at a rave in some jungle ruin and Speedy Chaz was now doing too much coke and running out of money. A bad combination and one that always ended in a mess.

He sighed, shaking his head. Pablo had probably spent five minutes looking for another gringo *cabrón* within the Coco Palms Bar. And not finding one, his knife had probably "revealed" that Al should be used as the *cabrón,* even though Al's services were soon to be rendered in a much more important way. Pablo was reckless. Impatient.

Pablo's knife spirits, of course, were foolproof.

"Yes, maybe we've got the other *chingadera* to plan, but maybe I don't need you for that one, so you're better off keeping things friendly with me, *cabrón,*" is how Pablo would put it tonight, while Al was trying to enjoy a cold Sonora. A Sonora was a good, dark, native beer. It amused Al to no end that Pablo, the Toltec warrior, drank blond ales exclusively. "If you want to help me in the future, *cabrón,*" Pablo would say, "You've just got to be the *cabrón.*"

Cabrón, used in one sense, meant a person was a fool or a creep or his wife was screwing around on him. Used in another sense, such as when one scored a goal in *fútbol,* or when one did something unpleasant with good cheer, it was an endearment. *Chingado*—fucked, adverb or noun—could also be a complimentary word. Al had never understood exactly why.

In any case, Al had seen the tanks on the beach, knew it was time for another drop to go down. The town got crazy during drop weeks; he could feel the pent-up craziness from here. Still, there was no way, no possible way, he was going to be roped into a wet move. Not with the rumors of a DEA sting. Not when there was an easier mark, a bigger *chingada*—almost ready to go.

He smoked again, feeling sad for Karl Von Tollman's imminent *chingadera,* sad for all *cabrónes. Cabrónes* couldn't help but be *cabrónes.* It was their fate.

In time, the writer came to his mind.

There was a long, floating feeling as Al watched the gulls line up over the azure, lazy sea. For many days now he'd watched the girl swim alone, or with Karl. The writer didn't seem to like water. This puzzled Al. Sea water was a beautiful thing, a free, floating, expansive thing; everyone should like it. As he'd watched everything the couple had done these last weeks through the binoculars—the tedious eating, sex, predictable drinking too much on the writer's part—it had been his opinion the girl was pretty enough, but her hands and feet were too large, monstrous really, and the writer could do better.

What the guy needed was less writing and more water. More air.

Al decided to tell him so.

Yes, it was sad the girl couldn't be roped into the wet move, but a *cabrón* just couldn't be female. Too much temptation for Pablo's guys out in the dark, warm jungle—especially after being primed with *pornografía* magazines and tapes where all the girls looked like Sarah. At least in the dark. At least the hair and the curves.

It was sad, yes. All of it. But with the closure of the town motel, the other guesthouse, the tension in Esmeralda, there weren't many gringos to choose from unless one went down to Chetumal or up to Playa del Carmen on a hunt. Hunting a *cabrón,* even in a tourist trap, wasn't easy. First you had to get a guy alone, a guy running out of cash. A desperate guy, say, who'd just broken with his girl, or lost his job, or hated his parents and didn't quite want his vacation to end. Then, you had to spend time with the guy, buying him drinks, listening to his life story. You had to play volleyball or foosball or Hacky Sack, or, more time-consuming yet, go to a rave with him, watch the nutbirds dance around under the moon on ecstasy.

Of course, Al could rustle up a Mexican in no time, but since last year someone high up had insisted on a pair of gringos for the wet moves. Revenge for someone's dishwashing years in Arizona or California; Al knew that's what the game came down to. Because they'd been treated like a cockroach in a menial job in the US, and because sooner or later they had to feed the DEA a sting, the unseen, unknown person insisted on white faces, preferably yanquis, to do the last bit of muling to the Chetumal airport, where it was said the sting would eventually take place. Saving Mexican honor, the Mexican *policía* would laughingly hand off the helpless gringo to the DEA for a photo shoot, then snatch him back to be tried under Mexican law. Fingers would wag at the evil yanqui menace, tongues would roll, life sentences would be handed down. No higher-ups would be caught or named, Esmeralda would sleep for a while, and it would all start up, fresh and clean for drug dealers. Or the hotels. Whoever won the war.

Al smiled a little less happily.

The easiest thing was just do the wet move himself—just to keep Pablo quiet and happy until the Gasthaus Esmeralda *chingadera* came down and he could finally take flight. But with the Radisson people putting pressure on all sides, who knew how close the end was now? A sting, a scandal-plagued Esmeralda, would be good for the hotel men. Which would be good for Castillo, if the rumors were true. Which would be bad for Pablo and Raul.

All of it was bad for Karl.

As he placidly flicked a beetle from his hand, looked at the ugly bulge under his watch, Al decided none of the long-range outcomes were of particular consequence to him if the writer did the wet move. "Wet" meaning that the stuff came from the water. Which, come to think of it, would be particularly rich in irony for Nick.

Al couldn't help but laugh to himself at the poor writer's poor swimming abilities. He never tightened his snorkel enough, he always sputtered water in his nose.

"I just hate the barracudas following me. I *swear* the ugly things wait for me. And I'm trying to write ten pages a day," the writer had said sheepishly to Al. "All work and no play is how I can get it done."

A particularly yanqui bit of logic.

"I fuckin' hate yanquis and their fuckin' *mayonesa*-faces," Pablo had said many times to Al. "Their faces jiggle, man. *Jiggle.*"

The personal nature of the hatred had puzzled Al, until he'd gotten drunk with the talkative Pablo a few times, and learned about the summer the Rodriguez brothers had spent as illegals. Being a dishwasher in a seafood place in Arizona could drive a man to rage.

"You shoulda seen the way they looked at us, man. Like we were fucking campesinos. We're from a good fucking family! Fucking yanqui bastards and their food-encrusted plates. Fucking uniforms with a fucking shrimp on the pocket."

Possibly due to his Catholic upbringing, Pablo used the word "fuck" solely as a quantifier. When he spoke of actual fucking he used silent pumping gestures, rolled-back eyes.

"My fucking brother sucked up to the yanquis because he wanted a raise, but I wanted to rip their heads off their fat, white necks. Those invading pilgrims and their fucking pantaloons and buckled hats. Who needs to buckle their hat, man?"

As it was, the Rodriguez brothers had returned to Esmeralda after just one unfortunate season in Arizona.

"Who in the fuck needs it, hombre? We make more cash from the *mayonesa*-faces down here. Land of opportunity, my ass. Land of fuckin' ugly fucks! I used to spit in their shrimp, man. Piss on their tires. I used to fart on their plates."

Back in Esmeralda, Pablo had become a policeman: it was his special duty and pleasure to help any American tourists who straggled in. As a sideline, he supervised the wet moves.

Castillo, upon his return, had become active in local politics. His sideline was to own a meat shop. Among other shops.

It was true Mexican culture dictated family over business, and that the Rodriguez brothers would probably not start a full-scale war over the subject of hotels and cocaine. It was Al's privilege to know, however, that since Castillo had become mayor in last month's elections, the men had lately been sitting far away from one another at family gatherings, and that their wives, two streaky blondes, avoided each other in town. Castillo's wife was suddenly the blonder wife, which might mean something in the Mexican societal hierarchy.

Then again it might just mean Pablo preferred brunettes.

Al wrapped his cigarette box in the Mexican poncho he kept in the shed, thinking of ways he might introduce the writer to Pablo tonight. The poncho was full of spiders and beetles, and it appealed to him to watch the many colorful shapes scurry out when he shook the thing.

The Rodriguez brothers' lines of work, policing and politics, also appealed to Al, and he thought he'd probably be good at either. At one time, he'd worried any line of work would annoy him, and had kicked around the idea of being an actor. Bored with acting school, he'd spent a few years pursuing a floater's standard choices: security guard, screenwriter, musician, dive instructor, roadie, model scout. For a year in Toronto, he'd worked in an exotic bird shop.

It was during that year, Al had come to understand there was no need to go crazy hunting for a paycheck. There was no need to pronounce oneself an actor—one could just act, just maneuver, get along fine that way.

In a bird shop, the answers to survival were all right there, all laid out, almost too easy to believe. The birds taught Al the importance of physical placement: feather-ruffling, head position, eye contact, all important indicators of one's likely position as prey. For small birds like Al, a position should always appear low—blending in was best. Plumage, of course, made the difference: raptors were often brown, inconspicuous. Speed, lightness, going for whatever moved. Listening was also key. Not only had Al failed in most of his young endeavors because he hadn't listened to people's words, but also because he'd not gauged their tone, pitch, timbre. Timbre was particularly important in a hunt. Too reedy, you became a fluttering prey, too squawky, you were noticed too fast.

Yes, Al had been particularly privileged to study the caged grays, the falcons, the double-yellowheads. From their clues, Al had learned to shed weight, *not* to load himself down with jobs, titles, furniture, land, hotels, wives, to take pleasure in a long, weightless glide through life, a sudden swoop, a bite, then a lifting-off again to the next mark and the next. He often thought of the long-ago birds, what they might feel if they were here in the Yucatán Peninsula. He had, of course, set them all free before leaving the shop with the contents of the register. It was true, the larger, tropical parrots with clipped wings had little chance, and the Canadian winter had been fast approaching. Still, Al did not doubt for a minute he'd done the right thing. Like Al would, they'd spend their last moments hunting, soaring, gliding. No more tiny cages, fluorescent boxes. No more laughing humans watching them defecate, fornicate, for fun.

After liberating his buddies, escaping the time clock, Al's travels on the cruise ships had brought him to Alaska, California, then Mexico. As a free bird he'd played out many lives in Anchorage, San Diego, Cancún, and now here in Esmeralda Beach. During those years, he hadn't looked for any one prey in particular but for everything that moved. He'd learned from the falcons to flap his wings, unnerve a possible mark, just for the hell of it, wink at the guy or gal, see what came down. What came down was usually nothing, but he'd had his share of laughs, he had.

Shells upon shells upon shells.

They dropped, broke. Meat. Pearls. Or not.

"Meat! *Ach!* Pearls!" And the word was not "poetical," Karl had informed him. The word was "poetic."

Al had been trying to explain to the old man how the poetry of survival worked, but Karl didn't listen. Karl almost never listened when Al talked about birds. Even when things got uncannily still. Especially not then.

"Nick! Don't shout at me. It's not going to help anything!"

"What! You think I should stay calm?"

When he heard the faraway voices carry on the wind, Al cocked his head, moved into position. His clear gaze swept the beach. The writer and the girl were arguing in the distance, he could hear them even over the sound of the outboard motor that was now at least a mile away. He smelled the scent of Cordula's bread baking—rye. He heard Karl raking leaves, flinging slugs into a bucket to feed to the coatimundis later.

"Nein, nein, nein!" Karl was muttering under his breath.

He was talking to the dogs, to the air.

Karl hadn't listened when Pablo cawed out the first warning. Pablo had been quite jovial about the matter, bringing a bottle of good Grava Alta wine to the rancho, then starting in on Karl's citizenship status, his lack of a Mexican passport. Later, Karl hadn't listened to Raul or the bow-tied government tourist *agencía* man when he'd come with a brimming fruit basket.

"I don't trink the likkids," Karl had said to Pablo.

"We're too busy here to be making hibiscus tea for politicians," he'd said to Castillo.

It had been a particular surprise to Al when Castillo himself had come to apologize for his brother's lack of manners. The vision of the fat man squishing along on the sand would never leave Al's mind. "I do admire the ingenuity of the German people. And yet," Castillo had said to Karl, "it would be safer for you if you leave us. Regrettably, my brother is not a polite man."

"This is Mexican land and *Mexicans* are free to repatriate it at a time of our choosing," Pablo had chirped to Karl the second time he'd come. The second time he'd shown up with Raul.

"Patrimony," Raul had called it.

"Patri-*money,*" Karl spat.

"I am truly embarrassed for the inelegance of my brother," Castillo had said, in his quiet, unruffled, way. "And yet, this land you have chosen to build on is a land that spiritually belongs to my people."

Castillo's "people" had remained unidentified.

His spirituality, too, had been left quite vague.

"Fuckin' German *huevón*. The knife spirits will tell me when the time is right," Pablo had told Al, soon after.

In his version, the exact amount of blood was described.

Castillo's people might and might not be local land speculators in favor of hotels. They might and might not be deserting him in panicky droves. For Castillo, it was said—since he'd been elected mayor by a landslide—favored both progress *and* peace, two not-quite-copacetic concepts when one's brother was Pablo Rodriguez of Los Nuevo Toltecas de Esmeralda. Until the unpleasantness with the bomb ten days ago, both the American and Mexican hotel scouts had continued to appear in Esmeralda frequently, each side chattering excitedly about the availability of "twenty, possibly thirty years," of fresh water before the lagoon was dry and they'd have to build an expensive desalinization system.

"My fuckin' brother has gone too far," Pablo said.

Sometimes he said, "But my fuckin' brother won't let it get further than this. He knows what I'd do if he did."

Zooming down the potholed roads in their blacked-out MexGov extra-long Suburbans, their GPS systems mapping possible tourist sites, the hotel men often made notes on water rights, and the depth and consumer friendliness of Karl's underground lake. Mechanized water sports in the lagoon, to their way of seeing things, were a selling point. Others included guided trips to Karl's old pyramids, a water park in his shallow beach, a zoo in Cordula's garden, and, of course, a long line of luxury towers and a highway and an airport.

"Fucking *un*-Mexican bastards. Let them make their notes. My brother says that's all they're going to do, make their fuckin' *notes,*" Pablo had said, laughing about the *mordidas*—bribes—Castillo was taking from hotel men. Pablo demanded half of the *mordida* money, and, it was said, got it. "And don't get me started on that crazy German fuck who started it all with *his* hotel. Lady Blood is going to see to him."

Because the long-haired, curly-nailed, serpent-eyed, Lady Blood was Pablo's patron goddess, and because Pablo's fondest dream was to repatriate Karl's hotel as his own personal estate, and because Castillo wished the matter to be solved peaceably and with a minimum of newspaper headlines, Karl Von Tollman's continued existence was not looking good. As Pablo saw it, he would keep burning candles for Lady Blood and her son Prince Knife the Cutter. As long as the candles burned, as long as Castillo remained quiescent, the ultralight boats would keep coming through the lagoons to the open ocean around Esmeralda. The plastic-wrapped kilos of cocaine would continue to be stacked into watertight canisters, tied to buoy floaters, dropped on the lee side of the reef by the Belizeans, picked up by Esmeralda men as had been done for many, many years.

With Mexican *cojones,* Belizean contacts, German architecture, Mayan curses, Karl's land would be "the fuckin' birthplace of the Toltec Renaissance. Lady Blood promised me this place. And my brother's gonna fuckin' help me get it. Whether he wants to or not." If this happened, Castillo would do his helpful mayoring safely from one end of Esmeralda Town, while Pablo would run the ever-expanding wet move industry from the main chalet, and his increasing number of children would populate the A-frame guesthouses. Together, behind Karl's formidable wall, the family would prosper, together they would rise up, lock-down, keep the hotel men from Esmeralda.

"And if my brother even thinks of going behind my back, I'll show his hotel friends how the Nuevo Toltecs fight a war! Crazy dogs!"

To Al's mind, the hotel men weren't particularly bad fellows. Partial to wagering large sums on cockfights, dogfights, poker games, they were just bored rich boys, fresh out of college, arrogant enough until someone had used a gelignite bomb to *sabotear*—blow up—one of their pricey vehicles.

Until the *sabotaje* ten days ago, the good-looking kids had been occasional fixtures at the town's Coco Palms Bar where Al had endeavored to have some fun with them. They were of the cupid-lipped, Yale-educated, "bringing capitalism to the Third World," variety who knew drinking tricks like how to put a peso coin on one's forehead and get it into one's mouth without the use of hands.

It had been just that game they'd all been engaged in when the Suburban had rocketed ten feet, bloomed in the air, then set itself down in flames. The peso coin had bounced to the floor, and Al had lost his bet.

"Did you see the look on that fuckin' kid's yanqui face when his stereo came shooting out of the window!" Pablo had laughed himself purple. "I've never seen nathin' better than that. I'm gonna die thinking about that! And I'm going to die a happy man."

Of course, Castillo was said to have been "greatly annoyed" by the "unfortunate" scene that caused the notice of a few reporters from the Mexican daily *La Atención.* A long talk between the brothers had apparently ensued. If "talk" was the right term for Pablo threatening his brother with a knife and a broken bottle, and a promise his boys in Belize would get nasty. Castillo had, according to rumor, backed down.

"Taken ill," was the term used to describe Castillo's sudden disappearance.

In any case, after Castillo's illness the locals had stopped calling the development Yanqui Beach.

La Playa Esmeralda is what the Yale boys had called it.

"Yanqui Beach is officially over," Pablo had declared the night of the *sabotaje.* "And no fuckin' Playa Esmeralda unless they like the taste of gelignite."

And yet, Castillo, it was said, had been mentioning La Playa Esmeralda from his sickbed.

"My brother is not a well fuckin' man," Pablo laughed. "If he wasn't my brother I'd put him out of his misery. And I may do it, yet. *Para la raza.*"

Of course, Karl still used the term "gasthaus" when describing the land in question. Because when Karl spoke of the land, he spoke of "my clean title," "my years of hard work," "my animals that depend on me," and it was immediately apparent to Al that Karl was not fit for life in this century. Maybe not any century, but certainly not this one.

A land title could be manufactured on any press: jaguars could be put into zoos, sold for pets, shot. Hard work? Al had to laugh sympathetically at the man's faith he'd scared the Rodriguez brothers off with a shotgun. Because Al sensed, and sensed in his very bones, Karl was coming into some bad times, Al had known it was a good time to give Karl a gold ring.

They'd been out on the sand earlier today, on one of the old man's crazy trash runs, when Al had flipped the ring onto the sand. "Look, old man!" he'd waved Karl over, winking at Sarah to see what she'd do. "I guess it's your lucky day."

The old man had gone half-crazy with joy, slapping Al on the back, telling him he was a genius.

Al *had* been intelligent about the matter. He'd covered the ring in salt, soaked it for eight nights just to get the right look. And Al had never seen the old man so happy, lecturing on the importance of looking through the sea's discards. The lecture had given Al a great deal of happiness. Especially the part when Karl told Sarah to "look and learn from our Al, here."

Of course, the writer's girl had been ridiculous about the ring, completely missing the poetry of Al's gesture. When she'd cornered him and whispered that what he'd done was "idiotic," Al had laughed at the angry shape of her mouth.

He didn't mind being idiotic and was quite good at it when the need arose.

"A dodo bird." He laughed. "Love it."

There was only one more cigarette in the pack he'd wrapped in the poncho, and the gulls overhead were now dispersing, telling Al it was time to forget how much he'd like to smoke it, and he should leave it where it could be found by Cordula.

He crawled out from his hiding place in back of the shed, ready to start in on the walls and fences with the enthusiasm expected of him. Usually the work was fairly easy, the climate agreed with him, and the good cheer was easy to project. And yet it troubled him, sometimes, that he'd spent the better part of a year constructing and repairing what he hated most—walls and fences, traps and locks.

More and more he felt the walls closing in.

The thought of the Von Tollmans being ambushed so completely did not please Al, and yet he'd always figured that if Pablo simply wanted him to leave the doors open one night, disappear into the wind, he would have to do it. Opening a few gates was the least Al could do in return for a large cash payment, and he had never minded doing the least where money was concerned. Still, it had never been pleasant to imagine how, when Al left into the wind, the knives would come out, the ancestors would start to whisper. The Von Tollmans would be all alone, probably asleep. Pablo would get stupid and scary. *Para la raza.*

Al shivered, stepping farther into the sunlight.

"I believe I will," Cordula liked to say, laughing.

Often, Cordula came and hid and smoked in the clearing with Al. As she smoked, she blushed and giggled, and told secrets about her marriage. Al enjoyed watching her draw the smoke in, shivering with naughtiness, with years of frustration. She seemed to take a great deal of pleasure in her secret from Karl.

"I love him, and I love the animals," she told Al.

"I love him, but I can't talk to him. He's going slowly mad."

During their smoking breaks, Al had used the opportunity to press Cordula about moving back to Germany, back to Mexico City. He thought some progress had been made—certain game plans had been discussed, certain tactics involving ever-greater physical ailments that couldn't be addressed outside of a big city—though mostly Cordula just giggled, shrugged, smoked.

"You don't know Karlchen." She would blush. "Not the way I do. He knows if I'm really sick. And we didn't even leave here when I caught the malaria. Karl simply made a salve."

But then Karl didn't know Al.

In a few days, after the couple was gone, Al planned to press Cordula harder, give her encouragement. In fact, he planned to scare her.

Introduce her to Lady Blood.

What he imagined for Cordula was a lone encounter on the road to Esmeralda Town. Two of Pablo's men in balaclavas, chanting in Mayan. Cordula's hen-eye hysterical. A little cut. A little drip. Flapping around and squawking, a woman could make a lot of noise. Surely, Karl would have to listen to his woman then.

"Just fuckin' run 'em out of the place," Pablo had said. "I don't give a shit, but it would keep my fuckin' brother happy, which would keep my mother and sisters happy, if they went peacefully. The guy is scared like a *ratón* of reporters. Like a dog, man. He shakes now when I talk to him."

Pablo had grabbed Al's neck and squeezed. It had been a friendly squeeze.

"My mother's gotta stay happy, hombre. But then she's an old woman, and I want to *relajar* in *mí casa nueva.* My wife's on my nerves for the place. She wants a fuckin' view. And get this—she wants a fuckin' horse ring. Arabians. Some shit she picked up from a TV show."

And so yes, scaring Cordula would be good for everyone. Good for the goose, good for the gander. It would be particularly good for Al. If he could get the Von Tollmans to leave peacefully there would almost certainly be money in it. That, and there would be pleasure.

If he couldn't scare her enough, there would only be money.

Either way, either way, he told himself now.

To put the unpleasant scene out of his mind, Al Greenley walked to his room in back of the property and began to think of topics of conversation Karl might enjoy this afternoon. It was his daily plan to come up with at least four or five topics of interest to entertain the old man and Cordula.

Coming up with the topics was a favorite part of Al's day, and within a few moments, he'd decided to talk to Karl about computers.

1. *How computers were tracking people's movements.*
2. *How computers were running the world's economies.*
3. *How computers were replacing parents.*
4. *How computers would soon sprout brains and get rid of humans.*

Of course the ideas would have to be refined, especially the last one. Karl had a second sense for when Al was pulling his chain: No one was trickier than a tricker. But then, no one was lonelier for conversation than Karl.

"Karl, Karl." Al laughed affectionately, having forgotten the annoyance of Pablo for the moment. Washing the smell of the cigarette from his fingers with a freshly cut lemon and then two cycles of soap and water—an action he performed each time he smoked because Karl didn't like cigarettes—he said, "Crazy."

Having settled the conversational topics, Al took out the apple Cordula had given him this morning from his pocket. Cordula had labored long and hard figuring a way to grow a northern plant in the hostile climate, then another way to keep the insects from eating the apple blossoms before they could bloom. Every branch of Cordula's specially fertilized, specially encased, *dauphin-pomme* tree was netted, wired, swathed in transparent gauze, and still the apples were mostly small—so many insects got through.

Since the writer's girlfriend had arrived, Cordula had taken to wearing Vaseline on her lips—just the tiniest amount—in an effort to compete.

"You're looking quite beautiful this morning," Al said every morning now.

Her pleasure pleased him, and he thought of it again as he savored a bite of her apple—the lemon, butterscotch tartness.

It was a good apple. He'd tell her so.

She'd smile prettily, heavily. "Not so good." She'd laugh.

And yet there was no use in dwelling on the fact he liked Karl and Cordula. In a perfect world Al would just slip out, slide on, hope for the best for them. In a perfect world, Al would not have to hear about bouquet-style killings, arms and legs cut at the stem, stuffed into the torso like a flower arrangement. He would not have to hear about bodies being primped and made up and set in an amusing tableau—such as a formal dinner party complete with ballgowns and candles—all the better to shock the finder into terror.

"Man, oh, man." Pablo laughed. "We could scare the shit out of my brother. Bouquets, hombre. Just like fuckin' roses! He won't dare invite any of his hotel buddies down here, then!"

During the last month, when awoken in the night by the unnerving, choppy dreams of Cordula in a bouquet, Al was sometimes tempted to forget Pablo's money, head south into Belize.

He'd had the same sensation before quitting the bird shop, the same series of sleepless nights, restless dreams. And yet, this time Al wasn't young and free and good-looking and floating. Easy money was like water or wind; beautiful when it came your way. Even more beautiful if it was the only thing you had.

He had to laugh, but it wasn't the kind of laughing one enjoyed.

"Hey man, how much do you figure if I get the Germans to leave by next month?" he'd said to Pablo last week.

Pablo had been engaged in scratching squat, toothy characters on the handle of his knife. He'd not even deigned to answer Al's question.

"In the Toltec tradition, certain sacrifices will need to be made." He'd laughed.

"And how are our German friends?" Castillo had surprised Al in town last week, after he'd warned Al about drinking tequila. It had been the first time the quiet man had ever mentioned his visit. He'd walked out suddenly from the room in back of his meat shop.

Castillo had smiled coolly when Al had inquired after his health. "How kind of you to ask, young Greenley. I had been feeling poorly, and yet as you can see I am much better now, since I've returned from my trip to *Tejas.*" He had given Al a particularly penetrating stare when relating the information about his trip to the US. "One should always thank the Lord for good health. It can always end so quickly."

"I'm happy to hear it—" Al had begun, but Castillo had stared him down with the pterodactyl eye.

"What you should want," he'd then said with a fat man's wink, "is to watch your health, young man. Remember the great lesson of the Toltecs." He'd smiled. "They lost."

And now, still remembering the short encounter with the fat man, Al shivered. Castillo, it was said, had taken to working the front counter of the meat shop. From there he did his mayoral business as a "man of the people."

Lately, *Americano*-style beef cutlets were on sale.

Pablo had given orders that any of his men seen patronizing Castillo's meat shop would soon find themselves "as, *pues,* meat."

Business, then, had not been good for Castillo. But it was getting a little better.

From far off, sausages were cooking. Al sniffed. Sausages and fuel and kraut.

His stomach humming and buzzing, he picked up his binoculars, swept the guesthouse. The sight was a welcome comic relief: the couple, fighting again. A birdy-looking girl, Sarah's Gustafsson's face was a long, sharp face; aquiline nose, hollowed widow's cheekbones. She had a crane's neck, long cranelike legs. Too birdlike, Al thought, for a human.

He studied the girl's long neck at leisure, turned the focus knob to zoom in on her deep, ovoid eyes. They were gray, stormy, endlessly full of fury and feeling yet, he thought, reminiscent of fowl. As a topic of conversation, how best to screw Sarah Gustafsson had been high on the list these last days, not just with Karl, but with Pablo, Chaz, Raul, all the men in town. Al didn't mind discussing various ways of fucking a tall woman; the secret was in making them feel you might just crush them.

He'd watched the couple fucking many times, and was of the opinion the writer talked too much, winced too much if the girl rolled over on him or bobbed too hard. A larger girl did not want to be reminded she was a ton of bricks. A tall girl wanted feather-lightness, then rough play, just a little smack to start. Just what Al would do.

As he swept over her jutting collarbones, her visible ribcage, he imagined dropping out of a tree, coming at her from the vines, laughing and saying, "Boo." Always frowning while running on the beach, Sarah would save her speed for the last twenty yards. As seen through Al's binoculars she'd get madder, madder, maddest as she crossed some imaginary finish line drawn in the sand. Her thin legs, jutting elbows, ferocious facial expression, made one imagine inner recitations of Hegel, Mao. Her habit of plunging into the sea after each run impressed him as kooky, frightening.

He now laughed when she tried to make up with the writer by holding his face to hers, kissing him. The writer started talking directly into her mouth.

It had become the second-best part of Al's day to spook the writer's girl. While keeping the writer cooped up in his pen, she flirted with Karl constantly, subtly, tipping her hipbones this way and that. From his bird's-eye view, Al had guessed everything about her—bored with the writer's endless talking and chirping, she'd begun to hunt the old man, looking straight into his eyes, asking questions about his life, standing very close. Then she'd go and screw the writer and make both men feel bad.

And so, for the writer, and just for the hell of it, Al liked to sneak up on the girl, ruffle her feathers a bit. He could not help wanting to fuck her. Crazy, tall-legged, flirting bird.

He often waited for her on the path to the beach, to the animals' pens. She often hummed, looked at her big feet, as she walked.

"Surprise," he'd say, in his quietest voice.

"Get lost," she'd answer.

"Hey, I'm lost. I might just need your help. You like to help people, don'tcha?"

Usually she'd jump. Then frown.

"It's awfully good of you to help the old man. Such a helpful person."

"Look," she'd say, "you're not scaring me."

"What am I doing to you then?"

Truth be known, Sarah Gustafsson didn't scare as easily as Al would have liked. From afar he could amuse himself by imagining her hatching from an egg, wet, naked, vulnerable—and in fact had enjoyed this divertimento several times. But up close, her good, shiny looks, perfect teeth, earnest squawking irritated him. As an irritant she couldn't help but arouse certain quick, animal-smashing urges in him. Still, a handyman could lose himself pleasurably in a suitcase full of secret thongs, scalloped camisoles; the kind of subterranean things a woman wore because she didn't want to appear frivolous. Sometimes Al took one of Sarah's bras, her thongs, and draped it over the bedpost. Twice he'd moved her shoes.

Now the couple was sitting far away from one another: the writer with his head in his hands, the girl folding socks into little eggs with a grim expression. All at once, the writer leapt up, pointing at the air, then dumping out drawers.

"It's not in there," he saw the girl's mouth move. She said the word "money" and the word "bank."

Al laughed.

She perched herself on the bench, as if guarding her little eggs while the writer went nuts, ripping through every bit of paper in the nest. The writer was really quite humorous when aroused, and Al put away the binoculars with much regret.

Cheered again, wondering if Karl would eat all the kraut before Cordula could hide some away for Al, he picked up the planer, the paints, the brushes, walked along the Von Tollman's *verboten* private pathway past the jute wash lines, stone washtubs, hand-placed irrigation pipes, spiderwebs, snake holes, and DO NOT ENTER signs in six languages.

As Al continued across the property, past the hammocks, trellises, and waterfalls, he was struck by the strangeness of a single fact. The language they spoke in Belize was the English language. Just fifty miles from Esmeralda Town, surrounded by Spanish speakers on all sides, the Belizeans had not given in. A few months ago, Al might have just skipped over this thought as mildly interesting, but now a strange detail occurred: The gelignite bomb had come up from Belize.

Since watching the writer and the girl, he'd been sure the morning would be a fine one, and yet the very act of unlocking gates and closing doors, being hemmed in by the enormous wall, seemed to always call the Rodriguez brothers to mind. More and more it was like this: little details poking out of nowhere, irritating facts that led to other facts.

All facts, somehow, leading to bugginess and bad days and the sensation of a trap being sprung.

"Our black brothers in Belize," Pablo had said to Al last week after the *sabotaje,* "came through for me. And the Toltecs pledge allegiance to them, man. Isn't that how it is, Raul? The *mayonesa*-faces are on the run?"

Raul Desquiniz, the go-between, had sighed and nodded and sighed some more, then taken more Tagamet for his ulcers. Raul had trained as a chemist and did not want to be a go-between—at least not going between Pablo and the Belizeans and the political *chilangos*—inhabitants of Mexico City. Which was exactly why Pablo had forced the job upon Raul: Pablo found it amusing to see his former childhood friend piss blood because Raul had once been, it was said, the better *fútbol* player.

"And your pal, Chaz, he's down with the hombres, Al. And as a *mayonesa*-face yourself, you better be getting down with us. Prepare to sacrifice."

Chaz, wanting points with Pablo, had designed the war's logo.

"I'm down with the Toltecs." Al had sighed. To make Pablo happy, he'd worn one of Chaz's crazy shirts.

"You don't know nathin'," Pablo had said. "Does he, Raul? But then again, he's a gringo."

Raul had chewed on Tagamet and nodded.

"Our black brothers," Pablo had continued, "are going to be running shit up here for us from now on. Not just product. Guns. Bombs. Good shit. Real shit. Shit my ancestors would have killed for. Shit! I could blow my way into the gasthaus with, hombre. With no help from you."

Al had felt a new fluttering in his pulse, and yet had almost laughed. The problem being that, having descended from Spanish blood, Pablo was no more Toltec than Al was.

"That would make a lot of noise."

"Yeah? Mexicans like noise, right, *cuate?*" He'd laughed. "Radios, car horns, firecrackers, church bells, gelignite. We just like the sound of *life.*"

All at once he'd stopped laughing.

"But this is your lucky week, *mi* amigo Al. I've decided gelignite is too good to waste on two old people about to die anyway. And maybe I do want your help for the repatriation of my new home." He'd looked up at Al. He liked to pause dramatically. "If you can get those fuckers out peacefully that's okay. But if you can't and I decide I want you to, you gotta do your part. *Para la raza.*" He'd winked at Al. "I'm thinking maybe you gotta do in those two old German fucks yourself.

In Toltec style. And you have to be *cabrón* this week. Or find me a good damn *cabrón*. Just to show me how much you care."

In the time it took Al to decide he could maybe, maybe, do Karl but not Cordula—not unless she was sleeping, but how would she be sleeping with so many dogs?—no, he could not do Cordula, Pablo had gone on to the next subject.

"*Mi mamá* is dying. And when she goes . . ." He'd crossed himself without irony. "The real war starts between my brother and I. I've decided Esmeralda needs a new mayor. Like Raul here."

Raul had nodded, tiredly.

"Para solidaridad," he'd said.

As Al drew the horsehair brush back and forth, back and forth, on the old fence, he saw a jaunty hat make its way over the shrubbery. Bobbing and floating, the hat seemed balanced on air. Finally the face appeared. Al looked uneasily at the rifle underneath it.

"*Ach.* You're daydreaming about birds. I've never met a man so obsessed." Karl regarded Al with disdain. It was all right. He regarded everyone that way. "Here, give me that brush. I'll show you how to paint correctly. And since you're thinking of birds, the ladies out back have to be fed later. I've got a few mice in the traps, waiting. Best to feed the two new hawks first, they didn't eat yesterday."

In fact, Al had been thinking of poison. That would be the obvious way to do the old people. And yet, Karl never accepted food or drinks from anyone except Cordula. He boiled his water, boiled his meat.

"Okay, show me how it's done in Germany." He looked at Karl in wonder. Christ, the man had never once invited Al inside his house. He always talked to Al through the window. Or they sat outside, on the flower-filled patio.

"They don't do it right in Germany, either." Karl took the brush from his hand, started painting furiously. Apparently the paint had not been laid on thick enough. "They're all lazy there now, too. Completely undeserved reputation. Skating off my generation."

It began to occur to Al that he might have to ice Pablo instead of the Von Tollmans. Or he'd have to fly. He started laughing. He'd always liked the word "ice" in the killing sense. Most likely he'd have to lower his price. At one point Pablo's stupidity and Al's price would converge. The gates would be opened, and he would fly with a lot less money. He laughed again, sure he could work something out with Pablo. And yet he was unhappy—every day seemed to hold more of these little snags. And every day the money shrank.

"Damn right I'm laughing," he said to Karl. "I'll never be able to paint like you, old man. But I'll get right on with the birds, next. I should be able to handle that."

Karl grunted. It was a sore subject with him that the hawks he'd raised from eggs were more affectionate with Al. Karl didn't mind pissing off the entirety of Esmeralda's population, but a bird's rejection hurt him to the quick.

"Slow down, old man. You're going to have a heart attack." Al was transfixed by the spider making its way up Karl's beard.

"*What* are you laughing at? All damn day, smiling and laughing and telling me lies to condescend to me. I don't believe a word you say." Karl glowered at Al. Soon he began laughing, too.

"The truth is"—Al grinned—"I'm laughing because I'm idiotic."

"*Ach,* you're out of your mind, boy," Karl said. He patted Al roughly on the back.

"That's what your new girlfriend said," Al said. "Apparently she doesn't like me."

"*Ach,* girlfriend! An old man like me. You make me smile. You're so strange, boy, in the head."

"She claims I'm following her. Just dropping out of trees to scare her. She thinks I run into her on purpose."

"Well, she's a nervous type." Karl smiled. Al knew he was seeing the girl in front of him. "Used to cities and all. She'll calm down.

They always do, out here. I've got her on my teas. And my exercise program."

"You're too kind to the ladies, Karl."

Karl shook his head slowly to indicate Al's sarcasm was supremely unimportant to him.

"And now I have some news, boy."

"Lay it on me."

Al smiled. In fact, he'd hit a nerve.

That ridiculous boyfriend of hers apparently lost his job." As Karl worked on the trim, Al's eyes scanned the horizon, recording certain things: the time it took for Karl to start sweating, the color of his face when he got exerted. At the same time he was happy not to be painting. It was a beautiful, violet day.

"He'll get a new one. He just has to stop talking so much. He even talks to himself all day. But come to think of it, so do you. Maybe you two should talk." He indicated the brush in Karl's hand. "Let a handyman do his job."

"But if we're *both* talking, boy, who'd be listening? What's the sense in that?" Karl smiled, blew his nose vehemently into a ficus leaf, an affectation of campesino mannerism Al indulged him in. In a particularly revealing photograph Cordula had shown him from Karl's successful Mexico City life, Karl was wearing a stiff tuxedo—at his right was a sleek matron, at his left was an elaborate cheese-fruit setup.

"Oh, he was quite the salesman. He used to be popular with the ladies," Cordula had told Al, with her stiff smile. "He probably had all of them. It was a small community of Germans in Mexico City, and we all stuck together. In a fashion. Karl was a drinking man in those days."

"And now I've got a mess on my hands," Karl was saying now. "The girl asked me if they could stay. What could I say? We operate a business here, and they're paying customers."

Al nodded calmly, even as his pulse speeded up. "Stay for how long?"

"Long enough to put a bee in Corde's bonnet."

Al tried and failed to calculate how long that might be.

"The problem is," Karl said, "I think the boy will talk her out of it. And then we'll lose the income. And Corde will be sorry." He tossed a despairing look at the sky. "My wife's not an inexpensive woman, you know, no matter how much she claims to be a simple person. With all her headache remedies and powders and visits to charlatans for her backaches and toothaches, and gold caps and platinum bridges, she costs me a bundle. If you ask me her teeth are fine. It's all in her head."

"Could be." Al had seen Cordula's teeth enough times to know pain was certain. Though he wasn't really interested, Cordula insisted on showing him her inflamed gums, her rotten stumps, almost every morning. Karl's homemade salves of goldenseal and myrrh did little except stain the whole mess an unattractive pea-yellow.

"Don't get crazy, old man. Let her go." The couple couldn't stay. Al would see to that. "It'll turn out fine. Next year we'll have a full house of pretty girls, and you'll be rich again."

"Rich!" Karl grunted and painted. "We'll be lucky if we can feed the animals *this* season. The couple's money can help out with that. Cordula thinks we should kick them out, dip into our capital. She doesn't know how low our capital is."

"Speaking of money, I'm going to go to town later," Al said, considering the news about the writer and his girl from many angles. "I thought I'd ask around tonight, see what someone's going to offer next. Word's out someone's prepared to give you two hundred for the place now. Maybe even two-fifty. So I'm afraid it's going to get nastier."

"Those *aphids!*"

Because it was Karl's habit to take a sputtering moral stance against those he called the aphids—the consumerist hordes munching their way through the world's resources—it hadn't been in Al's interest to point out Karl had once been one of those aphids. Besides, Karl's list of inferior people amused Al greatly, he especially liked to hear the tirade in Karl's accent. "Americans, French, academics, vegetarians, lawyers, car fanciers, television owners, computer buyers, air-conditioner users, politicians, Muslims, Catholics, actors, users of leaf-blowers!" That was, just about anyone without personal experience of crocodile attacks and class-five hurricanes.

"As for Pablo, you tell that human blood clot we'll be waiting with a rifle next time he comes with an offer. If I'm forced to shoot him it'll be a big mess."

Al nodded, unsure if Karl was speaking literally. "Two-fifty's a lot of cash. It would be one way to pay for some new teeth for your lovely wife. You could probably get computerized ones." He added, "Of course I'll tell them you won't sell. Not for any amount."

"*Ach,* those fools will turn around and sell it for double, and mow down the whole place," Karl said. "Ancient Mexican patrimony, my beautiful ass."

Karl's ass was decidedly skinny. Al told him so.

"I'll still fire you if you're insolent." Karl laughed.

Al consulted his Swatch. He was thinking it would be a good idea. "It's late. You haven't fired me even once today."

Well, I could point out Sarah's American. So if you're against them, she shouldn't be here."

He thought of what he'd done to her clothes last night. He'd been giving the matter of getting Sarah out a lot of thought.

Nothing concrete, so far, had occurred.

Still, Al was happy to move off the topic of local politics. They were onto Karl's third favorite subject: The "dogpile" of world events. In general, world events made Karl shout and made Al itch. Besides, Al had nothing much to say on the topic of Americans and their wars. To his mind, they tipped well, and were generally guilty and polite. In his years on the cruise ship, he'd come to appreciate their particular awkwardness. No one was more polite, less willing to accuse, than an American mark abroad. They were just too afraid of being an ugly American.

"But they have no business starting another war. They haven't even finished the last two."

Al scratched his chin. "But they make better razors." It was true. Mexican razors were crap. Like shaving with dull, broken glass. Mach one. Mach two. No difference. No machs.

Karl looked up quickly. His eyes narrowed. "And what is this between you and the girl? She calls you a stalker. You say she looks like a hawk."

"I said she looked like a crane. And she does."

"But do you *want* her?" Karl said suspiciously. "I know what all this nonsense is when two young people have attractions and pretend—"

"She wants *you,* old man. She's funny like that. A very funny bird."

Karl had swiveled his head. He was looking at Al sideways.

"I think she likes you. Because she says she doesn't want to work with you." Karl laughed suddenly. "She pulled me aside and said so."

"Oh?" A thrill of uncomfortable electricity ran through Al's spine. It wasn't altogether unpleasant. "She's working for us now?"

"I thought I'd put her in with the animals—the feeding and whatnot. She's good with them."

"She's too tall for me. Big birds scare the hell out of me. She's more for you."

Karl snorted. "I'm telling you I don't want any fighting. If you take her, the boy's liable to become angry and ridiculous and start wrecking the place."

"Let's just be honest." Al laughed, thinking of the many times he'd watched Sarah follow Karl around in a bathing suit, nipples sticking out. Wet nipples were something that a man in Karl's position had no defense against. Nipples—two little plugs of skin. Ugly, if you thought about it. "The girl is jealous. She wants you all to herself."

"Nonsense," Karl cried out, but Al knew he was pleased.

"Now you've gotten me to paint this whole fence."

Al shrugged. In fact, it was so. "I guess I know how to do it right next time."

"The wife's got a bee in her bonnet about Sarah."

"So you said."

He remembered the sensation of climbing a tree, splashing mud on the girl's clothing under a full moon. He hadn't been planning to do it. The impulse had come from the flapping noises of the fabric. The wind. Maybe the moon. Certainly from the arrogant placement of the coy lace in front of Cordula's sturdy cotton.

"There's a war on. Why shouldn't the poor girl stay here where it's safe? Why should she go back? Who knows what those maniacs will do? Talk to the wife, Al, she'll listen to you. God knows why."

"Maybe because, well, I listen to her." He added, "And maybe when you talk to Cordula you should say 'they' not 'she.' Just some advice from an idiot."

Karl gave him a tired glance.

The mud had splattered perfectly onto the writer's girl's clothes, nature's weird patterns. That was my kiss, he now thought. My kiss to Cordula. And it may be my last one.

"Ah. Just as I thought—it's love. And you're due for another wife, Karl. They say it adds years." Al shrugged. "Or maybe it's spice, I forget."

"You just stop that now. One of these days Corde's going to hear you."

"Okay, okay." Al filled his cheeks with air. He then fished a book from his pocket.

"Give this back to your pretty wife. Tell her thanks, I enjoyed it. Read it cover to cover." He winked.

Karl looked at the book warily. "Philosophy," he said.

"That's right."

Karl was looking at Al and smiling. "You didn't read a word of it."

"Nah," Al said. He winked slyly at Karl. "But did anyone ever tell you that you look like a great horned owl?" It was true. The long, pointed fingernails completed the picture.

"Whooo, Whooo." Al laughed. In fact he had enjoyed the book. He'd gotten the phrase "nature's weird patterns" from it.

"According to Aristotle we shouldn't be painting, anyway. It's a pointless, human endeavor."

"I thought you didn't read the book."

"I have to talk about it with Cordula, so I picked 'a' for 'Aristotle.' And 'm' for 'monotheism.' And I studied up on certain patterns that seem to do with 'n' for 'nature.' "

"You're too good to the wife."

Al agreed he probably was.

"Maybe I plan to steal Cordula away—a good German wife. You can have the American crane, envy me later."

"You touch the wife and I'll bury you under the lettuce patch." Karl swung the paintbrush in mock anger. He said, Al noticed, exactly nothing about the American crane.

"Now you start in on the next fence before you go to town. We're going out looking for orchids tomorrow, so you can finish it then if you need to."

"We are?"

Karl flushed nearly purple. "Our new tenant wants to learn solar and cooking and gardening and whatnot. I told her she should learn to shoot a gun. While her man glowers and hunches and writes his hate *buk,* she expects me to keep her busy. That's the life of an innkeeper."

There was something about the way Sarah Gustafsson stood, on one spindly leg, head cocked to the side, that made Al sure she should not have access to guns.

"*Ach,* she doesn't want my body. She wants wisdom and she thinks I have it."

They both laughed.

"At my age that's what they come to you for, Al. Wisdom." For a moment Karl's mouth swerved, and then it was smooth again. "You tell yourself it's enough, that you should take what you can get," he said. He then hesitated, "Don't do it, boy. Don't buy it. It's not enough. Don't let yourself get old."

Cordula Von Tollman was of a certain older type Al had studied closely on the cruise ships. Years of frustrations and silent suffering made these women meek, riddled with physical complaints. And yet, no one, Al was sure, was physically heartier than Cordula. In bed, she would probably turn pink, joyful.

Al had watched the Von Tollmans a few times at night—not in their bedroom, the bedroom had no convenient windows—but in the den. As seen through the window, Karl would be carving or sawing or gluing and Cordula would be neatening and straightening. The less Karl looked at her, the more violent her gestures would become. If need be, she'd resort to a coughing fit, doubled over the plank table, pounding on her chest.

Karl would get up from what he was doing, get a glass of water, set it on the table, and then go back to his project: all without looking at his wife once.

From what Al had gathered in his years at the rancho, the Von Tollmans had been married forty years. Their pairing, Karl seemed to believe, was a successful project long since completed. Karl knew everything about his bird, was content with the way she fed and watered him, was happy to do the same for her, and did not need to give the pairing much further thought.

"I wouldn't say he's selfish," Cordula had confided to Al.

"*Ach,* depending on the day, I might say he's selfish," she'd confided further.

Once Al had kissed Cordula using his tongue, just to see what she would do. She had laughed. She had a beautiful little laugh when smoking.

"You don't have to make an old woman feel good, Alchen."

Neither of them had ever mentioned the kiss again, and Al had never tried to repeat it. For one thing, Cordula's bad teeth had left an unpleasant flavor in his mouth. "Just you being here is enough."

"Why not go away without him?" Al had said on that day. "I'll help you find a new place."

"Because *er ist ein sehr verletzlicher Mann.* He'll get himself into trouble." She'd smiled. "He's so hurt by the world, Alchen. He thinks everyone feels as deeply as he does. He thinks he has to set an example."

Karl, she'd told him, had once been a shoe-shine boy in Germany, then a shoemaker, then had started his own shoe factory in Mexico City. Al could just imagine the place—a sweatshop with minimum comfort and salary, the finest equipment but no lounge, no one daring to complain because no one worked longer hours than Karl, or made better shoes.

There would have been an unspoken, infuriated sense of machismo. Plenty of antigringo racism boiling under the surface.

Karl wouldn't have noticed. He wouldn't have paid more than the barest wages, considering it against his code to purchase the affections of his workers.

"I tell you the Mexicans are born clever enough, but they're all damaged from the sun," Karl had told Al once. It was one of Karl's beliefs that his woolen hat protected him from the fury of the tropical Yucatán weather—his threadbare Alpine hat, and the superior German wool it was made of. "You can't protect your brain with straw!

"If you give the Mexicans a good hat, they sell it for a peso!" Al could just see it, a legion of local guys, laughing confusedly at their gifted woolen hats—hats so hot and itchy only a gringo could invent such a torture.

And so it was Karl's reasoning that Mexicans could not be trusted on the gasthaus property. "I've seen them work, boy, and I'll tell you, if you're not one of them, they target you. You have to watch them every minute, or they'll walk off with everything not tied down."

It was true Karl had been robbed many times at his former factory.

It was also true he refused to give out personal loans, a common gesture in Mexican businesses, which were run, Cordula had explained, very much like feudal lordships. Stealing, the workers claimed, was the only reasonable way they could make ends meet with such an inflexible *cabrón* for a boss.

In Mexico City Karl had been assaulted twice, kidnapped once. He'd taken to bringing three large shepherd dogs wherever he went. A not undashing gesture on his part, Cordula had pointed out.

"I swear that man loved his dogs more than anything," Cordula had told Al. "They slept in bed with us. He probably brought them to bed with his mistresses, too."

The old injury of the mistresses was still one of her customary topics. One small guzzle from the flask and she was off and weeping. Apparently Karl had favored blond, tall women.

"Oh, he tried to treat his workers right. But right by his standards, not theirs. He wanted them to *care.*"

Cordula had secretly given the workers small amounts of money from her housekeeping budget to encourage them to stay on at the factory.

"They'll never respect you that way, Corde!" Karl had shouted at her on the occasions he found out. "And if they don't respect you, they'll kill us both in our sleep."

"And so we moved," Cordula said, "out here."

"Out here" being a place so remote they would never be robbed or cheated again.

"But I'm frightened, Alchen," she'd confessed. "He's not being sensible. I think those hotel men mean what they say."

"This is a good story, boy," Karl had said once to Al after a particularly jolly day collecting shells for grinding into garden mulch. Karl's mulch, he claimed, was the secret to the delicious produce in Cordula's garden.

"*Totaler* nonsense!" Cordula whispered to Al. Her whisper was both harsh and pleasing. He'd grown to enjoy it against his ear. "Weeding and whacking—that's the secret!"

"Now you listen up! I'm going to tell you a secret," Karl had continued. "After the war, all the Germans thought they had to bow down to their conquerors. They wanted us to learn the yanqui language, eat yanqui foods, take part in yanqui baseball nonsense. 'They'll take the entire world, Karlchen,' my father said to me. 'You can't escape them, so you must become like them.' I fought him. After I made some money, I began to look for a place the Americans would never occupy and ruin. I wrote to my father to tell him of my plans. 'You will not find such a place,' he said to me."

The rancho, he'd told Al, had been the culmination of a ten-year search in Mexico's farthest corners. As soon as he'd laid eyes on it, "I knew my father had been wrong, and that there was a place they wouldn't want." He'd sold his factory in Mexico City, said good-bye to his German friends there. "And I wrote my father. Told him to go to hell. And he died in hell. A little apartment in Munich with no sunlight! Like a snail! That's what he wanted for me—to die like a snail in a shell."

The story, especially the ferocious pleasure Karl had gotten in besting his father, entertained Al. Apparently the man had been a fan of the German strap. Karl had never forgiven him the use of the strap, or the weakness he showed in front of the yanqui army.

"First my father was a Nazi, then in the blink of an eye he was a yanqui. He was nothing! *Nothing!* And he dared say I shamed him!

He, who died on the commode after eating an entire box of *Backpflaumen!* Prunes!"

When Karl spoke of his father, he had the tendency to lapse into German, a language Al found too difficult—all the impossible verbs piling up at the end of the sentence. Al would often bring him around by clapping him on the back.

"Okay, old man, okay. He died on a shitter. You got your revenge."

It was Al's policy not to attach any particular importance to his own father's existence. Mr. Greenley was off before Al was born. Having known his wife, Al's mother, Al decided it had been a good choice.

"My father would have sold his own left buttock to the yanquis if he thought they'd told him to," Karl had once told Al. "And that's why the yanquis will get nothing from me."

And so, Karl would not accept the offer of two-fifty. He would not accept an offer double that. He would just not give in to his father.

"As you notice," Karl had crowed to Al, "they respond to force down here."

"As you notice," Pablo had said to Al, "the German is old and stupid. You could probably take him in your sleep."

Though official word from Mexico City and New York was that development plans were "slowed" in Esmeralda only because of Mexico's national elections, and America's war, and *not* because of the *sabotaje,* it was no secret to Al that the men in black Suburbans, flown in on private jets to Chetumal, had stopped coming to Esmeralda lately. It was said Castillo had hoped to play the development game on all sides, taking his *mordidas* from the drug dealers, promising development was many years away, while welcoming the hotel men's "courtesy payments," telling *them* the land would be theirs soon after the election.

All in all, thousands of kilos of cocaine were moved through Esmeralda every year, and were even now making their way to *gringolandia* where Al hoped they were being used in the service of fun and pleasure.

But thousands of tourists would pay thousands for a snorkel on the reef of Yanqui Beach for fun and pleasure.

So who had more money? Cocaine businessmen? Hotel businessmen?

Al had to laugh. As usual, it was just too many zeros for such a beautiful day.

Now Cordula joined them, as she often did when she'd finished the washing. Al walked alongside the Von Tollmans, delighting Karl by bringing up the computers. He thought of Pablo again, while looking at the shepherd dogs. A shepherd was not an easy animal to take by surprise. At the same time he was pleased a beautiful wind was blowing through the palms, and that Cordula's gray hair had a magnificent sheen to it. Her skin was as soft and translucent as a girl's.

He was glad he'd flung crap on the writer's girl's clothes.

"Buy the Frau some candies when you're in town. That's what a woman wants—a lazy life, a slap on the backside, and plenty of candies," Karl said, pinching her cheek.

"I'm reducing," Cordula protested. "No, Al."

"*Ach,* if she doesn't have her candies, she'll get thin again! And when she's thin, she's grumpy, so by all means get some candies."

"They say the Americans will invade Iraq within twenty-four hours. They say even the bombs are computerized now."

The computerized bombs had not occurred to him as a topic of interest until this moment. Like Pablo, he enjoyed the aesthetic image of them. An aficionado of fireworks, Christmas lights, lightning storms, another thing that irritated Al about Sarah came to mind.

The girl claimed his job on the cruise ships must have been "depressing." There was nothing more generous, more easy, than a twinkling cruise-ship Christmas with Americans. For a moment, he remembered the good, best times.

Cordula bit her lip. "Surely if the war starts, the couple will want to go home."

"*Du, du, du!* Put your claws in, Corde," Karl said.

Al searched for a new topic to distract them, before they started speaking in their Spanish-English–German patois, and he, Al, would be left out of it. The patois had been perfected by the Germans of Mexico City in order to keep the Mexican workers under constant surprise. Al found it unnerving, himself.

"I've got something to say," Al said.

"Go on then, boy. Tell my wife, here, we need their money. Everyone needs American money."

" 'And out of his mouth goeth a sharp sword, that with it he should smite the nations: and he shall rule them with a rod of iron: and he treadeth the winepress of the fierceness and wrath of Almighty God,' " Al said, quoting from Revelations.

Karl laughed. "Okay, okay. Stop it, now. Before you eclipse my tirade."

"It took me all night to memorize that," Al said. The Bible could always be counted on as a conversation-stopper. Karl had taught him that one. He in turn, had taught it to the writer, who had laughed.

"To rule with a rod of iron," Karl said, still laughing, "is not a bad idea at all. Especially to keep the wife in line."

"What do you think, Cordula? Shall we take him? I'll get the left side."

Cordula looked away, smiled, tapping a syncopated stick against her palm.

"Let's get him later." She giggled. "Let's get him while he sleeps."

The first drops of rain began to fall. They heard raised, angry voices from the guesthouse.

"Ah, the fights again!" Cordula exclaimed. "What do two good-looking young people have to fight about?"

"I like the fights," Karl said. "All the scintillating, nasty dialogue."

They heard the sound of things being thrown around.

"They say good-looking people fight more because they think they deserve more," Al said.

"Who says that?" Karl frowned. "I think you made that up."

"You're good-looking, Alchen, and you don't fight," Cordula pointed out.

"Why thank you, Cordula." Al smiled.

"Don't be flirting with the wife, young man," Karl barked. He swatted his wife quite lovingly. "It's my little experiment, that room. Couples come so lovey, lovey. But they can't take such a small space for very long." He winked at Al.

"Really, that couple fights too much," Cordula said, in a stronger voice. "I can't listen to this for a year. I'll go mad."

"I've got the girl working for free, *meine Frau!* I've got the girl paying to work for me! What else could you possibly want?"

"Do you think she's as intelligent as Karl thinks she is?" she asked Al.

Al affected a yawn.

"She thinks Jesus was a communist."

Cordula smiled at her husband. "See?" She took Al's comment for a "no."

Al felt the tension rise in the air. He smiled at Cordula.

"Cordula, how would you like to take a walk with me tomorrow morning?" he asked, winking at her. "What you need is a younger man. A beautiful, wise woman like yourself."

Karl shook his fist at Al in mock anger. "I'm going to have to shoot you, boy. You know I will."

"I would like that very much." Cordula blushed furiously. "I haven't had a date in approximately forty years."

"Good, then," Al said. "Maybe I'll get you really, really drunk."

Karl was still shaking his fist and grinning, no doubt happy that he would be free to spend time with the girl. Shooting. Collecting orchids. Or whatever.

A happy feeling descended on the group, and they walked in silence.

"Oh, yes. Don't spray in the tourists' room anymore," Karl said casually to Al. "Sarah thinks she's missing a few things. Probably misplaced them herself. But—"

"She can't accuse our Al!" Cordula said incredulously. "That's a terrible lie! I'm telling you the girl's out of her *mind*."

Al stiffened. "I hope you don't think—"

"Al, my boy"—Karl put a warm hand on his shoulder—"I don't think anything except that the writer's probably drunk and knocking things about. How we're going to put up with such a nitwit is beyond me." To his wife he said, "But you don't see me complaining about his personality. His money is as good as anyone else's."

"The girl has a lot of nerve." Cordula was glaring at the sky.

"What she's got," Karl said, "is dollars."

Greenley!" Al looked up from the lock set he was installing, having completely forgotten his anger at the writer's girl in the absorption of his task. Karl and Cordula were gone to feed the animals. Al had already decided the girl had to go before the gelignite arrived from Belize and things got hairier: a guilty little affair with Karl was probably the most expedient method to get rid of her. Al smiled to himself, wondering if the old man would have a heart attack mid-pump. Probably not; they'd play out their daddy game, and each would come out a little ashamed, hostile toward the other. Cordula would guess, and wouldn't say a thing. But Al would make her say it. He would make her leave.

Anyway, the writer almost certainly wouldn't want to stay around after the wet move.

Two birds. Two stones, he was thinking, and two more birds to go.

The sky had clouded over; a fine, gray mist the locals called *chipi-chipi.* The mist was supposed to portend troublesome things.

"Greenley!"

Through the *chipi-chipi,* Nick Sperry was coming toward him in a half-run, grimacing from the effort. Each stride made his look of anxiety more distinct.

"Hey, writer. What's up?"

"I'm having the worst day of my life. The absolute fucking *worst.* I don't think I could even begin to describe it."

Al waited for him to describe it.

"That's scary, all right," he said, when the writer finished. "Must be the *chipi-chipi.*"

The baited, terrified look on the writer's face was familiar to Al. Swim, he wanted to tell him. Fly. Or you're down.

The writer hyperventilated for a moment.

" . . . and then I try to start my car, so that I can go to town and stop the whole thing from getting worse, but the fucking car is *shot.* The engine won't even turn. I've got to call my boss—God, it's a nightmare—I didn't even mention that I lost my job—"

Al nodded sympathetically. But his mind turned a slow circle, slowly caught.

"Let's just take a moment here. Let's just think this out."

Quite to Al's surprise, he'd begun to think of the writer as the best part of his day. Though Nick Sperry had at first seemed wrapped up in himself—sitting all day in the guesthouse, playing a guitar without knowing how to play, or any sense of rhythm, then walking in circles, fighting with the girl, or staring at a piece of paper, then balling it up, then staring some more—his increasing furor had a comic edge.

Just this morning Al had watched the poor guy fighting butterflies. Al had watched him windmill his arms, wanting to tell him there was no use in fighting out here. There were far too many butterflies. And other things.

"It sounds like a battery problem—at least the car."

"Criiiepp. Criierpp, cutty, cutty caw," said Nick.

What Nick was, was a cockatiel. Chattery, harmless cockatiels were among Al's favorites. His mother had kept such a bird, and one of Al's very first memories was of the bird warning him from the lighted fireplace with its *cutty, cutty caw,* and then later following each of young Al's movements with its eye.

"If there was just a goddamn phone! E-mail. Something. Can I use *your* car? Just for a few hours."

"Remember? My car's shot, too," Al said. "But we'll go to town later in the Von Tollmans' Jeep, if that helps. The old man will give me the keys."

"Christ." Nick's jaw trembled. "Is Karl going, too? Because I swear I'm going to just—"

"The old man doesn't leave the place," Al said soothingly. "I do most of the town runs these days if Cordula can't go."

"Did Karl mention anything about us staying on? Because I think he—"

"Your nose is bleeding," Al said calmly. The blood was just a thin trickle. Still, he didn't like it.

"Nerves." Nick swiped at his nose. "It always happens. Shit. I mean, I don't have any money if he fires me! I used my savings for this trip!"

"That's bad."

"That's one way of putting it."

"Cutty, cutty caw."

"What?"

"Just a local way of saying, 'Holy shit.'"

Al had joked with him, because he knew the man in front of him had meant to say, "These are problems a handyman could never understand." He didn't fault him for it. For birds like Nick, one's own problems were colossal, unparalleled in all of history. He smiled.

"Try to breathe. Go clean up. We'll get to town, and you'll call your boss, get it all straightened out. I'm sure it's not as terrible as it sounds."

"It *is.* Believe me. Things couldn't get any worse!"

"Okay." Al continued wiping the tools with the rag. He wanted the writer to go. The blood called to mind pictures—not ideas yet, just the pictures that proceeded them. He shivered, his heart began to beat a little faster.

Lady Blood developed in his mind like a photograph. She was dripping, drunken, holding out a red, accusing finger. But it's not a done deal, Al thought.

"If they can't get any worse, then you're in a good position, buddy."

"Think so?" Nick looked dubious. He often looked this way when talking to Al.

"I'm sorry, I have to get back to work if we're going to make it to town later."

The guy kept talking anyway. When Al closed his eyes, listened to the voice blur against the whirr of the electric planer, the nausea grew. Four birds, two birds, what did it matter. Long hair, curly nails. Fingers pointing. It was nothing. Not up to him.

"Sarah only has two weeks left on her visa. Of course she says she doesn't care," Nick was saying. "She thinks—" He was goggling his eyes. Al half-believed he'd start pecking at the ground. "I don't know what she thinks. She's not thinking at all. And it's not like her."

Al, himself, was thinking of bones and skin and metal. Certain sounds. Incense being lit. Cordula's hen-eye.

"Nick!" When the wood was smooth he switched off the tool. "Slow down. You're bugging me out."

Nick did, finally, stop his talking.

"My friend, the cop I was talking about, is a very interesting cat. If there's any help to be given on the visa problem, he can do it."

"Thanks, Greenley. *Thanks.* You're the only sane person in this entire town."

As the writer stomped off through the trees, Al looked at the whorls and patterns under his fingers.

Glide, he was thinking, glide. Anything could happen. Almost there.

Nick was loping along the jungle path, each step falling to the rhythm in his head which was *No, no, no, God, no, no.* Thank God Al Greenley had agreed to drive him to Esmeralda Town, yet he couldn't quite believe, couldn't quite wrap his mind around the fact, that he, an adult in the twenty-first century—had to beg a ride to a horrible palm-infested town just to use a goddamn *phone!*

Who knew what Larry Scakorfsky would say when Nick begged to keep his job, and then how long he would be stuck in the Coco Palms Bar, talking to Al's "trippy" cop friend; a word that could mean many things, but mostly meant "druggy," "stupid," and "unpleasant." How much would the trippy cop charge for a bribed visa extension, not only for Sarah, but also for Nick if Nick had to wait it out in Esmeralda?

The irony was not lost on him: He'd be paying for a stolen visa with stolen money.

He thought of Phil, laughing. He almost screamed.

Even now Sarah's credit cards were accruing interest, and she thought the concept laughable. Larry Scakorfsky had fired him *and* had possession of his computer and Mondrian chair, and had very likely located his pornography collection. In what world was that a reasonable outcome?

Nick imagined how their conversation might go.

"Larry, this is Nick Sperry, and I hear we've got a problem."

Nick would explain over the phone that he would stop drinking immediately and irrevocably—no questions asked. Nick had heard Larry's own wife suffered from some kind of kleptomania, or bulimia, he wasn't sure which but Larry, he thought, Larry would *have* to understand Nick's own weaknesses.

It would work because Nick would work it. He had to.

For this moment, what he needed was a drink.

He shielded his eyes from the pellets of rain. It was falling sideways now, making the horizon a brittle, tablet gray.

"*Mein Gott!* Why are you running! You're upsetting every beast in the jungle, boy!"

A long shadow fell over Nick. His heart beat rapidly.

"There you are, Karl."

"What is it, boy? You've located the Loch Ness monster in our lagoon?"

"What did you say to Sarah to make her do it?"

Cordula was looking at him with great surprise. Karl was looking at the horizon and sighing.

"Well, let's see. I've been talking to the girl about throttle potentiometers today. And subsistence farming. And the mating habits of the endangered gull-wing bat."

With great effort, Nick kept his voice calm. "You know what I'm talking about. I don't believe for a minute you didn't encourage her."

Cordula clutched her cardigan sweater to her bosom. She looked at her husband fearfully, then back at Nick.

"Look at the boy. He's got blood on his face." Karl addressed his wife, "Do you think he's been raiding our chicken coop?"

"You think it's funny. It's all a big joke to you." Nick wiped his nose savagely.

"*Ach,* I don't think it's the end of the world."

"Mr. Sperry, please!" Cordula exclaimed. "Why are you upset with my Karl?"

"The money Sarah paid you," Nick's voice rose a notch, "is from her credit cards. She'll never be able to pay them off. Your husband apparently thinks that's okay."

Karl took a deep sniff of the fragrant air—just to annoy him, Nick thought. *"Ach!"* he finally said. "Miss Gustafsson is certainly old enough to make her own decisions. And she simply took out a loan. That's how it is in your world. Everything on credit. Pay if you can, if not, the insurance companies pay. It's all rigged to get you good and scared and buying more. The girl saw right through it. I say good for her."

The words left Nick's mouth. His tongue felt forked, raw. He knew it wasn't right to blame Karl—not for all of it—but if Cordula wouldn't have been there he might have taken a swing anyway. "You've been working on her since we got here. She's using your phrases. Wearing your clothes." He turned to Cordula. "You see what he's doing to her. I know you do."

"Don't clench your fists, boy. The dogs get nervous." To his wife he said, "As I see it, Frau, she's taking a stand just the way we did. They're the ones making indentured servants out of people, offering them credit when they know very well it's a trap."

"But, Karl?" Cordula paled. She was looking at Nick with a distant and yet utterly helpless expression. "I don't even know why we're here if all we have is one problem after the next. Every day it gets worse."

Karl turned to his wife as if he'd been slapped.

"And stealing," Cordula continued to avoid her husband's eyes.

"The boy is right to think it wrong. We didn't *steal.* We worked very hard for our money." She finally let her eyes rest on Karl's. Her jaw was trembling. "And why is she wearing your clothes?"

"*Ach,* now." Karl stepped slowly between Nick and Cordula, blocking their view of one another. A purple flush spread up the back of his neck. *"Nicht vor den Gästen!"*

"Don't shush me. We don't need her money," Cordula persisted. "And you're being reckless, Karl. With her safety. With both of them."

"Ihr benehmt Euch wie eifersüchtige Kinder." Karl's voice was tight, dangerous.

"But your wife is right," Nick said. "She's not safe with you. That's clear enough."

Cordula gasped, turned slowly away.

"Watch yourself, now," Karl slowly replied.

"Oh, I'm watching you," Nick said.

The road to Esmeralda was still and warm. At night, the jungle seemed sleek and perfect, but under daylight the trees and vines displayed their tattered, broken-looking leaves. The road seemed to go on forever, the only break in the gray-green monotony an occasional glimpse of sea through a clearing, an Indian carrying a basket full of heavy fruit or wood.

Nick jounced along, seated on top of a milk crate. What he needed was a drink, but he couldn't even have that: Larry would sense the alcohol in his voice. A frog leapt from the dashboard onto Nick's chest. As he beat at it, his molars crashing into one another, he realized how unlikely it was, in the scope of his life as he'd planned it, that such an event should be taking place.

Calls to the US cost five dollars a minute from the *caseta*—even if Larry took his call, he'd have to wait, on hold, for an indeterminate time. He was precariously short of cash.

"Nice windy day, isn't it?" Al Greenley broke into his thoughts.

"You've got to be kidding me."

"Let me tell you something."

Nick said nothing. He was going to anyway.

"The worst is that you leave your girl here. You leave her. When she's gone, you'll think of her maybe five hundred more times. Maybe a thousand. A blip. Then you'll start thinking about what you want for breakfast, what kind of coat you should wear, whether you should take the crosstown express or pony up for the tollbooth. Pretty soon those thoughts will take up your brain space and she won't matter."

"Right." The man knew nothing. Los Angeles didn't even have a crosstown express.

"I've left 'em a million times. You just move on, man. Later you laugh at yourself, wonder what you ever saw in them."

Nick smiled tightly.

Nearer to Esmeralda Town, small shack-settlements came into view. The landscape went by as if on a loop: a thatched roof house like an overturned basket, a spotted cow, a pig, a scattering of children. A Mayan woman came into the picture. Her basket of firewood was piled impossibly high, she was bent nearly in two under its weight. Nick leaned his head far back, watching her.

"She's got it pretty bad," Al said, humming a placid song. "That's gotta hurt. Dragging that thing for ten, twenty miles. Did you know they walk all the way into Esmeralda Town? If it takes us, what? Fifty minutes to drive, how long do you figure it takes to walk?"

"I know what you're getting at, Greenley." Nick didn't want philosophical discourse from a man who unplugged toilets for a living. "But let's not."

"Even when she gets it home, she gets it." Al drummed his hands on the steering wheel. "All the señoras here get it. They go back to their palm-thatch huts and get their lips split by drunken old Mayans who want to go back to the way it was back in prehistoric times. Makes you wonder if they wouldn't be better off cleaning toilets in a big hotel. At least they'd have some cash."

"What's your point?" Nick tried for exaggerated calm. His words came out as a long shiver.

"Hey, I'm just thinking about the crazy shit that goes on around here," Al smiled. "Just passing time."

"Look. Can we just drive?" Nick said.

What you're needing is a good, stiff one," Al said cheerfully. "There's a fifth in my backpack, in case you agree."

Nick thought of Larry, opened the beige pack. Tipping the bottle to his lips, he smiled at Al gratefully. In fact, he'd decided, Greenley hadn't been lecturing him, and had been making conversation. The bottle clanked against his teeth as he swigged from it.

"We can go back and get the old woman if you want." He didn't want to, and yet a good deed might just turn his luck around. He thought of Sarah, what she would do. She'd probably give the old woman not only a ride, but everything in her purse. The woman would tell her friends about the crazy gringa giving out money, and soon everyone in town would be beating at the gasthaus door, and Sarah would pace and sleep badly, and then decide not to leave the grounds. Karl would second the motion.

"Nah. That's just the crazy shit I'm talking about." Al smiled. "The native gals won't take rides from gringos—they won't even talk to us. In case we sell their kidneys to our rich gringo friends." He swung the wheel to miss a large pothole. "That's what we gringos do when we're not flying over the pueblo on evil *shuk-shuk* clouds at night, looking for Mayan children to make into sausage. I don't know what they're going to do when they're overrun with us down here." He looked at Nick. "But there's nothing to do about any of it. It just works itself out. Always does."

"God, God, God." Nick's stomach hurt. Without his glasses, he couldn't see more than twenty feet in front of him. He had no idea where they'd fallen: sometime during Sarah's mea culpa. "It's all such a nightmare."

"I'm telling you, buddy, give it a week. Let your girl think you don't care what she does. Something good will happen, then. You just have to not care, and she'll come running."

"Except, I *know* her," Nick said. "I know her very well."

"Hey, look at that." Al was pointing at what seemed to be a stork or crane of some kind.

"What?"

Al kept staring at the crane, seeming to find something profound in its flapping motions. The car was running off the road. "What does that remind you of?"

"Want me to take the wheel? I'll drive. You can look at all the birds you want."

"Look at her," Al repeated.

"I see a low-flying bird." Nick clenched and unclenched his fists. "A fish-eater. A goddamn fish-eater on a mission. Meanwhile, we're about to end up in a ditch." He laughed unconvincingly to soften his tone.

"Holy-o." Al laughed. "A goddamn fish-eater. That's all you see?"

Just ten miles inland from Esmeralda Beach, Esmeralda Town was a hundred times more sweltering. At the beach, the sea breeze occasionally pushed the insects away, but here, the nearby lagoon and swamp formed a sort of pincers that squeezed mammoth mosquito habitats into being. To walk was to be assaulted.

"Do you have a phone here?" Nick was shouting to the bartender in the Coco Palms. In answer, the man cocked his bald head, bowed, swept his arm toward the selection of liquors behind him. Behind the bar, a music video played, drums beating, voices wailing, and it made him angrier to be fighting for conversation in between the beats. Every once in a while, the bassist emitted a fierce howl.

The howl made no pretense of being melodious, it was just a scream of anger whenever the fancy took him. The video clicked off suddenly. The next channel showed the outline of a ticking clock superimposed over a map of Iraq.

"No, not a drink! A phone!"

When he'd tried the phone at the *caseta,* he'd been told to come back tomorrow. The line was down due to a *travieso*—a "mischief-maker"—cutting the incoming wires from Chetumal.

"A mischief-maker!"

Only Al's bottle had kept Nick from jumping the desk, throttling the clerk who loved *Scarface.*

"*Sí! Traviesos!* Bad people. *Hay muchos aquí en Esmeralda!*" the clerk had said. "No newspapers—you get it? No *reporteros.*"

"A telephone!" Nick made a receiver out of his thumb and forefinger, trying one more time. It was his first afternoon visit to the Coco Palms Bar. Every single person in Esmeralda seemed to be there. The bartender looked at him, made a face at his pal, then handed Nick a key, indicated the proximity of the bathroom. The pal laughed.

A sound system, with huge hair and fuzz-encrusted Berensford speakers dominated the far wall. The roof was made of some kind of spiny grass, the floor dirt, covered in crushed shells. Large, taxidermied bonefish hung over the portals. As if hoping to inject a bit of glamour, an enormous, spinning disco ball cast an eerie light over the patrons: aging local beach bums, miniskirted chubby girls, a single wintry foreign matron—almost certainly European—in a long dress.

"Excuse me, do you have a phone in your home?" he asked the matron. The older woman looked at him and laughed. "You Engres from Engran?"

"Yes, I'm from England," Nick said angrily.

"How many years?" She was watching the Navy destroyer on the screen, shaking her head.

"Five hundred years."

"You not Engras. You yanqui."

"I need to call someone. I will pay you."

"You wees that mans?" She was pointing at Al.

"What's wrong with you people?"

"You go 'way, *Americano.*" She made a face like a cat choking. "We don't want wars. *Bam, bam.* That's what happens in wars, little boy."

No beer for me, thanks," Al said, when Nick sat down on the leatherette stool next to him. "I'll stick with my soda. At least for a while."

"When it finally comes, it's two for me, then." Nick was incredulous at how long the bartender was taking with the bottles. He held up his finger, waved it. "Doesn't anyone in this *entire* town have a phone in their *house*?"

"Nah. If you had a phone, you'd have all the neighbors at your house all day talking to their relatives working in the States." Al looked at Nick with his robotic green eyes. "And when the bill came, the neighbors wouldn't or couldn't pay. A blood feud would start, and, hell, blood feuds might last for two or three generations." The eyes blinked slowly as Al yawned. "It's a delicate social ecosystem, man. You definitely don't want to have anything your neighbors want. The nail that sticks out gets it bad."

"Christ," Nick said. "What's the point of Esmeralda, then? Live shitty and have lots of friends that way?"

"I think they think they live pretty well."

"Awl! Awl!" A young, drunken couple—also on pills by the vigorous, bright-eyed look of them—called to Al from under the disco ball. They were laughing, making complicated, graceful, yet wholly disturbing movements. Nick guessed they were each married to someone else.

Al held up his 7UP to the couple. *"Oye, Rocío, cómo estás?"*

"Rocío? The hairdresser?" Nick looked up hopefully. "Does *she* have a phone?"

Al shook his head, translated Nick's question. The couple laughed and laughed.

The woman in the long dress passed the table. She hissed at Al like a snake. *"Bam, bam,"* she said, slurringly, to Nick.

"What's her problem?"

"Old Hilde? Nuts." Al smiled. He drew small circles around his head.

From the corner Hilde sat, still looking at Nick, nestled under her hood, a crow in a nest. She said, *"Sssssssssssssss."*

"Drink, buddy. Relax. There's nothing else to do."

Al watched an elderly couple get up from a booth, begin waltzing under the ball. The couple was very formal, serious, though the music was Billy Joel.

"Or you could eat. The menu here features *lengua frita*—fried tongue. In its own gravy, whatever that means."

"You could take me to Chetumal. I'd pay you." The town was hours away, but it was at least a large one with many, many phones.

Al nodded, still watching the old dancers. He seemed to find a great deal of pleasure in watching them. " 'Fraid not. Karl's careful with his Jeep."

"Is there a bus? Christ, something? Some kind of technology?"

"The buses left this morning."

Finally the beers arrived. Nick stared at them long and hard. He emptied one and then the other. He shouted to the bartender, "A tequila. *Dos* tequilas."

"Hey, you're getting it, now. Mexican time. *Relajate,*" Al said. "Hope for the best, and it'll probably happen." He lifted his palms in a what-the-hell gesture. Al poured the beer for him, lifted his 7UP. He looked up, swished the ice around his glass. He had eyebrows so blond they were invisible. "If you call your boss today or tomorrow, what's the difference?"

Al waved lazily to another couple who entered the bar.

"And tell me, does that man resemble an old toucan or what?"

Nick looked up. An hour had passed and he was getting very drunk. Inebriation didn't go well with the startling, glossy turquoise color of the Coco Palms walls. In fact the entire room gave the impression of a giant pool with furniture, bodies, floating in it.

For a while, now, they'd been talking about Sarah.

"I don't know, she's a do-gooder. One of those who takes every damn problem in the world personally. It's like a sickness. Hell, it *is* a sickness."

Nick sighed thickly, a watery sound. Even through his anger, he felt he had to defend her. He could not find the words.

"A real champion of the underdog, huh," Al said.

"Believe it or not, it's usually a charming trait. I keep hoping it'll rub off on me."

"Gotcha." Al smiled.

But he didn't, Nick knew. Going through the story of his meeting with Sarah—how she'd been at the Zero Bar, playing darts alone—brought to mind her tenderness and courage. She was good at darts. Was good at most games involving skill. It was everyday life she had no knack for.

"Who's throwing peanuts at me?" He swiveled his face to take in the Coco's patrons. At the same time he shook his head like a dog to get Phil's laughter out of it. "What in the hell do they want?"

"So what are you?" Al chewed ice from his drink. "One of your gal's causes?"

"Jesus, that's cold." Nick made a disbelieving noise. He hated the word "gal."

"Hey, I'm talking about the book. She wants to be your muse, I'm guessing. She wants to see her name on that dedication page."

"I don't know what she wants." Nick shivered. Al had quite possibly just hit it dead-on. Some of the tenderness evaporated.

"Ah, now, just drink. Pass the time. Don't think." Al said, "And the Von Tollmans are pretty tight. The old man would die without Cordula. You've got no worries there. I take it you think she's fucking the old man. Behind the solar panel or something."

Put that way, with Al's calm grin, the situation seemed unlikely again.

"I've got a worry in every port." Nick laughed into the bottom of his glass. He wanted to indicate the fates were busily stalking him, fucking up his life. This time he would fight them. He lifted the next glass, drank. "Money, for one worry. I can't even pay for these drinks."

"I got them, I've got money. And something tells me you're going to have plenty of money, too. You're the type." Al laughed.

He then said, "Are you going to puke, buddy?"

"Yes I'm going to puke." Nick was laughing. Then suddenly he was sobbing.

"Hey, now," Al said.

A low ray of sun pierced through the window and into Nick's eye. He imagined it had come very far to find him, to spotlight his failure.

He was getting fat. The thought outraged him.

"I could try for fifty years, and I still won't be able to write anything good, and she knows it." He shifted his weight with a tiny smile. "And she'll just move on to the next guy. There's always going to be a guy to rescue Sarah. I should know. I was that guy."

"Sperry?"

"Listen." Nick snapped his eyes open. "I've got a woman who thinks bankruptcy might just be good for the soul. What do you say to a woman like that?"

"I'd say adiós," Al said. "And there's my friends."

As the cowboy-style door swung open, the room was illuminated for a split second. The light appeared, dimmed, appeared, dimmed. Nick felt himself sinking into the chair.

"I didn't mention that my friends and I might have to speak in Spanish for a while," Al said as the two figures came toward the table. The two wore pressed chinos, a high, lacquered hairstyle, dark glasses.

"No *problemo.*" Nick was wiping his face. The surfeit of alcohol made his movements very slow, deliberate. "I'll just drink until I think I understand Spanish. That way we'll all be very comfy."

A whooping noise came from Nick's left. He dragged his eyes across the table. A grown man sat on the bar stool, reading a comic book. Nick's eyes rested on the open page, a naked cartoon blonde in the jungle, her legs splayed, while a thousand or so Indians knelt down before her. A common pornographic fantasy, but a disturbing one, considering the numbers involved.

He felt his stomach heave.

"One more thing, if you're going to puke, don't do it in here. Alfonso the bartender will make you eat a chili. I'm not kidding." Al made a half-hearted gesture of disapproval. "See that gumball jar of chilies on the counter? If you puke, Alfie'll hold you down and force you to eat one. A habanero—hottest chili in the world."

"Good. I've got something else to worry about."

"Hey-o," Al called out.

It's hot," the smaller man said.

"Hot like bitch," his friend agreed.

"Fucking hooot. Like beeetch."

"Fucking," his friend agreed.

"What's this guy doing here?"

"Nick, this is my friend Pablo. Pablo, this is Nick," Al said. The larger one took a seat at the next table, sat with his back to the group. His eyes scanned the patrons, who studiously looked away. "Nick's having problems. I thought we could help him out."

"The kid with the BMW? I like that car. Feel high above your fellow man in that fucking thing, Nick?"

Nick sighed. "A BMW is a low ride, comparatively." He was seeing triple. The man's badge seemed like a toy.

The *comandante* didn't respond to Nick's outstretched hand.

"You know why people shake hands?" Pablo said, looking at Nick. "To show they've got no hidden weapons."

Pablo finally put out his hand.

"Yeah. My old man told me that one."

Pablo withdrew his hand.

"You drunk?"

"Yeah."

"Good for you. Some of our nice, cheap Mexican booze. Everything's cheap in Mexico, isn't it? Just cheeeap."

"Okay, okay." Al laughed. "I told you he's having problems. Let's let off him."

"Cut, tit, shit, shut," Pablo said to Nick with a friendly expression. "That's what your language sounds like, Nick." He made a sympathetic face. "Caaar. Baaar. Beeer. Waaader." He made a flatulent sound with his cheeks.

Nick was drunk enough to find great humor in such sounds.

"Excuse us, Nick." Al smiled. He and Pablo spoke in Spanish for a long time.

Nick couldn't help being fascinated by the scar under the man's chin. It was as round and red as a button. One more drink and he'd push it.

"Quiz." Pablo turned to Nick again.

"Shit," Al said. "Not this. Give the guy a break. I just explained everything."

"Who would win?" Pablo closed his eyes. "In a war between the USA and Mexico?"

Nick looked out at the room. Pablo's friend had gotten up, started whistling. The room was emptying quickly.

"I don't know much," he said. "The French."

"Come on. Ten thousand Yankees against ten thousand wetbacks. *Mano a mano.*"

More tequila arrived. Pablo tossed his down without expression. He signaled for another to the bartender, who stood nervously behind him. "Well, what's your answer?"

Al's face expressed anxiety.

"Not me."

"Good answer," Pablo said, delighted.

"I told you he's good people," Al said. "He doesn't deserve to have these problems. He's a good man."

Pablo grabbed Al's hand, upsetting the 7UP. "Money problems," he said, looking at Nick. "You're a bad boy, Al. Crazy bad. And Nick, you're a good man, it seems."

"He reads palms," Al said easily to Nick. Pablo had not let go of Al's hand, and was, in fact, bending his fingers backward. The situation might be funny, and it might not. Nick couldn't decide.

"I see no problems on your horizon, Al, but check with Raul first. Get his read." Pablo was teetering on his chair. Just when it was about to fall he snapped it back. Al used the moment to wrench his arm free.

"What did I tell you?" Al said to Nick. "Pablo's a seer."

"But wait a minute." Pablo was looking at Nick. He took out his knife, immersed it in the tequila. "Do you like Holland, Nick?"

It took Nick some time to understand Pablo was referring to a low geographical region. "Never been there."

"Too bad." Pablo pinched Al's cheek. "They say Dutch people are pretty dumb."

"Who says that?" Nick was beginning to feel certain he would puke. Somehow he looked forward to it. "I thought they ate cheese."

"Nick doesn't know any Dutch people," Al said. "So let's not worry about it."

Pablo's big paw clapped Nick's back. "I believe you this time, Al," he said. He raised his hand, made a fist. He regarded the fist for a moment. "I believe Nick's a good American, and I'm going to like him very much. Let's see what Lady Blood says."

Nick lifted his glass.

"Absolutamente," he said.

And that's when I knew there wouldn't be even one fucking hotel on my beach," Pablo said. "Let 'em come. We'll show 'em floral arrangements for their lobbies."

"That's a thought," Nick said.

The repetitious, confusing conversation had been going on for an hour. Every so often Pablo would swizzle his knife around in the tequila, address a female spirit. Every time he did it, the guy muttered an unintelligible phrase about blood. Nick, who had excused himself to puke, felt better afterward. The day's events were now at a watery distance, and he aimed to keep them there. Toward this aim, he drank slowly and steadily, interspersing each beer with glasses of ice water. He played a slow game of Ping-Pong in his mind.

"I'm telling you, my drunk friend, you'll want to hear this." Pablo shook Nick's shoulder. "Listen up—this is a good story."

Pablo, it was ascertained, had consulted a certain *brujo* on the matter of Esmeralda's future, and the future for Pablo looked very good, indeed. A *brujo* was roughly equivalent to a warlock, Al explained to Nick, who couldn't care less.

"A fucking warlock! You insult my country," Pablo spat. The bartender looked up nervously, hurrying over with a full bottle of tequila, which he left on the table. "This isn't movie shit. This is Mexico, and a *brujo es el hombre más poderoso.* The Man Who Knows."

Al turned to Nick. "A *brujo* isn't anything like a warlock."

"Okay," Nick said. The cop's machismo was definitely on his nerves. There was a safe world just in front of Nick—a soft, quiet, boozy, watery world. The cop's voice, the stabbing knife, was disallowing him from entering.

An elbow poked into Nick's rib.

"The lady likes him."

"*Pues,* good," Al said.

"Do you believe in the knife spirits, Nick? The Toltec renaissance? Things that go bump in the night?"

"Wholeheartedly," Nick said. He was thinking about Sarah, alone with Karl. "I want a Toltec renaissance shirt. I like Al's shirt. I told him so."

"Good, good. I like you. My country welcomes you."

Against Nick's express wishes, Pablo went on to describe the meeting with the *brujo* at length. The meeting had apparently included not only Pablo's fortune being told by the reading of a broken egg, but also a blessing over his knife. The whole time he spoke, Pablo was looking at Nick, gauging Nick's reaction. "The knife spirits are saying full-out war." Pablo patted his knife. "With the yanks who want to come and grab our nice land for cheap. What do you think of that, yanqui?"

Al mouthed the word "careful" at Nick. He was laughing.

"Nick's a little wasted to be discussing geopolitics," Al said. "I believe."

"Nick's a fucking cuckoo clock," Pablo said. "What does Nick think of the next big guerilla war? The next Chiapas? Serious shit if they try to fuck with Esmeralda Town. I'm talking the next Bogotá. I've got backup."

Pablo looked at Nick, who said, "Hmmm."

"Nick, you listen to me, my friend. Fucking blood worming through the air."

Nick, considering the image, almost puked again.

Pablo kicked a chair so that it went spinning across the room. "That's an illustration of history, my friend."

"And a good illustration it was," Al said. "Let's drink to it."

Man. What was that all about?" The men had finally left. With every drink Pablo had moved closer to Nick, once even putting his hand on Nick's thigh. Approximately ten times the man had told Nick he liked him. At one point he'd asked Nick if Nick wanted a line of cocaine and Nick had drawn back. "Of *course* not. I hate the stuff."

"Good answer. I'll keep liking you," Pablo had said.

"I don't even have a *single* Flemish ancestor," Nick had said later. "So I don't know why you keep asking me.

"I am not familiar with particular Mayan goddesses, no, but I have total respect for all of them."

"So you got money problems," Pablo had said at another, more coherent, point. "You got girl problems."

Pablo had also said, "That old German fucker has no right to go after another man's woman. There's no honor in it. I'll get the *cabrón*. I'll do it faster than I was going to. Since I like you."

"I wish I wouldn't have mentioned Karl," Nick said now. He'd attempted to politely decline the man's help. "I don't want some maniac coming around the rancho talking about blood fucking 'worming through the air.' "

"He got you a new visa," Al said calmly. In fact, Pablo had taken one from his shirt pocket, scribbled on it, shoved it into Nick's hand.

"And that's a favor you owe me, yanqui."

"That was a real threat, wasn't it? Against Karl?"

"That was just Mexican tequila talking. He won't do anything. He can't. The guy's a big lip-flapper around these parts. And he and Karl have hated each other for a long, long time." Al grinned. With his small pointy ears, he looked, Nick noticed, a little like a leprechaun. "You should see them passing each other in town. Two pit bulls with their ruffs up. For an old man, Karl can emanate far and wide."

Nick rested his head against his forearms. The buzzing in his chest was starting again. "You're sure, then. *Sure?*"

Al raised his blond eyebrows, yawned.

The wind had stopped, and the clouds were beginning to stack up again in the shimmery blue sky. In the morning, Nick had thought it might not rain, but now he wasn't sure the storm wouldn't be a big one, disallowing Sarah a planned jaunt to look for sea turtles laying their eggs. She hadn't mentioned Karl, but then she hadn't had to. Very carefully, she'd mentioned Cordula would be there.

Sarah now cracked eggs into a pan, extricating a moth that flew into the yolk. "Poor guy," she said to Nick. "Can moths fly again if their wings get wet?" He watched her wash the soft creature, then put it on the sill. "It's some kind of powder coating, I think, that allows them to stay aloft. I hope I didn't make a mistake."

"Anyway, the crap is in the eggs now," Nick said. He'd been trying to settle on a way of being with her. "Not frightening" was the way he'd decided. But not yet.

"I'll eat the eggs, and make you something else," she said. "And I'll try to hang netting around the stove so it doesn't become the Bermuda triangle for flying insects. Maybe I could get some hooks from Karl." She said quickly, "Or Cordula. She asked, by the way, if we need anything. I said we might need another lamp. They can take one out of the other guest cottage."

Nick didn't answer. During the night, he hadn't looked at Sarah and had slept in a pile of sheets and clothes on the ground. But the more he sobered, the clearer it became that he never should have met Pablo the Knifeman. Each of his dreams had incorporated a knife; Sarah had featured prominently in all of them.

"So, apparently, you didn't understand me. Esmeralda is not the place to be right now," Nick replied in a tone that struggled for calm. "Greenley says it's set to blow. We don't want to be here when it does, believe me."

"I don't really like the town, much, anyway. I'm going to avoid it."

As she stirred the eggs, set them aside, he felt more lonely than he ever had in his life.

"The guy last night brought up Chiapas. Guerillas. Hell, he was talking about handheld rockets."

Sarah rolled her eyes, then looked at the moth with a worried glance. "It's not looking too good for our friend here," she said. Then she said, "Your policeman talks to his knife. That's reason enough not to take him seriously."

She tried blowing air on the moth.

"And yet," Nick said in a harder tone, "crazy people with knives tend to *need* to be taken seriously."

"I'm going to try something on you," Sarah said in her most soothing voice. Nick might have been a child, a bird with a broken wing. "Just a stab in the dark—no pun intended." She turned to him, snapped the dishtowel, folded it. "Have you ever wondered why everywhere you go it's war?" Her tone was still loving, soft, but there was an edge underneath it.

"This isn't a pop psychological euphemism." He waved his fingers in a wild denunciation of her absurd analysis. "This is a *real* nightmare. That Pablo guy is *fucking* scary. He thinks God—excuse me, *Mrs. God*—told him Dallas is spiritually Toltec." When he slammed his hand against the table, she jumped, looked at him.

"Should I assume you don't want any eggs?" she said.

He got up, started to pace the floor.

With every step, he felt the tuning fork vibrate ever more insistently in his chest. Early this morning, after his restless sleep, he'd returned with Al to Esmeralda Town, made the call to Larry Scakorfsky. Before he could even speak, he'd been ambushed.

"We're all proud of you, Nick," Larry had said. "Never knew you had it in you. So you're going to write your novel."

"Larry—"

"You've got balls. The artistic life. What a set on you."

"I want to—"

"Balls, man. *Cojones.* And don't worry about it, I've got all your valuable stuff in a Quik Storage downtown—you owe me for that. Nice porn collection, man!"

"No, Larry, I want my job back. I've stopped drinking . . ." His voice trailed off. "I need the work."

"You don't need us, friend."

"I'm *saying* I've stopped drinking entirely."

"Good for you, man. Keep up the—"

"Larry, don't fire me. Don't."

Nick heard the sound of nicotine gum being chewed. "Your job's gone, Sperry. To tell you the truth, I promoted Jay. You're more of the artiste type anyway."

"If I proved to you—"

"I'm trying to let you down easy here, pal, and you're not letting it happen. So I'm going to go now." He'd gently hung up the phone.

"I'm going to work," Sarah now said. She'd finished the eggs, eating them straight from the pan with a spoon. As she spoke she stretched, bringing her long arms into a steeple above her head. He knew she was not as calm as she strove to appear—her left eye twitched uncontrollably. "It's a little bit of a walk, so I should be going. Later I'm going to work on my sketches."

The moth Sarah had washed was almost dead now. Nick watched it raising and lowering its heavy wings, helpless. "I, me, my," he said.

She pretended not to hear him.

"Hello in there," Nick cried out. "Are you listening to me? Even if we had to go somewhere else. Back to Vallarta." The nasty words came out before he could stop them. "There's probably an orphanage you could commandeer there."

She sighed.

"Don't yell, please. Cordula apparently has acute hearing." She held her hand over the moth, as if trying to draw life back into its body. In a small voice she said, "And please don't threaten Karl anymore. Because he'll throw you out. He warned me he would, and I believe him."

He clenched his jaw against the implicit threat in her words—that Nick would go alone. Very softly he heard her say, "You can't go on threatening people. Larry said you almost had a go at Jay, just because he made a joke about your shoes. I'm seeing the look he described in your eye right now. It's, well, unnerving. I don't think it's Esmeralda that's about to blow." She looked up. "To answer your previous question."

Nick imagined Pablo's boot coming down on Karl's face. He savored the image.

"You see, Nick, I'm hearing you. Karl's not afraid of that cop.

No one's going to get in here. Crazy people live everywhere."

"Shit. Deepest, darkest shit," Nick said.

Instead of arguing, she simply shrugged. "That's an ugly image." She was now taking the moth off the sill, dropping it into the trash. She seemed to hesitate, then extricated the corpse from the trash, this time throwing it out the window. Birds, he knew she was thinking. Recycling. Nature, Karl says.

Even through his anger, he felt the need to keep her from seeking out the old man, engaging his sympathy.

"You don't have to come with me. It's not something you signed on for. In fact, it's pretty gruesome." To illustrate her point, she extricated a Hefty bag from the refrigerator. As she swung it around her shoulder, rivulets of blood dripped from the bottom of the bag, flecking her ankles. "Sorry about the chicken carcass in the refrigerator. But I didn't know where else to keep it until feeding time. I guess I'll have to buy a cooler."

There was no need to point out that Karl should be buying the coolers. Instead he feigned interest. "What in the world requires an entire chicken carcass?"

"Oh." She laughed secretly, her eyes bright. Anytime Nick expressed interest in the animals she seemed to pounce on the subject. "It's amazing, really, how much food they need. One isn't even enough. And it's just for the cat."

They passed the Von Tollmans sitting out on the veranda. Cordula was drinking sparkling water in the heat, rubbing Karl's smooth back with Mentholatum. When she saw Sarah, she smiled stiffly, politely.

"Thank you, girl!" Karl cried out.

"I like doing it," Sarah said.

"Please don't argue in front of the animals," Cordula called out. "They're nervous enough as it is."

"Wouldn't dream of it." Sarah's mouth tightened.

"And you've enlisted a foot soldier!" Karl called gleefully at Nick, who was carrying the bag.

"Actually, he volunteered." Sarah laughed, relaxing her mouth again. "And so we're off. Absolutely calmly."

It was a long, muggy walk through the jungle behind the guest-house. The path cleared through the vines was marked with conch shells shiny white against the early moon. Now and then a palm tree came visible, bent under the late-afternoon breeze. The virgin jungle had been shaped to Karl's liking. Unpruned, wild bougainvillea predominated; explosions of fuchsia, pink, and where the leaves had begun to rot, a silvery moldy gray. They passed tall, slender papaya trees with long, draping leaves and bulbous, udderlike fruits. Green, hard, and bitter berry trees slapped at his ankles. Pitcher plants hung from moist cavities in the rock.

Flies followed Nick, attracted by the smell. As he swatted out at them, he dropped the grisly bag.

"Here, I'll take that."

"No. I got it."

But it was in Sarah's hands before he could protest.

When the path came to a swamp, they continued over slippery pine planks laid over the mud. Nick held his breath, walked through a giant web. Looking at Sarah skip across the planks, holding the heavy bag, he had a churning, sick, poison feeling in his stomach. Every so often the leaves parted and sunlight pierced through. In those spots of bright sunlight Sarah was thrown into negative, sharp and dark. The bag steadily dripped fluid.

"So things are a little tense between you and Cordula, I see."

Sarah shrugged. "Apparently you intimated certain things in front of her. That didn't help."

Nick watched a grasshopper leap from flower to flower. Like everything else in the jungle its neon-green color, its mammoth size, seemed to sound a silent alarm.

"The Von Tollmans have to keep the animals way out here,"

Sarah continued in a pacifying tone, "because when the females go into heat no one can sleep."

"I've heard them." Many nights, through his sleep, Nick had heard yowls, screams, wails. His dreams tended to assimilate the sounds so that all he felt in the morning was the longing. Or the fear.

They passed under an enormous beehive. The metallic din was of a million zippers closing at once.

"Every time I pass under that thing I get a rush." Sarah laughed. "Fear. Endorphins. I'm not sure."

"How many times have you been out here?"

"Oh, ten, maybe. Eleven. At first Karl didn't want me to come with him. He doesn't like the guests getting involved with his projects."

"But now you're involved."

"I am," she said firmly. "Yes."

"Your life is more meaningful now that you're carrying heavy bags of slain animal parts."

"Particularly hideous for a vegetarian," she said serenely. "And let's not fight. Cordula's right about that."

It seemed to him the walk had slowed to subreal time. He again thought of drugging her, wrestling her into the car. A black bag over the head, arms wrapped in duct tape: The image of childhood games with Phil made him feel physically ill.

"And here we are. Just go in through the gate." Sarah gestured to a walled-off enclosure. Taking a huge ring of keys from her pocket, she opened the lock, while scanning the area. The heavy iron door groaned, giving way to another walled enclave. Nick stepped forth, sinking to his ankles in soft mud, petals, and leaves. A series of large mesh cages, concrete runs loomed up before them like a hidden village. Interspersed throughout the space were small *palapa* huts, each containing food, cleaning implements.

"Incredible—eh? I couldn't say anything either when I first saw it. The natives call this particular place Kombu-ha, the Evil Place. They think there's a doorway to hell here; some kind of evil spirit that lives in the cenote." She laughed. "They think Karl made a pact with it, and that's where the noises come from at night. Actually he put the animals here because he knew the natives would never enter, try to poach. Because they'd sell anything for ten pesos if they could."

"Whoa, there, lady." Nick took his eyes off the erstwhile village in front of him. Even the cages had a German flavor: pitched roofs, flowerbeds. "You're sounding a lot like him."

"Cordula bought an endangered night monkey for ten pesos from a local kid. The kid had been keeping it in a cardboard box. So, the price was a literal one."

He wanted to shout at her, but instead focused on the mud with as intense an expression of revulsion as he could muster.

"Go in, meet everybody," she said. "You might just start to understand."

In each cage was an animal or two or twenty. Fur smells, feather smells, the smells of hooves and nails crowded the air. The noise was incredible. Other smells of rotten bread, frangipani, dung began to enter Nick's nostrils. Sarah headed for a particularly large enclosure, gesturing for Nick to follow her. From a *palapa* she extricated a pair of yellow dishwashing gloves, then grabbed what looked to be a large turkey carcass from a green Rite-Aid cooler. She laid the carcass next to the bag, then dumped the bag out, looking away.

"I never know where to start," she said. "It seems unfair some of them have to wait. I try to mix it up. I keep a chart, actually."

"Sarah? This isn't—"

She sighed. "Don't."

Nick clenched his fist into a ball, holding it in.

"Kitzel, she's called," Sarah then said, indicating the large black shape, which paced, endlessly, in a cage. "She gets fed first today. She's been smelling the food all day, but she couldn't get to it. It must make her crazy."

"Karl keeps a jaguar in a cage." Nick filled his cheek with air, expelled it. "That's his idea of saving her. *That's* his grandiose refuge for animals?"

"It makes him sick, too. He lets her out on a leash sometimes." Sarah regarded the jaguar sadly, then looked away as she used a shovel to sever each carcass into three pieces. "But he has to tranquilize her with ketamine first. It must be like walking along while on LSD. But at least she gets out. The boars, poor things, never do. We were thinking of—"

"Why doesn't he just let them go?" Nick snorted dirt into his sleeve. He was trying for concern, but knew he was projecting only pity and vague despair.

"Let them go where?" Sarah said pleasantly. "Cordula took Kitzel in when she was hit by a car on the road to Chetumal. The poor thing wouldn't survive any other way. She eats forty pounds of meat a week. Karl's got to hunt for the meat himself. That's one thing I'm *not* going to do."

Nick, dutifully, looked around. His head was pounding. Suddenly he stepped in front of her.

"Sarah, please just stop chopping that thing up and take a minute to understand how crazy this is. This is the old man's fantasy. Not yours. You're trying this life on, and you think it feels good, but it's not going to change anything. You can't waste yourself like this."

There was something flat and skeptical in her eyes. The jungle was dark, unyielding. "To my mind, the Americans *should* pay. And I'm one of them."

Nick looked at her sadly.

"Here, have an . . . intestine if you're going to stay." There were large wet stains on her shorts. "Put it right there in that slot. Just shove it on through. Don't make her wait."

The meat slithered off the trowel and fell in a lump onto the floor of the cage. Sarah abruptly smiled, handing Nick a large chunk of feathers and meat, retrieving another dish from the burlap bag at her feet. The flesh was cold and gelid in his hands. After she placed it carefully on the dish, her hands were smeared with grease.

"The problem is that I said something to Pablo I shouldn't have. I think he's going to come after Karl now. And I don't think I can stop it."

"Let it go." She was talking about the food.

"I'm not proud of myself, but—" Sarah was looking at him, exasperated. "But Pablo took some kind of insane liking to me. Now he's going to, Christ, 'help me' is what he said. I'm afraid he'll hurt *you*."

"Oh, Nick, stop," she said with a little laugh. "Please."

Because he would not let go of her arm, she slammed the shovel into the ground. "Let me *do* this. Fuck it, Nick, I *am* going to do this."

Sarah stood back, looking at the animals. She lowered her voice.

"So you want to talk about scary people?" The lowered voice wasn't any less disquieting. The pulse on her temple gave her away. "The wild boar in that cage were shot with air rifles by the local kids. Just for fun. Because they see it on television. Make something die or blow up. Eat Chee·tos. Game over."

She glided quietly to the next cage, keeping the tense smile in place.

"This harpy eagle? Karl doesn't *want* her to be in a cage, but she can't fly. She was shot with a BB gun through the backs of her wings. Some hunters thought her head would look nice on a wall. Or maybe they wanted her feathers for a mattress. Or they wanted to look cool in front of each other—who the fuck knows what they wanted?" Sarah was looking at the eagle with desperation. "Look, blame Karl, but he came when there were no *cars* in Esmeralda. Cars brought the hunters. Hunters brought the stupidity. And the locals all have so many kids, and each kid is going to have more kids . . . and you're not supposed to mention that fact because it's somehow racist, when it has nothing to do with race, but sheer numbers, and ignorance, and religion." She laughed, smelling of sweat and patchouli and rubber. "God, you can't say anything that's real. Because it always hurts someone."

She touched the shells hanging around her neck.

"And now *you're* making up these stories, trying to make me afraid. And I can't even get angry with you because you're doing it out of duty. You're saving a damsel in distress."

"Of course I—"

"Stop!" She caught herself before the emotion could escape. "Let me tell you what you're about to say." She was leaning close to him, the vein throbbing mightily. "You think I'm doing the wrong thing with the money. But to my mind everything is wrong. *Everything* people do." She looked at Nick warily. "And I'm even thinking about getting my own tubes tied. Yes, I'm not going to ask anyone to do what I won't do myself." She smiled shakily. "Heck, I look forward to it. You try inserting a dinner plate into the tender spots. It gets old."

The joke fell flat and she shivered. The wind raised small tendrils of her hair, slapped them against her forehead.

"Don't do it. Don't even think about it."

"But why not? I won't teach a kid to be ruthless. So what kind of mother would I be in this world?"

There was no answer. There was no logic. The logical was tubular and twisted with no certain end point.

"Robin Hood," Nick said to the air. Liquefactious sounds issued forth from the monkey pen. The furry creatures were pissing in frustration, waiting for the food.

"Yeah. That's about it. What in the hell happened to old Robin Hood in the end?" Her laughter was nervous as she moved toward the monkey pen, making soothing sounds. "They probably shot him—right?" She began to throw fruit a little wildly. Suddenly she shook the wire mesh to dislodge apples and bananas.

"I know what you're doing and I thank you. But I'm not buying the story about Pablo. Karl already told me all about Pablo. The guy's a common drug dealer who wants this land like everyone else. Join the line. And I'm going to help them not get it."

"You're going to go up against them? With Karl?"

Something shivered in a tree, scorpions or lizards. He shuddered, watching the largest boar take all the coconuts Sarah threw into the pen. The smaller boar waited, just out of the larger's eyesight.

Quickly she moved off to grab the fruit for the monkeys. They were next on the chart.

"You're funny," she said, not laughing.

"Why?"

"Because you actually think I might do that. You still think violence interests me."

They worked in the silence, filling empty bowls. Finally she said, "I've been thinking maybe you should go back to LA." She put up her hand.

"No, really. I'll give you some money. If you aren't going to write the book, or at least try to understand what I'm doing here, what's the point?

"Let me answer that," she then said. "You can't let me leave you because your father said I would."

But look at me. Why else would you want me?" she said. "I used to wonder in LA. I mean, why a Sasquatch? You could have a nice girl who doesn't wear size eleven shoes. A girl who doesn't break teacups just by holding them." She laughed quickly, unhappily. "That's what happened when the Von Tollmans invited me in for tea, by the way. I cracked one of Cordula's antique cups. The nicer she was about it, the worse I felt."

The last afternoon light flashed with the intensity of an X-ray booth. Nick sneaked a look at Sarah, who was engaged in trying to pass sly coconuts to the smallest of the boars. Each time, the larger boars charged, stole the fruit. Finally, the two largest of the animals were lying on a mound of coconuts while the rest waited, alert, in the corner. Throwing sticks at them, Sarah sighed. She was looking at her hands.

"Phil told you I would leave you." She pushed a sweaty tendril of hair behind her ears. "You want to prove him wrong. That's what this is about."

"I can't believe this. My father has nothing to do with this," Nick said when she'd finally looked at him.

"And he *wanted* me to leave you. He was just *waiting* for it." She dusted off her hands. "He pulled me aside, asked me what I was doing with 'someone like you.' At the time I just thought him sad and fucked up." She laughed, shaking her head. "Now I'm not so sure Phil wasn't just evil. It might just be that simple." She continued, wiping her hands on her pants. "No wonder you don't want to write about that. Because there's no moral in it. No stunning revelation about human nature. No ending that gives us all a little hope."

"What are you talking about, Sarah? So your feet are *big?* Who cares?"

She waved off his comments. "Look at his track record. Who's he to give advice to you?"

"You can't hide out here because—"

"Because people are crazy? And maybe evil?" She laughed. "Why not? I'd say it's a wonderful reason."

Nick swayed.

She continued. "Look at Phil. And then look at me. Ask yourself why you're with me."

Nick took an uneasy step toward her.

"No. Really. Think about it. For once, would you please think about your life, instead of soldiers you never knew? Think about things that happened to you."

Because she would not talk to him until he considered her point, Nick stood with the shovel in his hand, tamping the dirt and sand with its bloodstained tip. It had been a long time since he'd thought of Phil's dating advice.

"Racially borderline women."

That had been Nick's father's suggestion.

"Marry a white woman, and they'll think they're too good for you. A white woman has no fear anymore. They're too much in demand—they've all been spoiled, you see."

Of course, there were criteria within criteria: blacks were going too far, Japanese were sneaky, Chinese, too. They might turn on you.

"You get yourself someone who's almost white and *knows* they're almost white," Phil would say when drunk enough. "You'll better their race; they'll appreciate you and keep your house clean. They wouldn't dare leave you, and that's the key to it. You're doing a favor for these people and they know it."

And so, Nick's dark-haired, olive-skinned mother had died in a car accident when Nick was five, and then for a long while there had been no one special in Phil Sperry's life. Nick had been long gone, in college, when Phil had met Alia. If anything, the remarriage of his fifty-year-old father had seemed impossible. Phil had been known to date blond gin-drinkers with hard mouths, cut it off in a few months.

Alia was from Iran, had lost her money before coming to America, was working as a clerk at a department store when she met Phil. She had soft, wide hips, blue contact lenses, a slight fuzz over her lip. She had acquired blond hair on Phil's direction. When Nick thought of her, he thought of long, thick fingernails coated in a lacquer of brown-red. Sadness. The smell of rice. An ancient Toyota car. The sense of a clock ticking.

The boxes and boxes of Clairol Born Blonde in the cabinet.

In deference to Phil, Alia adopted the American-sounding name of Allie. She used the word "Persian," never "Iranian."

This switch had been necessary because during the hostage crisis of 1979, Phil had been among those calling for the immediate deportation of all Iranians from American soil. Phil had given money to a group supporting such an aim, and had picketed at the federal building, bringing young Nick along.

Father and son had walked concentric circles bearing angry signs. Nick had had a lot of fun waving at the passing cars, getting honked at, and later his father had been proud of him.

"This is Alia, she's from Persia. A lot of Arabs are white-skinned," Phil had introduced the woman to Nick.

Nick had been mostly embarrassed and shy and tongue-tied in front of Alia, and hadn't seen much of her during the years she accompanied Phil to air shows, space conventions, naval shows. Still, there had been signs things were going okay: Phil was always pulling out Alia's chair, buying her jewelry, choosing her clothes, and complimenting her cooking. Phil's house had been redecorated in shades of gold and red, a den had been added on next to the bedroom so that Alia could sit in it, with the door closed, speak in Farsi to her family.

"A Persian woman knows exactly how to treat a man, son," Phil had said. "You get yourself a light-skinned Persian when you're ready. They appreciate you, because they don't want one of their own. They've got it bad back there, and they know it."

It had never been explained, the circumstances under which Alia had gone. One day Phil had called Nick, "She's gone." A long, bitter court case had ensued, whereby Alia was granted half of Phil's money.

Soon after the divorce, Phil had gone back to dating his blondes, using the word "Iranian."

In due time, Phil had consulted several Russian matchmaking services, several Latin-American services, but then the cancer had struck, and he did not marry again.

"Don't let them go blond," he'd said. "Then they think they're just as good as you."

"Date blondes," he'd said. "Just don't marry them. They'll leave you on a dime."

"So, it doesn't matter if you love me. It doesn't matter if you even like me," Sarah said now. "You're just not going to let Phil win."

"Wrong. *Ridiculous.* That's so ludicrous I can't even believe you'd say it."

"The harpy gets puppy chow," Sarah said, into the silence. "Unless I catch mice."

"*Wrong*. I mean. Just wrong!"

"Is it? You listened to him for a lot of years, but you never talk about those years." She shook grime from her hands. "Maybe you think you're proving something against him, being with me. But that's the part you don't get. *This* is what you win. Look at me."

Nick watched the giant bird attack and shake each pellet as if the food were fighting back.

"I love you," Nick said. "This is *sick*. You're an amazing, intelligent, beautiful . . ."

"Except," she cut off his list hurriedly, "right now you're afraid I'm going to touch you and get slime on your shirt." She was picking dung out of the eagle's cage with a rigged-up set of enormous pincers, tossing the large pellets toward the trees. "And I will get slime on you. I can't blame you for thinking it's ugly and wanting to get away from ugliness. Not after all your years with Phil."

Nick watched the bird's gullet move up and down. She was right. He wanted to be far away from ugliness of all kinds. Especially Phil's.

"Blood, guts, ooze," she said. "Fat. I understand. I remember how people looked at me."

They had finished feeding the pigs, eagle, and jaguar, were standing in the last light of the evening. The sky had darkened quickly under the canopy of trees, but already moonlight made tiger stripes across Sarah's golden skin.

He reached out to her.

"I know what people are capable of, and so do you." She regarded the pigs with care. The smaller ones were now eating a few leftovers. Looking at him, she wiped her hands on her pants. He saw the fat glisten on them and recoiled. She turned away from the look on his face.

"Except." She looked at him, shaking her head tenderly and distantly. "You scream at slow drivers, Nick. Your skin bubbles, your nose bleeds. You shout obscenities. You kick in your sleep. But Phil has nothing to do with it. And Phil has nothing to do with your wanting to be with me."

Nick looked at the jaguar behind the bars.

"Look at me," she said again. She put out her hands. "Ugh." When she laughed, the mud slid off of them.

"I'm not some big, blond *thing* that will prove you right if you can just pretend enough." She then collected the buckets, the cooler. "And I can't be a bet between you and your father anymore." She started walking.

"It's not good for either of us."

He looked at his watch. The rain hit the window. Sarah was reading under the mosquito net, giving him guilty little glances.

"I've felt so guilty because I don't want to prove Phil right, either," she'd said. "But is that a good enough reason to stay with someone?

"I mean, can you admit I, at least, might be correct?

"You've been laughing at me, here. At least admit that."

Nick looked at his watch again. Somewhere, overhead, Phil was shaking with laughter. A few yards away Karl was rubbing his hands together. Five thousand miles away, Larry Scakorfsky was rooting for him.

Sarah now raised her index finger, let it fall. "So you're going for a drink? That's the plan?"

"Something like that."

They'd walked back from the animals' pens in embarrassed silence, only occasionally touching elbows or fingertips: sharp, unsensual parts of the body. Lines had been drawn. For now they would be "housemates." Sex was up in the air, but, she said, she knew he was scrutinizing her body for sand and mud, and she didn't want to feel bad about it anymore. Hers was a dirty job and she was willing to accept that.

"I take showers," she'd said. "Swim. Wash my hands . . ."

"The problem is," he'd said, "a job is something you get paid for."

She'd ignored his comment. "I've been trying to turn around when we make love, but I start thinking you're just looking at the skin on my back critically. Finding fault. But maybe you're not looking at me that way. I don't know."

"Yep. You *don't* know."

So sex was up in the air. The way it always started. She was willing to pay him to leave, Karl saw her soul not her body. He was up, up, up, revolving outside himself. Phil did a sharp salute inside of his head.

"You're going with Al Greenley?"

He looked up. Her pajamas were light pink, mannish, tailored. Underneath she was soft, smelling of plums and wood smoke. And there was the sand. He didn't have to like *sand* to like her. It was difficult to meet her eyes without flinching.

"That's right," he said in his new housemate voice.

Feeling the wetness of his hair, each strand of it tapping against his face in the hot evening wind, he gazed out at the ceiba trees. They looked new and shiny like they'd just been placed there that day. The dunes were acute. Even the wind had a sheen.

"Let her see you don't care," Al had said. Al had probably been right.

Al didn't care, and Sarah didn't care. Phil hadn't cared. Nick was the only one who cared, and look where it had gotten him.

"I thought I'd draw tonight. Snails are what I'm into at the moment." Her voice caught, lost its jaunty edge. "Oh, Nick. This is horrible. Every minute it gets more fake. I wasn't saying that I didn't like making love. Or that we couldn't. Just that I don't know what's going to happen in the future. I don't want to be scrutinized and found spoiled goods. I don't want you to be disgusted because I have sand in my toes or because my stomach is a little blubbery. I'm not going to change because you think I'm better if I do. I'm not going to be like Phil's wives."

"No. Don't." He hated the term "making love." The sand didn't matter, not too much, the rest of it mattered, and she wouldn't say it.

She put a protective hand over her flat stomach. Pinched it, grimacing.

Nick's skin felt raw, worked over, his lips swollen and alien. Even the slight breeze seemed to leave a deep imprint on his skin.

To keep from looking at Sarah, he fell into watching one of Karl's dogs, sleeping under the moon on the porch. The bitch twitched, having fallen asleep on her side, back legs crossed as if trussed. Her graying muzzle, undignified posture touched him. He thought he might cry.

"Nick?"

He glowered.

"Be careful with that guy." Sarah looked painfully into his face. "Karl says Al isn't involved in anything weird, but I can't help but wonder. I mean, Al just showed up here out of the blue a few years ago. And now he's everyone's best friend. Everyone loves Al."

"Your buddy Karl sure does," Nick said. "What does he do? Tell you you're fat? Is that how he got you hot for him?"

A wind came up, the first drops of rain began to fall against the screen. The air didn't cool off.

"Is that creep Pablo going to be there?" she asked, turning the page. He noticed she'd read the same page many times.

"Maybe. Is Karl going to come in here when I'm gone? He doesn't mind sand, I'm sure. His father is no excuse, and he'll tell you how fat and awful you are so you can finally have an orgasm."

Let her answer that.

"I don't know what Karl's going to do."

And so it was out.

She continued to read the same sentence. Pat her belly. Frown.

Nick walked away from her, his legs broken glass. With every step they shattered a little more. On the porch, he sat down, facing the sea. As he thought of Pablo's scar, he shivered, lay back against the deck chair, lifting the glass of tequila to his lips. The idea had been forming itself ever since he'd watched the jaguar stalk the meat.

"Pablo, buddy," he imagined himself saying. "What I need is some help."

Any new trouble, and Cordula would see to it that Sarah was thrown out of the rancho. Help, he thought. A buzzing began in his stomach.

Pablo wouldn't *hurt* Karl, just scare him a bit. He certainly wouldn't hurt a girl. There was no honor in it.

Help.

Drinking the warm liquid, an image came to mind. An acquaintance from his college days—Joe Gibee. Gibee used to wear black eye makeup, read aloud a certain horrible kind of story in the paper—things that had to do with post offices, McDonald's playgrounds.

Now he conjured up Gibee's hurt, little face, triangular and wan, bobbing up and down to the heavy metal music he favored, wearing one of the black concert T-shirts he collected: lugubrious drawings of skulls, melting monsters, skeletons, grim reapers. The night of Gibee's funeral, Nick had actually cried, sifting through the Metallica and Megadeth albums on the altar. Gibee, who'd annoyed the shit out of him in life, was sorely missed after his suicide. So many times he'd lectured the kid, "There's nothing more bourgeois then being afraid of being bourgeois." Half the time he was just rambling, blotting out the kid's annoying nose ring. After Gibee killed himself, he'd regretted the glib Andy Warhol references.

Meeting Pablo, he felt, would have scared the hell out of Gibee. There was a salient point there, but the buzzing in his stomach prevented him from exploring it.

Pablo would just not hurt a girl.

"Hey writer, ready to go?" It was Al, pulling up in the van.

"The van? So you got the fan belt worked out?" Nick said in an odd, quiet voice.

"Everything's worked out, buddy," Al said. "You're going to have some fun tonight. You look like you could use it."

"Hey, Nick," Sarah said in a low voice. "No. Karl's not going to come in. But I just think you should start to think about Phil. . . . Maybe I'm wrong, but . . ."

He turned toward her, thinking to take her bony form in his arms. Instead he looked at the perfect little face and said: "The war started today. They sent a cruise missile into Baghdad. Phil would be proud. I'm not."

Sarah looked away.

"Out of sight, out of mind. That's one way to conduct a life." The bitterness in his tone was unmistakable. "And so, I'm going now."

As he walked down the path to meet Al, he caught a glimpse of Karl, sitting on his bicycle. The way he hunched over the bars, elbows at right angles, reminded Nick of a gargoyle.

"You boys be careful, now," Karl said. "Don't trink too many of the likkids."

"Aye, aye, Captain," Al said, jingling his keys.

"Karl." Nick's eye caught Karl's blue one. "*Gute Nacht.* The lady awaits."

"Now, now, boy." Karl was still watching him warily. He grinned with the teeth. "You look like you just bit into a lemon. I don't particularly fancy that look."

Nick saluted, goose-stepped away.

"There's not going to be any trouble," he heard Al say. "I'm going to set it all straight with Raul—tell him to tell Castillo exactly what you told me."

Nick heard Karl suck on his teeth.

He heard the word "aphid."

He squeezed his knuckles. He heard the rush of blood.

Orange

Al's van was one of the earlier Dodge models, square and blocky as an adobe brick. It was brick-colored, primered in spots, smelled faintly of wood shavings, forest air freshener, burlap, cigarettes. The tobacco smell put Nick in the mind of whiskey.

"So we're going back to the Coco Palms Bar? A little fun with Hilde and her gang?"

"Nah, another place. Tonight's bad tuba night at the Coco. They call it *norteña* music," Al said. "Besides, I've got something to take care of for Karl. A handyman's work is never done."

Suddenly Nick wished the entire night were already over. But the minutes would tick louder with Sarah nearby. Karl would be alone with her now, all evening. Either something would happen or it would not. And yet, Nick's absence was going to make something happen. *He* was not going to humiliate her. *His* pleasure centers were not built that way.

"Your mother's race was a race of cowards. You didn't find many of them hacking Vietnam."

"It's cold all of a sudden," Nick said to Al. "Are you cold?"

"It's eighty degrees, man."

"The Israelis are all animals," the French girl had said. "They fight because they don't know anything except brutality."

Nick breathed deeply into his lungs. "Maybe it's the air-conditioning. I haven't felt cold air in so long, I forgot what it's like." He looked at Al. "And man, I've got to talk to Pablo again. I hope we see him tonight."

"Race does not exist on a DNA level," said the scientists. A blob of DNA, and there was no black, Jew, white, Iranian.

But a blob of Karl DNA. Nick imagined blobs of slimy spit that Karl would make, kissing Sarah. He gagged.

"Stop worrying, buddy! This is Mexico—if Pablo even remembers what he said to you, he won't get around to doing anything about it for at least five years." He nudged Nick's elbow.

"Yeah, well, I've got to talk to him. I need his help."

"We'll see if we can find him, then. But around my pals, don't mention Pablo. It's one of those delicate social ecosystem things. A big, bad cop and all that. They're from different tribes."

"What should I talk about?" Nick was rubbing his hands together to warm them. "Since we're planning a conversation all out in advance." His voice was bitter.

Al smiled. "With Raul, talk about Mexican culture. Use that phrase—'Mexican culture.' He likes that one."

Nick felt something cold spread in his stomach. "Right."

"He doesn't speak much English anyway."

"The possibilities, then," Nick said, "are endless."

So where *is* this other bar?" They'd pulled off on a street behind Esmeralda Town's rows of shops. The pueblo was surprisingly large with houses—if windowless, doorless concrete boxes could be called that—that bookended one another, stretching on for almost two miles. Under the harsh yellow glow of irregularly placed street lamps were dusty, sagging armchairs on communal lawns of reddish sandy dirt. The stuff lay a foot thick on rickety porches and old playground equipment. Dun-colored animals huddled together under broken tables and awnings, children slept in hammocks strung between trees.

"No way. Don't tell me this is the festive place."

After several left turns Al had finally parked on someone's lawn.

Old Ford trucks and newer VW *bochos* crowded the asphalt driveway. "Hey. This is your chance for a little real Mexico, writer. But if you don't want to go in, you can wait out here, and we'll hit the Brava Cantina later. But I warn you, it'll be a long wait. A Mexican social visit has its standard rituals."

"Hopefully one of those rituals is tequila."

"No doubt."

The mobile home was plunked on the dirt, a few concrete retaining walls added on as an afterthought. As Nick walked toward the door, he saw a few cheerful touches—a bright orange hammock, a Mayan rug on the porch, a decorative hedge around the fence.

"Your friend's got a righteously lush pot plant on his front porch." Nick shook his head in wonder. "And what's up with the Coca-Cola sign over the door?"

"As the town entrepreneur, Raul wears many hats." Al smiled. "In fact, one of them is a small grocer."

"What are the other hats?"

"He's also a pharmacist. And a realtor. In his mind."

"I'm getting the picture," Nick said. "Let's sell some real estate, then."

Qué pasa," Al called softly, though the front door was half open. Moths and mosquitoes swarmed the light. Geckos twitched under the awnings.

"Ándale," a voice said. *"Y quien?"*

"Al Greenley y mi amigo."

Al whispered. "Oh, yeah. Try not to smile too much. Mexicans think Americans smile too much. They think we're laughing at them."

Nick nodded. "Great. Now that you said that, I'm going to laugh." Nick laughed nervously. He needed a drink. "It's bad enough that I'm going to have to pick through my limited Spanish. Which consists, basically, of menu items."

"If Raul's got company, you're in luck. A lot of these locals won't speak Spanish—only Mayan. They call Spanish 'the language of the knife-fuckers.' "

Nick felt the buzzing in his stomach again. "There's actually a word for 'knife-fucker' in Mayan?"

"Eight distinct terms for fuckers—motherfuckers, kid-fuckers, goat-fuckers, cat-fuckers. You get the idea. And so I'll stop speaking English for a while. I don't want to offend anyone."

"Not in the land of fuckers, you don't."

It was only when they reached the door, Nick realized Al must speak the incredible language. He'd never mentioned it.

"Where'd you learn Quiche?" he asked. "Jesus. I can't even understand people from Australia."

"I don't know much of it. But languages are easy, buddy. Just a matter of listening."

"Man, you need a better job," Nick said admiringly. "You don't need to be picking up sticks for Karl."

They entered through a kitchen, low-ceilinged, constructed of plywood and concrete blocks. On a bare Formica table was a giant wooden bowl full of green oranges and a small natural gas–operated refrigerator in one corner. A few mismatched pots hung from hooks in the ceiling. There were bare hooks next to them, and shelves holding fancy vinegars, children's toys, empty jars of mayonnaise, a chipped mug picturing a teddy bear that read: I LOVE YOU UNBEARABLY.

Sarah would have wrinkled her nose at the mug, laughed in her pretty way.

"This way." Al waved Nick toward a room thick with cigarette smoke. In it an extended Mexican family sat around a gigantic television. The women were dressed in housecoats, or loose, homogenous floral affairs, the men favored button-up shirts, sneakers, pressed jeans. A little girl in a pair of sheep pajamas was making fanatical circles with a crayon on a pad of paper. She looked at Nick suspiciously, then went back to the circles.

A sudden smell of Lysol hit Nick's nose. The old grandmother was spraying an ant with it, and shaking her head. The grandfather sat upright in a La-Z-Boy recliner, regarding Nick with a raw, senile gaze.

"Uh, hi."

Nick might have just walked into the Mexican *Howdy Doody* hour. His stomach sank. Karl, Sarah, he was thinking. Sarah, Karl, Pablo. No one gets hurt. Or just the right people.

"Awl! Qué milagro! Encantada de verte! Y quien es tu amigo?"

As Al shook each of their hands, Nick tried to believe he would be stuck in the suburban scene for the next hour, grinning ghoulishly at the couch-sitters while picturing the old man on top of Sarah. Other than the television, the La-Z-Boy, a blue-striped couch, a blindingly white rug, the room was bare of decor. Linoleum lined the floor, giving off an ammonia smell. A plastic rose, doily jammed underneath it, sat in its prim vase on a single wooden shelf. The only wall decorations were gold-framed family photos of chubby, bland children and what seemed to be a calendar displaying different breeds of dogs for each month. The smell suggested hypercleanliness, Lysol, sponges, mold spores lurking under cabinets.

The couch was plastic-sheeted. It crinkled and sighed as legs crossed and uncrossed.

Al sat on the couch, apparently very comfortable. The girl held up the drawing for him, and he gave her the thumbs-up.

"Memo here swears you're the actor who always does the space movies."

"No, no," Nick demurred. Discomfort and anxiety caused him to hunch.

"Well, he says you are."

"Jesus Christ," Nick said, remembering not to smile as he shook each hand in turn. "Then I must be."

As Al continued to talk to the men in the impossible language, Nick sat on the knife-edge of the couch. A *Monopolía* game, edges worn and dog-eared, was produced, and three of the women started playing. Every so often the grandmother would hold up the can of Lysol, use the stream to target ants. The spraying would go on for many, many seconds after the ant was dead. The family would look at the grandmother indulgently and laugh among themselves. Finally the fluid seemed to run out.

"No, *gracias.*" Nick declined a position at the *Monopolía* board.

Hairy balls swinging. "Let me help you undress, Karl." He was going to die.

"Oh, absolutely. *Sí, sí.*" He accepted the tequila offered by an ancient auntie on a plastic tray. Pretty soon, she came with another.

"Um, Al?" He tried to keep his voice even. "You know the guy we were talking about . . ." It was ridiculous not to be able to say Pablo's name. These people had no more in common with Pablo than they did Nick.

"Why don't you hold off there for a moment, buddy." Al held up a finger. "Just, uh, relax. Watch some TV with the clan."

On the TV a dubbed version of *Quo Vadis* played.

The air smelled of corn, plastic, static, crayons. Two more women came in from the anteroom, one thin, nervous-looking with a large, soft, giraffelike nose, the other round and gentle and long-haired. They stood poised over a CD player, touching random buttons. Nick's instinct was to explain the problem—from where he sat, he could see the thing was unplugged—but he didn't want to seem to be paying undue attention to the ladies. He knew enough about Latin culture not to make *that* mistake.

He crossed and uncrossed his legs many times, each time setting off a series of sounds reminiscent of disturbed Saran Wrap. Each time he moved, the women looked at him expectantly, and he mouthed the word, "Sorry."

Fat, Sarah had said, no one wants to look at fat. She'd been fat as a kid, and in her mind was still fat, and was mentally waddling around the world trying to save it from cruelty, and now she'd made a big, fat mess. Detox. He started to laugh. That's how Karl had started it with her. Of *course.*

Let me clean your DNA, my pretty.

"My friend has a question, Nick," Al called out. He appeared to be arguing with the thinner man, who was making impatient noises under his breath. To Nick he said, "Raul here wants to know if you like Mexico more than California."

Nick's first thought was to laugh.

"Just nod. I'm going to say you love it."

Nick nodded.

The men appeared to discuss his answer. Finally, they all smiled.

"You're a hit," Al said happily.

I will never see a stranger pairing, Nick thought. Al in his pukka shells. The thin, clean man in his drip-dry socks.

An old man and a beautiful, smart girl. That was a stranger pairing.

"Excellent."

The CD player switched on.

"And now the family has something special for you," Al was saying.

"Perfect."

The kid started to dance with castanets.

He was now on his fourth tequila. The drink had been given no less politely than the other three, and yet, he knew the women were starting to get uncomfortable, lowering their eyes. *"Sí, sí, gracias,"* he said with all the dignity he could muster. The Monopoly game had been abandoned, and they were all now watching Romans slay other Romans with a jazzy soundtrack.

"Muy bien tequila," Nick said.

He knew he was talking like a caveman.

"Gracias, señor. Gracias!"

A commercial came on. The disembodied announcer was saying, *"Limpia más rapido con Kleer Skies!"* The old woman smiled at Nick with delicate distaste while pouring yet again. A damn thimbleful. A sip.

"So, howzit?" Al finally said. "This is real Mexico."

"Have you ever thought about that fact that 'real' Mexico doesn't exist on a DNA level? It's all some made-up shit to explain pigmentation and corn-based foods?"

"I never have quite thought about that," Al said. "But maybe you should slow down on the tequilas, buddy."

"Let's think about, um, hitting the other place soon." That was right. Give Karl and Sarah a good, long time. And where would Cordula be? Cordula would be knitting. Sharp, little dropped stitches.

"Oh, yeah. Yeah." Al smiled, making no move to leave. "Right-o."

Two cats, stick thin, slunk outside the window, with starved, feral expressions. He thought of Phil's second wife's cat—a lazy, plump Siamese who lay on a blue satin cushion all day, only deigning to stir when it heard the sound of the can opener. The woman had treated it with utmost solicitousness, even buying it a rain suit for the occasional wet California weather. The cat had gone with her.

Karl kept tigers. He kept lions and bears and pretty girls. Oh, my.

"Raul wants us to go outside," Al finally said to Nick. The music was now blasting over the sound of the TV set. No one else seemed to mind.

"Yeah, uh, how much longer?" Nick asked.

Al's voice came into his ear. "Not much longer now. By the way, Raul thinks you're a real estate whiz, and I'm asking your advice. So just nod your head when I look at you. I'm trying to let him down easy that Karl still won't sell."

"Sell it."

"You're crazy." Al laughed.

"Could I get another tequila, you think?"

The buzzing noise had spread to his ears.

"Come out here and Raul will get you another."

As he bent to wipe a spot from his boot, a silver object fell from Al's pocket. He retrieved it, covering it with his palm. Nick stared at it hard, while Al slipped it quickly in his pocket. One of the ladies watched the scene and laughed.

"Uh. What's up with the gun?"

"Everyone's armed in Esmeralda," Al said, keeping his friendly smile. He ushered Nick out. "That's why things are pretty peaceful in our little 'burb. Good neighbors stay good this way."

"I think the gun lobby uses that exact logic."

Don't talk, he was thinking, sell.

"Do they, now?" Al said. "Well, good neighbors are a good, good thing. That's the spirit of Esmeralda Town."

Al Greenley was moving across the lighted porch, careful not to step on a crack, change his luck. It was only slightly disturbing to him that Raul had commented that Nick was drinking too much. The *cabrónes* all drank, Al had said quickly. That's how they got through.

What was worrying Al was the superlong truck he'd seen parked at the entrance to the ruins. The truck had no markings, was glossy jet-black. Its thick, long antennae could signify television, government, Pablo's guys, many things. Still, bad things came to mind.

"I think the kid will work out fine," Raul had said, speaking in code in front of his family. "But Pablo doesn't want the BMW involved. Too flashy. Too many eyes."

It had been decided Nick would drive Chaz's old Pontiac. "But he better not be drunk, man," Raul had said. "You keep him off the sauce tomorrow."

"Your *Americano* certainly likes tequila!" Raul's wife had said, disapprovingly.

"His girlfriend just left him," Al explained.

"Ah, then he *needs* tequila," the woman had exclaimed.

"So is it interesting, buddy? A slice of life here?" Al said to Nick, who'd followed him onto the porch.

"*Quo Vadis* is even more impressive in Spanish," Nick was saying. "But like I said, I wouldn't mind finding the little cantina you promised."

Al's head was throbbing. The whole time Raul was arguing Nick's cut, Al had been thinking Raul had been strangely unconcerned about the presence of the truck. "Hotel goons," he'd said, shrugging. "Or a government thing. Pablo's not worried, so I'm not worried."

"Pray to Lady Blood and Cut 'im Up, or whatever the son's name is."

When Raul appeared with the tequila, he handed it to Nick with a dubious look. "The son's name isn't Cut 'im Up," he said angrily to Al. "Not in front of Pablo."

"I was thinking about that truck, man," Al said to Raul, after an apology. "I don't think it's the hotels. They don't carry sat phones."

"Some Americans, maybe." Raul waved it off, unconcernedly. "CIA, or spooks of some kind. Fucking Pablo and his gelignite. He had to rock the boat. When the yanquis are already paranoid about terrorists. But not DEA. No worries there."

Raul looked at Nick, who smiled.

"The kid doesn't speak Spanish at all, does he?" Raul asked, laughing. To Nick he said, "No *español?* Nathin'?"

Nick shrugged, looking helpless and wasted. Then he took another drink.

"So you *don't* think they're DEA?" Al asked carefully. Something was not quite right about the truck. Or about Raul's calm. "There's no chance of that?"

"Al, my friend, that sting shit takes a long time to set up, and we would have heard something. There's no DEA in Esmeralda—not this time around. If there was, would I be here?" He watched Nick with a wide smile. "Besides, what do you care? You got the kid to do it."

And yet, something was not right. Raul had been grinning at Al all evening. Grinning and calling Al "my dear friend."

"He doesn't know a thing? You're not going to tell the poor bastard?" Raul then said. He answered his own question with a strangely effervescent smile. "Better if he doesn't know, eh?"

Nick was sighing, stubbing his toe against the floorboards. When Al looked at him, he stopped, straightened up. "Did that guy just say 'DNA'?" Nick asked him. "Is the guy, like, reading my mind? What's he saying about DNA?"

"This kid is like a yanqui classic." Raul switched to Maya, just in case. "If the shit did go down tomorrow, they've got their perfect newspaper article. Polo-wearing kingpin arrested in Mexico." He laughed. "But don't you worry, it's *not* going down tomorrow. Your friend's all right." He laughed again. "Tell him I like his shirt."

"No one said 'DNA.'" Al looked at Nick. "But Raul here thinks you're an elegant dresser. He thinks I should take pointers from you."

Nick laughed. "Is that why he keeps looking at me?"

"Too bad, though," Raul was saying. "The powers up high will never have a better chance to drag the yanquis through the dirt, man. The kid's, like, perfect. Better even than you."

"No one wants a Canadian kingpin. There's no satisfaction in it." Al laughed. "Raul says you should be married," Al said to cover the laugh. It wasn't easy keeping all the conversational balls in the air. "He's got a cousin. A real *bonita*."

Nick smiled. He looked slightly ill.

"The sting's got to happen sometime this year," Raul said, looking at Nick with a sad smile. "It's been too quiet too long. I wish to Christ they'd just get it over with, go away, so we can get back to sleeping easy. And Pablo could calm down."

Al didn't believe anyone in Esmeralda would ever sleep easy again. "You know it," he said. "Absolutely."

The air was bone-dry and warm, and the sweat dried in Al's armpits almost immediately. He was seeing spots in front of his eyes, the ground was too soft under the wheels of the van. The minute Raul had signaled them to the end of the driveway, Al had groaned. Al, who'd sucked without inhaling much, had been sorry to see the writer coerced into actually smoking the strong stuff Raul favored. Then again, Nick had gotten less nervous, and that was a plus.

"Some kind of terrorist shit!" Raul had kept assuring Al with the toothy grin. "They're paranoid up there, man. Word got around Pablo's been talking about meeting with the sheikhs is all. Dumbass had to open his big mouth to the Radisson guys, and they think he's serious. A sleeper cell in Esmeralda. *Jesús Cristo,* the man's got too big of a mouth."

"Steady enough hands. Clueless. Perfect," Raul had pronounced of Nick. He had never spoken to Al in such a friendly tone. "Give the kid a little *muj* before the run tomorrow. Just keep him off the booze. He babbles too much."

"I'm stoned. How embarrassing." Nick shook his head roughly like a dog releasing water. "I kept thinking your friend was a mind-reader."

"That was some strong *muj* all right," Al said.

"It's not even fun to be stoned. It's like . . . time. Keeps. Stopping." Nick was still clutching on to the handle of the window. "I should have said no. I hate the stuff."

"Raul's got a thing for weed. He's got stomach problems. Nervous problems. Among other problems."

"Mr. Cleaver smokes a doob. Who woulda thunk it?" Nick giggled. "Man, that was one of the weirder nights I've ever had. And I didn't think Mexico could get any weirder."

"It can always get weirder," Al said.

I did the pothead thing in my youth." Nick's eyes were closed, remembering. "I wanted to be mystical, but I mostly felt nauseous. Nothing's changed."

"So he liked you. Invited you to a poker game tomorrow. It's going to be at my buddy Chaz's place. You remember Chaz?"

"There's no way Raul could be poker buddies with Chaz." Nick laughed.

"Raul's a secret maniac," Al said. Which was true enough.

Nick was tapping his fingers together in a certain pattern and rhythm, no doubt trying to find a point of perfect equilibrium.

"I don't know about going out again. Maybe it's not a good idea to leave Sarah alone."

"Pablo will be there."

"Shit, I forgot all about him. Yeah." Nick bit his lip. "Yeah. I gotta talk to him. But I thought you said Raul and Pablo aren't copacetic."

"Poker, man." Al laughed. "The great social equalizer."

The writer was quiet for a time, and Al started to drift off, wondering if Raul was going to put a sting on Pablo tomorrow—that's what the smiles were about. Maybe he meant to work a deal with Al, move into Karl's land himself. *Of course, of course.* Little, defenseless sparrows always survived in the largest numbers. And there would be no Toltec shit with Raul. He started to laugh. But Raul wouldn't dare.

"It's not funny, man."

The writer's snort wasn't a happy sound.

"You're thinking about your gal?" Al looked up. He watched the writer shiver.

"I'm thinking about the word 'housemate.' " Irritation gave the writer's face a fatherly—no a grandfatherly—mien. "Why doesn't she just cut my balls off?"

"You could just drive outta here tomorrow morning, buddy. Let her keep house herself."

"Nah," the writer said. "Not cool."

"So you said it." Al watched the rearview mirror. Not for anything in particular. "Be cold, man. Cool. Ice her out. You can write inside my place, if it feels too crowded in the guesthouse." He added, "Hell, why don't you sleep on the cot tonight. Let Sarah sweat it a little. That's a sure way to get a woman back."

Nick was now smiling the wide, spacey smile.

"That's not a bad idea."

"And be gone all night tomorrow." Al grinned. "So how are you at poker, buddy? Because Chaz takes his game seriously."

"I've got nothing to lose," Nick said after a long time. "Actually."

"Except your shirt," Al answered. "Which is something Raul wants.

"Tell you what," Al then said. "I'll take you there early so you can get in a few extra games. I'll slip in a hundred. Whatever you win, we'll split. And if you lose, you help me paint the last six sheds."

"You're a dog. Because you think I'm going to lose."

"Actually what they call me out here is *ratón*. Rat," Al said easily. It was also true.

"Watch your money."

Al closed his eyes for a moment, locking on to the glide of the wheels. The whole night had proceeded perfectly, easily. Too easily. And yet sometimes that's how it was. A speedy, metallic flavor rose in his mouth.

"On second thought I think I'll give you my place tonight." He was thinking of the scorpion in the sheets. "I'll sleep outside in the hammock."

"You are a gentleman and a scholar." Nick laughed.

"And a *ratón*," Al said.

When they passed the ruins where the truck had been parked, Al felt the steering wheel, warm and smooth under his hands. Everything, the night air, the wind on his face, the pale yellow light of the headlamps, felt watery, unsure.

"The old man taught me how to play soldier's poker. Meaning:

winning. So what I need to know is how bad is it to win with Pablo? I mean, what're the consequences?"

Al laughed for the writer's benefit. "I've come out eight hundred, nine hundred ahead. Pablo threw a chair at me—that was about the end of it."

"What's his thing with chairs?" The writer was off and laughing now. "Was the chair heavy or light?"

"I'll watch your back. Count on it." The chair, in fact, had hit Chaz. Knocked him out.

"I mean it. Don't be sure you won't lose. I might seem like a sap, but I'm pretty good. That's one thing I can thank the old man for."

"Yeah? I'm quaking."

Moment by moment he was watching as the writer emerged from himself. If he somehow made it through the wet move, he would never be the same. Al had seen it happen to plenty of guys—like a switch being turned, their confidence grew, the *demonio* came out. The *demonio* of easy money. Looking at the writer's goofy smile, it was Al's instinct to look away. For a moment he saw a fuzzy image, the writer going down, down, down, the girl, Karl, Cordula. It made him think of cold blue water. The image extended to his immediate surroundings; for a moment they were driving on the bottom of the ocean.

"Man, that was some strong ganja."

"Man," Nick agreed.

The van pulled to a halt around the next corner, where a crowd of young men was gathered, holding pitchforks and scythes. The men had angry expressions, were holding out white plastic buckets, jingling the captive coins and chanting. An old, old woman was before them. If she hadn't been shrieking, Al would have guessed she was dancing.

"What in the fuck!" Nick sucked in his breath, flattened himself against the seat.

"Well," Al said. "This again."

Nick was reflexively clutching at the door handle, looking around wildly. But there was nowhere to go.

"Is this the part where they sacrifice us to Chac Mool?" He saw Nick tried to keep his voice neutral. "Or are they *selling* those fine garden implements?"

"This is the part where we enter into Third-World alternative finance. In other words, we're on a homemade toll road."

Al considered old lady Alvarez, her wizened, wild eyes. Her sons worked for Pablo sometimes, doing patrol. The Alvarez boys were a little dopey, but alert enough when coked up. They'd worked as kitchen prep boys in Texas for a few years, and were handy enough with knives.

"They want a toll for driving on a dirt road?" Nick was laughing unsurely.

"That's their prerogative." Al handed the woman a few coins. "They've got to buy candles for their gods."

"There's a lot of delicate systems in place here."

"You have no idea."

And still she was not ready to let them go. She pointed and wailed at Nick, who looked, concerned, at Al. While Al waited, curious to see what Nick would do, the old woman pounded on the windshield, shouting something about her youngest being in jail.

The calmer Al got, the more Nick seemed to accept the situation. So he was the type who looked to others for clues. Al would have guessed so, but it was better to know. Not particularly helpful when it came to working with Chaz. Especially not in a sting.

He let the situation escalate, keeping an eye on Nick.

"The gringo's got money," the old woman screamed. "He should pay. You *make* him pay! My son needs some help!"

"So what's she saying, then?" Nick said. He now looked more confused than scared.

"She's just going on and on about her kid." Al, shrugging at Mrs. Alvarez, continued to let the situation rise. He tapped his elbow, a typically Mexican gesture that told the old woman Nick was a cheapskate. She howled.

"I guess I'll let you handle this," Nick said.

At that moment Al recalled Raul telling him some kid had taken a few hundred from one of Pablo's guys when the guy was drunk. Now the Alvarez boy would die like a Toltec, nailed to something. If he hadn't already. Stupid and scary. He shook his head.

"Um, is it still okay? I mean, should I just fork the money over?" Nick was staring as the men formed a line in front of the car. Suddenly a board studded with nails was plunked down behind the back tires. "She's looking at me like she'll rip me apart."

The nightmare increased in tension and volume, until suddenly Al gave the guys a few large bills, explaining they were from the cheapskate gringo. The board was lifted, and the men smiled and waved Al along. They made the devil's horns at Nick, who stared grimly straight ahead.

Not bad, Al thought. But Raul was right. Nick needed a little tranquilizing first. Absolutely now.

"It turns out she needs money for one of her kids," he told the shape next to him. "He's got some kind of health problem."

"A little less hostility might work better." Nick was breathing hard.

"A Norplant gun would work best," Al said.

Al sheltered his eyes against the blowing sand. They were skirting the edges of the town, almost at the turnoff for the road to Esmeralda. There was no reason to worry about the truck. Black trucks arrived in Esmeralda. They turned around. They blew up, or they did not. Still, he had a slippery feeling in his stomach, his headache wouldn't quit. A DEA truck wouldn't park itself so calmly.

But a hotel truck wouldn't be in Esmeralda. A spook truck, then. Maybe. He looked at the writer who was silently staring at his feet.

"How're the mystic thoughts going?" he said to Nick.

"I'm seeing triangles fold into triangles fold into triangles." He jerked his head upright. "I'm seeing pyramids in Karl's head. This shit sucks."

"That's why I need a gun, by the way." Al punched the gear again, Nick was thrown against the door. He watched Nick blink.

Nick laughed into his pyramids.

"Back there, you might have just escaped a kidnap, whereby you'd be driven to your ATM every day until your money ran out—which in your case would have really pissed them off."

Nick was smiling. "Hey, you should be the writer."

"Happened to me once in Vallarta at a roadblock much like that one. Nothing too elegant. A chair, some rope, a gag, a bad Mexican radio playing for days. They emptied me out."

He didn't mention what he'd done to them later, but the sound, a little *pop,* came back to him quite clearly.

"I hate guns. I had my first one at twelve. A rifle for shooting rabbits."

"So you can shoot then?" Al felt himself come awake, alert.

"Of course I can shoot. I didn't want to kill rabbits, so every damn weekend I shot paper people. Me and the old man. Bullets through the heads. Fun at the range. Make sure I'm tough. Not 'inferior.'" Nick was hitting his fist against the dashboard. He seemed to be following a particular tune. The tune was fast, nervous, maybe punk. "That's the other thing the old man left me with. A profound knowledge in the ways of pointing and clicking. Karl's not the only old guy with armature on the brain."

"Hey, buddy. I'm surprised."

"You've got me all wrong. Most people do."

"And I like the word 'armature.'"

"I don't know if it's even a war word. It might mean a piece of furniture."

Al held his silence. The larger part of him wished things had gone the other way. But this way was good, too. Nothing would probably happen, and at least the guy could shoot. Better if Nick didn't even know anything until it was right on top of him—but not knowing was a luxury that didn't often happen.

"I don't want to know what brain matter looks like up close. I don't want to suck on adrenaline, get the red mist, go for the throat, chest, throat." Nick was faraway, and Al left him there. "That's what my old man couldn't understand."

"So you and your old man have problems?" Al finally said.

"No problems now."

Al drove slowly, nodded.

Along the road to Esmeralda, they passed the ruins of what had once been a Mayan sacrificial pool, a dark green, murky, plant-smelling basin, half-filled with water and vines. There were at least eighty species of birds living in the surrounding forests, monkeys, cats, a few families of long-tailed coatimundi. Part of the land was wetlands, marshes filled with cattails, sinkholes from the prints of drinking deer, the occasional big cat, who roamed, looking for prey. The slopes were tangled with vines, hiding the aloes that lived beneath, poking their spiny tendrils upward for the sun's warmth.

Al could not shake the feeling the van was being watched.

Raul had definitely been strange about the truck.

They passed a hillock so denuded of landscape, it could only be coconut disease. The denuded landscape, though only intermittent, was not uncommon. To the Yucatán, in the past years, had come not only coconut disease, but also mango rot, banana blight, palm fungi, strawberry worm. It was said by the locals the beachfront land had been cursed to thwart the *extranjeros*—foreigners—from coming. That only ugly things would grow. Al had to laugh sympathetically. Not that the *extranjeros* would have discriminated between producing

plants and not—bulldozers and earth-movers were just as effective against ugly plants.

"Did you see headlights—or anything—behind us?" he asked Nick.

"Don't tell me you think the old woman's coming after us for more cash?" Nick's grin was a rictus.

For a second, Al saw a woman with long hair. Red nails. But no.

"Man, pot makes me paranoid," Al said.

"Al, my friend, I've never seen you anything except happy. And slightly less happy. It starts to wear on the nerves. Make me wonder if I'm not eating the right breakfast or something."

Al knew exactly what Nick ate for breakfast. A splash of secret Kahlua in the coffee probably wasn't nutritionally optimal.

"Happiness," Al said. "They say it puts hair on your chest."

"And that's why I'm bald." Nick laughed.

And so it would be. The writer would try to hang on to his girl, Karl would try to hang on to his land, Pablo would hang on to his ideas about *la vida pura,* Castillo would watch and wait and sell meat.

Why in the hell did the truck have a satellite hookup? Reporters? That was another choice.

Al looked in the rearview mirror again, seeing nothing and yet unconvinced there was nothing to be seen. Because the writer had finally stopped talking for a minute, was staring out the window with a sleepy, slack expression, things that had been nagging at Al now came to the surface. For instance, why did Raul's wife have a brand-new CD player? Why did the kid have a new bracelet? The TV must have cost almost eight thousand pesos on Mexico's black market.

The pressure began to rise in his chest, beating against his throat, and as they rounded the bend near Rivas Cove, Al let go of the steering wheel, closed his eyes. If the van glided on, that was okay, if it didn't, it would all end now.

"Hey!" The writer grabbed the wheel. "Hey, Al! You're falling asleep."

"Am I? Sorry about that, buddy."

"Want me to drive?"

"Nah, we're almost there."

They'd reached the spot where the grass was short and brown. Locals let their pigs loose among the denuded spots—the pigs, it was believed, could eat the last, parched vestiges of the "wickedness" away—perhaps ingesting the Esmeralda curse. On the other hand, the pig's targeted rooting solved an ancient, troublesome local problem—where to let stock animals feed without recrimination. No one would accuse a pig owner of greed if the pig fed at the "evil" spots. On the other hand, no one would refuse to eat the pig afterward—the Yucatecos were far too practical.

Raul just didn't spend money on gewgaws for his wife and children.

Raul was a practical man.

The sand gave way. Al felt the soft familiar thump of the tires riding the collected leaves and earth. He was about to turn off the engine, unlock the gate, when he noticed Karl, just at the entrance to the lagoon, sitting in the shadows, arms crossed, a grim look on his face.

The unpleasant sensation of ambush ran through him; as he waved to Karl, the hairs rose slowly along the back of his neck.

"Hey old man," he called out to Karl in a friendly tone. "It's late."

Karl stared into the air. "Come here, boy. Leave your friend in the car."

A branch slapped Al against the cheek as he got out of the Jeep, made his way across the sand and soil. His movements seemed to happen in slow motion, his legs icing, heating up, then prickling with every step. Nearing Karl's shadow, he said, "What's all this about?" Karl seemed to be looking directly at the gun against Al's thigh. One of the dogs made a friendly move toward Al, head down, wagging its tail. He bent to pet it, made himself search out its pleasure spots, rubbing behind the ears, along the backbone. At the same time he was conscious of the look on Karl's face: pure animosity.

"Where have you been all night, Al, boy?" Karl said in a deadly calm tone.

"Spying. I told you where we were going." Al matched the tone, ice for ice.

"Where, exactly, son? Map out your movements. And was the boy with you at all times?"

Karl was looking at Al in a way he'd never looked at him before. The gun felt huge against Al's thigh. He had the sensation that he needed to run, but it was no use, with the dogs and the darkness, he had no chance. The air was close and iron-smelling. The fur was soft between his fingers and he concentrated on the softness.

"I was with Raul all night. We took the usual roads. You can check it out. A lot of people were there."

Karl's glare was penetrating as a radiograph. "So you don't know anything about a drawing?"

Al blinked. A word came to him: "Ah."

"A drawing?"

A shrug.

"Look at this, boy." Karl backed away, indicated the little machete scene scratched onto the wall. Three stick figures, two of them exaggeratedly female. The machete floated in midair, poised to strike. To the left, a lady with long hair held out her long fingertip. A series of well-articulated blood drips rained from it. A serpent was wrapped around her outstretched arm.

"Jesus, what's that?" Al's shock was well performed.

Karl considered him for a long time. All at once, his expression turned to sadness. "*Ach,* it's the aphids boy. Trying to scare us." He sucked in air. "They scared Corde. She's half-senseless in there."

Al could not look away from Pablo's handiwork. Underneath it, the footsteps had been carefully brushed away. There were no tire tracks. Nothing. Inside, he was starting to smile. His face remained stony, unreadable.

"What I don't understand is why there are three figures. Not five," Karl said to Al.

Al shrugged. "We knew it was going to get worse. They're trying to make you suspicious. They probably saw me in town with Nick."

Karl continued to regard Al with the boring eyes. Finally he threw up his hands.

"I'm sorry I even questioned you, boy." Karl sighed deeply. "This nonsense can make the sanest man unhinged." He handed Al a paper bag decorated with inked Mayan symbols. Inside the bag was a pair of silver wire eyeglasses. The glass was intact, wrapped in layers of cushioning toilet paper.

"These are the writer's glasses," Al said, confused. "I'm not sure I'm getting this."

"I found them here. Apparently the boy's been making friends. I'm not as sure of him as you are, Alchen."

"Nick?" Al's disbelief went up another notch. It was almost too perfect.

It *was* too perfect. He would never have another life like this one.

"Apparently things are not what they seem with our young friend."

"Wait a minute," Al said. "That couldn't be."

Karl indicated the Jeep with a tired glance. "Either way, he's a danger to us now, and Cordula's not going to let this one go."

"So what should I do with him?" Al asked.

Oh," Sarah cried out, when Nick knocked on the door. She walked back to the bed, sitting under the mosquito netting, poised in a wrinkled white T-shirt, hunched as if she'd been waiting a long time. The lights were dim, the wind generator only working at half power.

"Where have you been? I've been waiting so long. Karl found your—"

"I know, I know," Nick said angrily. "He practically accused me of conspiring with Al, then stomped off muttering. As if Al doesn't do everything for the guy." He sat on the bed, drawing little gulps of air into his chest.

"He found—"

"He 'found' my glasses under the hideous drawing, or at least he *says* he did."

"But where did you lose your glasses?" Sarah was looking at him intently. "You didn't tell me you lost them."

They heard raised German voices next door. Cordula's was louder. The dogs barked and continued to bark for a long time.

"So now you're accusing me, too? Jesus Christ, Sarah. I had other things on my mind than to tell you I lost my glasses on the beach." He looked at her expression of wariness with astonishment. "As if I'd be stupid enough to leave them there—all wrapped up in toilet paper!"

She looked away, listening to the loud voices. "Now we're making them fight. Karl asked me to talk to her, but I really don't know what to say."

She then put her hand carefully on his arm. "She thinks you had something to do with it. You and that cop. She says he left his sign."

"Oh, I get it, Sarah. *You* still think I'm trying to scare you into leaving. You do think I made the ridiculous drawing. That I would actually do something like that to two old people."

Her hand came up in a wild gesture. The gesture did not disallow agreement.

"And of course you told Karl your little theory. You told him what I told you *in confidence* about Pablo 'helping' me. He must have been overjoyed. You did his work for him."

He was throwing clothes into a bag. She watched him with wide eyes.

"Where are you going?"

He smiled at her expression of surprise. "You want me to live a little, get adventurous, well, I'm doing it. I'm going to spend the night out, housemate. And I'm not going to indulge you by telling you you're fat. You looked better with some weight on you, actually."

She opened her mouth, closed it.

"I think I'm going to start doing a lot of things I've never done, like telling you the truth, even if it bores you."

Very clearly they heard the name "Sarah" being shouted. With a German accent, the name sounded like a poison. He walked for the door.

"And by the way, Mexican law says it's illegal for foreigners to own beachfront property. So Karl's going to lose this place quite legally. He doesn't need my help."

"Who told you that? Pablo?" She was looking at Nick warily. "Were you with him tonight?"

"Ambos!" Cordula was shouting. Nick knew that word. It meant "both of them."

Al was not inside his room. Nick knocked twice, then walked in.

The room was bare, spare. A chair, a desk, a bird book, more books: *Introduction to Zen Buddhism, World Religions, Dream Interpretation.*

For a while Nick listened to the Von Tollmans arguing. Sometimes Cordula shouted in English, sometimes Spanish, sometimes German. In any language, Karl was losing.

"Al?"

Nothing.

He walked to the window, found Al's binoculars in a disturbing spot. Holding them to his eyes, standing on top of the chair he found pushed near the window, he trained them on the guestroom. Sarah could be seen quite clearly, checking to see if the

BMW was still there. After checking she sat at the table crying. He was still watching her when Al walked in.

"Nick, Nick, Nick," Al said, shaking his head.

"Tell me the truth. You look at her, don't you?"

"Nick, you're a nutbird." Al laughed. He raised the blond eyebrows. Laughed again. Nick watched him go very calm. "Of course I look at her. I'm stranded out here. Put yourself in my situation."

The room went strange. Nick started to laugh.

"You beat off to her."

"Honestly, not very often."

"What in the world am I supposed to do?" Nick started to laugh. He started to make a move toward Al at the same time. "Beat the shit out of you? Kill you? I mean, practicality dictates I need one goddamn friend tonight. But, gross, man. *Gross.*"

Al regarded him slowly, not making any move, and yet Nick had the feeling he was, in his mind, making one.

"I mean, what am I supposed to do?"

"Why don't you just stop giving a shit, since nothing really happened?" Al actually grinned. He then turned his back on Nick, put his hands up.

"Or you can always shoot me. I'll put my gun here on the bed table. I'll be asleep on the hammock." He walked out of the room.

Nick could not adjust his thinking to Al getting off on Sarah. Al, his friend. No, not friend. His ally. He could not adjust his eyes.

Now Nick stood in the darkness, watching Sarah through the binoculars. She was drawing furiously, eyes furious. She'd given him three minutes of tears, but was already off in Sarahland, drawing. Or no. She was writing something. Probably to Cordula. Almost certainly.

The sea was hitting the shore with huge, cracking sounds. The sounds mirrored the pounding in his chest. He would get no notes of apology from Sarah. He was her chauffeur. Her warm cock. One of her little craft projects. He was see-through, almost delirious. In Los Angeles, she didn't even work for a single company, preferring to be freelance. So many offers, she could pick and choose. The whole time he'd been at *Lucid* magazine working for her, she'd been working for her, too. And now she got to skitter off, skate into the sunset. Everyone needing her.

He watched her seal the note, walk out the door, down the path. Her flesh pulled against her bones.

"Because no one else takes care of them," she'd said. "Because they're helpless."

"Because you have to work harder because your blood isn't the best blood," Phil had said.

When she returned, he watched her behind the glass. The icy, cool aquarium. Being watched. Her logic for leaving Nick was this: *glub, glub, glub.*

He masturbated into his shorts. It was an angry river, a lonely, little swim.

He watched her write another note. Seal it. Put it on the kitchen table. Then she ripped the note in two and trashed it.

Al had the best idea. A train. That was how Al put it. Let them jump on. Jump off. Better yet, don't even let them on the train. Just look at them through the window: imagine. Get off. Zoom.

She was writing again.

He imagined Al, watching her, getting off.

Did he hate Al?

Yes, he did.

Did he want to kill Al?

Fucking ram horn crashing against ram horn.

He laughed until he cried.

He tried to sleep, to imagine himself leaving without Sarah in the morning. He could leave her the car—get on a plane and be back in LA tomorrow.

He should just leave her. Let Phil win. Let Sarah win. Let her starve to death.

And yet there was this love. This need. Even from here he felt it. The solar lights, low on energy, only ran at half power, giving Sarah's room a candlelit, antediluvian appearance.

He watched two clouds join together, separate. He heard Cordula screaming in pain. There was a half-mad machete on the wall, a madness, now. Every last thing was coming unspooled. In a battle zone, there were two guises under which to operate. Camouflage. Aggression. What you do, son, is blend in. Lay low. Then throat, intestine, throat. Don't let them see you coming. Never put yourself in an ambush situation.

"You can rise above your blood.

"She's too good for you, son.

"She's going to leave you for something more interesting."

He tried to believe he was going to fight this and win. Throat, intestine, throat didn't answer the love he felt for Sarah. Not the love. He didn't want to love her. He heard Cordula raging on.

Sarah sat, icily, thinly, behind glass. Karl was circling, circling.

He looked at Al's gun. Fully loaded. Semiautomatic. Small and light and clean. Probably kicked a little, probably felt like a smooth piece of pipe in the hands. Probably felt like Sarah wanted to look.

Phil had kept his own collection of guns in the locked room next to the den. He'd purchased several more for the Y2K onslaught.

"What you need is a small gun so when those damn blacks from the inner city and those damn Mexicans and those damn gooks from China sneak over the lawn, you can surprise them," Phil had said. "Bring 'em on. I hope to God they come."

In the months before Y2K, Phil had suddenly purchased a piece of land in Nevada. There he had waited, hunkering down with his guns, his cases of food. January 15, 2000, he'd returned to his home in Yucca Valley, not ashamed but proud.

"I'm ready for 'em next time, Nicky. They come here and I'll be blowing them back to the ghetto. Let 'em take one step. Just one step over the line."

Nick closed his eyes after studying the gun.

Phil used to study his guns with wide-open eyes. A child's eyes. A drunk child. Thinking. One didn't want to start thinking like Phil. Nick laughed, he paced, he looked at the gun.

He'd avoided the man's thoughts with a special hat. Put his ten-year-old hands physically to his brain, blocking out the thoughts, then wrapping the head in a Met's hat for extra protection. Thoughts could infect; the dirt from Phil's hands might do it. Thoughts of cowardice: The need to scream and run and hide while guns and gooks were shooting.

He had bad blood. Dark blood.

No, he did not.

He looked at the gun again.

"What you don't ever do, son, is let your thoughts take over. You draw a line in your mind, stay on one side of it, and shoot back."

One didn't want to start thinking like Phil. One had to stay on one's own side. The light side.

He switched on Al's lamp. He switched it off again.

On.

Off.

On.

And yet, there was this pressure. This fishbowl. There was this fucking fishbowl with a thousand eyes diminishing you. Nothing in your life went the way you wanted it to. You wrote articles about movie stars, you were an insurance agent, you were a graphic artist, a cop in Mexico.

On one side you were ready to kill.

On.

He picked up the gun, and after a while he picked up the pencil. He waited for a voice to tell him how to start writing the feelings welling up within him, and as the sounds died away, they did. In time there was no sound except the waves, the insects, the pencil clicking hard on the pad.

"You were not in Vietnam. You were an insurance agent. You blushed when real soldiers asked which regiment you were in. You introduced me as your mixed-blood son. You said I was blond when I was born. You were so proud of this fact."

The words about Phil flowed and flowed, mixing with the desire to kill, to annihilate. It was not a book, it was a letter. It didn't matter, it had to come out. Phil had to die and stay dead. Phil didn't get to take Sarah with him. But just maybe he would take Nick. If the writing wasn't good, he'd take Nick. It was now. Die. Semper fi.

One bullet to the brain.

On.

Off.

On.

"You did not die in Vietnam, and I was your son . . ."

The letter went on and on, long after Cordula's voice died down. Many hours passed in an instant, and when the sun came up, Nick was still not ready to sleep.

By early morning he'd put the gun back on Al's table. He'd put his thoughts in order, written twenty-six pages, only this time the writing was good, and his mind was made up, and it was beautiful.

"Nick," Al woke him up softly, sometime around five A.M. Nick jumped, snarled, beat at the air.

"Get up. I've got to talk to you."

"I feel incredible," Nick said to the face of his enemy. They were all enemies now. It was all so fucking *easy.* Pick your flag. Wave it. Stay on your own side. Your side wasn't DNA. It was yours, alone.

Through the course of the night, Nick had figured out everything. He knew exactly how the drawing had appeared so mysteriously on the wall. He knew exactly how it had been done without upsetting the dogs.

"The old man wants to see you." Al pushed him up. "Nick? Are you listening?"

"No," Nick said. "And get your hands off me."

"Wait. Where are you going?"

"I have things to do today," Nick said. He would find the *Let's Go* book, get a haircut, a new legal pad, a set of working pencils. He'd place the desk high, to his liking. It would be a new desk Sarah would buy him. And soon, she would be leaving with him. Cordula would see to that.

"I'm going to have to ask you to remove that hand from my wrist. Unless you have a gay problem." At twenty pages a day, he'd be finished with the biography of his father in two months. Goddamn, he would be free.

"Karl's on the warpath," Al said sleepily. He was laughing.

"Karl," Nick said happily, "is my fucking innkeeper. Karl will take fucking orders until we leave for Vallarta."

Al didn't seem to understand they were leaving, off to a cheap room in Puerta Vallarta with a single clicking ceiling fan and a desk that looked over the water. Al didn't seem to understand the war was over and Nick was free now.

"Buddy, it was Pablo's boys," Al said. Nick imagined Al waving his penis at Sarah. His sad, little flag. "Karl thinks it was you."

"Funnily enough, you're both wrong. And you, Greenley, are an asshole."

They were standing under the eaves. The motionless, humid air hung heavy, like velvet. The trees glowed bright green.

"But matters are under control now," Nick said. God, Phil must have felt good saying the phrase. It shut them all up. It really did. Look at Al.

"If Karl finds out you put Pablo up to it he might—"

"Karl!" Nick laughed. "Karl is going to help me fucking pack."

"Take it easy, writer. We've got to talk this out. Cordula's lost her goose."

"Good," Nick said. "Good man. Good news." Everything was so, so good.

"Your nose is bleeding again."

"Excellent." Nick took off his T-shirt, wiped at his nose. Tipping his head forward, he regarded Al through lowered eyes.

It was all going to blow up in Karl's face. That was the beauty of it. Nick laughed, tasting blood. "There were *no tire tracks.* You said so yourself. Karl would be the type to wrap the lenses in toilet paper. A Germanic touch if I've ever seen one. And only he could have found my glasses. You know it and I do."

Al indicated Nick was losing his mind.

"But Cordula's not going to let Sarah stay now. That's the part Karl forgot. Fucking Karl. Not so Germanic. Not so great. He's going to lose everything. And if he doesn't help me pack, I'll tell Cordula about his little art experience."

He laughed.

"You know, for the first time, I think I could kill someone. But I'll just leave that for your pal Pablo."

"So it *was* you, boy."

The hat appeared and then the face. It was the old man's face that caused Nick to see the red mist. He looked into the misty red teeth, laughed.

"What is it that you've done?" Karl asked.

Nick laughed at the clever rat in front of him. "Hello, rat," he said.

"If you're in some kind of cahoots with that cop, I need to know about it."

"We all know the truth here." Nick shrugged the old man's hand away. "Screw Nick. Take his girl. Do it artfully." The hand came back, stronger. The fingers bit into Nick's shoulder.

"Is it drugs? Did you get involved in all that? Is that why they did this for you?"

"I'm going, I'm going." God, it was beautiful. "In fact, I'm going to tell Sarah all about your artfulness. Your handiness with a spray can."

"Sarah's with my wife, young man. She's not going anywhere."

Nick saw a red face, a red landscape. He saw red clouds running, rushing into a red sky.

"Come on. Let's just stop this now," Al was saying.

"Al, I believe you have chores." Karl didn't loosen his grip. "I believe I will handle this on my own."

To Nick he said, "I want you out. And the girl's not going anywhere near you. You're dangerous."

Nick stopped, slowly revolved until he was facing the old man.

"I'm giving you an hour to be packed and out of here. I should have listened to Corde in the first place." He stared at Nick, unblinking. "An hour, boy. Starting this minute."

" 'Listened to Corde'?" Nick started laughing and choking. "*Lis-*

tened to her? Don't think *Corde* doesn't know what's going on. I heard her."

"Now you have fifty-eight minutes."

"You're not going to get anywhere with Sarah," Nick shouted. "You lecherous old *bastard*. You *prick!* You blonde-worshipping Nazi *freak!*"

"Fifty-seven minutes." Karl nodded to Al, who sighed.

Nick looked at the bright blue eyes, the knowing grimace. All at once he was raising his hand. As it fell across Karl's cheek, the blood drained from the old man's face. He took a step toward Nick, fist clenched.

"You're a maniac, boy. I knew it from the first moment I saw you. And now the girl knows."

"Now, now." Al came between them, pulling Nick away. As Nick was maneuvered backward, he continued to flail and jab. Karl was holding his face where he'd been hit, smiling a strange smile.

"She's too good for you, son," Karl said.

"Nick, get hold of yourself," Al was saying. "This isn't going to help things go your way."

"I'm going to kill you," Nick screamed.

"Fifty-five," Karl calmly said.

As the van advanced through the cleared space, Nick saw a huge, glowing funnel. Upon closer inspection it proved to be a yellow school bus, ancient, with all the air missing from its tires, tinfoil in the windows. A wash line was heavy with piled clothing, mostly male underwear and socks. The clothing hadn't been washed as much as dipped in dirty water, then flung, as if from a great distance, at the line.

"This is it," Al Greenley said. "Unless you want to go up to Chetumal, grab a hotel room."

"I'm not going anywhere." Nick yawned ferociously. "As soon as

I get some sleep, I'm going straight back to the rancho. I'll bring Pablo with me. We'll see how calm the guy is then."

"All right. But I'm not sure how long it's going to take for me to find Pablo. I've got to get back to the rancho first, see what's happening there."

Nick yawned again. The muscles in his jaw hurt. He was still in shock from Sarah's betrayal. The way she'd stayed far away from him, behind Karl. The way Cordula had been standing behind the both of them, saying nothing.

"Don't look at me like that!"

Phil had looked at him, exactly, like that.

"Cordula, come on, now!" Nick had shouted. "You know he just wants to fuck her.

"Sarah, Christ! He doesn't *need* you." Al had had to stop Nick from seizing Sarah by the hair.

"Oh, my God, Nick, you have gone crazy. You're going to hit *me?* Oh, my God. You told Pablo to *scare* the Von Tollmans? And you hit Karl?"

When they'd reached the BMW, it was dead again. Al had forced Nick to put his things into the van, while Sarah, Karl, and Cordula looked on. Every so often Nick made a lunge toward Karl, Al would sigh, stop him quite easily. Once or twice Nick's blows had fallen on Al's arms and Sarah would look at Cordula nervously.

"He just wants *her,* Cordula! The man's scum. He wants her. He'll toss you out, too. He doesn't want you anymore."

Cordula had put her fingers in her ears. Sarah had turned to her, whispering, patting her hand. Cordula had looked at Sarah with purest hate.

While Karl stood, arms around both of them, Nick had made one last lunge. The rifle. He could do it now. If only he could get his fingers on Karl's rifle. Al had pinned his arms gently, walked him to the passenger side of the van.

"Don't make it worse," Al had said close to Nick's ear.

"You're dead," Nick had repeated to Karl.

And now they were at Chaz's lab. Here Nick would have to stay until Al could tow the BMW to town, locate Pablo, come back for Nick. From Pablo, Nick would secure a gun.

"Al, give me your gun again," he said now.

"Why don't you just keep your voice down?" Al said.

"This is *bullshit.* He thinks he's going to have them *both.*"

"Just get some sleep, and soon you'll be back with her. I'm going to help you, buddy. Just not the way you want."

"I don't believe you." Nick yawned again. He didn't know what to believe. His knuckles crackled and dragged. "Wanker."

"You're going to have to calm down. Chaz isn't going to let you stay in this condition. And Karl's going to be looking for you in town, so you can't go there. Your thinking is faulty, my man."

Nick took a deep breath. The corroded bus, the tinfoil antennae on the broken radio, the flapping, wet socks, yellowed shirts, dripping onto the hood of a beat-up Chevy Nova, seemed the very pinnacle of all his amalgamated fears.

"Why should I trust you? Wanking off to my girl?"

"Everyone loves a handyman." Al laughed.

"You're an asshole."

"It was just a wank." Al appeared to regard Nick with extreme mirth. "Or two."

"Fuck you."

Al's grin widened. "Okay, shut up. I'm about to blow your mind."

"Ha." Nick was laughing and laughing, sick.

"*I* made that drawing, buddy. Because me and Pablo want Karl out," Al said. "We want the land. We've been working on it a long time, buddy." He laughed at Nick's expression. "Don't worry. Nothing's going to happen to your girl. She'll be on her merry way to LA in no time. We don't want her there when the shit goes down.

"I told you to be patient, man," he then said. "But you had to go and fuck things up. Yanquis, man! They never think."

Nick's face almost split with the force of his yawn. He was looking into a grin, a hood of grinning bone.

"It's you. It's been you all along?"

"What did I tell you? Esmeralda has its secrets. Now you just lay low, let it all happen for you. And let's not be talking about guns." He winked. "Bad karma, man. If you believe in that stuff."

Hey," Al called out in a loud voice. "Buddy, Chaz, it's me. Hey. It's Al!"

The radio was abruptly shut off. It took a long time before Chaz came out. He stood in the doorway, enormously tall, darkly tanned, a beard reaching to his chest. He wore a yellow T-shirt and no pants.

"Fucking dude. Fucking Al! And your sidekick, too."

Nick was beginning to see dark spots in front of his eyes. His eyes opened feverishly as he yawned. What he wanted was for the man to put on some pants.

"Hey there," Nick's voice cracked through his yawn. He looked at Al with new fear. Felt a shiver on the back of his neck.

"Cool, man," Chaz said to Nick. "A fucking striped shirt! Like a boat man." He laughed uproariously. "I'm going to get me a boat. Drive it out into the ocean and keep fucking going."

"This man needs some sleep," Al said, winking at Nick. Nick pretended calm. "He's had kind of a rough one."

"My casa is yours," Chaz said. He was still laughing in wonder at Nick's shirt.

Inside, the bus was strewn with beer bottles, bits of rag, old clothes, light boxes, many, many potted plants. All the seats had been removed to facilitate a living space. There was a sink where the glove box might have been, lying inside it a sort of showerhead device, a bowl, and a rusty razor. The bathroom, no bigger than a coffin, was covered by a flowered shower curtain. Plywood was tacked up over the windows, a single oil lamp burned on a makeshift table. Crates of seeds and soil were piled high against most of the walls. The sweetish smell of marijuana hung heavily in the air.

"Boat Man, siddown. Al, you, too."

Chaz hopped to his other foot, which was curiously small, encased in an earthy, furred Birkenstock. His skin had burnt and peeled so many times it had the texture and color of clabbered snakeskin. "Have a morning beer. Sets the day off just right."

"I'm going to have to take off, but you take care of my buddy here." After repeating an abridged version of the story to Chaz, Al shrugged. "So he's got to have a place to cool his heels. But Karl can't know he's here. And he can't leave."

"Weird vibes," Chaz said, disturbed. "Just walking out of the vines like that. That can fuck with a man's mind."

"Vibes are what you make 'em," Al pointed out amiably. "And now I've got to go. Before Pablo comes and talks a mile a minute."

"So you're in on it, too," Nick said. Of course.

"Shh." Al made a displeased face. "No business, now. Don't think, buddy. Sleep. And don't be getting any thoughts about going back to the rancho. Your gal's going to be just fine. If you go, it'll just fuck things up for all of us."

"Ah, Boat Man's not going anywhere! We'll have a grand old time, won't we, Nick?" Chaz hopped around again. Nick began to see the man's smile wasn't friendly as much as automatic, possibly neurotic. There was some type of amphetamine involved.

"You like plants?"

Nick, unsure how to address a man wearing no pants, yawned again. In every corner were petri dishes, tubs of water, jars and jars of green, spreading goo. The smell was of swamp, sweetness, wet fur.

"Sorry about the mess, the maid doesn't clean until—hell—until

I finally marry her. Which will be"—Chaz consulted his nonexistent watch—"approximately never."

"He really needs some sleep," Al said. "So whatever you can do to help him out."

"The doctor is in, man."

Chaz laughed and laughed.

Red

Jesus. The Lord Jesus. Al stood near the church in the middle of Esmeralda Town, felt the nearby rustle of wings.

That was a close one. That was a bug.

Many hours had passed since Al had dropped the writer at Chaz's place. Many odd little moments Al had to consider from many angles. He stood under the statue of Jesus, a hugely unfortunately block-jawed rendering, smiling and shivering while going over each of the variables that had come to play in the last four hours. He was only a little alarmed by the sounds coming out of his mouth: In Mexico it was quite permissible to talk to religious statues. An old woman smiled at him approvingly through ancient teeth. He looked at the begging-bowl eyes on the statue and laughed.

He was about to be very afraid.

There had been cool, sterile silence at the rancho when Al returned for the BMW. The water had been flat, Day-Glo green, waveless, when he had taken a quick swim to wash the writer's sweat off of himself. Cordula, standing in the window, had waved to him with a choppy little motion. She was not talking to the old man. The girl was crying and pacing in front of her own window. Then all at once, she'd come to the beach, catching Al off guard.

"Whatever you did to Nick, you started this," she'd said, sticking her beak in his face, waving her talons for emphasis. "I've already talked to Karl—told him exactly what I think of you."

"Did you now?" He'd toweled off, watching Cordula watch the two of them.

"I know you helped him make that drawing. And Karl will find out sooner or later."

It had been a struggle not to grab her then and there, to drag her to the dim, hidden, muffled bushes where jungle struggles rightfully should take place. Her hair, floating as it did in the hot wind, had been a most beautiful sight, and he'd watched it throughout the exchange. She'd braided a single, thick piece so that it might fall over her crane-eye.

He'd touched the piece of hair ever so softly. "You're in a tizzy, little bird."

"Fuck you, Al. You psycho."

"If you want to fuck—sure. Since you mentioned it."

That's when she'd hit him, coming from the side, pounding and pounding, scraping her nails against his neck. As he'd withstood the assault, the instinct to take her little collarbone, to crush it, to feel the bird heart beating madly, to feel the heart and squeeze, had been so palpable. He crushed her to his chest, then pushed her away. She'd come back at him, fists bared, spitting and screeching.

A tall girl, he found out too late, could spit in one's eye.

"You. Bastard."

That's when Karl had come, taken her away. "Enough of this nonsense, girl! We've had enough dramatics here for one day!"

Cordula had continued to watch through the window.

Karl had apologized to Al many times for the bird's behavior. Cordula, of course, had taken Al's side in the matter.

"I want that girl gone from my home," she'd screamed from her perch. "She makes every man crazy."

"It's either her or me," she'd screamed.

"The boy was right," she'd told Al in a whisper, after Karl went to talk to Sarah, and Cordula had come to the beach to commiserate with Al. "My husband is in love with her. Maybe Karl did make the drawing."

"Run away with me," Al had said.

Cordula's laughter had been sad, wild, nearly crazed.

"But where would we go? An old woman like me?" Cordula had said.

"Not so old," Al had said.

Jesus. The statue wasn't weeping. It was merely a rivulet of bird droppings. Merely a birdy joke. A tern flapped its wings, settling in on the Christ head, lifting off again. Christ. What Al wanted to do was fly, lift up his wings and leave Esmeralda. He could get in the van, turn on the radio, keep going.

What were the birds telling him?

God, he was tired. So tired.

Though Al had gone through the trouble of hitching the BMW to the van's tow bar, once he'd gotten to town, he'd merely popped the spark plug back in, and the machine ran fine. Even now it was parked at the *mecánico,* gathering dust.

"Al, my friend, the yanqui's car is the least of your problems," he'd been told.

"Al, don't turn around," the *mecánico* had then said.

It had been right there, at the *mecánico,* where he'd been approached by the strange man in Escada sunglasses, the starched, white guayabera shirt. Castillo wanted to see him at his first convenience, he'd been told. Later he'd been told Pablo had been looking for him, too. Pablo, it was said, looked quite frightened.

"If something ever happens to me, you just grab your boss and go far away," Pablo had told Al once, when Al had been drinking with him. Pablo had laughed and laughed, disbelieving the day would ever come.

"I would be pleased to meet Señor Castillo," Al had said into the dark glasses.

"At your very, very earliest convenience," the stranger had said.

He'd been sucking on a pink, noisy mint. His accent was northern, his breath minty.

Al looked into the eyes of Jesus. "Jesus," he said.

The town of Esmeralda was stilled, hot, coiled. No one had seen Pablo all afternoon. At the *mecánico* he'd noticed the usual sounds of horns, bells, radios, firecrackers, shouting matches, were absent. The usual soccer field full of children was empty, all were inside, silent. Man, the air. It was in the air. Al wished he was in the air. The BMW had air brakes, air bags; driving the thing was like flying in air. Al could take the BMW, disappear into Belize. The car, parted out, could bring him thirty grand. Thirty grand could bring him a year, two years maybe.

For a moment he believed it was even possible.

"At once, actually," the guayabera had said. "If you would be so kind."

The tone of voice told Al Castillo would never let him fly; Al wouldn't even make it to the border. As he considered his options, dowdy, thick-ankled housewives crossed the street, carrying suspicious jute bags tight to their chests. Palms brushed against the side of a building. Al started to move, knowing Castillo was somewhere, somehow watching him.

As the bird flew, Castillo was probably less than a second away.

The boys in the *carnicería* were busy with a raucous game that seemed to involve strings of fat, freshly prised from the gray pig carcasses that hung on hooks over the door. The strings were hurled so that they landed in humorous positions on the opposing boy: gristle hung from the brim of the smaller one's hat, from the chin of the larger.

The young men wore butcher's smocks. On closer inspection Al saw what was odd about the costumes; they were made of orange, reflective material—stolen, no doubt from a road work crew.

Noticing Al, the boy said, *"Sí, señor,"* in an unaccountably grave voice.

"I'm here to talk to your uncle," Al said.

"Sí, señor," the boy said.

The string of fat wiggled as he nodded.

Al's throat bobbed up and down.

As Al had waited to talk to Castillo, an unseen order was given. Nearby shops were closed with hushed keys, plastic tarpaulins slid noiselessly off wooden structures, soft radios switched off, ending the barely discernible mush of marimba, *norteña,* salsa, jazz, pop. People began to slink out of every nearby doorway, not looking at Al, not looking at anything except the dusty horizon. The only sound came from the water truck that belched black smoke as it began its rounds. To alert possible customers it dragged a noisy burden of shaved metal rods on the pavement—the sound was of a million glasses breaking at once. Not a single customer waved it down. Soon enough a young boy came running to the truck, had a word with the driver. The truck melted away soundlessly.

"Ah, *qué onda,* my friend?" the quiet voice then said. "I've been watching you talk to our great shepherd, the Lord Jesus Christ."

"Amen," Al said, without irony.

They went through the pleasantries automatically. Mayor Castillo's family was fine. Al was fine. The weather was very, very fine. For a time, they sat in the dusky silence.

"It pleases me, as mayor, that our fine town will soon be pleasant. For too long, I've watched our more fortunate towns in Mexico grow as they should."

Al concurred that pleasure was a rare thing, indeed. He watched and waited.

"I must ask you if you've seen my brother," the fat man then said, without changing his polite tone. "Have you been seeing him, Mr. Greenley?"

"Why, I saw him just a few days ago. Two to be exact."

"What I'm going to need is everything he told you." Castillo's ancient lizard eyes closed. He seemed to be sucking Al's air.

For a long time they talked quietly, Al in the smaller chair, Castillo in the larger, comfortable one. When it was over, Al bowed his head and rose. It had been said, without quite saying it, that Pablo was now out of the picture, and that the picture had become quite inelegant, indeed. It had been decided, without quite putting it into words, that Al was going nowhere. That the writer was in for some wild times, and that Al, himself, would be held responsible for how an American writer held up under pressure. Beyond those unsaid facts, it was all still a mystery.

For a while they spoke of the mysteries of the gods. The mystery of Americans. Of nations. Castillo was looking more and more bored.

"And here is my dear nephew with your keys," he finally said. "I thank you for lending them to me while we've had our pleasant conversation."

"What a fortunate man you are to own a key shop," Al replied. They spoke of fortune. Al was about to make a fortune. A small one, but then Al was not a man who wanted for much. Pablo's error had been wanting too much.

"Yes, I find Esmeralda has been good to me," Castillo said, yawning.

"And to me."

"Ah, yes." Castillo slapped his forehead. "I almost forgot. The most important thing! Let us speak a little more, my friend."

Have a seat then, Nicky boy. Smoke a 'jay.' Run up an appetite." Chaz swept a pile of papers off the makeshift couch. Green geckos made screeching, metallic sounds as they moved across the wall in aqueous streaks. Nick watched a gecko stalk a moth, back and forth, in a comical, cartoonish display of patience.

"The lizards got their job in life. Cross-pollination, man. Pollen travels on their legs, man. Unbelievable." Chaz hopped again from leg to leg. T-shirts and women's dresses taped to the ceiling functioned as a room divider.

"We all got our jobs in life." He winked at Nick.

The gecko snapped. There was no more moth. What Nick needed to do was think.

"So you just tell doc here what seems to be the problem." He peered at Nick through a hole formed with his fist. Nick guessed he meant to simulate a doctor's scope. "Let's see. Crusty nose? Eczema? Funky lips? That's got to be connected to the optic artery." He curled the hole tighter. "Not good, man. Not at all."

"Maybe I just need some sleep," Nick said. As he planned ways of sneaking out of Chaz's presence, he looked at the pale bands of skin that denoted Chaz's daily wearing of flip-flops. The grime between the man's toes seemed built-in. The feet were enormous.

It was the forearms, however, that made him sit still.

"Nah. I'm going to come up with something righteous for you. Some protein binders—some afx accelerators. Something to soothe your head."

Nick nodded. "Sleep is more what I'm thinking," he repeated.

Chaz began to search intently through a sheaf of moldy papers. Still, he never seemed to leave Nick's line of vision.

"Ah, the recipe," he said after a while.

Nick was holding himself erect with a hand. Too many thoughts were swirling at once. What he needed to do was *think*. Think of the book, not of Sarah, or Karl. Al had given his word no one would get hurt. Sarah would be on her way to LA in no time.

There *would* be a book. It had been *pouring* out of him.

"Nah. Nah. Don't get up, Boat Man," Chaz called out merrily.

Thinking of Al, Nick felt the sensation of pinwheels, of caverns leading to more and darker caverns. He had to not let his mind wander off into certain directions because Al had promised the plans had been in place for a long time now: Sarah would be fine. Exactly *how* would Sarah be fine? Nick had Sarah's passport in his backpack, and besides, she was delusional. He had to think. He was about to be asleep.

For a while Chaz grabbed handfuls of dried herbs and sticks and threw them into a blender along with generous shakes of gin and vodka. As he strained the mess through a rusty spaghetti strainer, he kept nodding and modulating his facial expression as if Nick were talking and he, Chaz, responding. It dawned on Nick there was a full conversation going on in the man's head.

"So, should I just crash out here, then?"

Nick, starting to sweat in the closely confined bus, wiped at his brow. Chaz looked on, amused and jittery by Nick's every gesture. The antidote, Nick found, was to keep his hands still. The stillness seemed to comfort Chaz, who jumped every time Nick moved.

"Now the ice, pal. I'll fix you right up, man. Chaz's morning blend is righteous." While he whirred the ice, he handed Nick a thick booklet that seemed to contain drawings, recipes, and notes in handwriting so small and slanted it was impossible to discern. "That's the top-secret fungus papers. That's why they're looking for me in *el Norte*. Boy would Fish and Game love to get their hands on that shit! But it's all in code, man." He snatched the pad away. "No offense, but you never know. Who's looking. FAGs are everywhere."

Al and Pablo. Pablo and Al. Sarah. Nick shivered involuntarily.

"Now you just drink up, now."

Nick shouldn't be worried. He should be patient. He had twenty good pages in the backpack. Sure, it was just a letter now, but twenty good pages was more good pages than he'd ever had in his life. Twenty good talismans. Things could not go wrong now. Soon he'd be on his way home.

"Drink it." A measure of affability dropped from the affable voice. "You're about to hurt my feelings."

The taste was not so bad. What was bad was the way it had been handed to him. Chaz had stuck the jelly jar in his hands, hovered over him with the enormous face.

"You know what happened to Wee Willie Winkie, don't ya, Boat Man?"

"Uh. He slept?" Nick knew there was something wrong with the daiquiri. He knew it, even as he chugged.

"Nope. He drank." Nick heard the whirr of the blender. Crunchy, icy, delicious sounds ensued.

"You know, I'm not thirsty," Nick said. "Funny enough, I just have no appetite."

"Gong!" Chaz flicked Nick on the head. "That's not the right answer."

Under Chaz's insistent gaze, Nick took another sip from the sloshing jelly jar. Pinching his lips to give the liquid little chance to enter, he feigned more sipping. The aroma of anise, yarrow, something flowery, chalky, pleasantly bitter, rose to his nose. Because Chaz had settled beside him, thumping his head, he took another, larger sip. In time, he'd drunk all of it.

"Feeling anything?" Chaz guffawed.

"I feel . . . pretty strange actually."

Actually, he felt the walls moving.

"That's my insomnia special," Chaz said. "Man, FAG would kill for it. But that's another story."

And now the walls had disappeared entirely. There was no need for walls. Nick was on a river. It was moving downward and it was safe.

"Tok to me," Chaz was saying. "Tok! Tok!"

Very softly Nick heard himself say, "Ah." He really had no idea what Chaz was talking about, but it was beautiful. He called out to Chaz from the river. His voice was watery. Chaz was vapor, lace, a lace mantle of silver light. Whatever it was the man was trying to communicate fractured into dots of sparkly light. A surge of bright light, energy, nothingness.

"Nik? Nik. Nik. Nik."

The voice came from a long way off now. The river was metallic. Nick was floating freely on it, but the slightest veering off course and he would fall. Below the surface there were sharp stones, black throbbing holes. The careful modulation of Nick's voice controlled the holes.

"Ah," he said again.

He was transported over millions of miles, moving along as if in a suction cell. It would be perfectly pleasant were he not so cold. He had to stay away from the holes. Because in them were knives, machetes, ambush mechanisms.

"Kreezy."

Up close the face bending toward him was quite hairy. Like insect fur. Nick had a sudden image of the face on a trapdoor spider's body. There were spiders in the river. He started to laugh. When the face came down with its pointy beard, he felt the razor-sharp hairs touch him. The mandible.

"No."

"And he's out," the spider said.

The tears falling down Nick's face had nothing to do with him. They must have come from the river. He wanted to explain this strange phenomenon, but instead only wiggled his head from side to side.

"Shit, Boat Man, we need music!"

The music was soft, generous, voluptuary. Nick threw his head back, letting the silkiness descend. As it did, the river somehow emptied into the ocean; the current was pushing him farther and farther away. He tried to explain that the world was too far away, he could not come back.

"Fucking *norteñas.* Gotta love it!"

"Sarah, I'm sorry." Nick could not help her. Ah, but no. He was in something else—not a world. He knew in a flash that the harder his efforts to get back to his known life, the farther it would slide from him. He was entering the vastness of the ocean alone and it was unbearable. He grabbed out for the rope, held on, sobbing.

"Let go of my fucking beard, Boat Man! I'm not your fucking girlfriend. Jesus! Does your girlfriend have a beard?"

He dreamt of doors opening and closing, water spilling in. A bright splash of blood. The carved figures etched into Pablo's knife animated themselves and began hopping around. The BMW was approaching the Gasthaus Esmeralda, and Sarah was smiling. The walls started closing in. The trapdoors clapped open and shut.

"I'm sorry, Sarah. I did not know."

From somewhere in his dream, he heard two male voices talking and laughing. The dream incorporated the voices so that he, himself, was talking. He was talking to Phil over the whirr of a blender.

"So you lost her? Lost her to an old man?" Phil was laughing. They were in Nick's long-ago bedroom, Nick's face being pushed into the carpet. The blender was actually a saw, Nick noticed as he started to scream.

"You want to die for her? For *her,* but not your own country?"

He was flailing his arms to no good purpose, Phil was too big, too angry, too drunk. Phil did not understand. There was going to be a game of Vietnam and Nick had to run. Or hide. The sky opened and the rain fell down. His nose broke, and Phil kept pushing. The carpet was gooey, moldy. He breathed in great quantities of swamp.

"Fucking son. Run, run, run. Goddamn you shame me."

"Fucking Nicky. Run. You're the gook. Why? Because you're the one with bad blood."

Phil was suddenly gone, and then Nick was running, alongside Al Greenley. They were hunting. They were soldiers.

"Wait! I don't want to do this," he was crying out. There was a gun in his hand, a swamp smell.

He didn't want to kill anything in this murky light because that thing might turn out to be Sarah.

But he had to kill something, because if he didn't, it would kill him first.

"Finalmente! El huevón!"

Nick was fighting his way from deep under the sea. When he opened his eyes, the danger had passed, everything swam, blue and beautiful. If he could just shake the water from his skin, he would emerge. He had to break the surface. They might still be waiting, anywhere.

"Ya sí levantó, el yanqui."

"You do it, woman. He was trying to kiss me. And Chaz don't swing that way."

As Nick came to the light, he reached out. The face was female. She had lazy, black eyes, deep lines around her mouth, lank black hair coiled in several rubber bands. To no good effect, she wore a shimmery blue skirt, a T-shirt, and tennis shoes. The overall effect of the shape of her body was a football resting atop a sack of potatoes.

Nick could not stop blinking.

"Ya, ya, ya, levántaste," the football said. She laughed.

"Hey," Nick said, after a time. He wasn't sure if the word had actually formed, or if it remained a bubble in the air overhead. It must have been spoken because the woman nodded curtly. If only she would stop shaking him, and he could go back to sleep. She was *hurting* him.

"Hey. No. Don't."

"Ah! You're finally up! You slept like a beached whale, man!" A bearded sea creature came into view. A subterranean discomfort rose in Nick. It was all coming back, soon enough. Chaz. The drink. He closed his eyes.

"None of that, none of that!" Chaz said, slapping Nick's face to rouse him. "This here's my maid. She says howdee-do and la-di-da. Hope you enjoyed your Ipazine trip."

If it was possible, Chaz was even more animated now. Nick watched distantly as he bent to a table, sucked up a line.

"What time is it?"

"Pacific Standard Time is"—Chaz beat at his chest happily—"five o' fucking clock."

Five? Nick, even through his haze, knew it couldn't possibly be true that he'd slept for eight hours. He started to protest.

"But time has no meaning. Time's a man-made crock. If you think about it, which I *do.* Which is the point of Ipazine, man."

Nick began to think about it, drift off again, but the woman shook him roughly. He grimaced up at her. "Um. Is Al here? Pablo?"

"That friend of ours is pissing me off, man. He knows we've got a party tonight." Chaz sucked another line of coke with a flourish. "He knows he's on for it. Fucking Al."

Nick sank farther into the pillow. Crumbs and sticky things adhered to his face.

"Get up! Get up!" Chaz did a little dance over Nick's head. "You're doing the Ipazine shuffle, man, but you've got to come back to the land of the living." Nick considered what the Ipazine shuffle might be, and all at once his heart began to beat too fast.

"What was in that . . . drink?"

"Man, how many times can I tell you? Ipazine, *toloache,* bitter herbs. A little rough with the smooth. But you've got to get *up, up, up.*"

Nick shivered, icy and hot. He was aware of being more confused than he'd ever been in his life. But Chaz kept yammering away.

"I told Ava here about your lady friend. She says to take green-colored salt and vinegar and splash it on the front of the woman's door. Then she'll get sick. After she vomits six times she'll come back to you." Chaz was raising and lowering the blind on the window, frowning and smiling in turn. "Ava's a *bruja.* They're all witches here, man."

"I don't understand. You haven't heard from Al?" Nick said. "Pablo hasn't come?"

"You think you've got a gal, but what you've got is a witch. Take one of Ava's *limpias,* man." Chaz peered through the blinds again, twitching. "Twenty pesos, you can't beat it. And don't worry about the dark energies—the egg gets fed to the dog outside, so the shit gets trapped in him."

Nick nodded as if he understood what the guy was talking about. His ears rang steadily. The feeling, at least, was coming back to his limbs. In a few more minutes he would rise, run. Suddenly Chaz jumped up, flailing his arms.

"Al better get his *ass* over here. He's the *cabrón*. He can't be doing this shit, Boat Man. Not tonight. You got to tell me where he *is*."

"I don't know." Nick had a wholly unpleasant sensation things were about to get worse. Every time he looked at Chaz, the sensation grew.

"I don't like this, man. Not at all." The blinds got caught in Ava's long hair, came crashing to the floor. Chaz screamed, then laughed, then began to hang the things again.

"The van, man. He's driving it. He better be. The Pontiac's low on gas. The Pontiac's not a *cabrón* fucking vehicle."

Chaz was now wiping the blinds with clumps of Ava's hair. She was staring sullenly ahead. All at once, Chaz loomed over him.

"Take a line, man. Get up."

"No." Nick looked at the line of cocaine as if it were a serpent. "Thanks."

"I'm going to have to insist you take a line." Chaz pointed at Nick, who blinked. To be forced into taking an unwanted drug made no sense. That is, he could find no context in which to believe it might be happening. And yet it had already happened.

Chaz grabbed the back of Nick's head in a friendly bear lock. "Do it. Because if Al doesn't get here, I guess you'll have to be the *cabrón*. You're white enough."

Nick continued to look at the cocaine with disbelief. Chaz forced his head downward.

Very carefully, so as not to breathe on the weightless powder, Nick spoke through the side of his mouth, "Let's just wait for Al." He tried to smile reasonably. "You heard Al—he's coming with my car. Me and Pablo are going to—"

"Boat Man, you just shut up now. Take a fucking line because it might be you and me. Me and you. Sailing off to Cashlandia." Chaz laughed, paced some more. "The place where South and North converge. Dig it." Al consulted his wrist. "Dig it. The convergence. Now don't make me hurt you."

It was a funny thing, Al was thinking, that the writer was in the thick of a writerly journey now, and Pablo was probably dead, nothing too dramatic, nothing worth writing about—shot twice in the abdomen from what he could assume, then dragged off to the boat, where he'd be dumped into the sea, over by Mantel Reef. *"Mantel"* meaning tablecloth, because the reef was shallow and flat there, and a favorite feeding ground for sharks. Lots of meat. For a while. Then a clean tablecloth again.

That was it. Man, that was it. Castillo resembled a *buzzard.*

Castillo hadn't used the word "dead," but then a buzzard wouldn't. Castillo had used the word "unfortunate," as in "My unfortunate brother. He was never a happy man."

Al felt spooked when imagining the look of surprise in Pablo's eyes—Pablo would have had time to guess what was happening long before it did. He felt sad for the image, yet not the man, for Pablo had it coming ever since he'd gone against Castillo's wishes, ordered the gelignite. Though it surprised Al to learn Castillo had taken the heavy step of killing his own brother, he shouldn't really be startled at all.

"Piquant." He thought of the writer. "Harsh. Spicy."

Killing one's own family would only cause sleepless nights if a man believed in karma, which Al didn't think Castillo did. Castillo was a Jesus man. Sins could be confessed, wiped clean. *Mantel.*

A much buggier way to go.

"How do you find the meat?" Castillo had said. They'd eaten from a clean, white tablecloth. They'd eaten small squares of sausage while they spoke of Al's future.

Every hair on Al's neck had stood up when Castillo laughed and chewed.

"To put things into the simplest possible sense, your future, my young friend, is up to me. And I find myself in need of a good man."

Al banged his fist against the dashboard until it hurt, the pain temporarily taking away his sense of uneasiness. He was now in the van, and he wondered if he might pass the writer. Nah. It was too early. At least the writer knew how to shoot. He'd meant for the writer to get to know Chaz a little, to be eased into the man's sense of humor. He'd meant for Nick to enjoy the many facets of Chaz before the night got started, but when they'd arrived Chaz was all coked up, and Chaz, in his state, had a tendency toward seeing bad signs and omens, so Al had paid Chaz for the Ipazine, and split.

He banged his fist again. Castillo had indicated the wet move still on, the kid was perfect, Al had done well, and if Al kept doing well, there would be a longtime friendship. The hotels would come, and the drugs would *still* run. A little farther south. Would Al enjoy to move south?

And how did Al enjoy the meat? Castillo, himself, enjoyed meat grilled simply. Salt, maybe.

"I like it here in Esmeralda," Al had said. "Actually."

"I, myself, enjoy the southerly regions," Castillo had said, moving a little closer. "Though, sadly, as *diputado* of a growing town, I cannot plan on spending much time there. A man such as yourself, a non-Mexican man, might consider a move. I would consider it a personal favor."

Al stared at the wedge of sea coming up in the distance, felt the pressure begin to build, crush him. It was all happening too fast, and he, Al, had been caught unaware, flapping, naked, snared. There were two kinds of gliding—and he was in the middle of the bad kind, the uncontrolled kind, where the slightest current of air might knock him senseless.

Goddamnit, the man was a bug.

"When the time is right for you to leave your job with our German friends, I will provide you with a new job," Castillo had told him, "As it pleases me."

Al did not want to be muling Castillo's shit for the next ten years. He did not want to work and work and then be set up for a giant sting. He just did not want traps and cages and handcuffs. He turned on the van's radio, loud.

"The problem with your staying in Esmeralda is that it's unfeasible after your close acquaintance with my brother," Castillo had said. "And you would find it a very changed town. Pleasantly changed, and yet, not for you."

Al swerved to miss a strutting gull walking on the side of the road. He then consulted the sky—counted the gulls overhead, five—and watched one as it dove, headlong, into the sea. He pulled over, watching the errant gull stagger across the sand, its fat, unsteady body so unsuited to walking. He blew the horn suddenly, just to see it take off again.

He felt better.

It could be assumed Raul and not Castillo's new guayabera friend would be handling the move tonight for Castillo. He shivered, thinking of the truck he'd seen again in town today, parked by the church. The truck was almost certainly not a hotel truck. The guayabera man had crossed his legs at the ankles. He'd been leaning up against the truck's bumper.

The very constellation of birds above him now made him even more wary. It made no sense for Castillo to invite hotels to Esmeralda during a drop week. But with Castillo, anything could happen. The man was a bug.

Bad luck for Nick then, that someone new, not Pablo, would be at the airport, and under a new person the men would get paranoid and confused and twitchy. Al sighed, regretting the sting was almost certainly in place, and that Nick was their man. He was certain Castillo had something going after all—maybe they'd arranged to throw the Americans a little sacrificial bone—a little load of coke that would make the folks in the DEA happy. Had to keep those sacrificial bones coming to appease the DEA gods. It was almost Toltec.

"And now I'm going to need to borrow your set of keys,"

Castillo had said. "But I assure you, our German friends are quite safe now that they're dealing with a reasonable man."

The offer the Von Tollmans could not refuse would take place at a time of Castillo's choosing. Of course, Castillo hadn't used a mafioso term, he'd used the scholarly phrase, "Mexican patrimony." He'd thanked Al quite effusively for the keys.

"And of course it would be very stupid to mention our wonderful conversation to your friend Karl. There is absolutely no need to upset our German friends now. But I don't want that young friend of yours to enter the property again, upset our German friends further, and I'm entrusting that responsibility to you. And I am giving you a week to clear the Playa Esmeralda of any unwanted guests." He'd smiled, offered Al another slice of sausage. "The lovely, unfortunate American girl, for instance. I'd consider it a favor to me to find her gone."

Jesus, the guy was elegant. For a fat man, he knew how to glide.

"You might not understand, but you don't need to understand. After all, my friend, we are in Mexico, home of my people. But what I'm going to need is a good, calm handyman. A nice, calming influence on the rancho for now. What I'm saying is that I know about the stupid drawing my unfortunate brother made on the wall last night." Castillo had shaken his jowls disapprovingly. "And the rather inelegant plans he had for them later this week. I want our German friends to feel comfortable in their home. I want the transaction to be a remunerative, fair one for them when it takes place. One all sides can be proud of."

What he wanted was absolutely no trouble. No blood. Nothing the American hotels could get nervous over. Nothing even faintly reminiscent of stink.

Goddamn, the guy was a *bug.*

Al now imagined the writer's eyes bugging out—the way they would appear when the sting happened. "I did not do this," the writer would say in that staunch, correct way of his, a hundred kilos in the trunk. If the writer panicked and started to name names, he would probably be involved in something fairly gruesome as the night got longer, and the DEA handed him off to the Mexican authorities.

Al drove onward, upward.

He was bugging, bad.

Then again, the world was not of Al's making, not of Al's design, and his screaming and hitting the dashboard would do little to change it. He checked the rearview mirror, and was certain he was being watched, followed, even if he could see nothing.

Karl, on the other hand, had no perspective. Karl would never go quietly, no matter the sum offered by Castillo. Karl would scream and kick, face the night of the long knives. He would face Castillo down, and Al knew the knives would come out if they had to, quickly, quietly, in a way that would not cause annoyance with the Radisson chain. Lacking the need for Toltec symbology, Castillo's way of doing things would be to ask Al to shoot the couple quickly, provide a hot, deep burial on a still summer day. In Castillo's way of doing things, Al would be asked to "assist with some unpleasantness." Al could just hear the request now.

It would probably take place over a steak.

In the end, Karl would be buried under the lettuce patch, a hotel built over his outraged bones. Some odd, perfect universal craziness caused good men to come to the end they often came to, which was why he, Al, didn't believe in too much goodness.

And yet, he didn't believe he wanted Castillo trapping him in.

He just didn't want to mule Castillo's shit, join Castillo's army, join the bug brigade.

"What it's going to be, my friend, is whatever I want it to be," Castillo had said. "And now it's time for us to part."

Trapped in. For now.

Al had been snared. Just for now.

He looked at the mirror again, slowed down.

Still, trapping Al was not like trapping an unwitting bird—a bird unused to the hunt. He imagined trapping Cordula would be very bad for someone. Whoever it was would have to drink a lot of forgetful tequila after doing Cordula.

Yes, Al could still get away. It was just a matter of planning. Lie low. Stay small and brown. Chirp a little, just enough. Then fly.

As for the writer's girl, her tussling and cawing, Al had no sympathy.

She wanted Karl's life, let her live it.

He touched her face where she'd scratched him.

He had a night with her, and he'd use it.

The closer he came to the guesthouse, the more Al's stomach was humming and popping. Crazy, fluttery sounds hammered in his ears. He didn't know why he was going to do it. Maybe he wasn't after all.

But, Christ. He just couldn't be trapped in.

As a teenager Al had lain in wait, behind the front door, listening for his mother's heavy footsteps. Imagining all the things he might do to stop her from breathing, instead he'd say, "Boo!", scaring her again, and she'd scream at him.

How would she react to Al's showing up at the little farm in Canada with nothing? He had no idea, really.

The last time he'd phoned her was a year ago. They'd had the same chat about movie stars, frozen pipes, anticonvulsants, stomach pain, the neighbor's annoying cough. Al took pleasure in phoning his mother from time to time because it reminded him that like a parrot in a cage, she would probably live forever. The important thing wasn't to live forever.

He checked his watch.

The important thing was to keep his mind occupied.

Nick was in the thick of it, now. The Ipazine would be wearing off and Chaz would be bugging out, bad. In thinking about all the possible scenarios that might play out—Chaz biting the bullet and doing the run alone (never, it wasn't protocol); Chaz and Nick doing the run peacefully (unlikely); Nick trying to escape (success unlikely)—Al knew it was almost certain Nick was on the road at this very moment.

He was probably thinking to jump out at the nearest intersection, run to a kindly, native family who would take him in, shelter him. He'd probably even tried it.

As for running, there were no such protective, kindly families or towns on the mule route to Chetumal airport. Just jungle and rot and potholes, and lots of them, until the lagoon, and the shuttered buildings and nasty bars, and the road to the airport. Al felt himself nod when he remembered Nick's darting eyes, the quickness of the breath.

When one wasn't large, quickness was what worked.

For a soft man, Nick was quick. Al was quicker.

He looked in the rearview mirror again.

He slowed the van to a speed that agreed with him. He let Nick drop, falling, from his mind. It was all he could do to see through the dust on the windshield. It was all he could do to keep an even line. Yes, he felt that Pablo must have known—must have known for a good five minutes—why Castillo's men had popped out of the arroyo, following Pablo's battered Ford truck in their old green Windstar van. He could just see the surprise in the man's eyes, the disbelief—for didn't everyone disbelieve in those last few moments? Didn't everyone have the same sense of "not me, not me," even as it was certain the finger was pointing inextricably at them?

He looked up, half believing he'd see the finger.

Instead he saw a formation of night gulls.

The birds liked to trail the wake of the van. Al had noticed this many times. Go easy, go slow, go where the wake took you. Go with the birds. Just go.

North, south, east, or west?

Castillo's men would be stationed everywhere tonight. Everywhere except one place.

He continued toward the rancho, his pulse speeding up. While Pablo had been being followed by the Windstar van, then wrenched from the truck, then dragged into the bushes, Al had been back at the rancho, listening to the girl's harangue.

So many wasted moments today. What he'd have liked to do was paint the shed, smoke, take a swim, eat a peach. Screw a tall girl.

Now driving, he allowed the internal sound to come into rhythm with his breathing.

"No hard feelings, old man," he said, practicing.

"You're a good boy," the German had said many times.

It was this last phrase that made him smile now. As he led the birds into the night, he could imagine them all smiling down on him.

Eh, Al, going back home?" Rocia's kid brother, Miguel de la Rocha, slapped Al's arm, hard, with his elbow. Al had come to the roadblock without really seeing it. Some of the cops were fanning themselves with porn mags, others were lazily shooting automatic rounds into the sea. From now until morning the roadblock would be up, and the road to Esmeralda would be closed.

He idled the engine.

"You know I've got to do this." Miguel slapped Al's arm again.

"You like it," Al said, laughing.

After the feel-up was completed, Al punched Miguel back harder for the hell of it and smiled. Big guys like Miguel didn't get slapped often enough in life, and they liked it.

"I'm clean."

"*Claro que sí.* Of course you are."

"So it's all set," Miguel then said. He lowered his voice. Miguel considered Al a friend, because his sister cut Al's hair. "But I've been hearing some bad shit about Pablo."

Miguel crossed himself and shivered.

Al laughed. "*Mentiras,* lies," Al said, punching him again. *"Tú sabes como es."*

"I don't know, man. This sounded bad."

"Hey, it's *con el cielo,* with the sky, and we can't do anything about it."

He told Miguel to say hi to his sister.

Miguel was eyeing Al's Swatch with such an expression of raw hunger it almost made Al laugh.

For a moment Al considered giving the watch to him, but he liked it too much.

"That's a good watch, man."

"Yep."

As Al drove on through the misty darkness, he was not yet hungry, though he'd not eaten since the girl had hit him. The scratch made him think. He backed up, slowly.

In a few moments Miguel was wearing Al's Swatch.

"It's a good watch, man," Miguel said again. He then said, "Can I have your Nikes?"

"No," Al said.

"You sure?"

Miguel seemed to take the news badly.

Al sighed.

The more he thought about it, the more the Nikes made him feel friendly toward the kid. Al had taken them from a mark in Cancún, who'd probably stolen them from someone else. In any case, they'd probably been made in Mexico for a few pennies, shipped to the States, without delay. It must drive the locals to a murderous rage—it was their country, but the gringos had everything good and shiny and new, and were soon coming to take the rest. Playa Esmeralda. They'd probably drop the *"La."*

They always did.

As he continued to drive, certain other humorous things came to Al's mind. Dislike of one human being to another was so odd, so arbitrary. In thinking about it, Al knew it was the shirt Nick wore that had put Chaz off on him. Men like Chaz had little sympathy for button shirts with polo players, alligators, certain stripes on them. This prejudice for and against shirts amused Al to no end. Nick with his horses and alligators. Pablo and his scoutmaster shirts. Miguel and his proud, itchy uniform, carefully patched and repatched by his sister at home.

And now he sped up, hoping to reach the rancho before Karl and Cordula got into it again. The old couple had almost certainly taken a break from fighting. Karl would have demanded his bream with butter sauce, and Cordula, even angry, would have complied.

In any case, it was good the old man had eaten; everyone deserved a last good meal before bad news. Too bad it was Thursday. Fridays were sausage. Karl liked sausage best of all.

He yawned, wiping his brow.

If the plan worked out one way, Karl would have his dollars. If it worked out another way, Karl wouldn't need dollars. "Dollars," Christ, the word sounded goofy. Yen, sheckles, dollars, rials, euros—each sounded faintly ridiculous.

He couldn't help it. He wanted to yawn, to lie down and sleep.

When he pulled up a hundred yards from the clearing to the rancho, Al cut the motor. For a long time he squeezed his muscles, then loosened them, squeezed, loosened, to work himself into the necessary mindset.

All he could think about was sleep.

You better start talking to me about what we're going to do, because it looks to me like you're the other guy." Chaz held forth the wooden object—a broken picture frame concealing a younger portrait of a shyly smiling Chaz wearing a Member's Only jacket in front of the Statue of Liberty. The coke was piled on top of the statue's torch. "Take the fucking line. Because I can't talk to a guy who's doped up. We've got to get some flow here."

He knocked Nick on the head until there was nothing to do, except take some of the cocaine.

After snorting the powder, Nick felt a pure, cold vacuum.

"Listen up. What happened is this: Something happened to Al. He's been working too many sides at once and they finally got him."

"Who got him?"

The cocaine started hammering in Nick's chest.

"Pablo got him. Raul got him. The sea monsters got him. Who knows?" Chaz laughed, while twisting the edges of his T-shirt. "So it's going to be you and me."

"I honestly don't know what you're talking about."

"Honestly this, honestly that." Chaz poked him in the ribs with a ballpoint elbow. "Come on, Boat Man, you're freaking me out. You're starting to become a freak. They need two. That's what they say."

"Maybe I'm going to take a walk." Nick's mouth tasted metallic. A run, a sprint, seemed just possible if he could manage his legs right. "Just to clear my head."

"Take another line. And just stay where you are."

Nick looked up at Chaz, and shuddered. As soon as he'd taken the third line, a rubber band seemed to stretch inside Nick's whole being. His mouth seemed stretched, his lips could not stop moving. When he lifted his head, Chaz had his hand in a fist, was pounding out a tune on the arm of the chair. Ava was rolling the cocaine, smoking it. Large, watery tears were running down her face. Chaz smiled at her. She stuck her tongue out.

"It has to be," he finally said, "you and me." Chaz walked the circumference of the bus, nodding his head. He sucked up another line. "Don't you see?"

While Chaz giggled at the rhyme, Nick was absolutely still.

"Were you and Al and Pablo going to take the place? With Pablo tonight?"

"What place?" Through the sheen of sweat, Chaz was as waxy, shiny as an apple.

"Fucking Al, man," Chaz said. "Fucking guy. I liked him, man, but he had it coming. Pablo always said he was going to do in that guy sooner or later."

Nearly half an hour passed. Chaz and Ava argued incessantly, pointing at Nick, who kept trying to interject. Even to his own ears Nick's pleas sounded like nonsense—*Glibberty slip yi? Kippety kup fie?* In any case, Chaz's neck was too big, his forearms too huge. Ava seemed ready to fling herself at him, beat him senseless. Chaz's silences were punctuated by disturbing bursts of laughter: He kept pointing at Nick.

"Crazy man, it's me and the Boat Man," Chaz was saying, over and over. They'd been doing many, many lines.

"I'm *not* going on any drug runs. That's just ridiculous." *Flippity sipper gay.*

"Honey, sugarpuss. You kill me." Chaz snorted. "This is so surreal."

Nick swayed. For a moment he thought he heard Al's car. But he'd had many of those moments already.

"*She* can do it," Nick cried out. "*I* can't do it. I can't."

"Dude, the bad news is she can't do no wet moves. The good news is she's a *bruja!* She's going to read your egg."

Nick got up to run, but Chaz just laughed. A gun appeared and pointed in Nick's direction.

"I don't want to shoot you, Boat Man." Chaz gave the gun to Ava, who assumed the giggly stance of a Hollywood detective.

Nick sat down again.

So what's going to happen is you'll just ride on over to the airport. I'll be copilot most of the way, then I continue on, hand over the shit, and that's the end. Just hand it over, back up, and move on out. You got the easy job, man. Stop your crying."

Nick couldn't stop crying.

"Shut up. You're making me crazy, here." Chaz, even dead-serious, looked ready to laugh. He leaned forward, fixed Nick with pinned eyes. "When we get the cash, we bring it back here, and we'll divvy it up. You get half, but better keep it straight, pal. Bad deal if you don't. Bad moon rising." He continued to move his head to the music, pinched Nick's cheek.

"Chaz. Nothing's going to make me get in that car."

"I'm gonna make you." Chaz shook him again. "Dig it, dude. I'm going to make you."

Nick sucked up the line, thinking he'd drive the car as far as the end of the road, then run. The more coke, the faster he'd be. He'd fly.

"Honey, you should see your eyes." Chaz smiled at Nick. "Like a dinner plate with a raisin wiggling in the middle."

Maybe he'd run at the driveway, let Chaz shoot at him, try his luck that way.

"Nick." Chaz was shaking him. "You've got to get with the

program now. The time for fun is over." He snapped his fingers suddenly, then walked to a corner of the bus, unearthing a booklet marked "US Army Reconnaissance."

"This is what I used my first time."

Nick looked at the book and started to laugh. The same book had been on his father's shelf and he'd never once looked at it. He could not stop laughing, even if he tried.

> Things to look out for in a risk-assessment situation: silhouette, outlines, shiny surface (reflective), contrast (lighter green against brownish dirt), movement, spacing (fence posts, man-made if not the usual chaotic shapes in nature).

"What in the hell does that *mean?*" Nick jerked his head upward.

"What *I* got out of this manual—what you're lookin' for," Chaz continued in a speeded-up voice, "is *this.* Risk can be defined as the absence of the normal or the presence of the abnormal."

Ava was waving an egg around his head. She cracked it into a water glass, stared at it intently.

Finally she pronounced the egg *"bueno."*

"You got a good egg, so everything's going to be fine," Chaz said happily.

Nick was starting to cry again.

It was a chore for Nick to scream, he didn't do it naturally.

He was now tied to the chair. Chaz was still looking through the blinds, face just out of reach of his pile of coke. Because his eyes kept darting back to the pile, his tongue swishing over his lips, Chaz picked up the frame, shook the powder, started chopping.

Chaz sucked, groaned at the pain in his nasal passage. "Dude, stop making that racket. I'm warning you."

"I'll give you my car"—Nick cleared his throat—"it's a BMW."

"I can't take your car! The thing doesn't even run! Besides, I don't need a car, man. Here, take another line."

"Please don't do this."

"Boat Man!" Chaz was smiling even now, and Nick was glad of it, even if it was just a defense rictus. "Don't be planning anything sick."

Nick leaned over, was sick.

Ava shook her football head.

Still more time passed, and when Chaz looked at his watch again, Ava came out with a glass of orange liquid. Without removing his hand from the gun, Chaz said, "Up to you. Drink it or not. Though I can't say I'm not one-hundred-percent convinced you need a vitamin drink first."

When he didn't drink it, a needle was plunged into his arm.

"Ándale," Ava said.

"Ativan," said Chaz. "Or somethin' like it."

Nick was being untied, then retied. They were up, heading for the door. Because the room was spinning, Nick rested his eyes on a goldfish bowl for navigational purposes. He drew back, his eyes trying to calibrate the exact floorspace.

"What in the fuck? What in the *fuck?*"

"Keep breathing, man. I'll untie you when we get to the Pontiac. Then I'm gonna give you some beta-blockers. Cool—eh?"

Among other things, Ava was good with knots.

"I can't drive. I'm not even a good driver. You shot me full of drugs!"

"All you gotta be is a gringo. And you're as gringo as they get."

Because Nick was aware Chaz held the gun at his back, he had little choice but to let himself be pushed toward the bus's door.

"If it starts getting crazy just shut your eyes and drive," Chaz said.

"Uhnnn," Nick said, retching. This time they were outside, so he let the acid liquid rocket up his throat. Chaz held his back firmly, pushing his face slightly forward.

"Done then?"

Nick tried to believe the situation might unmake itself.

"Get in the car."

Nick fell down.

The unexcavated Temple of the Jaguar had seemed little more than a pile of dirty stones when he'd walked it with Sarah, but in the Pontiac, seated next to Chaz, it looked alive with thousands of edges, millions upon millions of stones fitted perfectly, painstakingly, for some purpose that had long ago ceased and that he would never know. With a quick look over his shoulder, Nick ascertained there was no one else on the road to Esmeralda, what might have been lights were only far-off fireflies, puffs of yellow dust in the moonlight.

"Hey, it's all good. There's nobody can see us. There's nobody knows what we're doing."

A bat reflected itself in the headlamps.

"Even if they knew, they wouldn't do a thing," Chaz said. "Believe me, Pablo's got it rigged up. Pablo fixes everything."

Nick bowed and looked ahead, trying in vain to project the dutiful diligence and penance Chaz seemed to be watching for. At the same time he was looking for a place to pull over, to kick, to slap, to bite, to run—anything to get away from the smile Chaz trained on him along with the gun.

"That's why I've got Ava, man. She can't clean for shit, but she knows when it's going to be a bad night. I got a good egg, you got a good egg, so it's all good."

Nick was thinking of a time, many years ago. Phil hiding among the trees in the backyard. He'd had a toy gun that made realistic sounds. "You're the gook, son." The purpose of the game was for the gook to die.

It was scarier when Phil was the gook.

It was even scarier right now.

"No, no, *no.*" Chaz cut into his thoughts, pointing to a dirt road, as Nick tried to speed the car toward the town. He cocked the gun—shooting a hole in the rear-seat headrest to show Nick he was serious. He then forced Nick to the side of the road, tied him to the seat with rope, muttering about bad vibes, and being late, and the hole in his Pontiac.

Other than his arms, Nick could not move.

"Don't try any more shit," Chaz screamed at him. "This does not have to be like this." Then, calm again, he'd patted Nick on the hand and said, "It's gonna be all right. You're just spooked, man. It could happen to anyone. But you owe me for my seat."

Now Chaz insisted on side roads, his body pressed against the far seat so he could face Nick.

"Yep." He nudged Nick, hard, with his elbow. "My seat. You owe me. But they do good upholstery work down here. Lucky for you, my friend."

Al found Karl at the place where the lagoon met the sea. Karl wore wading boots and stood in the muck, fishing out glass bottles. The piled-up bottles were in many languages, because the trash all arrived on the Gulf Stream. Karl raked at the water, chewing a piece of jerky. Heavy bones moved under the skin of his face as he chewed, tectonic plates coming undone.

"Hey-o."

Karl would not meet Al's eyes. Finally he said, "Well, I can't keep the girl here. I don't know how to tell her. And I'm not feeling well."

"I'll tell her," Al said quietly.

"I've got a pain going up through my cheek." Bits of algae swum in the puddle. Bubbles popped. "Never felt anything like it before."

Al said, "Old man, it's bad."

"Of course it's bad!" Karl spat a piece of jerky. "Six of the dogs are gone missing. That fool boy must have snuck around this morning, left a gate open." He clutched at his chest. "And now I've got to tell the girl she has to go."

"Karl, listen to me."

"I found the gate wide open! Cordula's out of her mind, but the aphids won't let us on the beach to look for them, of course! And I like that girl." His face was gray. "Al. I *like* the girl. *Ach!* I feel young around her. What's the sin in that?"

The rifle, Al noticed, was on the far side of the pool. On instinct he moved, putting himself between it and the old man. Karl took an unconscious step toward it. Al then moved away.

"Nonsense! Pure nonsense. The dogs won't eat tonight." Karl was grimacing. "No one will eat tonight. Cordula just picks at her food and glares at me. She says she'll leave. And something is squeezing my chest. I need a *Pfhefferminze* tea."

"Look at me, Karl. I have a lot to tell you."

"Goddamnit, boy! The girl says you made the drawings. She makes a good damn case." He paled, poked wildly at the trash. "And now my dogs are gone and the wife has gone mad. And my heart, goddamnit."

"Karl. I *did* make the drawing. Anyway, sort of."

Al moved to block Karl from the rifle as he told him the whole story, starting from the beginning. Soon enough Karl's look changed from sadness to rage to utter disbelief. He struggled for a moment, and then went grayer.

Al waded over to the side, took the rifle and held it behind his back.

"And now, they're coming for you in a week, and I'm going to get my things and try to get out of here," Al said. "I doubt very much I'll make it, but I'm going to try. I'm going to take this rifle, old man. I've already taken the other guns out of the shed."

Karl made a slow, convulsive movement.

"None of that, now," Al said. "It's over, old man. If you sell, Castillo will give you two-fifty. If you don't sell, well, you're dead. Take the money, old man. Then go meet the girl."

"But why, son? *Why?*" Karl asked. "We treated you like—" The rake dangled from his hands as the convulsive shiver happened again. Then he was lying in the muck, staring upward. All at once he looked very old. His mouth pursed into a strange shape.

"Because I don't want to work for Castillo," Al replied to the silent figure staring up at him. "I just can't be trapped in like that." He knew it was not the question Karl had been asking him, but it was the one that needed to be answered in his mind.

The Pontiac stunk of smoke, weed, the sulfur left over from the bullet. As they wound through a tiny opening that entered onto a dirt road overhung with ceiba trees, two or three giant land crabs faced off the car, claws raised threateningly.

Nick drove over them. The car jounced slightly.

"Now any minute we're going to see a light, like flash, flash"—Chaz opened and closed his fingers twice to illustrate—"and that's where you pull over." Chaz shoved the gun under the passenger seat with a quick sideways glance at Nick. "What you do is just sit there and don't say anything. They'll slip a blindfold over you so you don't see the important guys. It's all very cool."

Nick looked into the laughing face and saw pure, raw stupidity. The most horrifying, nightmarish creature in the world.

"Don't look at anyone. Just get into a zone, man. Just keep calm and steady. Keep your head, and I mean that literally."

Soon enough they saw the flash, flash of the light. Nick slowed the car, bringing it to rest under a hanging vine. A black armored vehicle could be seen, hiding among the jungle scene; farther off a boat hummed in the shallows of the lagoon. Shadows and shapes could be seen moving into position. Nick imagined thousands of guns trained on him. Whatever drug Ava had shot him with wasn't working. The beta-blockers hadn't materialized.

"Okay, now cut the engine, man. Put your hands in the air. Keep them up."

After a while, a figure stepped forward, watching Nick's upraised hands intently. The man's calm, sloped profile might have come from an etching on the Chichen Itza pyramids, though he was dressed in smartly pressed green fatigues. Other men came into Nick's side view, surrounding the car in a tight circle. Flashlights bounced around the inside of the car, laughter was heard over the sound of the boat's motor. Chaz slowly waved his raised hands and got out of the car. His feet, in their flip-flops, made squishy sounds as he walked off into the dim trees.

When the *comandante* ascertained Nick was tied to the seat and was not going to move, he made a tranquil motion, the kid's gun moved upward ever so slightly. He turned to his friend, appearing to say Nick was stupid.

His friend appeared to agree.

He indicated Nick lower his hands, put them on the steering column. The wheel was sticky with resin, old food.

Nick stared straight ahead as he was blindfolded. The blindfold smelled of gasoline, sweat, fried potato. In the utter darkness, heavy bundles were being loaded into the back of the Pontiac.

Ten. Twelve. Eighteen. Nick lost count.

He heard the sound of a slap, a chuckle, Chaz saying, "Come on, *Boat Man!* Skedaddle."

The Pontiac settled farther into the mud.

When Chaz got back to the car, Nick hadn't moved. The windows were rolled up and he was wet with sweat. He did not move until Chaz told him to. Then the blindfold came off. The Chichen man took it from him, smiling.

"And now we go to the *aeropuerto,*" Chaz said. "It's that easy."

There was a flash of blinding light. The boat moved away.

"Turn the fuckin' car on. Back up. Don't wig." Chaz was already smiling. "Don't fuckin' back up over anyone."

And soon enough they were on the dry road again.

"Boat Man! Mission fucking accomplished! Phase one is over!"

They were hurtling in space, locked in a metal pod. Nick clicked the controls.

He was not Boat Man. He was Space Man.

"Man oh man," Chaz said.

A sound could be heard, *whup, whup, whup,* overhead. The sound was coming closer, bright lights shone down, illuminating the jungle floor. Even from his position, he knew it was police surveillance.

And so it was with some shock that Al looked up from his standoff with Karl. Seeing the helicopter brought a sharp knife into him. Four men could be seen, seated in it. Two carried night-vision binoculars. The tops of the palm trees began to shake, delirious.

Karl shaded his eyes against the glaring spotlight, the paralysis from the demistroke beginning to set in. For a long time after Al had lifted him from the water, he'd been slumped on a log, staring wordlessly at Al, and Al hadn't been sure a stroke had occurred.

"So, you sold us out, boy," he'd said, many times, his mouth dragging slightly downward at the corner.

Al had agreed it was so.

"And for what?"

"Nothing," Al had admitted. "Nothing really at all."

As the helicopter began to lower its great black belly into the clearing, Karl used his remaining strength to hold out a single accusing finger. He stood, shaking it, as if the finger could command all the energy in the universe, force the helicopter backward. He did not move his left side. He could not.

"What in the hell?" Al said, in wonder. He still could not figure it.

There was an immense cloud of sand as the Bell sawed back and forth in the air.

"Get that thing off my land!" Karl was trying to shout in his newly garbled voice. Or maybe he was trying to shout, "You'll scare the animals!" The words came out "Gttttt sssssss lllaaaa." He clutched at his chest, swayed.

Al stayed low as the chopper descended into the Von Tollmans' land. It seesawed for a moment, then hit the dirt. Wind flailed at Al's face and hair.

"Shhh, old man, shhh," Al was saying. "You just take the money, now."

Karl was speaking in baby talk now. The words were soft, the cadence lost to the wind, the roar.

"Karl, Karl, it's a pleasure." The fat man called out from the passenger side. Al looked at Castillo and patted Karl on the back. Little star twinkles appeared in Al's peripheral vision, the flashlights being charged and switched on.

Castillo seemed to take Karl's slumped figure in stride. "I'm sorry to disturb you on such a lovely night, but my friends here are concerned about the illegal drug trade that has unfortunately overcome our lovely shores."

Two of the men were Americans, Al saw now. They wore Kevlar vests with the emblem DEA sewn onto the back in large silver letters. The fourth was the guayabera man. He now wore a semiautomatic, a bulletproof vest.

They were all going to die "resisting."

Al started laughing and shivering as Cordula hurried toward the helicopter, wearing a nightgown, shivering.

"Was! Was! Was ist los?"

She knelt by her husband, who was now leaning against a palm tree, staring vacantly.

"Mein Gott, Karl, was ist los!"

"Our colleagues, here, would like to have a look around, *señora,*" Castillo said. "Some of our other colleagues are now entering the property from the gates. You will meet them presently."

"What are you *doing* to him?" Cordula was purple. Her nightgown flapped and fluttered. "What happened to my husband? He's ill!"

"Your husband will be seen to." Castillo shrugged amiably. "And, *señora,* I must ask that you stand back. My men will do the utmost to keep your lovely garden intact."

The two men were jumping out of the helicopter. They spoke on radios to other, unseen, men. Soon enough, Al saw the others, walking in through the trees. There were wave upon wave of them. Karl watched the onrush with thick, glassy eyes.

"Mr. Greenley, would you be kind enough to empty your pockets?" Castillo gave Al a little wink.

"No!" Cordula shouted. "Alchen, Karl needs a doctor! Al, you must go to—"

Karl made no move to wipe the thin sluice of drool on one side of his face. He couldn't.

"My friend, why don't you escort our German friends to my men over there." Castillo's bow to Al was courtly. He was looking at Karl's rifle, Al's own semiautomatic, with distaste. "By all means carry the older man if he needs the assistance."

As Al picked Karl up, walked with him to the line of soldiers, he saw Sarah under the eaves of the guesthouse being handcuffed with thin plastic ties. She was trying to get to Karl and shouting, "No, no, no! Leave them alone. They didn't *do* anything. They're *good* people."

The girl's luggage was being thrown from two stories up. It had been packed, Al noticed. Underwear, paper, deodorant cans hit the dirt.

"You can't do this. They've done nothing," she said.

"Just sit down," Castillo told her. He was looking at an azure-blue thong that had landed in the tree. From the low vantage point, it looked like a bow tie.

"Just remain calm. Your embassy will be contacted. You will be apprised of your rights under Mexican law."

He then looked at Sarah, at the thong.

Something odd and ugly and prehistoric seemed to flicker across his mind.

The Pontiac hurtled toward Chetumal.

The whole drive to the airport, Chaz snapped his fingers, bobbed his head. The sweat had dried his hair into forked little tufts, giving him the appearance of a nightwing.

"Now what happens next is we meet the guys in the last dock. The plane's juiced up, ready to go. They might make you get out and help load. They like to see yanquis doing menial labor." Nick raised his eyes to Chaz's, at the same time conscious of a ridiculously giddy sensation in his marrow. Chaz's saggy pants, greasy forehead, added to the general sensation of a carnival-nightmare proceeding toward an inevitable conclusion.

"Hey, man. It's easy. It's cake. You'll laugh at yourself tomorrow. You've never made money as easily as this. Just think about what you're going to do with two grand."

Chaz's eyes closed, thinking about it.

"How much is in the trunk?"

"Fifty keys, man. Maybe eighty. God, I'd be liking some of that right about now. This is always the part when I get to thinking—"

"No," Nick said suddenly, violently.

"The voice of reason." Chaz slapped Nick on the back. "The Boat Man speaks! Right on! Keep my head."

Nick looked straight ahead. He fancied he saw a waiting *militaria* Humvee, but it was just the shadows playing tricks on him. With every branch, every twist in the road, he tightened his grip on the wheel.

"So what animal do you resemble, man?"

"Chaz, I can't talk."

"Come on."

Nick scissored his jaw. "Please be absolutely quiet."

Chaz didn't appear to hear.

"You've got to look in the mirror, move your face around, then be very still. You'll see it. Everyone's got their animal. Al told me about that one on a run we once did. Al says I'm, like, a fucking snake! A serpent! I told him he was fucked up, but later, I swear, I saw it!"

The coke thudded around in the trunk as Nick slowly shook his head.

"It was something Al started as a kid." Chaz laughed. He was chewing something, maybe his tongue. "Yeah. Al was crazy even back then. He says he's really a bird. He believes that shit!"

Nick's hands had come to rest at two and twelve o'clock.

"He used to see hawks wearing ties, man." Chaz laughed. "Hairy bears serving eggs. Grinning mice under fluorescent deli lights. I can see it too, man. He's not so crazy."

"What in the fuck does any of it prove?" Nick said.

He was talking about everything.

Yeah, yeah, that's it. Trippy, man."

During the point between Ascención and Playa Valverde, it had been ascertained Nick resembled an eel.

"It's those teeth, man. Little rice teeth. You ever seen an eel? Crazy little fuckers. Just a tail with a mouth."

It was impossible. Even if Nick went to the *policía* in Chetumal, with the load in his trunk, he'd hang. The thing was to get to the airport without being stopped, without being noticed. His eye ticced wildly.

"Could you talk a little bit lower," Nick said. "In volume, I mean."

"Eel? You gotta stop thinking those crazed-out thoughts. We're home free now. Pablo's gonna meet us at the gate, and—"

"If you could just not shout," Nick said in a whisper.

"I can see that dark, doomed shit going on in your head. Your transparent eel-head."

"If you could refrain from waving your hands."

After a thousand hours passed, Chetumal loomed up in the distance—a second-world jumble of ultramodern buildings next to houses constructed of tin, cardboard. Nick drove slowly, yet not too slowly, past Banco Mexico, a sign in English proclaiming: CASH ADVANCES ON YOUR VISA! EXTEND YOUR VACATION ANOTHER DAY OR WEEK!

Steamy, industrial air came through the vent, trucks loaded with raw timber belched smoke into the night. AEROPUERTO, the sign said. On it was the outline of an old-fashioned plane. The plane was smiling.

"Eel! Eel! You gotta stay to the left. Christ, man! What do you think *aeropuerto* means!"

Nick jerked the wheel, the load crashed against the trunk. From here on in, he would just not breathe.

Upon entering the airport parking lot, the car was swarmed by a host of beggars. Most were female, swaddled in thick skirts, bundles of flesh pressed tight against their breasts. Babies, Nick thought. Teeth. Lumps of moving unhappiness.

Nick waved the Indian women away frantically, but hands continued to thrust forth, offering steamy things wrapped in banana leaves.

"Get these people out of here," he shrieked.

"There's something not right," Chaz was sniffing the air like a beagle. "Pablo should've taken care of those women. They shouldn't be approaching *us,* man. They should know us."

"Chaz. Stop."

They wound slowly past the far parking lot, past the last of the lights, to the area marked PRIVADO.

"This is not right. This is crazed-out."

A single old man guarded the gated entrance: He looked at Nick with no expression, spoke into a radio. The gate went up. A cluster of men could be seen under the farthest lamp; as Nick edged the car closer to them, they melted back into the shadows.

"Where the fuck is Pablo, man?" Chaz was saying. "Who the fuck are these guys?"

"What should I do?" The car stopped. Started. Stopped. A hand waved them forward. The gate had closed behind them.

"I don't fuckin' know!" Chaz screeched. "Pablo should be right *there.* He's always right *there.*"

"Chaz. Shut up."

There was no choice except to park the car next to the airplane.

"Yanqui," a voice said.

The voice then said, "Get out of the car."

Chaz was fetal now, whispering, "Not right. Not *right.* Don't get out."

"I can't get out of the car because I'm tied to the seat," Nick said in a loud voice.

"You shouldn't be fucking getting out of the car," Chaz whispered. "This isn't how it goes. We're under, man. This is a sting. This is a fucking sting."

Suddenly there was a bright flash of light, a beam aimed directly into Nick's eyes, and two large men were on them, opening the car, grabbing Chaz and dragging him out against the pavement. At the sight of Nick, they merely sighed.

"What the fuck is this?"

"Rope tricks."

"What will they think of next?"

The English was perfect. Accent from Texas. The one in the military T-shirt cut through the rope without expression.

"Don't tell me." He smiled at his buddy. "You got roped into this."

"Lord, yanqui, you're a sight to see."

Big, muscled. Cops. From Texas. Or soldiers. Nick put his hands on his head, leaned forward onto the steering column. At least they were laughing.

"Now get out." The faces were all Latin. Of course they'd have Mexican-American agents for an ambush in Mexico. Goddamn. What would they use—Aryan blonds? "Up, up, yanqui. And no running."

It was over and Nick was surrendering. He looked up uncertainly. How many years did one get for eighty kilos? What would it be like to have no sun, no air?

"If you guys are cops, another American might be in trouble. My girlfriend," Nick said. No air. No air. Sarah wouldn't believe a word he said. "It's my girlfriend. She's—"

"Hey, do your job, pal. We're not paid to hump."

They wanted his cooperation. Nick's legs coursed along, large, rubbery strides. His knees were hot, light. He kept repeating to himself the fact that the tone had been friendly. The men were going to arrest him in a civilized way, and everything could be gotten through, later. But no, they were often friendly, just to trick you. They were fighting a war and you were the enemy. You were scum, without soul, a drug scum, an enemy combatant. He walked toward the light, waited for the blow to the back of his head.

"Are you Americans?" he'd said. "Because I'd rather stay with the Americans. Don't give me to the Mexicans, man."

"Long may it wave, man," the chunky one had laughed.

"God bless it," another said. "God bless the Rangers."

When Al reached the Von Tollmans' gazebo, he lay Karl's stilled body against the cool stone. "It's probably better like this," he whispered to Karl. "Don't fight it."

He thought he felt Karl squeeze his hand. A thin sound uttered through the helpless lips. There was no mistaking it, the sound was death.

God, death took so *long.*

Upon rising, Al was immediately thrown to the ground again. Cordula was being ushered into a corner, while crying, "No, no, *nein*. We must have a *médico.*" Jackboots stormed past her, Mexican faces with grim expressions.

"So what do you say, can I have the Nikes now?" Miguel was laughing and laughing, standing over Al.

Al untied the laces. He heard female screams in the distance. Sarah calling for Karl. "I'm going to help you."

"These are the best shoes, man," Miguel then said. "I'm going to wear them out dancing later."

Al looked at the shoes being held up for perusal. Men came for Al's cap. His belt buckle. His cheap jute wallet, even.

"He needs a doctor," Sarah was screaming. "A doctor! Get him a fucking doctor!"

Miguel was now wearing the Nikes. They looked good on him.

"He's had a heart attack. Help him," Al heard Sarah say, before she lapsed into a stupefied silence again.

Perhaps someone had hit her.

"We got it," Al heard someone say in Mayan over the radio. "The whole place is crawling with it."

A general whoop of euphoria rose over the trees. As it did, Al understood the brilliance, the bugginess that was Castillo.

"It's all in the fucking sheds. The *cabrón*. He's got it everywhere. Tons of it. Must be eight hundred kilos."

Al closed his eyes. After a while, he opened them.

Chaz came swinging out the door of the bus, bobbing his head, snapping his fingers. The cocaine was now being sucked up through a five-hundred-peso note.

"God, I love this song."

For the twelfth time that night, the stereo played "Holiday."

Nick was sitting on the captain's chair, rubbing his ice-cool muscles. The plane had taken less than half an hour to load, to equalize the weight just perfect. The other guys had been pilots.

"You're under arrest, yanqui," one of the men had joked to Nick.

Another had laughed. "You must have pissed yourself, man!"

"Fuckin' DEA! *That's* what you thought?"

"Man, oh, man, that was some adventure. My blood is running *crazy!*" Chaz was laughing and grunting. The dance he was doing never seemed to end. "You drove the Pontiac like a champ! I thought we were gonna run out of gas for sure! Hey, get up and dance with Ava."

"Chaz, I don't want to dance. Leave me fucking alone."

"I've been hearing choppers, man." Chaz continued to poke at Nick, making the shimmying movements. "What the hell is going on? Is it in my head or what?"

Inside Nick's head, everything was calm and still. There was no room for anything.

"Esmeralda don't got no choppers. So I must be totally wigged out. Man, the vibes! Those were some strange vibes."

"I'm just going to start walking," Nick said suddenly. He narrowed his eyes. "Unless you object, of course."

"I wouldn't be walking tonight."

"I'm fucking *going.*" And he was.

Chaz watched Nick sympathetically. "I just can't allow that now, Boat Man. You don't even have a car."

"Yeah." Nick was sobbing. "Yeah."

"You've got a lot of money now. Just be happy. Just do the dance. Dance with Ava. Make me happy."

Do the dance. He had money. He kept repeating the sentences as he danced with a topless woman and a bearded man. He was trying to joke with Chaz.

"Like Sufis, man!"

"Ándale!"

"Religious!"

Nick danced and whirled and talked to himself. It all ceased to make any sense.

Yeah, but the problem is, it's not quite over. There's the race."

Chaz had taken off his pants again. He was sliding on a pair of board shorts.

Nick's eyes locked onto his. The dance had taken the breath from Nick. "If I can get through this night, you'll forget I ever existed, and I'll forget what happened. You don't know me and I don't know you."

"Do you think that can really happen, writer? I mean, they know who you are. Your passport is marked. Don't think the boys in *el Norte* don't know exactly what's going on. They're fucking with it all, man. *All* of it. And they're tied to the boys in Europe. And the boys in Katmandu. They're the fucking convergence. They control the fuckin' dance."

Nick ceased to feel a single thing.

"They run the hotels, the drugs, Castillo. Hell, man, they run Mexico. From now on you're on their secret list. They can get you anytime they want. That's why you gotta do the race. Let 'em know it's all cool with you."

Chaz left Nick standing alone for a long while. When he returned he had a daiquiri in his hand. "Chug," he said. "This one's on me."

Nick pretended not to notice the chalky powder floating in the liquid. It didn't matter. He didn't even taste it.

Al considered the shape standing over him. Some people looked like children when delighted, but the guard didn't look so much like a child as a furry animal. It was something about the ratio of hair to skin: in any case, no overwhelming affection occurred.

"Is it true the old *huevón* has a jaguar in here? I want a jaguar, man, as a pet."

"Mátame," Al said to Rocio's brother. Kill me."

The guard crossed himself, unrolled a length of duct tape over Al's mouth.

"I want to see what a jaguar does to a pit bull, man. My brother's got a pit bull."

As Al looked at Miguel to see if he still felt sympathy for the kid, he discovered he felt quite a lot less. Quite a lot.

"Agh." He was nudged, hard, with an elbow. The shape punched Al in the groin for the hell of it and smiled.

"Pablo was always saying a jaguar had, like, the spirits of the ancestors. Man, that would be some fight against a couple of pit bulls."

"Mátame," Al said again, through the duct tape. Miguel zipped off the tape with a little frown.

"Do it fast," Al said. "A bullet at the base of the skull, not through the temple. I gave you the Nikes. You owe me."

Miguel declined violently, redid the duct tape.

Al looked at the Nikes again, the silver stripe, the moon-walking waffle sole. Miguel would go out dancing in them, show them off. But that was in the kid's future, and his future could hold anything.

He knew a few things about what it would hold: tension, anger, and a quickening of the pulse when the Nikes were stolen by someone else. In one moment Miguel would be rich with Nikes, then he would be poisonous. Miguel and his pit bulls.

He started crawling.

"Kill me, friend, fast. Say I went for you. I'm just about to go for you."

He knew Miguel couldn't understand him, so he tried to raise his hand, thinking of the kid's future. Miguel would be pissed off, murderous, he would plan revenge. Beyond that Al couldn't say.

"Hey, loco! Shut up! The Germans are *chingado* but Castillo says things will go just fine for you," Miguel whispered, kicking Al's arm. "That's the word. You're going to be moving south. He also told me to give your stuff back."

"You just keep those Nikes," Al said, unintelligibly. He gestured the same.

"*Excelente,* man, just lay low. Castillo's going to promote you, man! You're big. You'll be working for him."

"Shoot me, man."

It sounded like "Ooooo eee aahn."

Miguel was grinning. "You're one of us, *cabrón*."

Al suddenly felt terror, greater than any he'd ever known.

Mop-Up

There was darkness, then light. Nick awoke to the sound of a coconut smashing down on the roof of the school bus. A stack of fast-moving clouds passed northward. The glass windows warped up as he yawned, his breathing was stiff, mechanical. He waited for a voice to tell him what to do now. Nothing sensible revealed itself.

Chaz was sleeping hard on his bare stomach on a gold rug. The stereo was still playing "Holiday."

Nick looked at his hand. It was blue, thick and blue. He really should be dead. Waterlogged.

"Swim!"

After the count-up, Chaz had initiated the race whereby each present male had to swim to the reef and back—the winner got a joint and two thousand pesos. When the men lined up on the shore, Nick tried to beg off, but Chaz insisted.

"You take their money, now, and you have some fun with them. I told you about the *race.* It's part of the vibe. To keep it cool for next time."

"No."

"Yes."

Chaz had then said, "With these guys you're either having some fun, or you're having less fun." He'd pondered his statement. "Yep. That's it. Those are your choices. Don't fuck it up now. Not when you're rich. Not when you're the new guy."

When Nick had walked to the shore among the squadron of shadow men, he'd fancied he could feel something shift in his own breathing—every pull of air containing more molecules of something that would get him through. As he breathed, he became darker, easier. It was a curious thing, not unpleasant.

You had to not care.

"Hey, you owe me for that seat," Chaz had said. "Don't think you don't."

"Just don't talk to me."

A gun had gone off.

The Ipazine had started to kick in when Nick was swimming back from the reef. There were men in front of him, men in back of him. Ah, he'd thought, and it had started again. He'd not been nervous when he started to choke, go under. His last memory was of a black, airless river. He had no idea how he'd come to sleep back on Chaz's couch.

"Ah, hell, Eel. You're up. You almost drowned out there. I saved ya." The face was strangely affectionate as it arose from the carpet. Indentations from the rug gave Chaz's face a thready, animal mien. "You up? Whatcha doing up? That shit's gotta stop. You gotta get on Mexican time, man."

"I'm not up." Nick cocked his head. He scrunched his shoulders. Thoughts were exploding in sequence. He'd survived.

"Get some shut-eye. Then I'll take you to town. The boys got your car ready. They're thinkin', maybe, we make a good team. The eel and the snake. Yeah, yeah, yeah."

"That could be."

"It is, man. It just fuckin' *is.* Now go to sleep now."

Nick kept his eyes open, seeing smoke, seeing the hole open. It was light. He waited for Chaz to start snoring again.

In time, he heard the sound he was waiting for.

He began to crawl across the paddies. The sun glowed.

The night had passed among a group of sweat-stained, rough locals in someone's house in Esmeralda Town. Al hadn't been told whose house it was, but had been given a plate of cold goat meat, a glass of warm beer. He'd been told he was not allowed to move until Castillo gave his orders. The order hadn't seemed a literal one—he'd moved from one end of the grimy hammock to the other just to fuck with the guys who jumped at his every movement, and had twice gone, escorted, to the bathroom. The goat had been too chewy and the beer had been a blond, in addition to being warm. The television noise was loud, unrelenting. He'd tried to sleep but had mostly spent the hours surveying the brown walls, brown beetles, the brown cigarette pall in the air.

The many men walking in and out of the house, poking their noses in and out of the cage, had eyed the television between beers, whooping and shouting. Mainly the Iraq War played, sometimes a shampoo commercial starring a sexy blond Mexican actress with a gap between her teeth. From what Al could gather, the war was apparently going well.

"I'd fuck her," the men agreed about the actress.

"I'd like to drive one of those fucking tanks really fast," they said of the war.

The article about Karl and Cordula would be lost in the excitement of the war. Castillo had blown it, there, a little. Al knew exactly how the article would read. He didn't need to see it; it was all right there in his mind:

MEXICO ARRESTS "DRUG BARON"

Mexican troops have captured a suspected drug baron last night wanted in both Mexico and the United States, officials have announced.

Karl Lustig Von Tollman was captured on Friday along with his wife, Cordula Ernestine Von Tollman, and Sarah Lancey Gustafsson in the southern Yucatán city of Esmeralda.

Mexican Attorney General Roberto Vazquez de la Huerta told reporters the group was suspected of being complicit in one-third of drug shipments from southern Mexico to the US.

The United States Drug Enforcement Agency has described Mr. Von Tollman as providing a key link between Colombian cocaine smugglers and the US border. More than eight hundred kilos were found on the expansive seaside property.

Mr. Von Tollman had been living in Mexico for twenty years, and is suspected to have purchased his land illegally.

The US wants to have the Von Tollmans and Ms. Gustafsson extradited, but Mr. Vazquez said they would face legal charges in Mexico first. Mr. Von Tollman was aiding a "cruel" and murderous cartel operating across the country, with strong Belizean and Colombian connections, said Defense Minister Moises Alcandón. "He has probably aided and abetted the transfer of literally tons of cocaine in the past ten years." Much of the drugs ended up in New York and Los Angeles, officials said. "These types of foreigners present the greatest menace to Mexican society."

In addition to the cocaine, one hundred forty-eight thousand US dollars were found hidden in the Von Tollmans' laundry room. Ms. Gustafsson was found with nearly twenty thousand dollars stashed away in a Mexican bank account. She is suspected of credit card fraud, and was a fugitive from crimes committed in the United States.

> The suspects were captured while hiding in a drug outpost designed to look like an eco-lodge, officials said. The cocaine was kept in several large sheds throughout the isolated property, before being picked up for transport. Several guns were also found. "It was a long-standing operation, going on for many years. Shame on these foreigners. The acts they've committed are unspeakable."
>
> According to Mexican officials, Mr. Von Tollman began working with the cartels in 1987. He is also said to have ties to the notorious Arellano Felix drug cartel based in Tijuana.
>
> "We will not tolerate drugs in our tourism areas," Tourist Minister Marvella Macedo said. Esmeralda Mayor Castillo Rodriguez agreed. "We will accept nothing less than zero tolerance. Foreigners be warned, we will deal with all drug-pushers under Mexican law."
>
> Esmeralda Beach is slated for heavy development. Radisson, Hilton, and Fiesta are said to be planning resorts there. The hotels would bring a change for the better, according to Rodriguez, "A place for the whole family," Rodriguez said. "Mexican Culture. Wholesome activities, not drugs. That's what Esmeralda stands for."

Al could see the photo of Karl in his mind, too. From what he'd gathered, they'd propped Karl up, half dead, and shot pictures of him. Ten rolls for good measure. Cordula had turned her face away from both the DEA photographers and the *fotógrafos oficiales mexicanos,* and it had taken quite a few rolls to get the required grim smile. The writer's girl had not yet been photographed. Apparently Castillo's men were taking their time with her—Castillo first.

Al knew the photos would be sent, via UPI, this evening, and that soon the whole world might have access to them. Spilling milk on the article, families would eat their Cheerios, talk about lacrosse, movie stars, the Iraq War. Probably, with a war on, the article wouldn't make much of an impression in the US and Europe.

In Mexico, it would be huge.

"Man, oh man," was the chorus going off in Al's brain.

Another chorus was "Caw, caw, caw."

Sometimes his mind was thankfully blank.

"Castillo says we move at noon," someone had finally said.

It had been in front of the *policía* office that Al had come upon Nick Sperry, probably for the last time.

"Greenley! Thank God!" Nick had said in the desperate voice. "I mean, I should say 'fuck you,' but that's secondary for the moment."

Al, who was simply waiting for Castillo's men to be finished with their lunch—fish tacos, no doubt—and to be taken to a beach where he would either be shot or trapped in Castillo's new regime, had listened to the whole story while keeping his eye on the men who'd been assigned to watch him. The two large men sat close to Al, on a bench, smiling in a friendly way. There were others, so many others.

". . . and then I hitched a ride to town after walking nearly an hour. On the way the truck driver passed Karl's place, and the gates were opened . . ."

It had been a chore to maintain interest in the writer's hysterics. What Al wanted was some fish tacos.

"The place was being guarded by the *militaria*. Jesus, that was fast . . . I kept asking and they wouldn't tell me *anything* . . . except something happened to Karl . . . he took drugs or something. It didn't make any sense . . ."

From what Al figured, Karl had suffered another stroke not long after Al had laid him on the cool stone floor. Someone had put peso coins over his eyes as a joke. The Mexican president had gleamed in the old man's sockets, a particular insult to Karl, Al thought. He would die, Miguel had told Al, before the day was over.

". . . and then the assholes told me the place was empty! The place was being 'repatriated.' I think that's what they were saying—*nacional*—right? I couldn't understand them. Jesus Christ, Al, so you got Karl out of the place. You got me to do your shitwork last night. Fuck you, but I don't care about any of that right now. Right now you have to tell me, did Sarah go back to LA . . ."

Wishing the writer would shut up, and knowing he would not, Al had gestured wearily toward the horizon. Let the kid figure it out on his own—*he* was the writer. He was also thinking he was sorry the old lady hadn't gone out like Karl. The dental care in a Mexican prison wouldn't be good. With her luck she would live forever. At least she was old and the men wouldn't want her. But then again, there were sick fucks. Sick fucking buzzards flying low.

"Christ, what do you mean. She's in that building?"

Nick's face had gone a strange shade of white when he'd seen a threesome of large men Al had never seen before. But then Al's night had been full of men he'd never seen before.

"Hey. Shit. Do you know that guy in the middle?"

"Never seen him before."

The men had Texas accents, though—even through their Spanish. They were talking about American football unfavorably. Soccer, it was agreed, was a much better sport.

"Jesus. Stand in front of me. Are you sure you've never seen him? That guy with the big teeth . . . He's one of yours . . ."

"He's just some guy, Nick." Al yawned. "And I don't know where your girl is. She probably just skipped out."

"No! *No!*" Nick had started to shake. "Al, this is all so fucking *weird*. Sarah couldn't have gone far. I have her passport. I mean, it's so *weird*."

"Shh." Before Nick could go on, Al had put his fingers over the guy's lips. The men next to him on the bench stirred uneasily.

"Go home, Nick, your car's down the street." Al had moved away from the writer, the writer's writerly journey. In some small way, he hoped Nick would get something out of it. "You lost her. Now just go the fuck home before they drag you into it, too."

The man Nick was afraid of suddenly looked Nick's way. His expression didn't change. "Yeah, but in *el Norte,* man," he was saying to his DEA pals, "you just live a lot better. They live too poor down here. It's creepy, man. Just wrong." He looked at Nick once more, then looked away.

"Did you just say I lost her? She's"—the writer's face purpled—"*with Karl?* Is that what you're fucking *saying?* He took her somewhere?"

Al wanted to smile at the yanqui cluelessness of the writer's logic. At that moment he was sure Nick would glide through this. The thought was pleasing. Al felt the chill deep in his bones when imagining what would be happening to the girl now. In time, she would just disappear.

"Have you got anything to eat, buddy? Peanuts or anything? I'm about to take a long, strange ride."

Nick was looking at the tall, broad Mexican and at the same time he was talking gibberish about Karl and Sarah and what Al *had* to tell him.

"Look," the kid had said with a crazy laugh, "it's not like I don't know a hell of a lot about you. You want me to keep quiet, then you just tell me where Karl took her."

Al might have answered that people always came and went in Esmeralda—it was that kind of place—and that it didn't really matter, but just then Castillo's boys had come for him.

"Ready, Mr. Greenley?"

"Al, talk to me," Nick had said.

"You write your book now," Al said. "Remember us kindly."

The men had grabbed Al's arms in a friendly way.

The writer had backed up a few steps. "Fuck, Greenley, what's going on?"

"You just forget about talking. *Stop* talking for once—believe me. You just get in that car and glide."

And now, Al was on a journey. He liked the south. It might not be so bad after all. There were gulls trailing the wake of the Windstar van. Five, six, no exactly seven.

"Boca Alacrán?" he asked the man sitting next to him. The man smelled like eggs. Eggs and sweat.

"I'll probably like it there." He already knew that was the name of the place they were taking him. He asked if it was wild.

"Sí," one of the men answered.

"I don't mind a wild place."

Wild and remote enough and Al would just sneak away and just start running. There were plastic surgeons in Belize. He'd get fat. He'd get a new style. Some bugs liked fat guys.

He blinked.

Or maybe he would just glide along for the next years, using Castillo's wake as a buffer. Maybe he could just get used to muling or organizing mules. Maybe it might even be okay. Not too much like a cage. Not too bad.

He looked at the big guys shoehorning him in. They'd put him in the middle, and were talking about who would win in a jaguar–pit bull fight. Someone was going to put money on the jaguar. The other was going to bet on the dog.

The middle. A position from which to be shot.

"Wild, huh?" Al repeated. "Lots of birds, then?"

At least it would be fast. From behind. There would be no warning. Castillo would do that much for him.

"I need a good man in the south," Castillo's last words had been.

They both knew Al wasn't a good man. For a long time Al considered the gulls through the glass.

"I'd say an eagle. And you—a falcon. Definitely," he said to the funny birds sitting on either side of him. Just to unnerve them a bit, he said, "What animal do you look like?"

The funny birds didn't look up. Which wasn't a good sign.

Al had to put things in perspective. The falcon was a lucky bird for Al. Castillo liked him. To believe in signs, one had to believe in a great guiding principle. Which was a pointless endeavor because . . .

The shot exploded.

Al died.

"Umm," Nick was gesturing to the police officer. It was a new guy he'd never seen before. The line had been long. "*Quiero hablar* . . . uh . . . Pablo?"

The officer smiled at a spot over Nick's shoulder, glanced tiredly at the TV.

"*Mi,* uhh, *esposa?*" Nick tried again. "Gone. *Ir.*" He pointed out the door in the general direction of nothingness.

"Esposa" was the wrong word. Sarah was not his wife. He was blowing this, making the wrong gestures. The cop was looking through him. The next people were shuffling restlessly.

"Sarah Gustafsson? She's a missing tourist. *Turista.* She was at the guesthouse. I have her passport."

Because the cop gestured to Nick that he did not understand, and then gestured to all the people waiting to be understood, Nick ratcheted his voice up a notch.

Of course, in louder English, the words made no more of an impact.

"Estoy ocupado tourist, *muy occupado no tengo tiempo para* tourists! *Vete! Vete! Me estás molestando. Todos estamos ocupados."*

Of course, in louder Spanish, the torrent of words made no impact on Nick.

"Um, wait. No, I'm *not finished talking.* Please bear with me."

When the figure walked past the office window, Nick ducked to keep out of the sight of the goon who'd untied him last night near the plane. And yet, the man did not look in Nick's direction at all. He was chatting amiably with a man in dark Escada glasses. *He* spoke English.

Nick shivered and laughed.

"My girlfriend! Damnit! This is a possible serious matter." The cop slowly put on a pair of mirrored sunglasses to signal to Nick their chat was over. Through the glasses the cop watched a tank cross a desert. The logo for Operation Iraqi Freedom turned slow circles on the lenses.

"She can't just *leave.* I have her passport. She might have come here looking for it."

The cop called the next person.

"An American could be in trouble! Do you *understand?* It's your *responsibility* to help me *find* her."

The next person elbowed his way around Nick and began to speak rapidly.

The cop talked over Nick's voice. Bombs fell. Nick put a five-hundred-peso note on the desk, elbowed his way in front again.

"Look. I'll *pay.*"

"No. That couldn't be right."

It had been a long, uncomfortable wait while the guy from the airport lurked outside, and the junior cop had brought in old Hilde to translate. The woman had taken her time getting there—apparently girding herself into the long gown, applying her makeup had caused an hour delay. The line drawn around her lips to emphasize the contours was thick and sloppy and suggestive of tequila. Every single thing Hilde said was nuts.

"Ziss *policía* say she mix up with drugs." Hilde added, fluttering her hand, "Bad girl."

Nick laughed.

"Ziss *policía* say yes. They found her wiss ze drugs. Very bad."

"Hilde, listen to me." The pounding had started in Nick's ears again. "If my girlfriend is in jail, they have to let her out. She has nothing to do with drugs."

"I want to dance," Hilde said. She started to tell a long story to the cop, who laughed. The story appeared to involve dancing.

"I have two thousand dollars if they let her out." Nick enunciated every word. "Right now."

"You Engres from Engran?" she said to Nick.

And now he had just given the cop two of his last five thousand. It wasn't quite clear how much Sarah was said to have been found with. Maybe a joint when they'd stormed the place. Maybe a long-forgotten joint in one of her suitcases. Perhaps a planted ounce.

"Yeah, that's right," he muttered to himself. "Squeeze every last dime out of the gringos while you can."

"Gracias," the cop had said, when Nick slipped him the roll of bills. As soon as he said it, Nick knew he'd made a mistake.

"And now what? When does she walk out of there? When! *Qué hora?*"

Sarah, he was told, would be "seen after."

"When!"

"You is crazy givink monies to these peoples," Hilde said.

She appeared to find the situation exciting.

"I like dancing," she then said, "in a gown."

Nick was staring at the old woman in front of him without seeing her. It had been crazy, rash to hand over the money without some kind of assurance. Christ, what kind of receipt could he have asked for with a bribe? Still, Hilde had seen the transaction take place. Nick had. And if Sarah did not walk out of Esmeralda with Nick soon, there were calls to the embassy. And calls to lawyers.

They were Americans.

No, he thought. No.

"And why you start troubles, little boy? Boom. Boom. Why you do it?" Hilde was watching the TV.

Nick put his head in his hands.

"Bam, bam," Hilde was saying. She watched the eighty-millionth replay of the "shock and awe" campaign.

The cop with Nick's money was studiously avoiding Nick's gaze.

"Hilde." Nick had to do something other than wait. "Will you come with me to the police in Chetumal? I need you to translate for me to the police. I don't trust anyone here."

He still had three thousand.

"Hilde! Christ! Please!" He was tugging at her hand.

"Stop it."

"I will dance with you if you come with me. I'm an English person from England. Christ, just come with me."

She looked at the television and nodded.

"You not Engres," she said sadly. "I know you."

And now Nick was on the road from Esmeralda. The heat in the car was nearly unbearable. The sky opened, a little rain fell down.

"The Engres put me in a camp during the war," Hilde was saying. "The Engres, they feed me. I was beautiful little child."

"Yes. I see." He couldn't see. He kept trying. But he couldn't.

"How could I have been so stupid?" he asked Hilde. *"How?"*

The BMW had been handed over to Nick without any questions.

The *mecánico* had tossed the keys to Nick and slammed the door like he had been anxious to be rid of it. When Nick had said Al's name, the *mecánico* had pretended not to understand.

"Go," he'd said. "Yanqui go home. It's bad for you now."

"The Engres are good peoples," Hilde now said. "They not kill me. They feed me puddings and meats. Very nice."

"What I *need* you to tell the police is that I have to speak to the American ambassador," Nick said. He was thinking of Al. Of the man with the big teeth. And then of Sarah. The pit in his stomach threatened to rise, swallow him.

The woman's perfume filled the car, mixing with the heat and disbelief.

"You sees, I am a dancer. I dance the 'Swan Lake.' As a child I comes to Engran. My family they all dies in the war."

Nick gripped the steering wheel in disbelief.

"Hilde? I understand about the war you were in. I'm sorry for it. But *listen*. We need to keep focused on *this* problem. Wherever the ambassador is, I need to talk to him. I know a lot about Esmeralda he'll be wanting to know. But I won't tell him *anything* if he doesn't get Sarah out."

Hilde smiled widely. "No ambassador man wans troubles. He wan monies and hotels like everyone else."

A blue Windstar van was coming upon the BMW fast.

"Where can I find the American embassy?" Nick was screaming at the woman now. "Can we get through to Belize? They've got to *listen* to me. Someone's got to *listen*."

Hilde smiled sadly. She looked out the window, tucked herself into her hood.

Nick looked at her, exasperated and shaking.

He pulled over to let the Windstar pass. It did not. It simply slowed down. The men were waving him over—six of them.

"Hilde, why are they stopping us? Who in the *fuck* are those people?"

"Bam, bam," Hilde said from under the cloth. "You yanquis think like childs. You so arrgant and so happy happy but you don't know nathin'."

Nick punched the gear. The van followed. He slowed. So did it.

"The dance," Hilde said, crossing herself. "The dance."

A single shot to the tire stopped the BMW.

"Get out of the car," the man in yellow said.

Around six o'clock the slow plane taxied past a stand of palm trees, cane fields, a wide blue lagoon, the slash-and-burn topography visible from the Chetumal airport runway. Nick sat in the first row of the DC-8 passenger plane bound for Orlando, Florida, with a connecting flight that hadn't yet been specified. A few rows back, sharing the first-class section of the plane, was a clique of young American holiday-makers—two blondes with dreadlocks, a young black man with a dyed blond Mohawk, a rail-thin brunette listening to an iPod. The group's sun-tanned good looks, world-weary posturing, added to Nick's sense that nothing that had happened in the past hours was real.

"See that!" one of the kids was whispering and pointing. "They still got him in cuffs."

"Is he an American?"

"I don't know *what* he is. Except bummed."

When the thin girl in the violet minidress started to walk across the aisle, the man sitting next to Nick intercepted her with a quick, practiced motion.

"Go back to your seat, ma'am. This section is off-limits."

"Man. What did you *do?*" the girl whispered, looking at Nick with great interest. She had a slight under bite. To the cop, she affected flirtatious insolence.

Nick put his hands over his eyes. The man sitting next to him was called Bingham. He had tufts of blond hair on his knuckles. His eyes were yellow and brown.

"Back up from the prisoner, ma'am. I'm serious," Bingham barked.

"Goddamnit," he said to the man seated just behind Nick. "This is so goddamn unprofessional."

"Standard Mexi-shit," the other replied. "Standard Third-World shit." His name was Ratcher.

The girl shrugged, then turned away. Her movements had a slow, underwater quality. Lines that should have been straight—the tray table, the edges of the plane's cockpit—were wavy and unnatural. Nick shook his head like a retriever dog. Objects remained warped, indistinct.

"You are not to speak to any of the passengers on this flight," Bingham said to Nick. "If you need to use the bathroom during the duration of the flight, you will be escorted."

"Look," Nick said. "I did not do these things I am accused of."

He was talking to himself.

"As Allah wills," Ratcher said. He laughed.

It seemed a million years had passed since Nick had been pushed into the Windstar van by the group of soldiers. After the tires of the BMW had been shot out, he'd tried to run into the jungle, but had tripped in the first stand on vines. He'd only fought for a moment before being overcome.

Back on the road, he'd been cuffed to a tree while the men searched his pockets and made notes on a pad. After being thoroughly ransacked, the BMW had been left, along with Hilde and a mustachioed Mexican driver, along the side of the road from Esmeralda. Hilde had been making wild waving gestures as the men pulled away from the dusty shoulder with Nick crouched in the middle seat.

"Poor boy," she'd called out. "Bad, bad boy."

"Hey, man?" The kid with the ring through his chin and the spiky black tattoo called out to Nick's seatmate with a conspiratorial tone. "You a narc? Narcs flying first class? That's where our tax dollars are goin'?"

The kid gave Nick a sympathetic thumbs-up. Nick didn't look at him. At any of them.

The Windstar had smelled of sweat, metal, the acrid smell of burnt nails, discharged arms. A ball of wadded newspaper had been stuffed in what looked to be a bullet hole in the van's upholstered ceiling. The Mexican soldiers—if that's what they had been—spent the drive to Chetumal looking through Nick's backpack with leisurely proficiency. From it, they'd taken Sarah's passport, Nick's visa, inserted both documents into plastic bags. They'd not answered any of his questions.

Removing a tape recorder from his shirt pocket, the English-speaking one had leaned over the seat, switched the device on.

"You know anything about any gelignite shipments? Mr. Nick Sperry? An anti-US terrorist ring financed by a certain drug-running operation here in Esmeralda?"

Nick had tried to gesture that the accusations were absurd, but two of the men had hold of his cuffed arms. His legs had been cuffed thigh to thigh, ankle to ankle.

"*Americano* trucks getting blown up? Plans to transport certain dangerous Arab nationals over the Mexican border?"

Nick had snorted in disbelief. The tape recorder recorded the sound.

"Do you deny you were seen having drinks on many occasions with known terrorist sympathizers? Pablo Rodriguez? Alfred Greenley? You deny plotting against your government and using our Mexican soil to further your political goals?"

"Greenley!" Nick started to laugh and scream. "That's so fucking *ridiculous!* Greenley has *no*—"

"*Tranquilízate.* And yet, *pues,* I'd say this writing is of dubious patriotism, my friend." The calm man had smiled at him, ruffling the pages, pausing now and again to reread Nick's first draft of the book. Nick's twenty good talismans.

"Ah, *sí*. You're one lucky hombre Castillo isn't going to deal with you here. Then again, Guantánamo Bay just isn't so hot, I hear." His tone lost a measure of kindliness, even as his smile widened. "They got photos of you last night buying up some gelignite at the lagoon. What were you gonna do? Blow up an airliner this time? Or just another truck?"

Even through his shock and fear, Nick had managed to laugh into the microphone. To explain the truck had been blown up before he arrived in Esmeralda.

"So you admit you *know* about the gelignite then?" The man shrugged. The recorder was switched off. "All they need these days is the suspicion of a suspicion, *cabrón*. They throw away the key. From what I hear, you don't even need no charges in Guantánamo. That's the *Nueva Democracía*."

Two or three men started to smoke.

"They got photos, *cabrón*. And your girlfriend *la droguista*? With the funny political leanings back home? The *comunista?* That one? See what I'm getting at?"

Nick began to gag.

"Oh, *sí,* you're in big trouble, friend. They'll be waiting for you on the other side. *El otro lado.* You make your deals over there. We just get you on the plane. Then our job is done."

Other than cigarette smoke, waves upon waves of nausea, Nick had very little recall of the remainder of the drive. The side room in the Chetumal airport had been green, freezing, filled with various officials who'd apparently been awaiting his arrival. Through his protests, he'd been frog-marched to a curtained corner where a nurse and a doctor waited with a pail, a tweezers, and a variety of metallic utensils. After the strip search, performed clinically and thoroughly with rubber gloves and assorted implements, two new men had waited with Nick in the lobby of the airport.

"We got nothing here."

"Take him for X-rays."

"Check his shoes for Bio DS."

They'd taken a sample of his stomach contents after he vomited.

"I just don't see why they don't send military transport!" he'd heard one of the Fiesta Airlines men complain. "We're not equipped for this kind of thing."

What "kind of thing" had not been explained.

"Bio DS" had not been explained.

"If the guy was going to op-run a suicide mission" had not been clarified.

The walls had started to dissolve during the wait for the X-ray machine to arrive. The residual pain in Nick's anal cavity had been dull, unrelenting, and yet, in time, it had ceased to feel like it belonged to him. When the voices began to drip from the ceiling, they'd brought him to another room, where a man in a moon suit ran a clicking, funnel-shaped appliance over every inch of Nick's naked body. Another combed through his hair with magnetic cellophane tape, while a third swabbed his mouth and esophagus with a yellow substance. He was told to spit into a bowl, urinate into a cup. The jumpsuit he was given was olive-green, baggy and greasy, used.

"As long as the airline isn't an American registry," he heard someone whisper.

"Paying passengers shouldn't have to ride with this guy."

"He's checked out nonradiological, so this is the way they wanna do it."

"Shitty," the man named Bingham had said.

Nick had only stopped shivering long enough to raise his head from time to time.

While telephone calls had been made back and forth, the group surrounding Nick had been given a special section of the lobby to wait in, roped off with yellow tape. After the argument had been settled—apparently three rows of seats had been purchased to isolate Nick from fellow travelers—a third man had crossed the yellow police tape.

He seemed to be a minor military official—his jacket bore the emblem of the Mexican navy. He was joined by a silent blond man whose emblem was ATF.

"As it turns out, *Talibano Américano,* you're going in first class. *Primera clase,* man! That's some yanqui luck. Up there drinking champagne, traitor."

"Was he read his rights?" the blond asked.

Nick had sunk slowly into the chair.

"Have you been *advised* of your rights?" the ATF man asked Nick.

Nick had closed his eyes.

Long before the plane officially boarded, eight officials from two countries had escorted Nick to the first-class section. Bingham sat in the seat next to Nick. Ratcher settled into the chair behind. The men's massive biceps prevented speculation they were anything except air marshals.

"When the civilians board the aircraft you are to keep your head angled exactly toward the window," Bingham said amiably.

"We've been advised to tell you we have no further information at this time," Bingham then continued. "You will be met by personnel appropriate to your case in due time."

As the plane soared over the ocean, then came back in toward land, Nick concentrated on the vision of an under bite, the sharp odor of air freshener, Scotchgard, plastic. The front of the in-flight magazine Bingham was flipping through showed a lazy scene from Cancún—a slatted deck chair under a palm tree, azure water, footprints leading to nowhere.

"I like the Cancún run, all right," Bingham said to Ratcher. "But Chetumal is usually crap. Rinky-dink."

Ratcher agreed Cancún was okay. Pretty girls. Did their parents have any idea?

Acid sweat dripped from Nick's chin. He tried to imagine the girl in back of him and saw nothing except a black hole.

"They're not narcs," he heard a young voice whisper.

He felt the distinct *ping* of a peanut as it hit his cheek.

"Wait?" There was a squeal. "A *terrorist!*"

Bingham turned around and glared. To his buddy, he said, "These Fiesta jackoffs should have the cabin roped off. This is not professional."

The fellow cop shrugged, agreed.

Nick's mouth sagged. He'd been tensing it for so long the muscles had given out.

"It couldn't be *that* guy!"

"He doesn't look like an Arab. It can't be him."

"As I said, keep your eyes forward," Bingham was telling Nick in the professional tone.

To the stewardess, who smiled unsurely when stopping with the beverage cart, Bingham said, "No drinks for the prisoner is the protocol. He could make a weapon from the plastic cup."

"Ah, you're right. I've never done one of these."

She looked tense.

As the plane bounced through the currents of air, there was no insistence in Nick's protests anymore. He closed his eyes, not a body but a protozoal mass. A blob of dividing cells.

"Lookit him sleeping." Bingham was saying in disbelief. "That's what Allah wants them to do? Kill babies?"

He'd pronounced the word "Al-lay." Nick blinked and sighed. He drifted off again.

"All those babies. Those little kids? And he *sleeps.*"

"They don't care if it's kids," the other voice said. "They're animals."

The voices were quite high, like helium, and for a long time Nick kept them at bay by fixing his inward gaze on the beautiful Cancún scene, the steps leading off to nowhere. His bladder slipped, then slipped again, and he felt the warmth.

In a few hours, Florida rose from the blackness to meet the plane.

Nick smiled and shuddered. He was dreaming.

"American peoples is like puppies. Too much arrgant, too much sure," Hilde had said.

Sarah was in Nick's dream. Sarah was wiping Hilde's mouth, playing nursemaid. He thought, Oh, Sar.

"But puppies is good," Hilde had asked him. "They nice and good, don you think?"

The ground was coming closer and closer. On the ground were buildings, lights. Palm trees, swamp. And the good that might come of this? Nick had to close his eyes and close his ears. He saw the nurse's under bite in his father's hospital room. HAVE YOU HEARD THE GOOD NEWS?

"Some politician—a mayor I think—turned him in." Nick heard the little air bubble burst.

Through the dream, he looked out at the lights.

"He was buying bombs. He speaks Arabic, I *think*."

The FASTEN SEAT BELT sign came on.

"He was always angry," Larry Scakorfsky would say to the reporters.

"He was a loner," Gay Jay would say.

"He must hate freedom." When Phil's voice came from the depths of Bingham's throat, Nick was up and running, tracing the footprints into the warm, clean, deserted beaches of Cancún. No one was following him. The plane disappeared.

When Nick got his speed going and passed through the plane's gray metal ceiling, Sarah was there, just beyond. Though he couldn't see her, he knew she was waving and smiling from the cool, clear water of the magazine photo. His damp hand slithered off the cushioned armrest into the sea.

"Get him up."

Just don't open them, Nick was thinking as the first wave hit.

"Orders are we wait ten minutes with the prisoner, then disembark."

Nick found he could run underwater. It was beautiful and strange.

"I know what *orders* are, Bingham. I didn't just fall off the potato truck."

If only the water wasn't so cold. If only he could open his eyes.

But no. No he could not.

"Christ Almighty, our towelhead—he's having a funny dream."

If Nick kept running on the wide, cold ocean floor with his eyes closed, the good people would find him, eventually. And Sarah was right there, just ahead. The thing was to believe and keep believing. And not to open his eyes.

Swim. He heard Sarah say it.

"Shake him, Ratcher."

Swim, Hilde said. The Filipina nurse said, Run.

"Shake him *harder* then. Like *this.*"

Nick held out until the very last stroke. But the pressure was too great. Too many slapping waves. Too cold, when it should be warm, endless.

As the plane reformed itself, as the magazine photo reconstituted, Nick's eyes struggled not to focus. The light, the glowing tunnel of light, might mean anything. Goodness. Escape. Heaven.

Even God.

A glowing, spectral light could mean "come." It could mean "safety." "Good news."

"Subdue the prisoner. He's starting to lose it."

" '*Subdue* the prisoner,' Bingham? How? We're on a commercial aircraft. If we hood him up, the liberal media will scream."

The hood, Nick was thinking. The camping trips. Yes. Of course. The hood again.

He struggled a little, while things went black. But he'd played Vietnam before. He'd come through.

"Just keep his head between his knees for a minute. Press the carotid artery a little, but not too much."

In his mind, Nick was cramped, waiting in the trees of the backyard in Yucca Valley. It would be a long night, but it would pass.

The thing was to find a hiding place, remain silent. Not to move a muscle.

"He's calming down now. Quick. Take my picture with this digital. I want to show my wife."

"Lift up his face," said Bingham. "Here. Snap me one, too."

Not to move. Not to deny. It didn't matter, thought Nick. The pressure on his neck grew. His face snapped up, a bulb flashed. He was starting to black out. Now would come the interrogation.

But the bad nights in Yucca Valley, too, always passed. The nurse had said there were good things to remember.

Nurse, he thought. Sar? Dad?

Run.

"All right, that's too much on the artery—he's passing out. Use your thumb. Like this."

All right, it would all be all right. Just agree, nod, stay silent. Nick nodded.

"All right, the prisoner is subdued. Let's get the show on the road."

"It's so cold," Nick said.

"It's hot and tropical where you're goin', pal."

Hot and tropical. Vines. Ambush.

"Oh," Nick said. "No."

"Move 'im on out."

Move.

Fight.

War.

Run.